THE YOUNGLINGS

SHADOWS & MAGIC

HELENA M CRAGGS

ISBN: 978-1-9196365-0-4

Cover design by Emily's World of Design

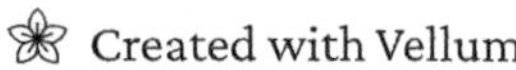

Barbara, my sister, my friend.
I love you every day
and still
I miss you every day.

THE TWO WOLVES

An old Cherokee is teaching his grandson about life.
'A fight is going on inside me,' he said to the boy.
'It is a terrible fight, and it is between two wolves.
One is evil—he is anger, envy, sorrow, regret, greed, arrogance, self pity, guilt, resentment, inferiority, lies, false pride, superiority, and ego.'
He continued, 'The other is good—he is joy, peace, love, hope, serenity, humility, kindness, benevolence, empathy, generosity, truth, compassion, and faith. The same fight is going on inside you—and inside every other person, too.'
The grandson thought about it for a moment and then asked his grandfather, 'Which wolf will win?'
The old Cherokee simply replied, 'The one you feed.'

CHAPTER 1
QUINN

Inside each of us,
There is the seed of both good and evil.
It's a constant struggle as to which one will win.
And one cannot exist without the other.
Eric Burdon

Unrequited love is a bitch. Especially when you're half-demon and the object of your desire is half-angel. Love is a complicated pain in the butt. Her name is Eve—the half-angel—and she's ... you know, divine in every sense. She's also my best friend, and, given her heritage, she's cool about my demon within.

Mortals rarely consider the fact that supernaturals

like me are real. I was one such human, up until my sixteenth birthday. But they do exist in the mortal realm —believe me. Humanity is unaware of what lurks in the shadows—a good job, to be honest. We can't escape the shadows, though, for they are the yin to the light's yang.

My circle of friends knows about my demon side too, and they stand by me. But most of them aren't exactly mortal either, which helps. We haven't always been friends. It's only over the last year that we've come together, but I honestly don't know where I'd be without them all. They have become like my family.

It took a while for me to accept who I was. But, eventually, I became pretty okay with the whole situation. I had a few complications here and there. I won't lie—the demon temper is *not* my best side ... it's probably best *never* to get me angry.

I always knew I was different; I just didn't realise exactly *how* different I was. On the outside, I'm an attractive, regular sixteen-year-old guy. On the inside, however, I'm a total super-freak. On the plus side, though, being half-demon comes with some pretty awesome, devilish powers. Got to look at the positives.

I like to think of myself as a multifaceted half-demon: badass but sensitive; ferocious but caring; angry but gentle ... and often confused.

Yep, I'm the secret, mighty half-demon who'll take on any adversary. Admitting to being in love, however ... a total snowflake.

The name's Carter. Quinn Carter.

I learned about my demonic blood when I met my estranged dad, and it didn't go too well. He was pretty to the point with his words: 'You're not entirely human, Quinn.'

Understandably, his words hit me like a juggernaut going at seventy.

It sounds really cool—you know, having super-demonic powers. Well, let me tell you, sometimes, yeah, it's fabulous fun. Until you get roped into fighting evil supernaturals, you have to understand, at that point, fun is *not* the word I'd use. But they say you should embrace your weirdness ... I had no choice, so I embraced away.

Luckily, my friends—a team of supernaturals—had my back. Turns out we were all destined to be Keepers—protectors of innocents in the mortal world—alongside worrying about Shakespeare and calculus tests. Believe me, weird was to become a way of life for us all.

So, let me first explain the series of insane events and how fate threw me together with my amazing supernatural friends. I think we need to start with Eve.

It feels like I've known Eve forever. We met at primary school when we were little kids; she was in my class. We weren't friends or anything. To be honest, she always seemed a bit strange. But then I was always a bit odd, too, so it must have been a match made in heaven—no pun intended.

I didn't realise I was half-demon—not then. The powers that came with my demonic DNA developed over several years. The first ability to develop was night vision. Strange, huh? The next was reading auras —the spiritual energy fields around people. Auras convey the feelings or emotions someone gives off in a range of colours ... and Eve's was different from anybody else's. Her aura fractured: one half dazzled white, flashed with blues; the other half was made of greens and blues. Reading auras comes in handy sometimes. I learned to avoid people with dark auras—these always equated to mean, devious, and none-too friendly.

I realised early on not to talk about my unnatural abilities—I just wanted to be like everybody else. I wasn't the brightest kid, but I wasn't stupid—it's called self-preservation. Anyway, these abilities were cool, so I kept them to myself. I just thought I was psychic or something.

I used to be small for my age, shy, and pretty antisocial. Yep, a perfect victim for the school bully. Noah King was four years older than me and a complete jerk. His favourite form of torture was flushing your head down the toilet, and the feeling of impending death by drowning was pretty horrific. I wasn't his only victim, but I was one of the easiest. I allowed myself to be bullied because I was scared. But Eve wasn't—she took shit from nobody, even as a scrawny seven-year-old.

Eve saved me from Noah one day when he was especially mean. He had grabbed me by the front of my shirt and lifted me off the floor, and there was glee in his eyes at the prospect of trying to drown me. But Eve kicked him in the shin, which made him instantly drop me. She's always been fierce and bold.

My knightess in shining armour.

That's how my mum, Helen Carter, met Eve's dad, Frank Williams: when Eve grassed up Noah for being a bully. Frank's a statuesque, slim man with russet, reddish-brown skin and hands the size of baseball mitts. He's a successful lawyer, a sharp dresser, and has the best laugh ever. I'd once overheard Mum describe him as eye candy; I tried not to think about that—it was just gross. Anyway, I digress; let's get back to Eve. Making friends with a girl at that age put me in a bit of a dilemma. Could I be friends with a girl? Would the boys laugh at me? Then I thought about it—no one ever bothered with me anyway. So Eve and I became best friends. Meanwhile, Mum and Frank became close friends too, and then officially started dating when I was about thirteen.

My mum is the best. And I mean *the best.* She's brave, beautiful, and selfless. She's not had it easy, what with my dad leaving her and everything. We live in a big town called Portaville, which is near enough to a few big cities but even nearer to the countryside. It was a pretty cool place to grow up. Apparently, Dad had at least left Mum quite a lot of money when he up and disappeared, which meant Mum could buy our high-end, two-bedroom apartment outright. It was always a cosy and modern place to live as a kid, plus it has a spectacular rooftop garden. When I was about one, Mum returned to work as a nurse at the local hospital, and our neighbour, Mrs D, would always look after me. Mum adores her job, and the extra money means she can spoil me.

Mrs D lived in the apartment across the hall from us. Her apartment was full of stuff, especially books. She loved reading. Her balcony was packed full of potted plants, which created a riot of colours in summer. Her apartment always smelled of flowers, cooking, and baking. Mrs D became like a grandma to me. She'd never had her own children, so she sort of adopted Mum and me instead. She *is* a bit odd, but she is also kind and funny. Her hair is always up in a bun, her clothes are always black, and she always wears short, black ankle boots. I used to think she must have something wrong with her feet because she walks really funny, like it's painful or something. But she isn't fooling me—I've seen her run like a gazelle when we are supermarket shopping and her favourite ice creams are on sale.

When I was really young, Mrs D was the only person I could talk to about my dad. I'd try to talk to Mum about him, but she'd only explain that he went away on business and never came back. What did that mean? Had he died? Had he left us? I stopped asking Mum about him as I got older because I realised that thinking about him made her sad. I couldn't remember him—he'd left when I was about six months old. I was happy and secure growing up, always loved by Mum and Mrs D. However, I still got an empty feeling inside when I saw other kids with their dads.

'Do you think Dad loved me? And if he loved Mum and me, why did he leave and never come back?' I'd ask Mrs D more times than I could remember.

'Life isn't as simple as you think, young Quinn. Your father worshipped you, but he had to leave. His job was extremely important. Then something must have happened because he just seemed to disappear from the face of the earth.' Was her standard answer. 'You must believe, though, that you were the best thing to happen to him.'

I'd sigh, knowing it was the best answer I was going to get. I learned to swallow the lump that always formed in my throat when I thought of him, and I let it go.

Mum's life improved once she met Frank, especially when they started dating. We'd spend a lot of time with Frank and Eve, going to their house almost every week-end. The house is massive, with a vast garden. I love our apartment, but it could fit into Eve's place twenty times over.

When Eve and I started high school, we were still

best friends. Even though Eve made some new girlfriends, she and I still spent most of our free time together. Eve was pretty popular—she was feisty and snarky, but not in a bitchy way. She was a hit with the boys too. I, on the other hand, was still a loner, which suited me fine. Most people annoyed the hell out of me.

My early teens were hellish as—I now realise—the demon hidden inside me fought to be released. At that time, I still had no idea about my supernatural DNA or the fact my demonic side was fighting for control. While I'd always struggled to bury my anger, the older I got, the more difficult it became. Fighting became a regular occurrence once I realised that a good chokehold or a sucker punch to the gut was quite an effective deterrent for bullies. So, usually, at least, I'd be fighting to protect people from bullies like Noah King. Not that that was an excuse, of course.

Whenever I got into a rage, Eve was the only person who could really calm me down. Half the time, I didn't know what came over me; I was seized by impulses over which I had no control. Subsequently, I was almost excluded from school for fighting. Miss Strickland was the school deputy head and the authoritarian. She had an amazing ability to evoke terror wherever she went, merely by narrowing her eyes at you. A rare talent, to be fair—well, unless you were on the receiving end of *the* look. But I was on my final warning with her, so things were getting desperate.

Mum was becoming stressed out with me getting in

trouble at school. As hard as I tried, once I blew, control was a struggle. People didn't understand; they thought I had serious anger issues. I was sent to see a therapist, but that sadly didn't really help. Looking back, though, I realise the poor therapist was no match for my demon within. One thing that did help was playing football. The intense daily training expended much pent-up energy, and I made some good friends.

In my early teens, I grew quickly to be well over six feet tall. I was strong and quick, and the lads who'd once shunned me for being a loner became friendly and accepting. I was also a hit with the girls. Once I hit sixteen, though, my temper wasn't the only thing I struggled with—things got seriously strange.

New powers started developing, and I could suddenly jump fifty feet into the air, seriously! What was wrong with me? Then there was running at super speed. I'd accidentally discovered how insanely fast I could run, thankfully when I was alone. I'd started jogging the trail through the woods near our apartment. One minute I was jogging along, gradually increasing my pace to build stamina; the next, I was running supernaturally fast. I mean, running like a phantom wind wasn't natural, right? I didn't realise how handy and liberating running like that would be—not then. I still had lots to learn about the paranormal world at that point.

My temper had also become fast and furious—I was losing it more often than ever. My anger seemed to have escalated, and my temper exploded in times of stress, and yeah, this was a particularly stressful time. And my strength? During an argument at school, I picked a six-foot-tall guy up as if he weighed ten pounds. I dropped him in shock, and he legged it. Thank God there wasn't anyone else around to see *that,* either. I hadn't been bitten by a radioactive spider or exposed to gamma rays, so what was I becoming?

I was turning into some sort of freak of nature, and it was seriously weirding me out. I'd kept my new abilities secret for months, and felt detached from the 'normal' world. I had no one to talk to about what was happening; who would believe me anyway? I'd probably be whisked away by the secret service or something, and I wasn't sure I was James Bond material. Plus, even though I could have proven my abilities, I felt like an aberration. I didn't want any of my family or friends to see me for the weirdo I really was. I was surrounded by people most of the time but felt utterly alone. The only calming constant in my life was Eve. One touch, one word, or even one look from her could quell my rage.

Mrs D was still a massive part of my life and insisted I have dinner with her at least twice a week. I never complained because she's an awesome cook. After yet another scrap on the way home from school, I decided to come clean with her. I needed help; otherwise, I was about to be expelled. I still had *some* control over my temper, but I was losing it more often, and God only knew what I was capable of. I couldn't worry Mum; she was already despairing of me. I needed to talk though; otherwise, I was headed for a meltdown.

As I came home from school, walking up the stairs to our apartment, I could smell Mrs D's baking—freshly baked apple pie. The scent of cinnamon, apple, and pastry tickled my nose and made my mouth water. Seconds before I knocked on her door, she answered it with a plate of deliciousness. Mrs D truly was an enigma—I also felt pretty sure she was psychic.

'I need to tell you something, Mrs D. You'll probably think I'm batshit crazy. But if I don't talk to somebody, I think I'm going to have a breakdown,' I blurted at her with a mouthful of pie.

Mrs D, calm as always, made me a cup of tea and sat down with me. Then I hit her with a verbal barrage. It poured out of my mouth like a raging torrent of words that couldn't be stopped. I explained about my new abilities and how freaked out I was. Mrs D just listened, a small smile on her lips.

'I don't know what's going on. I'm, like, ridiculously strong too. I'm not normal, Mrs D. Honestly, there's something wrong with me. And my temper's getting worse ... aw, man ... it's almost like I'm possessed. I try so hard, but once I lose it, I can't seem to control myself. I feel like I'm going insane.'

Just talking about my weirdness was like a champagne cork popping. The rush of relief from uncovering the buried secrets I'd been clinging to was strangely cathartic.

Mrs D's reaction totally shocked me. She wasn't fazed in the slightest and stayed completely calm. She just pursed her lips and said, 'Don't worry, dear, I'll help you sort things out.' She gave me a reassuring hug and ushered me out of the door.

I plodded back to my apartment, wondering how the hell Mrs D could sort an angry freak like me out. There was something else I didn't know then, though: my adoptive grandma was not all she seemed. Boy, was *I* in for a shock ...

CHAPTER 2

DISCLOSURE

While Quinn slept, the lower demon alerted its master of the news ...

Demons didn't need an airplane, a train, or even a car to travel. They could move from place to place by shadowing—one place one minute, another the next. Every demon had a different method of shadowing. The more powerful the demon, the further it could shadow. This demon literally went up in a ball of flames and reappeared where she needed to be, the fire acting as an anchor between the two locations.

When the demon arrived at her master's house, he was sitting in an armchair, brooding, with the curtains closed.

'It's time, sir,' the lower demon said as she bowed her head. 'He has hidden his powers for quite a while. I've just discovered the news, and he's asking questions.'

'Very well. We must act quickly. Our adversaries will be sniffing out the girl as we speak.'

'Yes, sir.'

'He must learn to control his powers. Otherwise, things could get out of hand. We don't want any outsiders to know about this.'

'Of course, sir.' The lower demon hesitated. 'H-he's not evil, sir. Far from it.'

'I know. But he's still my son. The last seventeen years have changed us, you and me. After centuries on Earth, how can one soul change us so?'

'I think it's called love,' the demon replied with a slight wistfulness to her voice.

'Be prepared for a difficult time ahead.'

'What of the Dark Lord, sir?'

'He's in hand. He doesn't care as long as he still gets his souls, and they are not in short supply. Leave me now. I will sort things out, don't worry. You do as you always have—protect and guide the Youngling at all costs. We have no idea how he's going to cope.'

CHAPTER 3
THE DEMON

The following day, I was on my way home from football training on a gloomy winter afternoon when a huge, black limo drove past, made a U-turn, and then stopped next to me. A man-mountain of a chauffeur climbed out of the driver's door. Over his enormous face, he wore a pair of wrap-around sunglasses. Strange, because it was almost dusk.

'Mr Atua would like a word.' His voice was deep and low, like rolling thunder on a stormy night.

'Erm, sorry—no idea who you're talking about. Th-think you've got the wrong guy,' I stammered as I started walking away.

'Quinn Carter?' he responded.

I stopped and turned to him. 'Y-yeah?'

'I have the right guy then. Get in the car. You *will* want to meet the person who awaits you. Believe me.'

I wanted to run, but I couldn't move. I bunched my

hands into fists, ready to fight, but I felt like I had grown roots and was literally stuck to the spot. My muscles tensed as I felt my heart jackhammering in my chest. Goose bumps raced up my arms, and my head began to spin. The chauffeur touched my back, but then he flinched and yelped. He took a step away. I stared at him with a frown.

I gulped as he moved around me, giving me a wide berth as he opened the door to the car. But he'd piqued my interest. Who wanted to speak with me? Who was this Mr Atua? I reluctantly climbed into the back of the limo.

It was pretty gloomy, but with my eyesight, I could see even the smallest detail if I focused hard enough, like the tiny hairs on a spider's legs. The perks of being a half-demon. Sure, I didn't know anything about my demonic blood right then, but I was about to get answers. Answers I had been craving. Answers that would drastically change my life.

I glanced at the man seated next to me, presumably Mr Atua. He wore a neatly pressed grey suit—the type you usually see on fancy lawyers and gangsters in movies. He had a sharp jaw and prominent cheekbones, and his raven-black hair glistened in the dim light of the car. His honey-brown skin shimmered, and his face was easy on the eyes—male-model handsome. He looked like he belonged on the catwalks in Milan. Yet his eyes were as black and liquid as ink, and his gaze was more fearsome than a tiger's. I gulped again.

The car started up ... We began to drive to who knows where. I felt my heartbeat booming in my ears as I chewed my lip with nerves. Mr Atua smiled, which made him a little less intimidating. 'Quinn.' His voice was rolling and rich.

'Um, yeah. Who are you?' I tried to sound confident.

'There is no easy way to tell you this, but I'm your father.'

'Sorry, are you on drugs?' Geez, what was with this guy?

Amusement clouded his face, and a small smile played on his lips. 'I'm not, no. But I *am* your father, Quinn.'

The way he said it caused me to hesitate—a feeling in my gut told me he was telling the truth. I tried to remember how to breathe. I could not speak. My brain stuttered for a moment as it attempted to process the information. My whole body tensed while my thoughts struggled to catch up.

'M-my dad? I don't understand. What are you talking about?' Now I could feel my temper prickling. According to what Mum had told me, he'd deserted us—went away one day and never came back. I examined his face and tried to remember the one photo she had of him hidden in her bedroom. He did look familiar.

'You're not entirely human, Quinn.'

I gasped, 'Wh-what do you mean?'

'You're half-demon, son. May I call you son?'

I gazed into his eyes, feeling like I was about to pass

out. I struggled to inhale, to exhale—to do anything. My brain was overloaded. His words reminded me of the rapidly expanding number of unnatural abilities I was starting to develop.

His voice shook me from my thoughts. 'I'm a demon. Your mother never knew about me—my demon self, that is—and I had to leave you both. With me in your life, you would both have been in danger from many creatures. I truly loved you both, but wasn't prepared to risk your lives. I often visited when you were a baby, believe it or not. I've missed you, Quinn.'

How could I be half-demon when demons don't exist? But I knew I was 'different', and even though all this sounded outrageous, I guess it sort of explained things. I still felt as though my head was about to implode, though.

'You are tall, muscular, and attractive. It's your demonic DNA—a trait of your demon blood. As you near adulthood, your powers will intensify. I'm sure you've noticed your powers, and you will learn to control them in time. I'm a powerful demon. You will be too.'

'I am *not* a demon,' I suddenly snapped. Rage was now bubbling inside. I needed to get away from this stranger.

His eyes glowed red for a split second, and then he sighed. 'Mrs Daemon will help and guide you. I'll see you soon.'

That's when I knew he was telling the truth. I mean,

glowing red eyes? Plus, power radiated off him in an almost palpable wave. He wasn't some delusional madman from Crazyville. And I was *terrified.*

The car stopped, and the chauffeur opened my door; my cue to leave. I climbed out as quickly as possible, realising we were now outside my apartment building. My head was spinning, and I was trembling from the combination of shock and anger. Then his words registered. *Mrs Daemon will help and guide you.* Mrs D? My surrogate grandmother?

I turned to ask him what she knew about it all, but I was too late—the car had disappeared. I raced up the steps and inside, heading straight for Mrs D's.

I didn't knock on her door before I burst through it. Mrs D was sitting on her sofa, waiting for me. 'Quinn, dear.'

'D-don't *Quinn, dear* me,' I shouted. Then I felt guilty. 'Sorry, Mrs D.' She nodded patiently. 'Can you tell me what's going on? Please. Apparently, I'm half-demon ... and you know all about it?'

'Ah, dear Quinn—you are, for lack of a better word, an anomaly. You are such a special boy. Yes, you're half-demon. The new powers we've discussed come from your demon within. As does your temper,' she added with a chuckle. 'Things will intensify now that you're nearing adulthood, and I'm here to protect and help you. I will guide you as best as I can. Everything will be okay, I promise.'

'What do you mean? Protect me? Guide me? And

how in hell can you promise me that everything will be okay? This is about as far from okay as it gets!'

She stood up, and I glanced down at her feet—only they weren't feet—they were hooves. Then, as she shook her hair out of her bun, it turned into tiny snakes. Purple, red, and black. *Snakes.*

As the room spun and my blood ran cold, I heard her say, 'I'm a demon nanny, dear.'

I passed out ... straight down like a tranquilised rhino.

I woke up to the sound of chuckling. I opened my eyes slowly, and a fuzzy Mrs D stood over me.

'Ouch,' I said, rubbing my head. 'Did I pass out?' She nodded. 'Was it a dream?' She shook her head.

Damn. My vision came back into focus, and I gazed up at Mrs D and screeched. The snakes and hooves were still there. I gaped at her, horrified. She scowled back at me. I'm pretty sure I'd hurt her feelings, but geez ... she had freaking snakes on her head and horse's feet.

'You've had a lot to take in tonight, Quinn. You need to go home and digest it all, and then we can talk properly tomorrow, okay?'

I nodded, stumbled along the hall to my apartment and plonked myself on the sofa. I was still breathing like I'd run a marathon.

'Dinner's nearly ready, Quinn,' Mum shouted.

'Sorry, Mum. I'm not feeling great. I think I'll go to bed early.'

The thought of food made me gag. Mum came

through and hugged me, ruffling my hair. The touch of her hands settled me a little.

I went to bed, belly churning, in a state of distress and confusion. *What am I?*

You're not entirely human, Quinn.

These words haunted me many times over the next few months. To quell the myriad of thoughts in my mind, I put my head under the pillow. At last, sleep came. But I didn't escape the demons.

I WAS IN A DESERT. The red sky shimmered, and the heat was oppressive, sweltering, and exhausting. The air was thick and hazy; each breath was like drowning in hot lava. There were sand dunes, colourful rocks, and tall mountains. Then I heard the screams. The kind that pierces your brain and makes your blood run cold. Screams full of hysteria, disbelief, and wild terror—human screams. I clenched my fists so hard that my nails dug into my hands, and felt the blood drain from my face The scene before me was gruesome, and the smell of burning flesh was an olfactory assault. Demons were everywhere, tormenting humans in the most hideous ways. I'm tempted to describe in more detail, but it'd give you nightmares.

'Ah, look. We have a visitor.'

I turned to see a demon stalking towards me. The rest of them stopped and stared, and a cacophony of screeching laughs assaulted my eardrums and made the hairs on the back of my neck stand straight up. The demon was tall, at least seven feet, and had the eyes of a serpent in its grotesque face. Its eyes were full of death and despair. It unfurled its bat-like wings and sneered at me, its jagged teeth glowing red with blood. Gross demon guy put a clawed hand on my shoulder, but when the demon touched me, it screamed and backed away. The rest of the demons backed away too.

'Who are you?' it muttered in a low, menacing tone.

I couldn't speak. My mouth was dry, and the burning sensation in my throat made me mute. I was terrified. I willed myself to wake up.

I was back in my bed, trembling like a building in an earthquake. 'It was a dream. It was a dream,' I whispered over and over to myself. However, deep down in my belly, I knew it wasn't. I switched my lamp on and looked at my hands, noticing the imprints from my nails in my palms.

I got no more sleep that night. Instead, I fetched my laptop and started researching demons. What I found made blood whoosh in my ears. They were hideous creatures. The more I looked, the more the trembling in my stomach increased. I found an alphabetised list describing each type of demon and their vast range of abilities. But there was one common denominator—they were all evil.

This realisation was like an uppercut to the gut and had me sucking in big, deep breaths. Was I going to turn evil?

I crept from the apartment while Mum was still sleeping and went to talk to Mrs D again. I'd gone from being a reasonably normal guy to some sort of super freak; I was in a state of emotional turmoil. My thoughts and feelings were colliding and running riot in my head. In other words, I was a mess.

I WAS STILL TREMBLING the morning after the dream. That, and, of course, finding out I was half-demon had seriously creeped me out. My talk with Mrs D had helped some, but my mind was completely mashed. I'd already had my fill of mind-blowing freaky, but if I thought my life couldn't get any funkier, I was seriously deluding myself.

Eve was still in most of my classes, which made my life at school easier. My attention span had never been brilliant, though, and I struggled a bit with the work. If it weren't for Mrs D and Eve helping me, I'd probably have had detention every day. So, later that day, we'd arranged to go straight to her house to do trig homework. I'd been struggling even more to concentrate recently—no surprise there.

Anyway, Eve was helping me out a lot. She also has the *best* basement ever, which Frank converted into a home cinema room. It was unbelievably good, and he never made use of it, so Eve and I assumed ownership. I was hoping we could have a game of *Fortnite* on the PlayStation after trig to numb my scattered brain a bit.

I was quiet on our walk as she babbled on, mainly about her new girlfriends. I heard her mention a boy named Jay and the new girl, Millie. I didn't hear most of what she said, though; I just grunted occasionally when she took a breath. I really was trying to pay attention, but my mind was elsewhere. What the hell was going on? Demons? Seriously? My almost grandma was a freaking demon! My *dad* was a demon, and God knows where I went in my dream, because that place was *full* of demons. I could still smell the lingering odour of burning flesh in my nostrils. *I'm a biological freak.*

'What's up with you, Quinn? You're too quiet. It's unnerving me.' Eve interrupted my thoughts and stopped to study me.

'Huh?' I said, nearly bumping into her.

'See. What's up with you? You've not said a word since the school gates.'

'I think you're doing enough talking for the two of us,' I grumbled.

'What's wrong with you?'

'Do you want a list?'

Eve glowered. 'Acting like a dick won't make yours grow bigger.'

I stared at her, amazed, then burst out laughing. Eve never really used bad language. Well, unless she was angry. She rolled her eyes, sort of growled, and then she carried on walking.

A tiny, white dog with a curly coat, a bit like a poodle, appeared on the other side of the road. It was dirty and scruffy, like a stray. The dog spotted us. Then, when it looked at Eve, its ears pricked up. It ran across the street towards us, but a car came around the corner and ... *bang*. The car didn't stop after hitting the dog—it just sped off.

Eve screamed and rushed over, tears streaming down her face. The poor dog didn't look too well, and blood was dripping from its mouth. I knew it wasn't dead, but it wasn't far off. I realised sensing death was probably another new demonic power of mine. At this point, I decided to stop questioning these powers; I determined that dwelling on the demon stuff would send me heading toward a meltdown. Plus, so far, most of the powers were cool. I'd concentrate on what I could control, not what I couldn't.

Eve picked the dog up and carried it to the pavement. 'Call my dad. Tell him to come now,' she yelled at me.

I called Frank, who told me he would be on his way as soon as possible. Eve glanced up and down the street, and then she did something that totally blew me away. She closed her eyes and laid her hands on the dog's chest, and a golden light glowed and shimmered from her hands. It was like magical sunbeams; the dog's body shimmered with a myriad of gold and ambers.

At that moment, Eve's whole aura dazzled in brilliant white, tinged with blue. Her eyes opened about the same time as the dog's. The creature let out a tiny yelp and wagged its tail. Eve's face lit up, and her smile was the prettiest thing I'd ever seen. I gazed into her intoxicatingly wide, sea-green eyes, and what I saw melted my heart. Eve was beautiful, inside and out. Her ethereal beauty took my breath away.

In that moment, I wanted to hold her face in my hands and kiss her. At that moment, my feelings for Eve changed to a whole new level. My heartbeat quickened, and my blood surged as I looked at her. Then I got a peculiar feeling in my gut. It was almost as if I was seeing her for the first time, and it confused the hell out of me.

As I studied her, I knew I was done for. Toast. But while we knelt, staring into each other's eyes, we were jolted back to reality—Frank had turned up. I scooped the small dog up, and we rushed to the vet.

CHAPTER 4
EVE

'That was so horrible.' Eve sobbed into my shoulder while we waited for Frank to finish speaking with the vet. 'The poor little thing. It's so tiny.'

'It'll be okay now, thanks to you,' I assured her.

'I don't know what's going on with me, Quinn. Please don't tell anybody about what just happened.'

I laughed. 'You don't need to worry. I'm as weird as you, honest.'

She glanced at me. 'I doubt it.'

You have no idea.

Frank came over before we could say anything else. 'The dog's fine—it's like a miracle. The vet's astonished. No broken bones, and all her vitals are perfect. They will try to find her a place with a rescue centre.'

'Dad, please let us keep her,' Eve pleaded. 'Quinn

and I will walk her before and after school. I promise I'll look after her. I want to call her Celeste.'

I stared at her open-mouthed ... walk a dog before school? Huh? Why was I getting dragged into this? Eve saw my face and elbowed me in the ribs.

'Erm, yeah, of course,' I said.

'Well, we need to leave her for now, so the vet can keep an eye on her and ensure they've missed nothing. Her chip is out of date, so they think she's a stray or has been abandoned. They need to contact the dog warden, but I'll see what I can do. This is going to cost me a fortune.' Frank rolled his eyes.

'Dad, you're loaded! *Please*, we need to give her a loving home.'

'Okay, if you promise to take care of her, she can come and live with us.'

Eve threw her arms around Frank and thanked him.

I needed to ask Eve about her ability to heal Celeste. Could I tell her about my powers? I wasn't sure. I mean, healing hands with a magical light show is one thing. Admitting you're a half-demon with super-freaky devilish powers was something completely different.

We drove back to Eve's house, and I stayed with her for a while. She was still pretty shaken up. We watched some TV and chilled out. I still hadn't broached the subject of her healing the dog, but I knew she'd talk to me when she was ready. I figured she'd probably bottled up her feelings about things, a bit like me. Talking about them wasn't easy—

pretending I was normal was simpler. But I realised that both of us were different, which, selfishly, made me relieved. Maybe that's why I'd become so attached to her? Perhaps that's why she had such a profound effect on me?

Eve has a perfect complexion: smooth and tawny. The white of her top popped against the light bronze of her skin, and her inky black hair cascaded over her shoulders. As I glanced at her, my blood surged again; something inside me was ready to erupt. I pulled a cushion onto my lap before she noticed. You get the drift—yep, it made me sit very uncomfortably, believe me. I looked away, horrified. What was wrong with me? Eve was my best friend. I needed to go home before I made a fool of myself.

'I'd best be off. I need to go and see Mrs D before Mum gets home,' I blurted out. I stood up and held my school bag in front of my groin area as I walked out with a bit of a cowboy swagger.

I left, thinking about the one time I *had* actually asked Eve to be my girlfriend. If I remember correctly, her reply had been something like, 'Ewwww.' For a seven-year-old boy, *that* had been a pretty devastating blow, I'll tell you.

I'd barely closed the front door when I realised I'd forgotten my phone. I walked back in, took a few steps back down the stairs to the basement, and then stopped —I could hear Eve talking to someone, and she sounded distressed.

'I can't, Eloise. He already thinks I'm a freak,' I heard her sob.

As I knocked and opened the door, Eve spun around, letting out a little squeak. She had tears running down her face, but she was alone. *Who had she been talking to?*

'Uh, sorry. I forgot my phone,' I said before trying to console her. 'Come here, Eve.' But suddenly, as I went to hug her, a girl's head popped through the wall. Actually, *through* the wall.

'Argh!' I screamed, stepping backwards ... and falling straight on my butt.

'Woohoo, you can see me?' the girl asked as she jumped through the wall. She looked about the same age as us and wore a long, white dress, that set off her flowing red hair ... but she was translucent.

Eve stared at me in amazement. 'H-how?'

The sparks in my brain were desperately trying to connect the dots, but instead they just caused a short circuit. I studied the ghost, and she just grinned at me like a loon. *I'm going insane.*

'Quinn.' Eve shook my arm.

'Who the hell are you?' I almost screeched at the spectre.

'Eloise is a ghost. She's been here for as long as I can remember. It's okay—she's friendly, honest. But I don't understand how you can suddenly see her?'

'What the hell's going on, Eve?'

I'd like to point out that I didn't actually say hell on either occasion. I admit I used a much stronger word—

but go easy on me—this was a particularly disturbing situation.

'I think we need to go and see Mrs D.'

Eve paused and looked at me like I was nuts. 'Mrs D?'

'Just trust me. Please?' I took Eve's hand.

'O-okay. I'll get my dad to drive us. We'll be back soon, Eloise.'

Eve helped me onto my feet, and I stumbled up the stairs on trembling legs. I was still trying to wrap my head around the fact I was half-demon, and now I could see ghosts? And how could Eve see ghosts and heal animals? This was insane, right? But little did I know then—things were about to get even crazier.

About ten minutes later, I was banging on Mrs D's door. 'Mrs D! Eve and I need to talk to you!' I shouted.

'Oh, Quinn, give me a minute,' she shouted.

I suddenly remembered the hooves and everything and just hoped she was putting her snakes in a bun and her boots back on. Those snakes and hooves freaked me out, so I was pretty sure they'd give Eve nightmares.

As she opened the door, Mrs D beamed at me but ignored Eve. She'd always been a bit uneasy around my friend. I'd just assumed Mrs D was being funny about me having a female best friend—you know what grand-parents can be like.

'Is it okay for us both to come in?' I asked.

'Of course. Let me make a nice cup of tea.' Mrs D

gave us a tight smile. As she tottered into the kitchen, I sensed she felt uncomfortable about this situation.

Eve and I sat on the sofa and waited. Eve was fidgeting, clearly nervous, and I realised the feeling of unease from Mrs D was reciprocated.

'She doesn't like me,' Eve said softly, but before I could answer, Mrs D appeared with a tray of tea and biscuits.

'Well, well—it's great to see you.' Mrs D smiled at me but gave Eve an odd glance.

'Mrs D, there's something strange going on ... with both of us. Those things we already chatted about are one thing, but ... well, I can see ghosts now too, and so can Eve. And she can heal animals. What's going on with us? Is Eve like me? A—'

'I'm a demon nanny, dear,' she interrupted, '*not* an angel nanny.'

'A-a what?' Eve stuttered, the blood draining from her face.

'Mrs D, we *both* need your help. I want you to help Eve too. Tell me what the hell's going on,' I hissed through clenched teeth. I could feel rage beginning to bubble inside me again, and my face started to burn with the heat.

'Control that temper, Quinn,' Mrs D snapped, but then she sighed. 'I guess the visions about Eve were correct.' She looked pointedly at Eve. I had no idea what she was talking about, but before I could question her, she started speaking again. 'I need to confer with the higher-ups before I can give you an answer. Give me a few minutes.' She left the room with a whoosh and a slam of the door.

Mrs D was a demon. If Eve was an angel of some sort, did that make them mortal enemies? If I was half-demon, was I fated to be Eve's enemy rather than her best friend? My insides started quivering, and my head started spinning. Demons and angels—what the actual funk was going on?

Eve groaned and closed her eyes. It was now or never. I needed to let Eve in on my secret.

'Eve'—I paused—'I need to tell you something. Please try and trust me, no matter how impossible this is going to sound. Erm, I'm a demon. Well, I'm half-demon. My dad is a full-blown demon, and, erm, I've only just found out.'

Eve's head snapped up, and she sucked in a startled breath. Her normally tawny complexion looked ashen. 'What the hell, Quinn? Don't be stupid. Out of everybody we know, I didn't think you'd ridicule me.' She glared at me with tense, angry eyes. Then she swiped a trembling hand through her hair. 'You're being absurd.' She shook her head in confusion.

I could sense she was furious with me, but somehow, I knew that deep down, she believed me. She didn't want to, and she didn't understand any of it, but I was sure she knew I wasn't lying. We heard voices approaching, and before I could say anything else, Mr Atua walked in with Mrs D.

'Quinn,' he said, his sharp eyes drilling into me.

'Erm, hi, Mr Atua ... Eve, uh, apparently this is my father.'

Eve gave me a sideways glance, her brow furrowed.

'And Eve.' He turned his gaze to her, scrutinising her like a bug under a microscope. Eve stayed silent but squashed herself into the back of the sofa. She seemed terrified and nervous, and something else I couldn't entirely identify.

Dad radiated a strange kind of energy and power, which permeated the room like a thick fog. 'It's time to discuss your parentage.' He beckoned to Mrs D, who sat on the sofa opposite us.

'Well, dear, after your father's indiscretion,' she started while Dad growled. 'Sorry, boss, but it's true. After the indiscretion that resulted in your conception, Quinn, the Omniscient One—as in God—wanted to restore the balance. So, Eve was conceived. Eve, your mother was an angel.'

'Well, yeah, I know. She died giving birth to me,' Eve said as her face crumpled.

'No, dear. That's what they needed you to think—that she went to heaven after you were born. In fact, she was merely a divine vessel to allow the balance the world needed. Your mother always was an angel, Eve.'

'Oh, sweet baby Jesus, this is ludicrous,' Eve snapped. 'It's like a bad movie or something—it's ridiculous. I'm going home.' She jumped up and went to walk out ... but found she was stuck on the spot.

'Eve,' Dad said in a quiet, growly voice. 'Sit ... down.' His eyes glowed red, and, in a split second, he went from looking kind and gentle to terrifying.

Eve gulped and sat back down. 'What's with his eyes?' she asked me under her breath.

'Eve, I'm a demon.'

Eve laughed, but Dad had a dangerous glint in his eyes. He looked like a panther watching its prey from the shadows of the undergrowth. His eyes shone red again, and he growled.

I suddenly found myself wanting to laugh—like, really laugh out loud, I mean, at the ridiculousness of the situation—but I managed to stop myself. The look on Eve's face was priceless—it was probably the first time I'd ever seen her lost for words. Plus, Dad appeared immensely cheesed off.

'I'm a demon, Eve. Quinn is my son. Your mother was an angel. This means Quinn is a half-demon, and you're a half-angel. Deal with it. I need to go.' And with that, he faded away and vanished to where only God knows?

Eve's jaw hung open as she stared at where he'd been standing. 'Where'd he go?'

'Oh, back to his house, dear,' Mrs D said to Eve. 'Now, let's have some sweet tea and cake, shall we? We have a lot to talk about.'

CHAPTER 5
THE NEWS

In a distant realm, far from the mortal world, news of the Youngling was on everybody's lips ...

'Have you heard the news?' Coralie appeared in front of Yvette. The angel closed her wings and ran a hand through her windswept hair.

'Yes, Coralie. The time has come. I've spoken to our Lord, and she has instructed me on how to handle things,' Yvette said. She appeared calm, but Coralie could see the worry in her eyes.

'Oh, the joy of a good half-demon.' Coralie giggled. 'And the irony.'

'Do not tempt fate, Coralie. Do not gloat. Our Lord is happy with the situation, as you may gather. But it must be handled sensitively.'

'I know. I can't believe the change the Youngling has made to the two most feared demons on Earth.'

'Do not be fooled, my sister. Those demons are still

dangerous. And if anything should happen to the boy, then I dread to think what they would be capable of.' Yvette shivered.

'So, you are to trust them with the most precious thing in your existence?' Coralie frowned at Yvette.

'Yes. Yes, I must. I have to trust that our Lord knows better than you or I, Coralie. Go back and keep a watch for me.'

'Yes, sister.'

Coralie unfurled her wings and disappeared into the sky like a shooting star.

CHAPTER 6
THE NEPHILIM

Being hit by a supernatural bombshell is pretty traumatic, believe me. Suddenly, demons were real. Ghosts were real. And now, apparently, Eve was half-angel. Was anything myth anymore? And did that mean other types of supernaturals actually existed too?

I shelved that final thought; my poor brain couldn't cope. I was on a cerebral merry-go-round, and the stormy commotion in my head was overwhelming.

I took one look at poor Eve, though, and felt a bit better. She looked like she was on the verge of a total meltdown. She was visibly trembling and had a glazed look in her eyes. She sat there, literally staring into space—I needed to get her to talk.

Mrs D handed her a cup of sweet tea and sat beside Eve.

'Will you tell me about your healing ability? And about Eloise?' I asked, taking her hand.

Eve regarded me with a close-lipped smile. 'About a year ago, I found a bird with a broken wing. Then, not long after that, a cat with a broken leg. I have no idea how I fixed them both—it just sort of happened. I've never tried it on a human, though.'

Eve's smile faded until she looked as bewildered as I felt.

'As for Eloise, I have no idea how I see her. She's been with me for as long as I can remember. She's my friend. Crazy, huh? I have a friend who's a ghost.' She squeezed her eyes shut. 'I don't see ghosts all the time, though. Oh, I don't know ... I'm confused.'

'So, if you don't believe you're half-angel, Eve, what possible explanation can you give for being able to heal these animals? And communicating with Eloise?' Mrs D's eyes softened, and she leaned closer to Eve.

'I-I don't know. I just thought it might be a gift of some sort? Maybe I'm psychic? I've never told anyone. People will think I'm a freak, and I just want to be normal.' Eve bowed her head and wept silently.

I hugged her, clasping my hands behind her back to resist the urge to touch her face. *Why have my feelings for Eve changed? Why am I so desperate to touch her?* Plus, I was half-demon, and if Eve *was* half-angel, then the chance of her ever potentially loving me had disappeared faster than a Magnum melting in the bowels of hell. I pushed the thought of wanting Eve from my mind. It was ludicrous.

'I have a few powers of my own,' I said quietly. 'Mine are a bit different, though, being demonic and everything. I can see in the dark, read auras, jump fifty feet, and run at super speed. But Eloise is the first ghost I've seen.'

Eve peered at me. I could almost hear her brain straining to compute the information. Selfishly, though, it felt great to unburden my secret to someone else.

'Run at super speed?'

'Yeah, crazy fast. It's pretty good fun too.'

Eve gawked at me like I was a purple flying horse, and then her eyebrows knitted together as she turned to face Mrs D. 'So, Mrs D, tell me ... why *can* I see Eloise and heal things?'

'Because you're a Nephilim, Eve. You *are* half-angel, dear. You need to accept your supernatural heritage.' Mrs D held Eve's hand as she continued, 'There are three planes of existence: mortal, spirit, and demon. Ghosts are real; demons are real. Supernaturals are as real as mortals, dear.'

I thought about my dream and wondered if I'd visited the demon realm. I swallowed hard, hoping the cheeseburger I'd downed for lunch would stay where it was. Eve took a shaky breath and rubbed her eyes with her fists.

'You are an anomaly, Quinn,' continued Mrs D. 'You have all the strengths of the most powerful demon, yet you're half-human. As I said, the Omniscient One—or God, as you know them—needs balance between good and evil to be maintained, hence half-demon and half-angel.' Mrs D swept a hand at us.

'But I'm not evil. Am I?' I snapped.

'Yes, we know that, dear. As does God—I'm sure they are all elated about it too. More importantly, we still love you,' Mrs D added.

Her words helped, but the niggling doubt still rattled around in my brain. This 'evil' thing was seriously stressing me out, making my brain scattered and unfocused. Gruesome images of the demons from my dream were burned into my mind.

Eve shook her head. 'This is all really messing me up —I can't think straight. Can we talk more another time, when I can concentrate? Can I stay with you tonight, Quinn?'

Mrs D stroked Eve's face. From my almost-grandma's expression, I could see that she worried for Eve, who was struggling to understand this supernatural bolt from the blue. I had a feeling my demon nanny was secretly quite fond of my half-angel best friend, whether she wanted to be or not.

'I think that's an excellent idea, dear,' she replied. 'I'm just across the hall if you need me. We can chat again in the morning once you've calmed down a bit. Okay?' Eve nodded slowly.

Soon after, Eve called her dad to ask if she could stay with me and Mrs D. Frank agreed and later popped her overnight bag around, and we agreed that Eve would take my bed and I'd sleep on the couch. Mum was working nights, so we were alone.

Neither of us said much that evening—I think we were both too bewildered. After Eve took herself off to bed, I crashed out within minutes.

My dream that night was extraordinary. I was sitting in an entirely white room—everything from the floor to the furniture, including the chair I was sitting on. It felt a bit like a waiting room. When I looked around, I found Eve sitting next to me.

'What are you doing here, Quinn?' she whispered. 'This is *my* dream.'

'I've no idea. Beats dreaming about the demon realm, though. That place sucks.'

'You dream about the demon realm?' Eve wrinkled her nose.

Before I could reply, Mrs D appeared. To say she looked pissed off would be an understatement.

'Oh, no, no, no, this will not do. This will not do at all,' she said, shaking her head.

'What's up, Mrs D?'

She was just about to answer me when the door opened, and a lady glided in, glowing as though she had a thousand-watt bulb behind her. She had blonde hair and ivory skin and wore tattered jeans and a sweatshirt. She was truly striking. I recognised her immediately, and I heard Eve gasp. Frank had a photo of himself with this lady in their sitting room. Eve's mum. I gazed into the same sea-green eyes as Eve's; they were like the ocean on a stormy day—green with tinges of blue, grey, and silver. Eyes that looked deep enough to hold the universe.

Mrs D took a step backwards, and I'm pretty sure I heard her hiss.

'Mrs D.' The lady's voice was like velvet—honey-coated, melodic, and hypnotic. My eyes were glued to her as she spoke.

'Yvette,' Mrs D answered brusquely.

'Mum?' Eve's eyes shimmered with tears.

Yvette walked over to Eve and sat down next to her. 'Hello, Eve, darling,' she purred in her velvety voice, 'I've been with you every step of your life. You must realise how much I love you. You have grown to be perfect in every way.'

'So why haven't you looked after her, Yvette? Provided her with an angel nanny, like Mr A did with Quinn?' Mrs D had venom in her voice.

Yvette laughed; it was a soft, enchanting sound. 'Ah, Mrs D, our Lord knew Quinn and Eve would bond. And they trust you.'

Mrs D's posture stiffened, and then she sighed. 'You're serious?'

'God knew that you would eventually care for Eve too. Quinn's and Eve's bond is strong. You may be a demon, but this young man'—she pointed at me—'has shown you and Edward a new feeling: love. God knew that Quinn's needs would surpass your own.'

I guessed Edward must be my dad's name. Mrs D's eyes glowed red, and Yvette laughed and shook her head at her.

'Mrs D, you cannot deny how you feel about Quinn and his happiness. Neither can Edward.'

Mrs D just pursed her lips and frowned.

Eve seemed to be coming around from her daze. She peered into her mum's eyes. 'Why did you leave Dad? He was heartbroken when you died.'

'I had no choice. It was God's will that I return. My mission was a success ... just look at you. And as Mrs D said, there must be symmetry between good and evil. No one is truly good or truly evil. Mortals have free will and a choice.'

She looked at me as she finished speaking. Was she insinuating that as half-demon, I was potentially evil? It was irritating, but in the back of my mind, it also worried me. *I think I'm becoming paranoid.* But to be fair, I'm pretty sure if you found out you were half-demon, you may well become crazy with fear and paranoia too.

'I dearly love you both. And your father will be fine now that he has the love of Quinn's mum, Helen.' Yvette's eyes shone with love, and then she stood up. 'I must go. Please find it in your heart to forgive me,' she said sadly.

She embraced Eve and stroked her face. 'Look after her, Quinn,' she murmured as she shimmered and vanished.

I woke up with a start and glanced around the apartment. A sliver of moonlight spilled into the room, so I guessed it was still the middle of the night. Just then, Eve burst from the bedroom. I averted my eyes from her long legs in her PJ shorts and the skimpy top she was wearing.

'I just had the weirdest dream. And you were there,' she said.

'I think we just visited your mum.'

'Oh, dear Lord. It's true then?'

I just shrugged in response.

We rushed to Mrs D's apartment, and she opened the door before we knocked. She had a pinched expression and still looked furious.

'Come in,' she snapped, and we followed her into her kitchen. 'The indignity of it, being summoned there. Wait until I tell your father.'

'So, it was real?' Eve said softly.

'Oh, yes, dear, it was real. Yvette is an angel. As I said.'

Eve burst into tears, and before I could get to her, Mrs D embraced her and held her tightly.

'Shh, it's all part of the plan, dear. Everything will be okay. Your supernatural heritage is something to be proud of. You are a beautiful half-angel. You will do so much good in the world.'

Mrs D grimaced a bit as she spoke but carried on stroking Eve's hair.

'But I'm half-demon. Does that mean I might eventually turn evil?' I asked, trying to keep my voice even.

Eve peered up at me with a tear-stained face. 'Quinn, you could never be evil,' she said as she stared fiercely into my eyes, then buried her head in my chest.

Mrs D sighed. 'Come on. It's time to have another chat.'

We drank sweet tea and sat with Mrs D. A heavy stupor clouded my mind, but Eve looked on the verge of a breakdown again. No surprise there—things were seriously spiralling into Crazyville.

Mrs D started, 'There are gateways between the spirit realm and mortal realms. Places like haunted houses, murder sites, and the like. Some people, like mediums, can sometimes catch a glimpse into the spirit world at these gateways. There are far fewer gateways to the demon realm, and getting there is much more complex.' I furrowed my brow as she spoke.

'These demons can possess both humans and spirits. They are dangerous to both and very difficult to remove once they possess a host.'

Eve was listening intently to Mrs D, who continued, 'Quinn, you have a connection to both the spirit and demon realms.'

I thought about my dream again and shuddered, but she carried on.

'Of course, you can visit the demon realm, but if you ever need to, you can also actually visit the spirit realm.'

'Huh? What? Like, become a ghost?'

'Yes, dear.'

'How?'

'Concentrate on your power, Quinn. Your mind is open now—just trust your instincts.'

Very helpful, I thought.

Mrs D turned her attention to Eve. 'Eve, as a half-angel, you can interact with spirits. However, you both only see spirits if you need to. If the spirit is stranded for some reason, then you may be able to help them sort out their unfortunate situation. Amongst other things, you will both become like liaisons on behalf of troubled souls.'

Mrs D paused, and I looked anxiously at Eve.

'Troubled souls?' I looked at Mrs D questioningly.

'Yes, souls that are stranded on the spectral plane. Souls with unfinished business.'

'What? It's our job to sort out ghosts' unfinished business? The mess they've left behind when they croaked? That's hardly fair,' I said with exasperation.

Mrs D shot me a disapproving look and ignored me. 'Eloise, the poor child, has formed a bond with you, Eve, and now your powers are developing, she will be able to follow you wherever you go ... if you invite her.'

'So, we can both interact with spirits?' Eve frowned. 'And we are both able to communicate with ghosts?'

'Yes, dear. Amongst other things.'

'What other things?' I interjected.

'You will find out, dear.' Mrs D glanced at me. I sighed through clenched teeth and rubbed my temples, but Mrs D ignored me again and carried on talking to Eve. 'You will only see spirits if there's a reason. It's the way it works, I'm afraid. You will be a go-between for lost souls. Things will become clear, eventually.' Mrs D smiled kindly.

'I thought you were here to help us? Why do you keep saying we'll find out eventually?' I said with a tight jaw.

'You will be fine, dear. You will know what to do when the time comes. So don't worry,' Mrs D replied.

Oh, yeah. We will be fine. Damn, she was so vague and annoying sometimes.

'Your powers will grow, Eve, in addition to your healing power, which is normal for an angel. So, be prepared, dear. Angels—and a few demons—are notorious for compulsion. Especially on mortals. That is another gift that you may develop over time.'

'Compulsion?' Eve frowned.

'It's the ability to suggest that someone do as you wish. Normally only in the short term.' Mrs D explained.

'That'd be a pretty neat ability, Eve.' I said, trying not to think about helping spooks with unfinished business or the 'other things', whatever they were.

'I guess,' she replied, giving me a weak smile.

'There's so much to talk about, my dears. I'm here whenever you need answers to your questions.' Mrs D smiled at us both.

'Erm, the visions you mentioned, Mrs D?' I asked.

'Yes, the visions. That conversation is for another time, dear. Come on—get some sleep. We have plenty of time to talk when you're ready,' she said as she stroked Eve's hair.

CHAPTER 7

A DILEMMA

While Quinn and Eve slept, Mrs D shadowed to see Mr A again ...

She was nervous—anxious, even. She'd waited until early the following morning, building up the courage to face him. The news she had to tell him was unheard of. She just hoped she wouldn't be punished.

'What is it, Lilith?' he snapped as she appeared in front of him. He was eating his breakfast and appeared to be in a bad mood.

'I have some sensitive information, sir.' Mrs D looked down.

'Out with it,' he snapped.

'I-I'm to be guardian of the Nephilim too, apparently.'

Mr A's reaction almost floored her. He bellowed with laughter, so much so that he had a coughing fit.

'God really does have the most twisted sense of humour. Worry not, Lilith—Quinn loves Eve. He just doesn't realise how deeply yet. His demon is drawn to her angel. The attraction is powerful, and their bond will be unbreakable. I have a strange feeling he may be her fated mate. Another of God's tiny snipes, I fear.'

'But does she feel the same, sir? Fated mates must have an equal attraction, and if she doesn't?' Mrs D's voice cracked.

'Of that I'm not sure. If not, the Youngling is in for a tough ride. We need to be there to guide and support him. We will care for the Nephilim as our own, the way it is adjudged.'

Mrs D almost collapsed with relief. 'Thank you, sir. She is actually a sweet little thing when you get to know her.'

Mr A harrumphed and carried on eating his breakfast, which Lilith took as her cue to leave.

CHAPTER 8
ELOISE

All in all, my morning at school was pretty crappy. I'd struggled to concentrate, which was pretty understandable given the absurdity of the whole situation. I figured that once I got home, the day could only get better. Geez, was I ever wrong?

I'd arranged to meet Mum at Eve's house after school, where Frank was cooking for us again. I was determined to find out more about Eloise. Not that I'd said anything to Eve, but I needed to know why even my demon grandma felt sorry for the young ghost.

Eve was quiet. I think she was still trying to process the dream from the night before and the fact that she was actually half-angel. She seemed far away and in her own little world. I wasn't much better, but tried to block demon stuff from my brain. If I thought about it too much, it sent me crazy.

Frank's culinary abilities are pretty impressive, so dinner was amazing, but Mum seemed a bit on edge. Eve seemed oblivious to Mum's mood, but I was acutely aware of the tension in the air. I started to get a bit twitchy—something was definitely up. We were sitting around the large oak table in the kitchen when Frank cleared his throat.

'Kids, we have something to tell you.' He paused, looking fondly at Mum, before saying, 'We're getting married.'

Eve shrieked and jumped up to give Mum and Frank a hug. I just sat there feeling stunned, my mouth wide open. My muscles froze, and I got a knot in my belly. How was my life going to change? I shook my head and chided myself. *Stop being a selfish jerk.*

Still, I only managed to utter one word, 'What?'

I mean, I liked Frank well enough and everything; he's great to Mum and makes her happy. He's grounded, sensible, rich, and a great fun guy. But even so ... did she need to *marry* him?

Mum took my hand. 'Quinn, it'll be okay, I promise. And we're going to move in here next month.'

Eve squealed again—at least she was thrilled about it. Frank laughed as she threw her arms around him.

'But what about Mrs D? We can't leave her,' I grumbled.

'Don't worry—we couldn't leave her, you're right, so she's moving here. That was Frank's suggestion. She has her own granny annexe. She's delighted about it.'

'Is she?' *Why hasn't she mentioned it to me?* I wondered, feeling a bit hurt. Then I thought about Dad. How would he take the news? I definitely didn't want him upset. Who knew what he was capable of?

'I want you to be happy, Quinn,' Mum said sadly.

Then the guilt set in. 'Oh, I am, Mum. I'm happy that you're happy, honest. It's just a bit of a shock, you know?' I got up and hugged her and Frank. 'Anyway, it'll be ace spending even more time with my bestie, Eve.'

I meant it, but—big but—I knew I wanted Eve as more than my best friend, so having her even closer? Now my love for her had changed—I wasn't so sure it was such a good thing, especially as she didn't reciprocate my feelings. Plus, Mum was now marrying Eve's Dad. It was all so screwed up.

After dinner, Eve and I went to the basement to find Eloise.

'I'm really pleased that they're getting married. You should be too. They're so good together, and I've never seen my dad so happy. I love your mum. She's the kindest person, and beautiful too,' Eve said as she took my hand.

'I know. Your dad's great too. I guess I was being selfish. I've always been the man in her life, you know?' I tried not to sound resentful.

'Yeah, I hear you,' said Eve. 'We need to make the most of it, though. Especially after meeting my mum and finding out who we really are. I can't dwell too much on all that—it hurts my brain. I'm struggling with it all, Quinn—really struggling.'

'Yeah, me too.'

'But at least now I'll have you and Mrs D here to talk to and help guide me, won't I? Which helps loads.'

I just sighed and nodded.

'I'm glad you're as odd as me.' Eve kissed me on the cheek.

I gazed into her eyes, and a crazy impulse to stroke her face almost overtook me. I balled my hands into fists. I was losing my mind.

'Hi, Eve and Quinn,' Eloise squealed as she popped her head through the wall.

'Geez, Eloise, you nearly gave me heart failure,' I grumbled.

'Sorry, Quinn.' She giggled, and Eve laughed.

Eloise talked and talked; I just nodded and listened to her and Eve's chatter. She was a talkative ghost, but then she was probably making up for years of being alone. Once she took a breath, I cut in.

'Anyway, what's your story, Eloise? I need to know more about you,' I said as the ghost sat down.

Eloise wrinkled her brow and pursed her lips; she looked upset. On impulse, I touched her arm in a sympathetic manner, and as soon as my hand made contact with her, she became physical, like a mortal. But, although Eloise appeared fully formed in a physical sense, the edges of her body shimmered with luminosity, like flickering starlight. I guessed this was her spectral glow.

Eloise looked at my hand on her arm, suddenly lost for words. It was probably the first time she'd been touched in God knows how long. That can kind of blow someone's mind, especially if that someone happens to be dead. Eloise looked at me with an expression of utter disbelief.

Not being alive—like, being dead—it follows that ghosts lack substantial matter. That's why they're translucent. So, it was definitely weird that I was able to touch her. I should have passed straight through her, right?

Eloise held her hands before her face and stared at them with her mouth wide open.

'What the hell, Quinn?' Eve gawped at Eloise.

My brain was officially fried—I couldn't even begin to comprehend it—so I just shrugged and accepted the fact that, as half-demon, I was definitely a bit of a freak. *We all feel like freaks from time to time, don't we?* I consoled myself with that fact.

'I've no idea how that happened.' I grumbled.

'Woohoo!' Eloise suddenly squealed, and she danced around the basement, laughing. Eloise was full of life—well, for a dead girl. Her enthusiasm was contagious. She was like a beacon of light and happiness, and when she was happy, her spectral glow was dazzling.

'Will she stay like that?' Eve gazed wide-eyed at Eloise.

'Who knows? I'll add it to my list for the freak-of-the-year award.' I blew out a big breath and smiled as I watched the crazy ghost dance and laugh.

Eve just chuckled at me. 'That's a pretty cool demonic power.'

'Yeah, I guess so.' I gave a resigned sigh.

At last, Eloise sat on the sofa, and began telling her story.

'Have you heard of the Pendle witch trials in 1612?' Eloise asked. We shook our heads. 'Well, my father, Nicholas Bannister, was a witch hunter. There were twelve witches, men and women, and ten were hanged for witchcraft.' She looked forlorn. 'I was seventeen at the time, and one of the witches cursed my father. Elizabeth Device was her name. She cursed him to lose a treasured heart and told him he would never be reunited with it again.'

Eloise started crying, but then she wiped her eyes and sniffed. '*I* was his treasured heart. I died not long after the trials and have never been able to pass into the spirit realm. I'm cursed to wander this mortal realm forever. I was so lonely until I met Eve; now I'm stuck here with her. Not that I mind, because you're my friend.' She sniffed and gave Eve a weak smile. 'But being cursed means I'll never see my parents again.'

Eloise then let out a wail, faded away, and vanished. Eve and I stared at the space where she had been sitting.

I swore under my breath. 'Poor Eloise.'

'Yeah, poor Eloise.'

'Eloise,' I whisper-yelled.

The ghost appeared in front of us again, still crying. Strangely, she was still in a physical form; well, apart from the constant flickering.

Eve got up and held Eloise's hands whilst smiling. 'I can hug you at last.'

'I've got some good news,' I said, trying to cheer her up. Eloise peered at me apprehensively from under her lashes. 'You have a strong connection to Eve, like a tied bond, so if Eve invites you, you can come anywhere with her ... with us.'

'Really?' Eloise's eyed me with suspicion.

Eve nodded. 'Well, you can't come *everywhere* with me, but yes. Why don't we try it now? It's still light outside, so let's go to the park and play on the swings.'

I laughed. 'What are you? Eight years old? I'm not playing on the swings.'

Eloise's face crumpled briefly, but Eve quickly put me in my place.

'Your lips are moving, but all I hear is "blah, blah, blah". Get your coat on, Quinn Carter—we are going to the park.' Eve gave me a friendly punch on the arm.

'Park? Swings? Oh, I'm so excited!' Eloise squealed, clapping her hands. And off we went to the park. I only hoped none of my football mates saw me—this would ruin my reputation completely. Geez, what we do to make a crazy ghost happy.

CHAPTER 9
MILLIE'S HOUSE

Eve seemed to have settled down, and she hadn't really mentioned angels and demons since the night we went to the park with Eloise, but I knew she'd visited Mrs D quite a few times. My adoptive grandma was a godsend for us both, helping us come to terms with our supernatural heritage.

On Saturday, a couple of weeks after Mum's and Frank's big announcement, Eve, Frank, Mum, and I went to the kennels to collect Celeste, the street dog. Apparently, the dog was a poochon, whatever that was. She was small, fluffy, and adorable. Naturally, Eve was ecstatic—that dog would be one spoiled pooch. Mum and Frank were quite taken with Celeste too.

As soon as we got her home, we all had to go for a walk through the woods. Even Eloise tagged along. Thankfully, Celeste liked Eloise. Mrs D had warned us that the dog may try to avoid the ghost because, apparently, animals are very perceptive to paranormal phenomena. But thankfully, Eloise bonded with the cute dog. Frank and Mum laughed when Celeste was chasing around after the ghost. To people who couldn't see Eloise, Celeste must have looked like she was chasing shadows. Mum seemed so happy, walking hand in hand with Frank, and I realised that their decision to get married couldn't be *such* a bad idea.

That afternoon, I had a football match, so I left Eve and Eloise to relax with the pampered pooch. After the game, I was running late and got to Eve's to find her waiting for me. Patience is not one of her better qualities. In fact, her impatience drives me crazy, but that doesn't stop me from loving her.

'Hurry up and have a shower, Quinn,' Eve scolded. 'I told Millie we'd be at hers in half an hour. It's a ten-minute walk, you know.'

I sighed and did as she commanded. A night with Eve, Eloise, and Millie—oh, joy. I decided I needed to spend more time with my male friends.

As we walked to Millie's house, Eve chattered away to Eloise. 'Yeah, Millie's lovely. She won't be able to see you, Eloise, but I wanted you to come anyway. I caught Mia and her crew giving Millie a verbal beating at school. I just walked up to Mia and told her to lay off, so she started on me! I put that biatch straight in her place, though.'

'What did you say?' I interrupted.

'Told her I hope she chokes on all the shit she chats.'

I cracked up laughing. Eve is hilarious, and her comebacks are legendary. It was a relief to see her back to her usual snarky and feisty self.

We got to Millie's house to find her outside on the front steps, which was odd because the sun was going down, and the early spring night air was chilly. Her parents were out, so movie night it was; I only hoped she had some decent food and drinks. I'd met Millie a few times at school. She was quiet and often seemed self-conscious and anxious. Eve was brilliant with her, though. Typical Eve—she was such a kind person—very angel-like.

Millie's skin had an almost alabaster hue, and her poker-straight blonde hair was pulled back into a ponytail. She was petite, seemed fragile and was dressed in her obligatory black. Her eyes were the colour of caramel, as were the freckles over her nose and cheeks. Millie's aura was hard to read, but I noticed she was stressed out about something. As I got closer, I noticed she looked unwell. Her skin was chalky white, with dark, bruise-like shadows under her eyes. It was as if she hadn't slept for a month.

'Hey, Millie.' Eve rushed to hug her friend.

'Hey.' Millie tried to smile, but it didn't quite happen. 'My parents are out, and they'll be late back. I'm so glad you've both come over,' she said quietly.

'Don't mind me,' Eloise huffed. I coughed to cover up a laugh.

I peered up at the house. It was large, old, and

gloomy. The trees surrounding it cast eerie shadows over the dark stone. The windows were oversized and divided into many parts, like the compound eyes of a fly. I felt like I was being watched, and a chill shot down my spine. Then I gave myself a mental slap. I thought I was being weirded out because of all the demon talk and stuff, so I decided not to think about it.

I followed the girls inside, and it was like entering a tomb; the house was freezing. I didn't say anything, though, because the girls didn't seem to notice the extreme temperature.

Millie fetched us Coke and popcorn, and we sat down to watch a movie.

After about thirty minutes, I felt at risk of hypothermia, so I braved up. 'Can you put the heating on, Millie? It's like a morgue in here,' I said politely. Millie's face fell.

Eve narrowed her eyes and made an exceptionally vulgar gesture at me. 'Suck it up, Carter. It's not cold in here.'

Eloise giggled, and Millie spurted out a laugh. I just curled my lip at Eve. I wasn't sure how they didn't notice the freezing temperature, so thought I must be coming down with a bug or something. I still felt like something was off, though, and it was giving me the creeps.

Eve and Millie started chatting, and I zoned out, unable to focus on the movie. I knew something was wrong. Don't ask me how, but the demon inside me was agitated. I eyed my surroundings—everything looked normal, like an ordinary family home. Comfy chintzy sofas, lots of table lamps, a huge flatscreen TV. Yep, everything seemed fine. But I somehow *knew* it wasn't. And I was bricking myself.

Suddenly, I felt a cold breath in my ear and whirled around. Sweat beaded on my forehead.

'You okay, Quinn?' Eve gave me a funny look.

'Mm.' I managed to nod, but a cold feeling had settled over me, seeping into my bones, and my heart jackhammered at my ribs. I was freaking terrified, and I didn't know why. I wiped the sweat from my forehead and grabbed my drink. Eve was concerned; I could tell she was trying to figure out what was wrong with me. And all I knew was that I had a horrible feeling in my belly and needed to get out of this house.

Eloise shivered beside me, saying, 'I'm going back to Eve's. This place creeps me out.'

And she's a freaking ghost. I watched her gradually fade away, wishing I could go with her. The two girls continued chatting, while I attempted to watch the movie. Millie looked much better and more relaxed. I felt worse and more anxious.

'Where's Eloise?' Eve mouthed at me. I shrugged my shoulders. My thoughts were as numb as my legs.

As I peered through the French doors to the kitchen, I could feel eyes watching us and caught a glimpse of a small, shadowy figure standing in the corner. Whatever it was, it radiated malice and meant us unequivocal harm. The demon within me became even more agitated. The eyes appeared to follow the girls' conversation but focused mainly on Millie. I felt sick. I had goosebumps up my arms, and my T-shirt was sweaty. I suddenly felt an overwhelming urge to get us out of there. I'm not a coward—not at all—but I'm definitely no fool. I think if you realise you are more than likely to be in mortal danger, it's perfectly acceptable to beat a retreat.

'Quinn, you look ill. What's up?'

I drew my eyes away from the kitchen and looked at Eve. I saw her shiver. Millie's expression changed too; she seemed scared.

'Get out,' a voice demanded. Eve's eyes widened—she'd heard it too. The voice chilled me to the core. *'I will kill the witch.'*

I leapt off the sofa and whirled around. Eve jumped up too. Millie now looked terrified.

A loud thump came from upstairs, making all three of us recoil. My stomach was in knots. Then there were loud footsteps: one ... two ... three ... four ... five ... six ... and then silence.

'Is there anybody upstairs, Millie?'

'N-no.'

Next second, the kitchen cupboard doors and drawers started opening and closing. Cutlery, cups, and glasses floated out and spun around the room.

'The poltergeist,' Millie whispered.

'What poltergeist?' I glanced at Eve, but she shrugged and mouthed, 'No idea.'

Millie sobbed. The opening and closing got faster, and so did my pounding heart. Eve and Millie gravitated towards me. Ironic, really—I'm pretty certain I was more terrified than them.

'Let's run for it,' I whispered, and we all bolted for the door.

'I'll kill you, witch!' roared in my ears.

Smack! Millie howled and fell to the floor. The furniture levitated and started rotating. Then came the menacing laugh, so loud it left my ears ringing—it was low and rumbling, filled with promises of pain and torment.

Eve and I grabbed Millie and hauled her out of the door. Then, just before I closed the door, I heard a child's voice say, 'Please help me. Don't leave me.'

Eve and Millie were stumbling down the steps. Eve was on the phone with her dad. I stopped at the bottom step, and Eve looked around at me.

'Come on, Quinn. Let's get out of here.'

I shook my head. 'Take Millie back to yours. I'll follow soon. Promise.'

From the moment I'd stepped into Millie's house, I had been terrified, but suddenly a blanket of calm wrapped around me. Or was it a blanket of temporary insanity? I wasn't sure. All I knew was that I needed to go back into that house.

'Quinn, please. Please come with us.' Eve was scared, but she ran back to me.

'Eve, you heard the voice. It's after Millie. You need to take her. It thinks she's a witch.'

Eve looked uncomfortable.

'What ... is she?' I asked, narrowing my eyes at Eve.

'I'm not sure ... maybe?'

I wasn't surprised, to be honest. *A half-demon, a half-angel, a ghost ... let's throw a witch into the mix, too, hey?*

'I heard a child's voice, Eve.' Eve seemed confused, and her forehead creased with worry as she stared at me. I felt sure she thought I was losing the plot.

'I did, Eve, honest. I need to help her. I'm going back in.'

Millie heard me and started crying again. 'Please come with us. You don't know how wicked it is.'

I paced around the drive like a crazy man. 'I have to go back in. I've got to at least *try* to help the kid.' I blew out a breath and attempted to psych myself up to go back into the demon house.

Eve gazed at me with wide eyes. 'No, Quinn—please don't go back in there. *Please.*'

I turned and glanced at the front door, but when I looked back, I spied Frank's SUV through the bushes at the top of the garden. He was pulling onto the roadside outside of the house.

'I'll be okay, promise.' I gave Eve a half-grin.

Of course, I didn't know I'd be okay—quite the contrary, truthfully. So, I clenched my jaw and squared my shoulders, then frogmarched her and Millie down the drive and out of the gate to Frank's car. I made them get in, but Eve halted.

'Hey, Quinn,' Frank shouted. 'You all okay?' he added, narrowing his eyes at me.

'We're fine, Dad,' Eve interjected quickly. 'Millie's just feeling unwell, so I thought I'd bring her back to ours.'

'Yeah, but I'll walk back if you don't mind. Need to clear my head,' I said as cheerfully as I could.

Frank shrugged but gave me a strange look.

'Look, get in the freaking car,' I ordered Eve sharply under my breath.

She knew I was serious, so she climbed into the car with grim reluctance. As the car drove away, Eve and Millie stared through the back window, worried looks on both their faces.

Once they'd left, I walked back to the front door, struggling to swallow the ball of dread in the back of my throat. The house was silent, and I eyed the red door for a few seconds before opening it again. Then I took a deep breath and stepped inside. Everything seemed normal, like I'd imagined the furniture doing acrobatics. The kitchen cupboards and drawers were closed. The silence was oppressive.

Suddenly, I heard the young girl's voice again.

'I'm glad you came back,' she said happily.

The other voice was silent. I knew I had to help this child.

A sudden, blood-curdling scream and a demonic laugh resounded throughout the house. A feeling of dread built up in my chest. BUMP, BUMP, BUMP came from upstairs again. I took a breath and legged it up there, stopping at the top of the stairs.

'Can you hear me?' I shouted out to the child.

'Yes,' her faint voice called back to me.

I opened a bedroom door to find the ghost of a little girl sitting on the bed. She wore a white pinafore dress and black shoes. In her hands, she held a gruesome-looking doll. She looked at me and started humming a nursery rhyme—one I couldn't place.

'I'm so glad you can see me, Quinn. My name is Victoria. Pleased to meet you. Are you a witch too?'

'Erm, n-no, I'm not, Victoria.'

'Ah, good. We don't like witches, do we?' she said to the doll. 'Do you want to play? It's been so long since I had someone to play with. You can stay here with me forever.' She smirked. 'I'll have to kill you first. Then we can kill the witch together.'

Her voice was sweet but venomous, like cupcakes sprinkled with poison. *She's psycho* went through my head a few times. It was like a scene from a horror movie. Adrenaline flooded my system. Then her eyes glowed yellow, not red, but the hairs on my neck stood right up—demon alert. I was pretty sure I was dealing with the demonic possession of a ghost, essentially a poltergeist.

'Talk to me,' I shouted. 'Who *are* you? Stop hiding

behind a little girl, you complete wimp. Show yourself.' I tried to control my racing heartbeat and struggled not to gasp as the girl's mouth opened wide, revealing rows of sharp teeth like tiny daggers.

'You will die. Then you will help me kill the witch.' The voice of the demon was guttural and echoed with cold brutality. Then it laughed—a burst of thunderous laughter that reverberated through my brain.

'Okay. So, you're a freaking lunatic? I get it. But I'm really not in the mood to die today,' I growled, trying to stop my voice from cracking.

The next thing, the girl lunged at me like a ninja. She had a huge carving knife in her hand. Where the hell that came from, I had no idea. I put my hand up to shield my body and felt a searing pain in my arm. The little vixen had sliced me. Raging anger surged through my bloodstream. I growled and jabbed my fist hard into her face. She turned opaque at the touch, and stumbled backwards, becoming translucent again.

The girl looked at my face and said, 'Uh ... oh.' Then she gradually faded away.

The house started banging and thumping again. Furniture danced around the bedroom, and photos and lamps flew through the air. That's when I knew I was in trouble. I had zero idea of what I was capable of —well, apart from jumping high, running super-fast, and seeing ghosts. And I was pretty sure that reading the demon's aura wouldn't enlighten me—it was clearly an evil entity. Its energy was consuming me; I felt it like a thick, freezing fog enveloping my whole body.

'Great ...' I said aloud, 'this was *not* on my to-do list for this week.' The odds looked dismal. I tried not to think about potentially getting my butt kicked by a deranged demon.

I glanced down at my arm, which had stopped hurting. No blood. No cut. That's when I realised the demon couldn't harm me. Slowly, I opened the bedroom door and poked my head out. *Smack!* A lamp lay broken on the floor. I ducked, only just avoiding being decapitated by a huge knife from the kitchen. I could feel the demon's energy intensify. It was close, but it had dematerialised.

Then I thought about Mrs D's words. *I'm capable of visiting the spirit realm and the demonic realm*, I told myself, so I decided to give visiting the spirit realm a go. I concentrated and felt myself shimmer; static pulses fired over my skin and through my very core. The whole of my body tingled with a strange type of energy. Then I looked at my hands ... and I was translucent. I was able to see the demon; it was standing right in front of me, frozen to the spot, it's eyes bulging in shock.

'Come here, you little ...' I growled as I seized its arms. When I touched it, I felt like I'd been plugged into a wall socket; electricity surged through me. I couldn't have let go of her if I'd wanted to, and believe me, I *wanted* to. I was stuck to it like a barnacle.

The girls face contorted in agony. The demon's voice panted and growled, *'What are you?'*

I could see a face within hers. A face with black, cracked skin, yellow eyes, and those dagger-like teeth. It made Stephen King's imagination look like rainbows and unicorns.

But the demon was scared—scared of me.

I felt myself soaking up the demon. Blind panic surged through me, and my heartbeat drummed in my ears. What the actual? It was a truly horrifying experience.

The demon released an agonising scream as I drew it out of the girl. I felt it circulating through me, still screaming. The screams became quieter and quieter until they were almost like whispers, and then they stopped. The young girl collapsed, and I turned around and almost threw up all over the carpet.

Shakily, I turned back to picked Victoria up. I was in my physical form again, and so was she. How could I make ghosts opaque? It confused the hell out of me. I laid her on the bed and plopped beside her, holding her hand. Gradually, she opened her eyes.

'Thank you, Quinn,' she uttered weakly. 'I've been trapped here for so long time by that demon. How did you do it?'

I looked at her in a daze, just as I noticed that the temperature had risen and the eerie feeling in the house had disappeared.

'How did you do it?' she repeated.

I shook my head. I felt like I'd been hit on the head with a piñata stick a few hundred times ... *maybe that's what absorbing a demon makes you feel like?*

'I have no idea,' I croaked in response to Victoria's questions.

She sat up and hugged me when a man and woman dressed in old-fashioned clothes appeared in front of us. I gasped and jumped up. Victoria screeched and ran to the woman, hugging her.

'Thank you, son.' The man smiled kindly at me. 'We have waited many years for Victoria to be released. Now she can come with us to where she belongs.'

Victoria waved happily at me as they all faded away, and then they vanished, leaving me feeling anxious and unsettled. I'd just rescued a ghost and absorbed a demon. My skin was still thrumming with energy, and I was trembling. The demon was right. What *was* I?

I walked down the stairs on shaky legs and glanced around. Everything was normal, with no signs of a demon trashing the house. It was as if it had been a bad dream, but I knew better. Then I screeched and stumbled backwards as Eve, Millie, and Eloise appeared out of nowhere. Well, actually, they walked *through* the wall.

'What the hell?'

'Sorry.' Eve rushed over and hugged me. 'We'll explain when we get back. We've come to rescue you.'

'You're shaking, and you look sick,' Eloise said as she touched my arm.

Millie was scrutinising the sitting room, looking scared. She had a small knife in her hand and looked ready to use it.

'I'm sorry, Quinn,' Millie murmured. 'I shouldn't have allowed you to stay here. Nobody would believe me when I said this house was haunted by evil.'

'It's not anymore,' I muttered.

The tension drained from Millie's face.

'Come on. Let's get back to my house. You can fill us in when we get there,' Eve instructed.

'I'm aching all over. I don't feel great. I'm not sure I can walk that far.'

'You don't need to,' Eve said. 'Take my hand.'

Millie touched the knife to the wall and murmured strange words. The wall shimmered blue, and part completely disappeared, leaving a large, gaping hole. Through it, I saw Eve's basement.

Then, everything went fuzzy ... and I lost consciousness.

CHAPTER 10
THE KEEPERS

I woke up a while later on Eve's sofa in her basement. I felt almost human again ... well, as human as a half-demon can feel.

'Eve?'

Eve ran over to me. 'Quinn, you okay?' She stroked my forehead.

Then I thought about absorbing the demon and only just managed to control my gag reflex as my stomach convulsed. Niggling worries made me jittery. What *was* I? I couldn't tell Eve—I'd repulse her. A heavy ache twisted at my heart.

'Yeah, just a bit woozy.' I lied.

Eloise and Millie squished on the sofa with me.

'You can see Eloise?' I narrowed my eyes at Millie.

'Um, yeah. I'm not sure why, and I knew she was friendly. I thought she'd tagged along, and you didn't realise. I didn't say anything because I don't normally see ghosts, and if I'd told you, I worried you would have thought I was crazy,' Millie said softly.

'Oi.' Eloise playfully slapped Millie's arm, and then the crazy ghost jumped up and danced around the basement.

I reckoned that, after hundreds of years of being alone, she was just so happy another person could see her.

Let me explain something. For mortals, ghosts are ethereal beings, lacking substantial matter—most of you walk straight through them on a regular basis, completely unaware. You may feel a cold spot or get a chill down your spine—you get the drift. But for whatever reason, even though Eloise appears in a physical form to us—well, apart from the flickering and shimmering—she's still invisible to mortals.

Mrs D explained this to us—she's a font of weird information. So, I couldn't fathom why Millie could see Eloise; maybe it was the witch thing? Who knows?

'Tell us what happened.' Eve looked into my eyes.

'I-I've got to go.' I jumped up, leaving a confused-looking Eve.

'Shall we meet in the morning?' she said in a small voice.

'Sure, see you at ten o'clock.' I closed the basement door.

Of course, I should have come clean with them there and then, right? ... Instead of delaying it. I guess the whole finding out you're a demon-absorbing-biological-freaking-weirdo thing had really gotten to me. All I could think about was seeing Mrs D and finding out what the hell was happening.

Thanks to my ability to run supernaturally fast, I bolted through the woods and was back home in no time. The thought of that yellow-eyed demon inside me made my heart beat so fast, I thought it would jump from my chest. Never in my life had I been so scared. *Never.*

'Mrs D,' I called out as I banged on her door.

Mum was still at work but would be home soon, and I needed to talk to Mrs D before then. When Mrs D opened the door, she had her snakes in a bun, but her shoes were missing. Those hooves were, frankly, creepy.

I was momentarily distracted and pointed to her head. 'How do your snakes look like hair, anyway?'

'Oh, they're glamoured, dear.'

I scrunched my face at her. 'Glamoured?'

'Glamour interferes with the field of perception, Quinn. Like a smokescreen. But I can't bear putting my boots on tonight, sorry.'

I mumbled a *whatever* as I walked past her into the apartment. 'Mrs D, I must talk to you about what happened tonight. I'm so confused,' I said, pacing around her sitting room.

I explained about the demon possessing the little girl, giving a step-by-step account of every minute I'd been at Millie's house. 'Demons are real; ghosts are real. I know that now. I can interact with both of them. I know I'm half-demon, but this is seriously weirding me out, Mrs D. I managed to turn myself translucent, like a ghost, like you said I could. But what's all that about? And that freaking demon is inside me somewhere.'

Just thinking about the demon caused me to melt-down faster than a tub of Ben & Jerry's left in the midday sun. I tried to control my breathing and forced myself to calm down. Then I plopped myself down on the sofa, closing my eyes.

When I opened them again, Mr Atua was sitting in the chair opposite me. I jumped up and let out a gasp. My nerves were completely frayed. He looked at me, his eyes enigmatic.

'Can you help me understand, please, Mr Atua?' I pleaded.

'Yes, Quinn—I'll help you anytime, son,' he said quietly.

'I became a freaking ghost. And that hideous demon is floating around inside me somewhere. How is that even possible?'

'You can enter the spirit realm, as Mrs D said. This means you disappear from the mortal realm, as you did at Millie's house. You can travel in and out of the realm of death without actually dying yourself. You become a shadow, and no mortal will see you when you're in that state. Or very few demons, unless they're as powerful as me.'

'So, I became a ghost? The demon saw me, but it had possessed a spirit. That's probably why, then?'

Dad nodded. 'You became a spirit without death. Don't be afraid of using this gift, Quinn. You have complete control. It's a useful ability—you cross the veil and walk in the shadows; you are completely invisible.' He gave me a serious look.

'I guess being half-demon is pretty cool, sometimes,' I muttered.

'As a half-demon, you're capable of many things. Your powers are growing, son, although you must know that I have no idea if you will inherit all my powers.'

'But absorbing a demon? Will it make me evil? You're right; I'm not entirely human. But what am I, then? I'm worried, Dad.'

He grinned at me. I'd called him Dad without thinking; if that made him happy, I wasn't about to burst his bubble.

'Quinn, you are innately good, despite my being your father. Being a demon myself, I felt slightly disappointed at first, but now I'm proud of you, and there was a divine purpose for your birth. I see that now. God has a wicked sense of humour sometimes.' He raised his eyes to the ceiling, a twinkle in his eye. 'You are so like your mother. Such a beautiful soul ... she changed me in many ways.'

He paused, and a sad smile twisted his lips. 'But, *because* of my status, God needed balance, hence Eve. With me as your father, you're destined to be more powerful than most demons. It is unusual—almost unheard of—for a demon to conceive a child with a human. Maybe it's because your mother opened my heart to love.'

I felt my face flush. 'So, there might be more half-demons?'

'Maybe, but they're unlikely to be as powerful as you,' he replied. 'To answer your question, Quinn, you are not evil. You are a strong young man in many ways. Humans have a choice, with no divine interference, and this choice is called free will. You have chosen your path, Quinn—of integrity and compassion. Believe me, no matter how hard your demon self tries to take control, you can control it. On the contrary, absorbing demons will ultimately make your powers stronger.'

'Really? It won't possess me?'

He laughed. 'No, son. I'm one of the three most powerful demons in existence. I am a demon king, and because I'm your father, you have my demon DNA. Earth is my domain, and my world is full of supernatural beings—more than you can imagine—as well as demons. Portaville and the surrounding area are convergence points for mystical energies.'

'What?' I blurted.

Dad ignored me and carried on. 'Due to this, it's a favourite hangout for supernaturals. They are drawn here. Most go about their lives like normal people—you would never even know that they were supernatural.' He paused and let out a breath. 'You are destined to be Keepers. Protectors of innocents in the mortal realm.'

'Innocents?'

'Yes, mortals and other unfortunate supernaturals may need your help.'

I thought about Mrs D's talk. 'Like ghosts?'

'Amongst other things, yes.'

He was as vague as Mrs D had been. I couldn't get a straight answer from either of them.

Dad paused and looked me in the eye. 'You and your team of Younglings may have a few challenges ahead.' His tone snagged my nerves like a barbed hook.

'Me? What team? What challenges? You're joking, right? There's only Eve and me. Well, and Eloise, but she's a freaking ghost!' My head was reeling.

He shook his head, and his mouth was set in a rigid line. The breath caught in the back of my throat.

'Son'—Dad's voice was low and cold—'you'd be surprised how often supernatural beings are the source behind the headline news in mortal newspapers.'

'Oh, come on! No way. And you want us to sort it out?' I laughed with zero humour. 'Why can't you sort it out?' I took a deep breath through my nose.

'Quinn, son, I'm a demon. The balance between good and evil is important. But I can't be seen to interfere, especially on the side of good. I'll guide and help you as much as I can. You have my word.' A ghost of a smile played on his lips.

This information overwhelmed my already challenged brain. I steadied my breathing, gritted my teeth, and changed the subject before my brain imploded.

'How do you just appear, anyway? Like, from out of nowhere?'

'Ah, that's called shadowing, son. It's normal for a demon. The more powerful the demon, the further it can shadow. As a demon king, I have many powers.'

'Can I do it?' It sounded like a pretty cool ability.

'Yes, son ... eventually. Your powers will become stronger with age.'

Maybe being half-demon wasn't so bad. I tried to look at the positives. Then I thought about shadowing in my dream.

'I think I shadowed to the demon realm while I was asleep,' I started.

'Yes, I know you shadowed to the demon realm, son. It's easier to shadow in dreams. You will be fine there—you are powerful. They will not harm you.'

I squeezed my eyes together and took a breath. 'I know I'm half-demon and trying to get my head around it, but why do I have to visit the demon realm? It's dismal.' I rubbed my sweaty palms on my jeans.

'Quinn, the demon in you is part of you. You will be drawn to the demon realm, and you can visit the realm by choice if you ever need to.'

I was horrified and pretty sure I wouldn't be visiting the demon realm by choice anytime soon. 'How come some demons live here like normal people, but some live in the demon realm? The ones in the demon realm definitely don't look human. Is that where, erm, Lucifer is too?'

'Well, again, it's a choice, son. The demons in the realm are vicious and purely evil. Their idea of fun is to torment human souls. Not that the humans sent there don't deserve tormenting. And no, the Fallen Angel does not reside in the demon realm.'

Dad paused, and before I could ask more about Lucifer, he continued, 'If a portal to the demon realm were to be opened, then all humanity would suffer. And believe it or not, that's not what I want in my domain. Souls maybe, but not total destruction of the human race.'

'Uh, well, taking people's souls sounds bad too. Why would you want that?'

'Some humans will sell their souls for many things —power, money, talent. Some humans are easily corrupted and devious, and the price for this trade-off must eventually be paid. Payment for the price of success keeps us in business, I'm afraid.'

I narrowed my eyes at him. 'Who are you? What's your name?' I said through clenched teeth.

'Quinn, son—my name is not important. The name *Dad* is the one I cherish. I never thought I was capable of love, not until I met your mother. And since you were born, that feeling has grown with every passing day.'

'Mum's getting married.' Childish, I know, but the desire to try to hurt him overtook me.

His eyes glowed red for an instant. 'I know,' he sighed. 'Frank will look after her, and you too, but I will always be your father. If you ever need me, no matter where you are, all you need to do is call my name. I'd prefer you call me Dad,' he said wistfully. Then he faded away, and the chair was empty again.

'Come along, Quinn!' Mrs D shouted from the kitchen. 'I've made your favourite brownies. Let's have some before your mum gets home.'

I reluctantly walked to see Mrs D; my eyebrows knitted together in bewilderment, but I chatted with Mrs D as if everything were normal. Which it wasn't. At. All. I felt like I was on the train to Crazy Town, wondering if I'd bump into Alice and the Mad Hatter when I arrived.

CHAPTER 11
MILLIE

I hadn't slept well the previous night after my very unusual chat with Dad. I'd had way too much on my mind. That and dreaming about a yellow-eyed demon that had invaded my body and turned me into a serial killer had resulted in a pathetic two-hour slumber. So, when I got up, I decided to run in the woods to clear my head.

My feet barely touched the ground as I flew. I was faster than any car. Running supernaturally fast was fantastic fun. When any walkers or joggers appeared, I'd simply leap into the treetops and jump from tree to tree, like a human sifaka. My abilities were seriously crazy.

As I left the apartment to meet Eve, I shouted goodbye to Mum.

'See you this afternoon at Frank's,' Mum called. 'He's picking me up in a while. We're trying to sort out a wedding venue.'

My heart stuttered again as I thought about Mum getting married.

I walked to Eve's in the early morning spring sunshine to soothe my frazzled nerves. Once I arrived, I hurried down to the basement to find the three girls waiting for me with Celeste. Millie looked a thousand times better. She was new at our school—had only been there for a few weeks—and was often picked on. Every school has them—bitchy girls walking around like a pack of lionesses stalking impala, looking for emotional blood—but Millie's life had been better since she'd palled up with Eve and me.

'Cool—Frank's blueberry muffins,' I said before stuffing one in my mouth. 'I love coming here.'

'You'll be living here soon.' Eve looked at me a little nervously.

'Yep, we move in a few weeks, and I can't wait.' I grinned, but secretly I was dreading it. I'd lived in our apartment my whole life and had Mum and Mrs D almost always to myself, and truthfully, I sort of quite liked that. Was I resentful? Well, I tried really hard not to be. So, I put on my best happy face and swallowed the ball of apprehension stuck in my throat.

We all sat around on beanbags to exchange stories with Millie about who we were and what we could do.

'So, tell us about yourself first, Millie. We're all part of the supernatural world. Maybe that's why you've been drawn to us?' I started.

Millie scraped a hand through her hair and started

fidgeting. 'I'm a solitary witch, and nobody knows apart from my grandma. I think my mum suspects, but she turned her back on witchcraft when my real dad died. She's never practised since. That was a long time ago. I've never had friends—I've always been a loner.' She paused and peered down at her hands. 'Mum remarried … my stepdad is an ambassador. For the last five years, he's been posted in the Middle East. He and Mum returned home about a month ago. While they were gone, I went to live with my dad's mum in Boscastle, Cornwall. I loved it there,' she said wistfully.

'And now you're unhappy?' I asked.

'And?' Her eyes flickered with annoyance.

'It just seems a bit harsh, that's all.'

'Yeah, I suppose. Don't they say, if life throws you lemons, make lemonade? Or something like that.' She smiled grimly.

'At least you've got us now. So, life won't be quite as lonely, hey?' Eve pointed out.

'Yeah.' Millie smiled widely, flashing her teeth.

'Eve and I are different too.' *I'm very different*, I thought to myself.

Eve explained about being a half-angel, meeting her mum, and healing Celeste, giving the tiny dog a kiss on the head as she spoke. Millie let out a small 'Whoa …'

'I'm a cursed ghost.' Eloise went on to tell Millie about the Pendle witch trials without crying this time. 'I know you're a witch, but I think I'm going to like you anyway,' Eloise added.

'Thanks. I think.' A small smile twitched on Millie's lips.

I hesitated. Being half-angel sounded pretty cool; being half-demon, not so much. I was worried about Millie's reaction. She watched me expectantly, and I swallowed, unsure how to start.

'Quinn's half-demon,' Eve declared.

Millie's mouth fell open, and she jumped up and backed away from me. Which made me feel a combination of, *Oh, for God's sake, give me a break* and extremely hurt. What can I say? I'm a conundrum.

I took a breath and explained about my super-freaky demonic powers. I left out the bit about my trigger-happy temper ... I didn't want to scare her. 'Plus, I've just discovered I can absorb demons.'

All three girls looked at me with wide eyes.

'You absorbed a demon?' Millie grimaced.

'Yep. The demon in your house.' I recounted about the little girl and freeing her from demonic possession. Seeing their faces scrunching with disgust was painful, but in reality, I was as repulsed as they all looked.

I continued with desperation in my voice, 'My dad says it will strengthen my powers. The demon can't possess me, so don't worry.'

'Nobody could ever say you were dull,' Eve intervened, a smile tugging at the corners of her lips as she watched me. 'He's a good guy, Millie, honest. Half-demon, but with the heart of an angel.'

I smiled too, and Millie relaxed but then peeked at

me suspiciously from the corner of her eye. I knew she was unsure about my demon within, which hurt—a lot.

'I'm so glad I've met you all. I feel like a kindred spirit. I feel such a deep connection to you, which I've never had before,' Millie said, although I noticed she was looking at Eve as she spoke.

'We all feel our way as we go along. You have us *all* now,' Eve reassured, 'including Quinn.'

Millie gave me a nervous look and took a breath. 'My dad died when I was small. He was murdered.' Her voice cracked, and she wiped her eyes with her hand.

I swore under my breath. 'Sorry, Millie. That's brutal.'

Millie gave me a small smile and continued. 'I've always known I was different. When I was small, I could make my dolls move just by thinking about it. Mum would get upset if she caught me, so I hid my powers. I thought there was something wrong with me—that is, until I went to live with Grandma.' Millie paused and took a drink.

'Grandma's a powerful witch. I learned all about witchcraft from her. She thinks my powers are even stronger than hers.'

She cracked a subtle smile, stood up, mumbled a few words, and then put her hand in the air. A massive leather-bound book appeared in her hand—from out of nowhere.

I looked at her incredulously. 'H-how the ...'

'Oh, the book is kept in a dimensional hollow—it

must always be kept safe. Only Grandma and I can retrieve it,' Millie said before I could finish. She said it as if it were the most normal thing in the world.

'This is the *Book of Shadows*,' she declared proudly, before I could ask her about the dimensional hollow. 'It's been passed down in my family for hundreds of years.'

We all gathered around to look at the book. It was deep green, and the leather was cracked with age and smelled faintly of lavender and dust. The front was covered with gilded golden symbols, and the symbols surrounded what looked like an eye. Then Millie mumbled again, and the eye opened.

I let out a small yelp and took a step backwards.

'You big wuss.' Eve sniggered at me.

I stepped forward again for a closer look, but the book screeched, and the eye closed again. *Charming*.

Millie looked embarrassed. 'The book can sense the demon in you. Witches and demons don't normally get along.'

'Hey, I'm not sodding evil, though.'

It was exasperating. Mention the word demon, and suddenly, you're hell and brimstone. Honestly, demons have such a bad rep.

'Hold on.' Millie moved away and seemed to be talking to the book.

Eve and I glanced at each other, slightly amused, and Eloise stifled a snicker. Then Millie returned with the book. The eye was now open, and it was observing me suspiciously.

'Hi.' I waved at the eye. 'I'm not evil, honest.' Eve snorted a laugh, and I felt my face flush with embarrassment.

'The *Book of Shadows* appreciates your explanation,' Millie noted dryly.

'Whatever.'

Together, we leafed through the pages of the old book. It was unbelievable—when I touched it with my finger, a small shock made me pull my hand away. My skin tingled and became all goosebumpy.

'I think the book really does like you, Quinn—demon and all,' Millie said with insulting astonishment. I just shrugged.

'The book contains spells, incantations, potions, and information on evil and the supernatural beings my ancestors once faced. It also includes spells for vanquishing demons. Sorry, Quinn,' Millie uttered worriedly.

I just grunted and carried on looking. On the first page, there were symbols that I'd never seen before and a text written in cursive writing:

A Witch is at one with the universe,
A Witch is nothing and everything.
The Moon and the Stars,
The Sea and the Storms,

Fire and Earth will know me.

I'm a healer, giver, teacher, and protector of all things.

Sutton Witches walk your path of Majick with love, light, and integrity.

Blessed be.

'Sutton?' Eloise asked.

'My paternal family name,' Millie explained.

After a long while poring over the book, Millie returned it to the dimensional hollow.

'How'd you *do* that?' I asked.

'With magic, of course.' Then she mumbled a few more words and brought a knife down from the air. It was in a sheath and had an inscription on the handle, like a circle with two crescent moons butting up to it. 'This blunted knife is my athame.'

'What's an athame?' Eve asked as I handled the knife and checked it out. Once Millie permitted me to touch it, that is.

'It's my ceremonial dagger. It's used for directing potent magical energy, and it's my most treasured possession,' Millie answered.

'Don't you have a wand, like Harry Potter?' I asked.

'Harry who?' Eloise asked.

'I'll explain later,' Eve said, hugging the ghost.

'I don't need a wand. I use my athame and incantations. Sometimes just incantations. I'm a real-life witch, Quinn. Some witches can be dangerous, but don't worry, most are good.'

'Nice to hear.' I laughed nervously and gave her the knife back. 'Right, there are two things I wanted to ask you. First, how you both got me to the sofa when I passed out?'

'Well, you weigh a ton—no offence—so, rather than drag you, I used a levitation spell.'

'Huh? You can do that?'

'Easy—watch.' Millie muttered a few words ... and I started rising up in the air. In shock, I pinwheeled my arms and yelled. Eve and Eloise dissolved into laughter, and Millie brought me back down gently.

'It's much easier when you're unconscious.' She laughed.

'O-kay ... second thing. How the hell did you come from this basement to your house? That's some serious magic.'

'Ah, it's a teleportation gateway—my athame and a spell can take me anywhere,' she said as if it were completely normal. But hey, I'd just discovered that I could absorb demons, so I just went with it.

'Can we try it?'

'I need somewhere that's deserted. We don't want to just appear right in front of people, do we? We may give someone a heart attack.'

'I know,' I said, 'Mrs D's apartment. I'd like you to meet her.' I told Millie the address and described the location of the apartment, and then she simply hovered the knife against the wall and drew a circle. The wall shimmered blue, opened up, and within seconds we were looking into Mrs D's sitting room.

'Intense,' I whispered. Then I shouted, 'Mrs D. We've come to see you.' I hoped she would put her snakes in a bun and her boots on.

Mrs D appeared; thankfully, no snakes or hooves in sight. I also had a strange feeling she was expecting us. She examined us through the gateway.

'Ah, the Witchling has finally joined you,' she said. 'Would you all like hot chocolate and cookies? Except you, Eloise, obviously.' She smiled as she stared at the ghost.

We all piled through the hole in the wall, which closed behind us.

'How did you know we were coming, and how d'you know this is Eloise?' I asked, looking suspiciously at Mrs D.

'I can sense you coming, Quinn, dear. I'm your demon nanny. Eloise appears physical, but she is still a ghost, and, like I told you, she's still invisible to mortals and other supernaturals. Plus, her spectral glow is a bit of a giveaway.' She chuckled at her own humour.

'Every supernatural that has a close link to any of you, however, will be able to see Eloise,' she added before shuffling off into the kitchen.

Eloise frowned. 'I wish I could have hot chocolate and cookies.'

'Demon nanny?' Millie whispered.

'Yeah, demon nanny. Our lovely neighbour, who's looked after me all my life as a grandma, is actually a demon.'

Millie appeared uncomfortable. 'Demons hate witches—we are one of their main adversaries, one of the few supernatural beings that can vanquish them.' Her face was ashen, and she looked ready to leg it.

'Millie, she's like a grandma to me. She's not going to kill you, honest. She's adorable. Well, apart from the snakes and the hooves.'

'Serious?' Eve gasped, and I laughed at the look of terror on Millie's face.

'Come and take a seat.' Mrs D reappeared before we could talk anymore. She placed a tray of drinks and cookies on the table.

It wasn't long before Eve and Eloise chatted happily with Mrs D. Even Millie seemed okay in her company. After inhaling a few cookies and a mug of hot chocolate, I asked Mrs D about Millie's ability to see Eloise.

'It's because she's part of your supernatural team, dear.'

I scrunched my eyebrows together and glanced at Millie. 'Cool, a witch on the team.'

'Er, what team?' Eve asked.

'Erm, well, I saw Dad after, you know, Millie's house and everything.' I gave them a rundown on the chat and what Dad had said about us being Keepers and protecting innocents in the mortal world. 'He told me that often supernatural beings are the source behind the headline news in mortal newspapers. So I think it might be up to us to help.'

Eloise clapped with delight. Eve whispered, Huh?' but the blood drained from Millie's face, making her look even more dead than our resident ghost.

'Er, wait just a minute—I'm a solitary witch. I get anxious about things, you know? I'm not sure I can help,' Millie said softly, wringing her hands together.

'Aww, come on, Millie, please. From what I've seen, you're a pretty brilliant witch. Plus, we really need you. Having a talented witch on the team is going to be major. It may mean the difference between life and death. Well, apart from you, Eloise,' I said, wondering if it really might mean the difference between life and death.

My gut tightened up into frigid knots at the thought. Eloise giggled, Eve's eyes widened, and I heard Millie gulp. Mrs D winked at me.

'There is a reason that you have all gravitated towards one another, kids,' Mrs D intervened. 'The purpose of your births.' Mrs D looked at Eve and me. 'The reason Eloise formed a tied bond with Eve'—she gave the ghost a kind smile—'and Millie, you're stronger than you think, dear. Much stronger.' She gave the witch a weird look.

'But you're a demon. Aren't you evil?' Millie asked.

Mrs D laughed. 'Oh, I do like a bit of conflict here and there. But ultimately, I quite like humans. I admit I wasn't happy at first coming to the mortal realm and leaving the Dark Kingdom. Especially to be a nanny. That was until I saw his pudgy cheeks and his squidgy toes.'

She nipped my cheek, and I felt my face heat as the three girls spurted a laugh.

'At the sight of you, dear, something strange overcame me. I think it's called love,' she said wistfully. 'My job *was* to protect you when you were younger, Quinn. Now it's to guide you all.'

Millie visibly relaxed at Mrs D's words.

'I know it's hard to get your head around, but I think we make a great team,' I said, wanting to change the subject from my pudgy cheeks and squidgy toes. 'And having Mrs D guide us will make it much easier.'

Millie squared her shoulders and appeared almost determined. 'Maybe ... I've never had the support of a team before.' Then she wobbled a bit. 'I-I'll think about it.'

That was a yes from Millie, I hoped.

'I'm in.' Eve beamed.

Eloise jumped up and danced around the apartment. 'This is so exciting.'

And that's how Millie, the timid witch, became the fourth member of our team of supernaturals. A talented witch on the crew was an ace on the Keepers' side of things. Can you blame me for being optimistic? Things were going great, for a change.

Yep—deluded is my middle name ...

CHAPTER 12

LEO

The following couple of weeks went by in a flash. Mum and I moved in with Eve and Frank, along with Mrs D. Frank's house is enormous and impossibly pretty. It's a listed building with mullioned windows, inglenooks, and stone fireplaces—you get the drift—but it's modernised and luxurious. It's also set in half an acre of gardens.

My bedroom is huge, with an en suite, and, to be fair, having more space is pretty cool. Plus, having my adopted grandma live with us makes me and my friends feel safer. Eve and I see her every night; she's effectively become like our housekeeper. She cooks, cleans, and joins us for dinner, much to Mum and Frank's delight. I've never seen Mum happier, so I sucked it up.

Once I'd realised what was wrong with me—like, literally, having a demonic side—my trigger-happy temper was a *bit* easier to control. Well, most of the time. This was primarily thanks to help from Mrs D.

I wasn't like the Hulk; that guy becomes an enormous, green humanoid monster when he's enraged. At least I didn't turn green; so I guess it could have been worse.

Our team of supernaturals met most nights in Eve's basement, mainly to hang out and be normal teenagers. We didn't mention being part of a team after visiting Mrs D that day, but it was always in the back of our minds. I knew it was. Millie was fine with me now, demon and all. We all had this extraordinary connection to one another, which none of us really understood. Maybe it was synced brain waves or something; who knew?

One day after school, Eve and I were chilling in the basement while Millie was teaching Eloise how to dance, much to Eve's amusement.

'Oh, my football team buddy, Jack, has invited me to a party. It's at his house this Friday. I wondered if you all wanted to come with me?'

'Um, no.' Millie stopped dancing and shook her head. 'I don't much like parties, and the bitch pack will be there. Mia is Jack's girlfriend, isn't she?'

'You're coming with us, Millie,' Eve stated.

'But I haven't got anything to wear,' Millie complained.

'But I have. Come on, it'll be fun. Let's go and find you a nice black top to borrow to go with your jeans.'

Millie caved and followed Eve upstairs.

'Oh, a party. I love parties.' Eloise jumped around and disappeared to join Eve and Millie, leaving me alone. While alone, my mind went straight to the fact that we were to be Keepers and what that would entail. It couldn't be *that* bad, could it?

Boy, was I ever in denial ...

THAT FRIDAY, we all walked to Jack's house. Millie had permission to sleep over at Eve's that night and was with us too. Mum and Frank were on a weekend away, leaving Mrs D in charge.

'Back by 11.30 pm—no arguments. And stay together,' Mrs D said. I went to argue but thought better of it when she gave me one of her looks.

We strode up the long, tree-lined driveway to Jack's house. I was looking forward to chilling with my friends—in theory. Recently, things have never quite seemed to go according to plan for me, though. 'Whoa, this is a mansion,' I whispered.

Jack's house looked like a photo in some sort of fancy modern magazine. It had a vast, grey slate roof and polished steel windows covering entire walls. An oak porch covered the door, which is as wide as it is tall. I rang the bell with some trepidation but relaxed as soon as Jack opened the door. Inside, loud music was playing, and we saw groups of people standing around and chatting. The air was hot, and the bass of the music rumbled through my feet and into my chest as we walked in.

'Quinn.' Jack gave me a one-armed hug.

'Hope you don't mind ... I brought my friends?'

'Nah, all welcome,' he replied. Jack's the captain of the football team and loves me because I'm one of his best players.

'Go and grab a drink—beer fridge is in the laundry room. See you in a bit.' He started walking off, then turned again. 'Oh, the games room is that way.' He pointed. 'Game of pool in fifteen?'

'Sure.'

Eve, Eloise, and Millie followed me into the vast, swanky, white kitchen and into an oversized laundry room, where a colossal fridge was stacked with drinks. We all helped ourselves to Cokes, except Eloise, of course. The smell of cooked onions tickled my nostrils.

'Hotdogs!' I grabbed one from a tray, wolfing it down in three bites.

'I don't know where you put all the food you eat. You eat more than a football team.' Eve laughed at me.

'Maybe being half-demon gives you a bigger appetite?' I said with a wolfish grin.

Eloise was prancing around—then she picked up a hot dog. 'Oh, I wish I could eat this.'

I darted over and snatched it from her before

anybody noticed. Well, someone else, apart from Nathan—a guy from school who walked into the laundry room right at that moment. A hotdog hovering in mid-air isn't something you see every day.

He had a dim-witted *WTF* look on his face. 'What the hell?' Only he didn't say hell, if you get my meaning.

We all gave him a curious stare. 'I think I'd best not have any more beers,' he said as he stumbled back through the door. Eve spluttered a laugh, but I glared at Eloise.

'Do *not* touch anything else, or I'll get Eve to send you home.'

She stuck her bottom lip out. 'Sorry.'

To be fair to Eloise, it's not easy for a ghost to lift things, even light stuff. It takes a lot of practice, apparently. Obviously, she was quite used to the whole being dead thing—after all this time—so she was pretty skilled as far as paranormal activity went.

'Let's mingle.' I motioned with my arm.

'Let's not,' Millie muttered sullenly.

The girls followed me into a vast room full of sofas, where some people slouched in the comfy chairs, but most were standing. The room was full of laughter and chatter.

I soon spotted another teammate, Harry, who had moved up from London a couple of years ago and had become a close friend.

'Quinn, my man,' he called out, slapping me on the back.

'All right, Harry.'

He smiled at us, then snuck a look at Millie. I'm pretty sure he blushed. I introduced the girls and stood chatting with him for a while.

'Is that Harry Potter? Is he a witch too?' I heard Eloise ask Millie and Eve. Eve snorted with laughter.

It was hard to keep my face straight, so I pretended to choke on my drink instead of suddenly laughing insanely in front of Harry.

Harry turned to Millie. 'Um, I've tried to talk to you at school a few times.'

'E-erm, have you?' she said softly as she gazed up at him. Then she gulped and looked down at the floor.

'Yeah, never quite found the courage.'

Millie peered at him through her lashes and blushed furiously.

While we were chatting, I noticed a tall, dark-haired guy with pale skin. He was leaning against the wall and staring straight at me. I looked back at him, but he didn't drop the stare. His brooding eyes seemed to look at me with curiosity.

'Who's the pale guy over there?' I asked Harry.

'Where?' Harry glanced over in the direction I'd motioned. 'Oh, that's Leo Fernsby. He's from the US. I think Jack said h he was moving to our school. Jack's dad works with his dad or something. He seems like a good lad.'

When I turned around again, the guy had gone. I

changed the subject. 'I'm going to play Jack at pool if you fancy it, Harry?'

Millie gave me a hard glare, and I ignored her. Eve bit back a giggle. Eloise was oblivious.

Harry came with us to the games room, which turned out to be more like an arcade, with a pool table, table tennis, pinball, table football, and loads of other electronic game machines, plus comfy chairs and small tables dotted around. I joined Jack at the pool table, while the girls and Harry took seats nearby. I bent down to place the balls in their triangle.

'Mind if I play the winner, Jack?' a smooth, confident American voice drawled.

'Sure, Leo.'

I looked up to see the guy who'd been staring at me earlier. I took in his muscles, square jaw, weird electric-blue eyes, and hair, the colour of dark-roasted coffee beans. He was a looker, all right, but his skin—he was ashen; it was as if he hadn't seen the sun for years. I attempted to read his aura but failed miserably. He seemed friendly enough, but something about him felt off.

Leo went to join Eve, Millie, and Harry, but strangely, he hesitated before he sat down on Eloise. The ghost jumped up and scowled at him. Eve smiled sweetly at Leo, and they all started chatting.

I felt a pang of jealousy and mentally kicked myself; I kept watching him surreptitiously. I didn't trust him;

he gave me a bad feeling in my gut. Something about him made me feel agitated.

Eve leaned closer to Leo, and he went rigid in his seat—his posture changed, his eyes widened, then he scooted backwards. Eve frowned and bit her lower lip. Leo turned to talk to Harry, but the whole time, his dark-eyed gaze was riveted to my face.

Maybe he likes guys, I thought. I knew my friend Ollie did, and that was cool. The pang of jealousy faded. I concentrated on the game, and after ten minutes, I'd whooped Jack's ass.

Leo stood up to play. He set up the balls and broke, sinking three on the trot. Then the game became the shoot-out at the O.K. Corral, with both of us determined to win. I don't know what came over me.

He sniggered a few times when I missed a ball. 'I think you need pool lessons,' he drawled annoyingly.

I had a feeling he was trying to rile me by ridiculing me—and I *really* don't like to be made fun of. Bullies in school used to do it all the time until I got older and realised how effective the threat of a fist connecting to their nose was in shutting them up. But I wasn't ready to hit him—not yet, at least. It was close, though.

When he wasn't playing a shot or trying to rile me, Leo gazed at me intensely with dark, brooding eyes. He started creeping me out. He whooped my ass in the game, smiled smugly, and extended his hand. When I shook it, his face darkened; he pulled away and walked off.

'Wow, the amount of energy some people expend on being jerks astounds me sometimes,' I said to Harry as I watched Leo walk through the doorway. But, joking aside, Leo had left me with a clenched jaw, a dry mouth, and a peculiar feeling in my gut.

'Come on, let's play doubles. Eve, you're with me. Millie, you're with Harry.'

Millie seemed nervous at first but relaxed after about ten minutes and started chatting with Harry, who is awesome—easy-going and loveable. Meanwhile, Eloise danced happily around the games room, invisible to everybody but us.

After a couple of games, Harry and Millie wandered off together to get some food. I left Eve and Eloise to go get more drinks. As I was walking down a hallway, Leo appeared. He grabbed my neck with one hand and pinned me to the wall—he was freakishly strong, and I struggled to breathe. He was strangling me single-handed.

'Who are you? What are you?' he growled.

A rush of anger fired through my belly. This guy was seriously getting on my last nerve, but I controlled my temper enough to decide not to punch him in the face. A decision I'd later regret. When I knocked his arm away, he looked startled. He may have been strong, but as a half-demon, I'd say I had him beaten.

'I don't know what your problem is, you jerk, but do that again, and you'll be sorry,' I snarled in a low tone.

We glowered at each other in silence—then he

walked back toward the sitting room. My mind started racing, my pulse hammering in my ears. What was his problem? How did he know I was different? I decided that dwelling on him would ruin my night, so I focused on breathing slowly to calm my temper as I continued to the kitchen to get the drinks. I snaffled another hotdog on the way back.

When I returned to the games room, part of the bitch pack, Jessie and Chloe, were there—looking perfect, from their immaculately styled hair to their Jimmy Choos. (I know; how do I know about Jimmy Choos? By spending way too much time with girls. Don't judge me.) The bitch pack was supremely confident and popular, but they were also shallow, vain, and totally self-centred. Jessie's tongue was so sharp, it had the ability to cut and slash as soon as she opened her mouth.

Anyway, Jessie and Chloe stood over Millie and Eve, while Eloise scowled at them.

'I love the outfit, Jessie. Did it come with a pole?' I heard Eve say in a sweet voice.

I swallowed a laugh as I walked up to them. 'Hey.'

'Quinn,' Jessie said in a smooth voice, 'why do you hang around with these losers? You'd have much better fun with us.' She licked her lips teasingly as she spoke. Jessie was hot, and I felt my blood surge to my extremities. It's really embarrassing for guys sometimes, believe me. We have no control over certain appendages, generally at the most inappropriate times.

I surreptitiously wandered behind Millie's chair.

'Yeah, Quinn. We'd be much better fun to hang around with,' Chloe added.

'Mia goes out with Jack, and she's just the best, right?' Jessie continued. 'I've watched you play football, and your arms are totes amazing. Soooo muscly ...'

Jessie paused as she walked towards me and touched my arm, gazing up at me, fluttering her long, obviously fake eyelashes.

I glanced at Eve and saw a flash of anger in her eyes, which confused me a little. Eve was just my best friend, wasn't she? Surely, she didn't feel the same way I did about her. Nah—being protective, maybe? I knew she hated Jessie.

'Is your drama going to have an intermission soon?' Eve sniped. Jessie gave her a withering look.

'Eve!' I exclaimed as I sat down next to her. 'What is wrong with you? Don't you know that Jessie is the centre of the universe? That the rest of us merely revolve around her?'

Eve and Millie laughed, while Jessie and Chloe gave me daggers—then they swung their hair and stormed off.

'Whoa ... they're a breath of vile air,' I murmured.

'Do you fancy her?' Eve murmured to me.

'Well, she's a bit bitchy, but that aside, she's really hot.'

Eve gave me a slashing look, then turned away to talk to Millie. Apparently, she was oblivious to the fact that you can actually think about boning someone even if you don't particularly like them.

'What's going on? Chloe gave me a proper black look back there. Huh, Quinn?' Harry said as he came back to us, eating another hotdog.

'They were being their typical bitchy selves,' Millie answered. 'Quinn and Eve merely told them to do one.'

Harry chuckled and slapped me on the back.

'Hmm,' Eve said. 'We are forced to spend too much time around synaptically challenged individuals, who care more about lip gloss and handbags.' Millie nodded in agreement, and Harry guffawed.

We all carried on chatting and relaxing as we played pool and table football. Millie really came out of herself. I had a feeling in my belly that Harry would be a strong ally, too—his aura was clean and honest. Maybe one day I could even let him in on our secret? I'd need to ask Mrs D about that.

Everything was going well until Mia decided to exert her authority. Mia, the prim and perfectly groomed bitch, from her designer clothes to her flawless make-up. 'I think you all need to be going,' she declared, grinning like the cat that got the cream. 'You can't offend my BFFs and stay.'

'Your whats?' I asked in confusion.

'My best friends, Quinn. They are so upset. Jessie has the hots for you, you know.'

Harry almost spat out his drink, and Eve appeared ready to rip somebody's head off.

'Mia, please keep talking. I only yawn when I'm super-fascinated,' Eve snarked as she covered her mouth and pretended to yawn. Mia crossed her arms and raised her eyebrows. I choked on what could have been a cough or a laugh.

'Well, Mia, I apologise. Your pack just isn't too pleasant sometimes, you know?' I explained. 'Mean girls are really not cool.' Mia gave me a perplexed look.

'Hard truth, Mia,' Harry said.

'Not you too, Harry!' Mia looked horrified. 'I'm going to get Jack!' And she stormed off.

'That girl brings so much joy to the world ... when she leaves the room.' I sighed, and Harry guffawed again.

Eloise's eyes shot daggers at Mia's retreating back. 'Why are they so mean?' she asked angrily.

'Because they're gorgeous and think they rule,' Eve replied.

At the same time, a mirror on the wall near us started to shudder slightly. This was due to Eloise's agitation and her kinetic abilities. Ghosts can be very easily angered sometimes.

'Stop with the mirror, Eloise,' I whisper-growled so Harry didn't hear me.

A minute later, Jack walked into the games room with a smug-looking Mia, closely followed by Chloe and Jessie. 'It's okay, Jack, we'll leave,' I said, expecting him to kick us out.

'Let me guess,' he answered. 'These three beauties

were being harpies again?' The pack of mean lionesses appeared mortified. 'Nah, all stay. It's my house.' He looked pointedly at Mia. 'And I like you, Quinn. You too, Harry—you're both good lads. Let's play pool again. Quinn, you first; Harry, you play the winner.'

I smirked at the three girls and followed Jack to the pool table. Harry, Millie, and Eloise followed too.

Eve pursed her lips and smiled sweetly at Mia, crooning, 'Enjoy your night.' She grinned as she flicked her hair over her shoulder and joined us.

Mia actually growled and stomped her foot before flouncing out of the games room with her 'BFFs' on her tail. We all broke down laughing, including Jack.

'She's a pain in the butt sometimes,' Jack said. 'Apologies, ladies.' He looked at Millie and Eve.

While we were playing, Jack whispered, 'Your friend Eve's gorgeous. Are you dating her?'

'Nah, she's my best friend.'

'Mm. Could you put in a good word for me?'

I nodded, but actually felt like breaking my pool cue over his head. Raging jealousy bubbled in my belly. What was wrong with me? I felt like I needed some space, so I left Jack and Harry playing pool and decided to find Leo. I couldn't get him out of my mind. He'd seriously freaked me out—something was definitely off with him, and I needed to find out what. Either that, or knock him straight out. As I walked around the house trying to find him, I caught Eve as she headed towards the door.

'Eve. I have something to tell you. Jack's into you; he wanted me to have a word.'

'Not my type, Quinn.'

Tension drained from my taut muscles ... *thank God.*

'I'm going to find Leo. He's outside somewhere,' Eve said, and I felt my fury kindle.

'There's something about him,' she carried on.

'Yeah, you're not wrong there. The guy's a jerk,' I said through gritted teeth.

'No. He's hurting, Quinn. He's lonely and confused —I need to talk to him.'

I gave her a stiff smile. 'Yeah, whatever,' I said sarcastically, then stormed off.

'Quinn!' I heard Eve shout in frustration.

I ignored her and went back to play pool, regretting the decision to not punch pretty-boy Leo's teeth down his throat. I walked away with a racing heart and what felt like the start of a blinding headache.

I had no idea how crazy things were going to get for me.

But I was about to find out.

CHAPTER 13

A MAJOR COMPLICATION

After returning to play pool with Harry, I tried not to think about Eve being with Leo. Still, my luck was in, and I was just about to take the winning shot ... when suddenly, I was no longer there. A vision clouded my eyesight, and I saw Eve outside. Leo was lying on the ground next to her with something sticking out of his chest, and Eve looked terrified. Then, as quickly as I'd been transported to that scene, I was suddenly back at the pool table with Harry.

'Y'all right, Quinn?' Harry put a hand on my shoulder.

'I ...' I attempted to answer, but now I was looking at Eve again. These flashes came and went, leaving me dizzy and nauseous.

'Millie, get back to Eve's house,' I yelled as I started running from the games room. As I barrelled through the door, I collided with a guy as another vision blinded me. I saw two men dragging Eve and Leo to a white van.

'Sorry,' I yelled at the guy, who was now on his butt.

I raced down the driveway and reached the road just in time to see a white van pulling away, its tyres squealing. I was desperate and panicked, but I was also furious. The chase was on.

I followed the van around side streets, keeping my distance to avoid spooking the kidnappers. They were only doing thirty, so it was like a fast walk for me. On each side of the road, the large houses had lit windows, their inhabitants oblivious to Eve being abducted. My heart was pounding so hard with stress that I thought it was going to crack a rib. The wide avenues and leafy trees of suburbia gave a false sense of calm and safety. If only that were the case.

The van took a right, and I bolted around the corner of a one-way street, which I knew would take me to the road they were on. My senses were on high alert—every colour seemed brighter and every noise louder—and I soon spotted the van, still within a comfortable distance. Then they came to the main road. At this time in the evening, the road wasn't too busy, so they put their foot down to fifty. I was still cruising, trying to dodge behind parked cars as much as possible to avoid being spotted. The pavements were empty, so following them was pretty easy.

Suddenly, I had a flash of a vision again and almost collided with a parked car. I saw Eve—she was crying and had Leo's head on her lap. I concentrated on Eve. I needed to hear what she could hear. But then she disappeared again, and I ran faster.

Finally, I connected with Eve—I could hear their voices.

'Look, Troy,' an American voice said. The voice sounded mean and gravelly. 'The guy is a vampire, I'm sure of it.'

Vampires—okay, this was getting a bit too Stephen King for my liking. Then I thought about it—*if demons, ghosts, and witches are real?* That's when the panic set in.

'But what if he's not?' I heard another American voice reply.

'Well, then, they're casualties of war, Troy. They'll both still need to die. We need to cover our tracks.'

Rage fired through my body. I'm blessed with superhuman strength, speed, and other things, but I'm also pretty good at headbutts, punches, and chokeholds—know what I'm saying? And God help this guy if I get him in a chokehold.

'We'll know when we pull that bolt out. If he's dead, he's not a vampire. If he wakes up, he is.' The guy laughed. 'Remember, a crossbow bolt through the heart only paralyses them; we'll need to burn him, but it shouldn't be too much of a problem if he wakes up—he'll be weak. Takes them quite a long time to heal from a stake through the heart.'

'But he can walk in daylight,' Troy said. 'I've seen him.'

'Vampires can, you idiot. I've told you this, boy. They just don't like direct sunlight. That's why they prefer England—always cloudy.' He howled with laughter. 'Man up, Troy. We're vampire slayers, not first-grade teachers.'

I just hoped Eve didn't pull out the stake. If Leo were a vampire, Eve would be an easy meal. I'd *known* there was something off about the guy.

The van veered off onto a busy dual carriageway, full of cars and lorries, with no pavements. The van sped up, quickly hitting seventy. Speed wasn't a problem—keeping up was easy; potentially getting splattered by a car or truck—not so much. My spirit realm powers came in handy again, though—just as a Mercedes 4x4 behind me blared its horn, its tyres squealing, I vanished to spirit and felt the car pass right through me. A 4x4 passing through you is not an experience I'd recommend ... it felt like my insides were turned upside down. I was pretty sure the driver of the Mercedes must have thought he'd gone mad, seeing a boy running at seventy then vanishing into thin air, but I didn't have time to worry about that.

Even as a spirit, I could feel myself breathing and my muscles working as I ran at supernatural speed, but there was no pain and zero fatigue.

I could see the van up ahead. I passed straight through cars and lorries—being half-demon really was pretty sweet sometimes. After what felt like hours, the van started slowing and turned towards Sherwood

Forest—a massive woodland area and an excellent place to hide bodies. We were back on minor roads now, and the kidnappers drove for another few miles before bringing the van to a halt but leaving the engine running.

A guy jumped out of the passenger side and used bolt cutters to open a chained gate. He seemed young; he was tall and thin with a thatch of close-cropped, ginger hair. His face was so pale, it was almost paper-white. After opening the gate, he jumped back in, and the van carried on slowly down a dirt track before eventually stopping. We were in the middle of nowhere, and the trees were dense. All I could hear were owls hooting and the occasional sound of an animal running through the trees. I stayed in spirit form, determined to appear to them only when the time was right.

'Let me out,' I heard Eve screaming as she banged on the back doors of the van. 'You've killed my friend!'

The older guy chuckled. He had a thin, high-cheeked face and a clipped, blond moustache. He wore a baseball cap, a black leather jacket, and jeans so tight you could see his muscles rippling beneath the denim. He was big. I gasped when I looked closer at his face—there were a dozen scars on his neck and around his cheeks. The two scars at the sides of his mouth, though, were stomach-turning. It looked as if someone had attempted to cut his face in half. His aura was a swirling commotion of greys and blacks. His spiritual energy field suited him perfectly—he was one *mean* mess.

'Get the flame thrower out of the cab, Troy. This is the fun bit,' the maniac laughed. Troy, the younger guy, didn't look too keen on the idea, but he did as he was told. 'Grab the crossbow, just in case the little lady decides to run.' Then, he laughed again—a deep laugh that turned my stomach in knots. I was freaking furious.

'I think you might be right, Troy. I reckon the dude is probably dead. Can never be too careful, though, hey?'

A flash of irritation crossed Troy's face.

I approached the older guy and felt like appearing in front of him, snatching the flame thrower, and torturing him. Then I stopped, realising that thinking like that made me no better than him. *I may be half-demon, but I'm not evil*, I told myself.

What are you? Those words went through my head again. I *knew* who I was. I was a good person. A good person who just happened to be, without a doubt, *furious*.

'Get ready, Troy. When we finish with the guy, you can kill the little lady. What do you say?'

'But if he's not a vampire, she won't be either, Scott,' Troy whined.

'Don't question me, boy.' Scott gave Troy a slap and knocked him on his butt. Troy was clearly incensed but didn't retaliate.

'Get up and open the back doors. Don't be a yellow-belly, boy,' the maniac snapped.

Anger thrummed in my belly like a fire. It was ready to erupt and cause an inferno.

'All right, let's get this party started.' Scott's eyes shone with glee. This guy was pure evil, coming from me, a half-demon—he seriously needed his butt kicking into next year.

Troy shuffled towards the van and grabbed the door handles. As he opened the doors, I think I was almost as gobsmacked as poor Troy ... Eve had obviously pulled the crossbow bolt out of Leo's chest because he flew out of the van and, within a split second, had his fangs buried in Troy's neck. Scott reacted instantly and aimed the crossbow.

As he squeezed the trigger, I turned to my physical form and yelled, *'Leo!'*

Leo moved like a blur, and Scott shrieked at the sight of me appearing out of nowhere but had still fired the weapon. The bolt hit Leo in the leg.

'Eve!' I screamed. She had curled up in the back of the van but raised her head at voice. She was like a deer in headlights; my heart stuttered at the sight of her.

Leo was leaning on a tree; he'd pulled the bolt out of his leg, but he was weak and injured. Scott smiled menacingly at the injured vamp. He was like a cobra about to strike.

'I knew you were a bloodsucker,' he snarled with an evil sneer as he picked up the flame thrower.

I managed to get my brain engaged and bolted towards Leo and the flame thrower. Temporary insanity? Probably. Was I fireproof? That's something I would find out if I didn't vanish again before he fired the flames. I shoved Leo to the side with such force that he flew ten feet.

Before I could disappear again, the jet of flames hit me. I screamed as the fire engulfed me, hearing the maniac roar with laughter. But I was okay. Could this be real? I wasn't sizzling ... I wasn't writhing in pain; the flames bounced off me. They actually made me feel *stronger*. The fire's energy pulsated through me. I absorbed the fire, just as I had absorbed the demon. I looked down at my clothes; I couldn't say the same for them—everything I'd been wearing was now completely charred, black, and raggedy. My Hollister jeans and Abercrombie tee were ruined, not to mention my new Nike trainers. A month's allowance down the tubes further enraged my already boiling blood.

Scott was speechless. He carried on firing the flame thrower at me, while I laughed like a desperate lunatic. When the flames stopped again, I glared at him and snarled a vicious, low, reverberating sound.

He was rigid like a statue. The moonlight had turned his face marble-white; sweat glistened on his brow, and he was panting. His eyes were wide, as if he was sure I was about to deliver a fatal blow. I was mad —I felt possessed—but thinking about it, I *was* sort of possessed. I looked Scott straight in the eyes and screamed, but the sound I made wasn't mine—it was demonic. This dirtbag had been about to kill Eve and bury her. Anger consumed me. I felt Scott's fear ... I absorbed it ... and it made me feel even stronger. That and my anger made the demon inside of me supremely powerful.

'What are you?' he yelled. I pushed that question from my mind as I disappeared again, leaving him frantically looking around. Leo and Eve were not even in my head; my demon side had gained control. I reappeared in front of Scott, who dropped the flame thrower to the floor as I clutched him around the throat with one hand. He fell to his knees, and as I peered down at him, I noticed a red glow on his face.

Suddenly, I felt Eve by my side and heard her gasp. I guessed my eyes were glowing red, but at that moment, the demon within me wanted blood. Scott shrieked a strangled cry of mortal terror. Rage consumed me, coursing through every fibre of my body. That is, until Eve touched my arm, and the fire in my belly instantly subsided.

My voice sounded different—deep and rumbling—and even scared me. 'Go now and keep running. If I ever see you again, vampires will be the least of your problems. Understand?' The red glow on his face got even brighter.

'Yes, yes. Just get the hell away from me.'

I let go, and he scrambled to his feet and ran off into the trees without looking back. Just as he disappeared, we heard groaning and looked around to see Troy struggling to his feet.

'You'd better get in the van and go. If you even *think* about a vampire, I'll find you, and I'll be your worst nightmare,' I snarled in a voice that was alien to my ears.

Leo bared his fangs. 'Yeah, next time we won't be so lenient,' he said. Well, slurred—his fangs made him speak funny.

Troy turned even whiter, stumbled to the van, and drove away.

I plopped down on the floor, shaking. I was worried Eve would think that I was a monster. That guy had been terrified of me. The thought screwed me up. *Was* I a monster? It was slightly reassuring when Eve sat down next to me.

'I need to sit down,' I said.

'You are sitting down, Quinn.'

'Does anyone mind if I pass out?' I glanced at Eve and smiled encouragingly, but she started to shake. As I took her hands, I noticed it—she had a bite mark on her wrist—two spots so tiny that a mortal wouldn't be able to see them. Leo's venom had closed the holes, but my eyes missed nothing.

Leo stood in front of us, opening his mouth to speak. That's when I hit him. It was like my fist had a mind of its own. One minute it was in Eve's hand; the next, it sank into Leo's gut. Then I dove onto him and smacked him in the face. 'What have you done to her?' I seized him around the neck and shook him. He didn't fight back. I could have killed him—ripped his head off.

But all he croaked was, 'Sorry.'

Eve screamed and struggled to pull me off him. 'Quinn, please—stop! You're scaring me.' She sobbed.

I stood up and turned away. What was wrong with me? 'The bite marks on your wrist,' I said quietly.

'Leo was injured. I couldn't heal him quickly enough. He needed blood. I'm sorry, Quinn. He was so weak. I thought we'd both die if I didn't help him.' Eve was crying.

I felt my fury subside with every breath as I turned back to Eve. My heart was aching because I'd frightened her. I pulled her into my arms, just as I'd always wanted to, and felt enveloped by her beautiful scent. She smelled soft and sweet, like jasmine, roses, and lilies, all blended together. I got a burning ache in my gut. That was the moment I realised I loved her unconditionally, with the very essence of my entire being. And I would give my life to protect her.

'Quinn,' Leo said softly, 'Eve's blood is a healing elixir for me. I only needed the tiniest drop to help heal me. I think it's because she's half-angel.'

I stared at him. How did he know? Eve had obviously told him.

'I don't drink human blood, and I never kill humans. You have my word.'

I looked blankly at Leo, feeling lost for words. I was drained, and I knew that I needed to get home. I thought then about what Dad had said: to call him if I ever needed him. There still wasn't complete trust there, though, for the guy who apparently loved me but had deserted Mum and me. My temper prickled just thinking about him. Then, my thoughts automatically switched to Mrs D.

'Mrs D,' I shouted and waited. I tried a couple more times and was on the verge of collapsing. I was exhausted. Eve and Leo sat silently among the trees. The need to get home overwhelmed me. I was just about to give up and call Dad when the air in front of us rippled blue and opened up. On the other side of the opening, we could see Mrs D's annexe at Eve's house. I sighed as I followed Eve and Leo through the teleportation gateway, and we were greeted by Mrs D, Millie, and Eloise. Millie's connection to us and her internal GPS was amazing.

'Gosh, we've been so worried.' Millie embraced Eve, and Eloise hugged them both.

'How did you find us?' I asked.

'When you called Mrs D, I used my crystal pendulum to scry for you on a map on my iPad. Took me a while, but I found your exact location as quickly as possible. It was my connection to you both that found you.' She turned her full attention to me, aware something was wrong. *Damned witches.*

'What happened to your clothes?'

Don't ask ... Long story,' I grumbled.

'Talk to me,' Millie told me softly. I shook my head at her and kept my mouth shut. I was still trying to get my head around being fireproof as well as everything else. I didn't even want to think about the *everything else* part.

Mrs D made drinks while Eve told everyone about the night's events. She didn't mention me being an out-of-control demon and scaring her. Was I becoming a monster? I felt a band of sorrow grip at my chest. I just sat quietly and listened.

'Well, dear,' Mrs D said to Leo once Eve had finished. 'I'm so glad you've joined the team, at last.'

I stared at Mrs D. *No freaking way.* I got up and walked silently out of her annexe.

'Quinn!' Eve shouted.

I ignored her and carried on walking. I needed to be alone.

About half an hour later, I was sitting on my bed watching TV—well, I was staring blankly at the screen—when there was a knock on my door.

'Go away,' I yelled.

Mrs D ignored me and came into my room anyway. 'Quinn, Leo is a good lad. You need to make an effort with him. He's destined to be part of your team, whether you like it or not. Eve seems happy about it.'

'Yeah, she would.' The thought of him biting Eve made me want to knock his fangs down his throat. Another knock on the door, and in limped Leo, followed by Eve. *Oh, for the love of God, give me a break.*

'I brought you a drink and some cookies.' Eve sat on my bed.

'I'm sorry. I just want you to know that, Quinn,' Leo

said, 'if you hadn't been there tonight, neither Eve nor I would be here now. You saved us, and I'm eternally grateful.'

I nodded mutely, and Eve took my hand. I felt so mixed up. I was a demon; she was an angel. My life sucked.

'I'm sorry if I scared you tonight.' I looked into Eve's beautiful eyes.

She shook her head. 'Quinn, you're the kindest and most loving person I know. I'll never be scared of you, not really.' Her words made me feel better.

When I diverted my gaze to Leo, I felt like he had a sense of loneliness and vulnerability about him. I got up and shook his hand.

'I bet you've got a thousand questions right now. So maybe come to my house tomorrow, all of you?' Leo asked. 'I'd like you to meet my family and learn more about you all.'

'Sure,' I said, a little reluctantly. 'I need to sleep now, though. I'm done in.'

'Cool, I'd best be getting home too. See you all tomorrow. And thanks again, Quinn.' Leo waved as he left, and I tentatively raised a hand in response.

'Do you want to talk about it, Quinn?' Mrs D asked when we were alone again.

I somehow needed to talk to Mrs D more than anything in the world, but exhaustion hit me like a physical blow. 'I don't have the brain power for communication. I'm exhausted, Mrs D.'

'Okay, dear. I'll see you in the morning when you've rested. It's important to talk about your concerns, Quinn. It's the only way you can cope. We can chat then, and we *will* chat.' Mrs D gave me one of her no-nonsense looks.

I nodded, and she kissed my head and left me. Then, slowly, I climbed into bed, hoping the demons would leave me alone for a while.

I had an insane dream. First, demons surrounded me, dragging at me and snarling. Some looked human; some like monsters from a horror movie. The next thing I was running, my lungs were near bursting, but I couldn't move my legs fast enough. It was like I was running through quicksand. Then I was being hunted by vampire slayers, who were shooting crossbows and firing flame throwers, and they were catching me. Next minute, I was in my bathroom looking in the mirror. My stomach clenched as I looked at my reflection—I'd turned into a horror-movie demon, with a gross face, red eyes, claws, and fangs.

I woke up with a racing heart and was soaked in sweat. I jumped out of bed and ran to the bathroom mirror. Relief washed over me; I was still me. I returned to my room and climbed back into bed. I'd had a solid five hours' sleep. I didn't exactly feel refreshed, especially after that dream. I could have slept for another month, but at least it was Saturday. Then I remembered we were going to Leo's house later.

I buried my head straight back under the pillows.

CHAPTER 14
THE FERNSBY FAMILY

After half an hour of pretending the day wasn't happening, I decided I couldn't hide any longer, so I showered, dressed, and went downstairs. The smell of eggs and bacon cooking wafted from the kitchen. Mrs D was humming while she popped the coffee machine on. Mrs D loved coffee; who knew demons would love coffee?

'Morning, dear.' She didn't even look around as I walked in.

'Morning,' I grunted.

I heard Eve, Millie, and Eloise chattering as they came downstairs. Celeste was barking with excitement; I think she wanted her breakfast too. 'Morning, Quinn.' Eve smiled at me. 'I can't wait to go to Leo's today. Can you?'

'Yeah, I'm elated.'

Eve frowned but ignored my sarcasm; she continued chatting with Eloise as she went to help Mrs D.

Millie grabbed a glass of juice and sat with me. 'What's happened, Quinn?' she whispered. 'Eve's saying nothing, and I need to know. You're not right, and I'm worried.' Mild and sweet, Millie was definitely becoming more confident.

I slurped my juice and lowered my eyes. 'I lost it, Millie. I lost it with the slayer, and I lost it with Leo for biting Eve. I know I'm ... I'm not entirely human, but I feel like a monster. A demonic monster.' I looked down at my hands, feeling tears prick at my eyelids.

Millie took hold of my hand. 'Quinn, I've learned that, half-demon or not, you're a beautiful person with a beautiful heart, and when you have a good heart, there is no way you could ever be a monster.'

She gave me a serious look. 'You had a bad day. You're not perfect—nobody is. If it weren't for who you are, you would never have been successful, and Eve and Leo would be dead. You are an amazing guy, Quinn, and meeting you all has made my life so much better. I'm proud to be your friend.'

I gave Millie a small smile. 'You're pretty special yourself.'

The talking-to from Millie helped alleviate my worries. We chatted while we ate.

Eve found my hand under the table and squeezed it gently. 'We don't have secrets, Quinn. We've been friends for too long. Talk to me if you need to, please,' she whispered.

'I'm sorry I scared you,' I said again.

'Yeah, you did a bit. It's the first time I've seen you properly angry,' she laughed. 'But, Quinn, I know you. The demon is half of you, not all of you. You will never not be my Quinn, even when your eyes glow red, your forehead goes lumpy, and your voice goes weird.' She laughed again.

'My forehead went lumpy?' She just nodded and hugged me.

I sighed. Damn ... a lumpy forehead, red eyes, *and* a demonic voice. Was I turning more demon than human? I got a knot in the base of my gut but resolved not to dwell on it. Plus, when she said the 'my Quinn' bit, my heart did a little flip-flop in my chest. *Geez, why am I so pathetic?*

'Quinn, we *are* chatting before you go to Leo's. I'll drive you all there at ten o'clock,' Mrs D said. 'Chop-chop, girls—you've got thirty minutes before we set off. Oh, and don't forget your swimsuits—Leo has a pool,' she shouted as the girls dashed upstairs.

He would have a bleeding pool, I thought.

'Millie's parents are letting her stay here for the weekend,' she told me. 'Poor girl ... I don't think they particularly want her at home.'

'Really? Poor Millie.'

Mrs D tutted sympathetically, then sat down with me at the table. 'Talk,' she demanded.

I told her everything, starting with the visions of Eve and Leo being kidnapped. I mentioned quite a few times how horrified I was with myself for practically losing complete control.

'And ... how the hell am I fireproof?'

Mrs D laughed. 'Oh, you are your father's son, dear.'

Was that meant to be a backhanded compliment? She must have read my face, because she continued, 'He is a master of demons, dear. Capable of so much destruction, but his self-control is second to none. And you take after him—if you had properly lost control, you would have killed the slayer and Leo.'

I gulped and must have looked horrified because she added reassuringly, 'You are innately good, dear. You have complete control over your powers. However, if you lose your temper, there is a very worthy reason. Don't ever question that.'

I nodded and sighed. Those words, along with Millie's and Eve's, made me feel loads better.

'And of course you're fireproof. You are half-demon. You definitely won't burn in the fires of hell.' She cracked up laughing until she had tears rolling down her face.

'Okay, at this point you're abusing sarcasm,' I grumbled at her, which made her laugh even harder. 'Anyway, the visions? What's all that about?'

Mrs D collected herself and dabbed her eyes. 'You have a strong psychic link to people you care about.

Especially Eve and your mum. If they are ever in trouble, you will know.'

'So, is anything myth anymore? Or are all monsters real?' I asked with a frown.

'All myths and legends are based on truth, dear. But not all of us are monsters.' Mrs D gave me a petulant look.

'Sorry. It's just—you know—a lot to take in. That's all.' I stroked her arm.

So, looking at the positives, I could add being psychic and flameproof to my growing list of demonic powers. And to be fair, I wasn't complaining. All of my new abilities had been pretty cool so far. Just talking about my concerns to Mrs D was strangely therapeutic, and it helped me sort my head out.

Once ready, we bundled into the car with Mrs D and set off. We arrived at Leo's twenty minutes later to find he lived in the middle of nowhere. As we approached the wrought-iron gates, we saw the house name: Whitewillows.

'Chuffing hell, it looks posh,' I muttered to Eve.

Leo's drive was broad and sweeping, with rhododendron bushes on either side. It goes on for at least a mile and is surrounded by forest as far as the eye can see. We swept into the large turning circle, with a big-ass fountain in the middle, just before arriving at the house. We all gawked, bug-eyed, including Mrs D. Leo's home was a huge, modern building, in every shade of grey, surrounded by lawns and gardens full of shrubs I couldn't name. We stepped out of the car and walked—well, my demon grandma tottered—up to the massive oak door, and Mrs D rapped the knocker. The door opened, and there stood pretty boy Leo.

'Hey. Please come in.'

We all followed him into the massive hallway, with a staircase in the middle. On first sight, I was blown away. The stairs twisted in a perfect spiral, like a child's slinky toy pulled from each end. Everywhere was decorated in fashionable, neutral tones.

'Your leg's okay?' I asked, looking at where the bolt had penetrated his thigh.

'Yep, accelerated healing. And you're fireproof?'

'Apparently so.'

Leo put an arm around Eve's shoulders and chatted with her as we followed, and I could feel myself getting irritated. Mrs D put a hand on my arm and gave me a look. You know, *the* face—the *behave yourself* look. I scowled at her but tampered my irritation. I just hated it when you had to be nice to someone you wanted to punch in the face.

'Geez, they must be loaded,' I whispered to Millie as we walked through the house. She elbowed me in the ribs, and Leo turned and looked at me. Damn, he had extra-sensitive hearing, a bit like me. I'm such an idiot sometimes. I just shrugged my shoulders and gave him a tight smile.

We walked into the enormous, spotless, pure white kitchen—a large table and chairs sat at the picture window, which overlooks the grounds. Eve, Millie, and Eloise went to look out over the gardens. 'It's beautiful,' Eve said as she turned to look at Leo. He gave a half-grin, displaying his pearly whites. I wondered what he'd done with his fangs.

'Let me get you all a drink. Mrs D, my parents will be down in a minute. My father has a day off, so they've had a late start.'

'What do your parents do?' I asked.

'My dad is a cardiac surgeon. Mom is a florist.'

'Huh? A cardiac surgeon. Like, in a hospital?'

Leo laughed. 'Yep, that's where they usually work.'

I couldn't get my head around a vampire being a surgeon. All that blood? Mrs D gave me that look again, and I shut up. Leo asked what we all wanted, then fetched drinks from the fridge.

'Don't mind invisible girl,' Eloise mumbled.

'Sorry, lovely Eloise. Can you drink lemonade?' Leo asked the ghost.

She seemed surprised. 'Could you see me at Jack's house?' She twirled around. Then, remembering the original question, she replied, 'No, I can't, but thanks for asking.'

'Yes, I'm not sure why I could see you. I knew you were a ghost, not a vampire, at Jack's ... no heartbeat, and no aroma ... but I just thought you'd tagged along as an attached spirit to Eve. I didn't realise your connection then, obviously.'

I frowned at Mrs D. 'He's part of the team, kids. Like Millie,' she said in response.

As we chatted, a gorgeous lady walked into the room, followed by a tall, striking man. Leo's parents, I assumed. *Geez, even they're beautiful*, I thought.

'Welcome,' the man said in an American drawl. 'Cordelia and Harrison Fernsby ... pleased to meet you all. I believe we owe you a debt of gratitude, Quinn.' He focused on me with obvious curiosity.

I stammered and felt my cheeks heat. 'I-it's fine. Anytime.' Seriously, that's all I could think to say—I felt like a complete tool.

'Scott Adams, the so-called vampire hunter, is an narcissistic maniac. He has killed many innocents in his quest. Too many.' Harrison paused. 'I've informed the ministry, and he is to be dealt with.'

I gulped, not even wanting to consider the 'dealt with' part of his statement, but noticed that Mrs D had a wicked gleam in her eyes. As Cordelia and Harrison started chatting with Mrs D, I studied them. Cordelia was about five feet seven and willowy, with a face cut right from the pages of a *Vogue* magazine. She had flowing golden curls, ivory skin, and piercing green eyes. Harrison was about six-two, with the kind of face that stops you in your tracks. Slim and muscular, with dark hair and blue eyes. They look like a Hollywood couple.

Leo was staring at me. He knew I was studying his parents, but I glared back; he didn't intimidate me. He just broke into a grin. I still wondered where he'd hidden his fangs. 'Let's leave the adults and go in the pool,' he said, and the girls followed him.

'I'll do lunch at one o'clock, Leo,' Cordelia said as he was leaving.

'Okay, Mom.'

I sighed heavily and followed the rest of them, wishing I was watching TV at home, alone.

'I'll come back for you at four o'clock, dear,' Mrs D said as I walked past her. 'Have fun, Quinn.'

I grimaced at her as I left the kitchen and followed the others down a long corridor. Fang boy directed the girls through a door, then waited for me, taking me to another small changing room. I started stripping and was down to my boxer shorts when, turning around, I saw Leo staring at me.

'You've got a great body.'

I frowned at him.

'Sorry.' He lowered his eyes.

I felt a bit uncomfortable, so I went into the toilet cubicle to put my swim shorts on. 'So, what's your deal, Leo? Are you interested in Eve?' I asked from behind the door.

I needed to clear the air while we were alone. If he said yes, I was sure I'd ignore Mrs D and punch him right in that pretty face. He didn't answer immediately, though. When I walked out of the cubicle, he stood there in his designer shorts, like a male model. A very pale male model, but still—he was annoyingly beautiful. He started laughing.

'What?' I glared at him.

'I'm more interested in you, Quinn.'

'Me? Oh ...' I felt my cheeks burning. 'Erm, I'm not, um ... you know?' Not my most eloquent response, but I was lost for words.

'I know.' He laughed and blushed. 'But having you as a friend is more than enough.' He gave me a half-hug, and I tensed up a bit but sort of gave him an awkward one-armed hug back.

I was loads happier when I walked out of there; like a weight had been lifted from my shoulders. He wasn't interested in Eve—best news I'd had all week.

I glanced around the indoor pool. I can tell you, it was pretty impressive. A naturalistic waterfall sat at one end of the pool, making a gentle *swoosh-plunk* noise as it hit the water. The tiles—a cobalt-blue mosaic pattern made the sparkling blue water beautiful all on its own. Laughter echoed around the building. Millie and Eve were happily chilling in the pool while Eloise watched them from a sun lounger. Leo dove in, and the girls giggled.

'Come on, Quinn,' Eve shouted.

I dove right in for the start of a surprisingly cool afternoon. I'd been dreading going to Leo's, but was a really nice guy. Plus, his being gay was a bonus, as far as Eve went.

Later on, we all sat around the pool with drinks and

chatted. I told Leo about me, Mrs D, my dad, and stuff. Eve, Eloise, and Millie filled him in on their stories too. I tried hard not to stare at Eve in her swimsuit. Her whole body, from her long legs to her beautiful face, was mesmerising.

Leo gave me a questioning look, so I scowled at him and shook my head. It was frustrating because I couldn't control how I felt about my best friend. Why had I all of a sudden become desperate to kiss her? How had my love for her changed? Geez, it was annoying.

'One thing, Leo,' Eve said. 'At Jack's house, why did you act like I smelled bad?'

'Your blood, Eve—the smell is divine. It's like moon-flowers. Made my mouth water.'

I curled my lip at him and narrowed my eyes. He raised his hands. 'Sorry, bud. It's because she's half-angel. I would never ....'

'It's okay, Leo,' Eve interrupted, giving me a black look. 'At least I won't have a complex now.'

The girls chatted while Leo and I fetched more drinks from the fridge.

'Sorry, Quinn. I would never harm Eve,' he said.

'I know—don't stress. It just worries me, you know? If her scent is so unique ...'

'If anyone wanted to harm her, they'd have to go through my family and me to get to her.'

'Yeah. Me too,' I sighed. 'Anyway, I could sense you weren't mortal, but how'd you know I was different?' I asked.

'Your smell.' Leo smirked. 'A distinct tinge of burning sulphur,' he said as he walked away.

'Huh?' I smelled under my armpits. The only smell I could make out was my Dior body spray.

'Ben said my legs were sexy,' I heard Eve whisper to Millie as we handed out Cokes.

'When did Ben see your legs?' I snapped.

Millie and Eloise snickered, and Leo gave me a quizzical smile. Eve frowned at me. 'When I was wearing shorts, Quinn.'

'Oh.'

I'd caught Eve and sleazebag Ben snogging in the basement, but thankfully the relationship hadn't lasted too long. Ben had gotten fed up with Eve always being with me. *Up yours, Ben.* It was the same with me, though —any girl I started seeing would be insanely jealous of Eve. I'd had my fair share of girlfriends, but I couldn't be bothered with the drama, so my relationships didn't last long either.

'Right, let's go and have lunch. I'm starving,' Leo said as he disappeared to the changing room.

'I hope he's not got a bag of blood for his lunch, or I'll barf,' I whispered to Eve and Millie.

'Behave, Quinn.' Eve wagged a finger at me. 'See you in five.' The three girls headed to their changing room, and I watched Eve's butt as she walked away. I gave my head a shake, shivered, and followed Leo to get showered and dressed. After we'd changed, Leo mentioned me ogling Eve and asked if I fancied her. I held my hand up.

'No. And don't say another word.' I glared at him.

He just shrugged and walked out. I followed him back into the kitchen to smell the fantastic aroma of steak cooking.

'I thought I'd do a few different dishes for you,' Cordelia said. 'I don't get to entertain very often.'

No surprise there, I thought.

The table was groaning with food, and Leo laughed at the look on our faces. 'Dig in,' he said, and I obliged. If someone had told me I'd be having lunch with vampires that weekend, I would have told them to get off the drugs. Yet, there I was, at their table, stuffing my face with pizza.

Cordelia plonked a big, fat, rare steak on Leo's plate. When I say it was rare, I mean it was almost still mooing. Ugh ...

'I'll leave you to it.' Cordelia beamed at us and walked out.

'I didn't think you ate food?' I asked, just as Leo put the last bit of steak in his mouth.

'Quinn,' Millie scolded me. Eve and Eloise bit their lips to try and hide their amusement.

'Yeah, I eat food, but I need blood too. I'm a dhampir.'

'I think I speak for everybody here when I say, *huh*?' I shrugged.

'A dhampir. I'm half-human, half-vampire—a bit like you and Eve—half supernatural.'

'Carry on,' I said.

'My mom was human, my father a vampire.'

'Let's finish eating, and you can fill us in.' I was certain Cordelia wasn't human.

Leo sighed. 'Okay. It may take a while.'

After eating, Leo led us to another fantastic room with big windows, massive sofas, and a fireplace wide enough to park a car.

We all made ourselves comfortable before Leo started his story, 'As you can probably tell, I grew up in the States, not too far from Buffalo. I had a pretty cool childhood and couldn't have been more loved. But, bringing up a child dhampir can be a challenge.' He huffed a small laugh. 'I wasn't an easy kid, so I was home-schooled in my early years until I was old enough to control my supernatural abilities.' He shook his head with amusement.

'And conceal your fangs, I guess?' I added.

'Oh, no. Dhampirs only develop fangs when they're nearing maturity. I think I was about fourteen when I got mine.'

'Really?'

'Yep, as our bodies develop, the need for blood becomes essential. It's bizarre, but that's the way it is.'

'Where do you put your fangs, then? You know ...' I asked.

'Oh, I just retract them. It's easy.' He smiled without

fangs and then with fangs. It was pretty weird, if you ask me.

'So, tell us about your parents?' I verbally nudged him.

'Well, I'm adopted—my biological mother died giving birth to me; I killed her,' he said, lowering his eyes.

Eve and Millie jumped up and sat on either side of him; both hugged him. Eloise let out a tiny whimper. Leo glanced up and saw my confused face.

'A human can't carry a vampire's baby and survive. Harrison found out about my mom a few weeks before my birth, and he offered to change her ... you know, into a vampire. But she refused—she was worried about harming me.'

He let out a mirthless laugh. 'Instead, she made Harrison and Cordelia promise to protect me after I was born. Which they have done ever since. Dhampirs gain most of the traditional vampiric powers without the vampires' weaknesses. The sunlight doesn't bother me, and I age slower too, but I have a beating heart.'

'How'd you survive a crossbow bolt in the heart, then?' I frowned.

'No idea.' He shrugged his shoulders. 'As a dhampir, I have accelerated healing and supernatural abilities like a vampire, but I'm sure, without Eve's blood, I would definitely have died.' He kissed Eve's cheek. 'Thank you. Obviously, dhampirs are extremely charismatic, athletic, gorgeous, and intelligent too.' He winked.

I threw a cushion at him, and we all dissolved into laughter. It lightened the sombre mood a bit.

'So, Harrison and Cordelia aren't your parents? And they're full vampires?' I asked.

'Yes, they are my parents. Not biologically, but they've raised me from a baby, and I couldn't wish for a better mother and father. I love them; you'll not find two kinder people. My parents *are* full vampires—but they're gentle and loving vampires, like my sister, and they don't feed on humans. Dad stocks the forest with deer and other wildlife, which is how they feed. Me too, normally.'

I saw Millie gulp. Eve had turned a bit green, and Eloise hid her face behind a cushion.

'Sorry.' Leo looked mortified.

'It's okay, Leo, honest,' Millie said. 'I'm glad you're part of our team.'

'So ... how old *are* you, Leo?' Eloise asked.

Leo hesitated. 'I've been alive for eighty years.'

'What?'

'Yes, a dhampir grows at a slower rate than a mortal. Normally, one human year is five years for me, until I'm fully grown. So now I age slower, but not quite as slowly. I'm actually eighty, but really sixteen. Crazy, hey? I'm not immortal, but I'll live for a long time.'

'Wow.' My head was spinning.

'What about you and Eve, Quinn? Will you live longer?'

'I've no idea. One to ask Mrs D, I guess.' Eve nodded in agreement.

'Oh, great,' Millie complained. 'If you all age slower, I'll be the old, wrinkled one. Cheers.'

'Grandma Millie,' I snorted.

'So how do your dad and mum cope with the sunlight?' Millie asked.

'The slayer was right. Vampires can go out in the sunlight—to say they can't is a myth—but direct sunlight is immensely uncomfortable for them. They avoid it, normally, but if it's a bright, sunny day, then long sleeves, hats, and tinted car windows. Easy. The slayer was also right about a stake in the heart. It merely paralyses vampires. Once it's pulled out again, they're in a weakened state and vulnerable, but they heal eventually. I'm pretty sure if Eve hadn't been there last night, though, I would have been a goner,' he said again. 'Your blood is a healing elixir, Eve. A vial full is all a vampire or dhampir would need, no matter the injury.'

Eve blushed.

I gave him a hard stare. The thought of anyone drinking Eve's blood made me want to rip their head off, and that included Leo. He held his hands up defensively. 'Just saying.'

'So, because you bit the vampire slayer, does that mean he'll become a vampire?' Eve asked Leo.

He laughed. "No, changing a human is much harder than just biting them. He passed out with fright, I reckon.'

'Oh.'

At that moment, a girl of about eighteen sort of floated into the room, her movements fluid and lithe. She stopped in front of us, graceful even in stillness.

'Hi,' she said in a lilting voice.

I heard Leo groan. 'Guys, this is my sister, Natasha.'

We all mumbled hello, but I couldn't take my eyes off her. I had to be reminded to close my mouth—I only realised it was hanging open when Eloise jabbed me in the ribs and frowned at me. Natasha's eyes were like liquid topaz, and her long, wavy hair hung around her shoulders, deep hues of mahogany against her pale face. Her frame was slight and willowy. I had to rip my eyes away and let out an involuntary whoosh of breath.

Natasha pouted her lips as she gave me the once-over. 'You must be Quinn. Thanks for saving baby brother from those sickos.'

'I-it's okay.' I felt my face heat. Eve frowned at me.

Then Natasha smelled me. Seriously, she came right up and smelled me. 'Mm, you do smell different—Leo's right. Oh, you're yummy.' She giggled. The sound was like tinkling bells, and as I gazed at her beautiful face, I felt my cheeks glow red. 'How old are you?' she asked, stroking my face. Her touch was like marble—smooth and freezing cold.

'Too young for you, Nat. Stop embarrassing me,' Leo complained to his sister.

Then she went around smelling everybody, except Eloise. She just peered at our ghost friend with a frown, seemingly a little puzzled. Then she wrinkled her nose at Millie, and I heard Millie mutter, 'Charming.'

'Oh, you do smell nice. So divine. Just like moonflowers, Leo's right,' she said to Eve. 'Thanks for helping baby brother, sweetie.' Natasha gave Eve a hug, and then she flounced out of the room.

We chatted for a while, all relaxing in each other's company. Then, when Mrs D arrived, we said goodbye to Leo, Nat, and their parents.

'Nat was pretty, wasn't she?' Eve said from the back of the car.

'Whoa, yeah,' I responded. 'She's really, really beautiful.' I heard Mrs D tut.

Something flickered in Eve's eyes; she let out a breath and turned her head away to look out the window. I saw Millie roll her eyes at me.

Was Eve jealous? Nah, probably worried Natasha was going to eat me or something.

'What?' I mouthed. Millie frowned at me and shook her head, and Eloise blew through her lips in frustration.

Girls. I'm serious. They're freaking weird sometimes.

CHAPTER 15

THE WEDDING AND

MR MONTAGUE

The following day at breakfast, Eve was still giving me the cold shoulder.

'What *is* her deal?' I whispered to Eloise as I walked into the kitchen.

But she just glared at me and said, 'Millie's right. Boys are stupid.'

'Huh?'

Eloise simply faded away, rolling her eyes at me.

Mrs D was making pancakes and brewing herself a coffee. While we ate, I told her about Leo being alive for eighty years but only being sixteen. Then I asked her whether we'd also age slower than ordinary mortals.

'Yes, dear. Both you and Eve will age slower than mortals once you're fully matured.'

'Cool,' Eve and I said in unison. Then Eve scowled at me.

'Sorry, Millie, looks like you'll be ageing before us.' I

chuckled, amused by her stony expression, but she glared at me.

'Why are males such jerks?' Millie said under her breath. Mrs D chortled.

'On behalf of the male population ... hey!' I groused.

Luckily, Leo arrived—perfect timing. He picked up on the tension around the table, so he and I decided to stay out of the way and disappeared to play Xbox in my room.

We saw Leo most days at school, and we'd all get together most weekends, either at Eve's house or his. Over the next couple of weeks, I became more relaxed with Leo, and even though I'd hated him at first, I was growing quite fond of him. He was loyal, a great laugh, and was one of the kindest people I'd ever met. Made me feel pretty guilty about sucker-punching him—you know, when he was nearly offed by the slayers.

Millie still spent a lot of time at Eve's. I think Mrs D was right; her parents saw her as a burden. But she loved being with us, so she seemed fine about it.

THE DATE for Mum and Frank's wedding was fast approaching. Yep, it *was* happening. Obviously, Eve was to be the bridesmaid, and I was to walk Mum down the aisle. Both Mum's parents had died in an accident when she was younger, so it had always been just me, her, and Mrs D. I was glad Mum was happy about her big day and all, but I couldn't get as enthusiastic about it as everybody else. My heart just wasn't in it ... Maybe I was just being selfish, but I honestly felt like I was losing Mum to another man.

A couple of days before the wedding, everything was chaotic—people running around organising this and that and who knows what. I decided to stay in my room most of the time; that is, until Mrs D knocked on my door and came in. She knew I was brooding—she knew me too well.

'Quinn, dear. You must let go of your feelings of doubt. Your mum is happier than I've seen her in a long time. And Frank loves you both very much. He's a good man. Even the big guy upstairs thinks so—they trusted Frank with Eve. Your dad is begrudging, but even he's fine with Helen marrying Frank. Yes, your father still loves your mother, but he knows he can't offer her a normal life. You have both changed your father, dear, you and your mum. He would do anything for you both. Now, put a smile on your face; there's a good lad.' And she walked out.

I sighed and thought about her words. I just had to look at Mum and Frank—like, really look at them—to see that they were completely crazy about each other. Time to take my head out of the sand, accept it was happening and be happy for Mum, at least. I turned off my TV and followed Mrs D into the chaos to help with the wedding preparations.

Eve was beyond excited about her grandma's arrival from St Kitts that day. Frank went to pick her up from the airport, and they returned home just before dinner.

We all went outside to greet Monique. She is a tall and slim woman with close-cropped black and grey hair, and she uses a bamboo cane when she's walking. When she saw Eve, she squealed and laughed, and her eyes shone with happiness. Eve rushed into her arms while Celeste went berserk, jumping about and barking. Eve picked the dog up, and Celeste licked her grandma's face. Then they turned to join Mum, Mrs D, and me.

'Well, hello.' She beamed at us all.

'Hello again, Monique,' Mum said as she hugged her.

Monique put a hand on my face and smiled warmly. 'My, my, haven't you grown, Quinn? What a handsome young man you have become, honey.'

I felt my face flush and gave her an awkward hug.

Some normalcy had returned to my world, which seemed to have gone into a complete tailspin in the last few months—believe me, it was to be short-lived.

The six of us went to the wedding venue; we were away for two nights, and Millie stayed with Leo to help look after Celeste. Millie's parents were cool about it, much to the witch's relief. And weirdly, Eloise had a link to Millie and Leo now—maybe because they were part of our supernatural team. I'd learned that sometimes it was best not to question things. Anyway, Eloise had decided to stay and haunt Leo's house.

As Gracewood Hall came into view, I gasped. It appeared awesomely ancient and absolutely massive. The impressive building was surrounded by hundreds of acres of land.

'Wow,' Eve whispered.

'You like?' Frank seemed pleased. Eve and I nodded our heads.

We walked into the reception area, where the ceiling must have been twenty-five feet high. Designs of fruits and flowers were carved into the mouldings, and sculptures of small, plump children with wings—cherubs, I guess they were—looked down on us from every angle. There were vases of flowers everywhere. After checking in, we found that Eve and I had rooms next to Mum and Frank, while Monique's and Mrs D's rooms were further down the corridor.

The two grandmas, who luckily got on like best friends, took over organising everything for Mum and Frank. It was going to be a small wedding, with about fifty guests.

Everything for the big day was in hand. Timings

were organised with military precision by Mrs D and Grandma Monique, who could have still run an army kitchen, given half the chance. Hair, make-up, dress ... blah, blah, blah. I switched off after about ten minutes. I started fidgeting, and Eve slapped my leg under the table and stifled a giggle when I caught her eye.

The evening before the wedding, we all ate dinner in the restaurant.

After the meal, I turned to Eve. 'Let's get out of here?' She agreed, and we made our excuses, saying we were going to bed.

As we left, the grandmas were *still* talking about the wedding. Frank's eyes were almost glazed over; I didn't envy him one bit. We decided—or should I say *I* decided—to go and explore. The hall was quiet, and not many staff members were about.

'Come on, it'll be fun,' I said.

'Maybe we *should* just go to bed?' Eve grumbled.

'Nah. Ten minutes. Promise.'

We walked around a few corridors until we came to the Grand Ballroom. 'Let's look in here,' I found myself saying. I had a strange feeling in my gut; I was drawn to the room.

'Erm, I'm not so sure about this, Quinn,' Eve muttered.

I opened one of the ballroom's big double doors anyway. The strange feeling was almost like an invisible force urging me to enter the room.

The room was enormous and surprisingly well-lit,

thanks to the moonlight shining through the vast windows. It had a glass-domed ceiling, a stage at one end, a ginormous chandelier in the centre, and dozens of round tables dotted around a dance floor. The room was stunning.

As we wandered around, there was a sudden drop in room temperature, and I smelled a subtle fragrance of flowers or perfume. A faint melody filled the air, but the room was empty.

Eve pulled on my arm; she seemed seriously spooked. 'Come on. Let's go,' she snapped.

That's when I got goosebumps all over my body. I could feel eyes watching us. I heard Eve whimper and felt her grab my arm, but I didn't feel scared, not like I had at Millie's house with the demon. Whatever was watching us gave me a sense of inquisitiveness—it bore no malice at all.

Suddenly, a man walked out into the middle of the room. He was about Frank's age and well dressed, in chinos and a button-down shirt. Eve let out a faint cry, and I pushed her behind me. We had no doubt that he was a ghost—translucent and radiating soft, understated energy. Every step he took felt like it was in slow motion.

'Hi,' I said, smiling at him.

To say the guy looked surprised to be addressed by me would be an understatement. He actually looked over his shoulder to make sure I was talking to him.

'You can see me?' he asked with amazement.

'Um, yeah.' I could feel Eve's body trembling behind me.

'Psychics have visited before. They could sense me but never see me. How can you see me?'

Before I could answer, he walked over and touched me. At his touch, he became opaque, but the edges of his body were flickering and blurred. He gasped and pulled his hand away, immediately becoming translucent again.

'Who are you?' he peered at me suspiciously. 'How come I can touch you?'

'I'm called Quinn; I'm half-demon, but—'

Before I could finish, he took a few steps away from me. Seriously! How rude. I felt my irritation prickle.

Eve stepped from behind me and rolled her eyes at me. 'Quinn *is* a half-demon, but he's a good guy, honestly. I'm half-angel, so we sort of balance each other out.' I just clicked my tongue at her. 'But we both see ghosts that need our help. So we are sort of liaisons for troubled souls.'

'And ... what exactly does that mean?' The ghost still looked at us suspiciously.

I cut in. 'Well, when someone croaks, we help them sort out the mess they left behind.'

Eve rolled her eyes again. 'We intercede on behalf of troubled souls and help guide them to their final destination, wherever that may be.'

'Well, I'll be damned.' He laughed. 'This is ... unbelievable.'

'Who are you?' I asked.

'I'm Lord Earl Montague. I own Gracewood Hall ... or I did.' His shoulders dropped, and he sighed. 'I should go.'

'Please ...' I cut in. 'Tell us what happened to you.'

'It's not important now. I'm drawn back here by memories of what happened to me. You could say it's unfinished business.' He started to shimmer.

'Don't go, please,' Eve shouted. 'Tell us about this unfinished business. I told you. We can help.'

He stopped shimmering and directed his gaze at her. 'I don't think you can help me, but I'll explain what happened.'

Mr Montague took a deep breath, a miserable look on his face. 'My nephew, he's a greedy man. We started renovating the hall about twenty-five years ago, and it was closed for a year. My wife, son, and I had our living quarters in the west wing, so we stayed here while the work was undertaken. One evening when visiting us, George left us a little surprise. He let his business partner in and left her hidden in the hall ... and we were all shot to death later that night. Thankfully, my son and wife were asleep. George had always thought it unfair that, as the eldest, Gracewood Hall had been left to me. Not that I knew that then—he certainly acted like the loving nephew. Of course, as his father was already dead, George inherited everything after he'd killed us.'

'But what did the police say?' I asked dubiously.

'They suspected George, but he had a solid alibi. He swore he was with his business partner, so, of course, they both accounted for each other. The police just put it down to a burglary gone wrong.'

'Aw, man. That's brutal,' I said.

'You kids are extraordinary.' He shook my hand. 'It's been a pleasure meeting you.' Then he faded away and vanished, leaving my mind in turmoil. Deep in my heart, I knew I needed to help Earl Montague get justice.

'Let's go and see Mrs D. I think we've got our first ghostbusting case.' I smirked.

I caught Mrs D just as she was going into her room. 'Mrs D, we have a problem.'

She sighed, 'You'd better come in then.' And we followed her into her room.

I explained all about Earl Montague, and Mrs D listened intently. A couple of times, her eyes glowed red.

'Oh dear.' She paused. 'I can see how distressed you both are, so I'll try to help you sort things out. I think we'll start by paying George Montague a visit.' She gave one of her wicked smiles, and Eve and I gulped.

Eve was still nervous, but her curiosity had been sparked, and she searched the Internet to find out anything she could about our new acquaintance. 'He's here tomorrow ... with his business partner. There's a big charity thingy on, and they're hosting it in the Grand Ballroom,' she squeaked.

We checked out the photos of the business partner

so we'd recognise her. As I looked at the picture of George Montague, I murmured, 'Great timing.'

TODAY WAS Mum and Fran's wedding. In my morning suit, with my hair gelled and looking pretty stylish, I knocked on Eve's door. When she opened it, I almost gasped out loud. She wore a pale blue dress with baby's breath flowers in her ink-black hair. 'Y-you look pretty,' I stammered.

Her cheeks flushed, and she smiled at me, looking up through her long, dark lashes. My gut twisted, and my hands fisted.

'You don't look too bad yourself. I'm going to your mum's room in ten. So, go and see her now, hey? She'll want five minutes with you, I'm sure.' I nodded and begrudgingly walked away from her.

I knocked on Mum's door and walked in, and my breath stuttered in my throat. She wore a long, white lace dress and had baby's breath flowers in her long, dark hair, just like Eve.

'You look incredible, Mum.'

She smiled at me. She was standing in front of a long mirror, so I went to join her. She cupped my face in her hands. 'Quinn, you remind me so much of your father. Tall, dark, and extremely handsome.'

As I embraced her, I noticed a shimmer from the corner of my eye. In the mirror, I saw Dad standing right behind us. He was translucent. I went to say something, but Dad put a finger to his lips. He was watching Mum, and the look on his face told me everything. I frowned, and my heart tugged; I felt sorry for him. Mum was happily chatting with me, oblivious to the man she'd once loved standing behind her. Then Dad faded away with a sad smile on his face.

The wedding went well. The banquet room wasn't quite as swanky as the Grand Ballroom, but it wasn't far off. It had a high-vaulted ceiling, elegant chandeliers, and panoramic views of the gardens. Everything had been beautifully decorated, and a grand piano was in the corner of the room, adorned with white roses A guy in a dinner suit played relaxing background music as the guests mingled and when we ate our meal. Everything was perfect—venue, food, company—and I was genuinely pleased for Mum and Frank.

As things ended, I heard Frank whisper, 'Congratulations, Mrs Carter-Williams.' Then he kissed her.

I looked away—it's not something I like to think about with Mum, kissing and stuff—definitely a ticket to Therapy Land. Then, as the guests started to dwindle, Mum and Frank left with a bottle of champagne. They had the bridal suite that night, but I definitely didn't dwell on the fact. I accepted that Mum was so happy, though, and having Frank in my life more wasn't such a bad thing.

Just then, Grandma Monique and Mrs D walked up to us. 'Right, kids. Let's go and sort out a couple of murderers, shall we?' Mrs D whispered.

I peered wide-eyed at Grandma Monique.

'Oh, don't worry, dear. Monique is well aware of everything,' Mrs D said.

'What?'

'I'm a seer, Quinn,' said Grandma Monique. 'For many years, I've had visions of you, Eve and your team. But worry not—your secrets are safe with me, honey.'

Two freaky grandmas. Insane. I burst out laughing when I saw Eve's face. She looked at Monique as though her grandma had just pulled a rhinoceros from her handbag.

'Why haven't you ever told me, Grandma?' Eve frowned at Monique.

'Well, Eve, honey. When I have visions, they are of the future. Not all come to fruition. It's very subjective—the future is not set in stone. Depending on the choices people make, no matter how small, their whole future may change. And one can never attempt to influence what happens. I'd spoken to Mrs D about the visions of you and Quinn, and she explained the rationale behind them.'

Monique glanced at Mrs D, who just pursed her lips. 'Oh, my wonderful granddaughter. I knew you had the support around you that you would eventually need, honey, when the time was right,' Monique said gratefully.

'Oh,' Eve murmured. 'Mrs D didn't know she was to be my guardian, though?'

'Ah, she had an idea.' Grandma Monique smiled wryly.

Mrs D just clicked her tongue and harrumphed. 'Thought it was a load of codswallop, though. No offence, Eve.'

Then I remembered Mrs D talking about visions and Eve, which suddenly made sense. Monique had seen that Mrs D would be Eve's guardian too.

'You know Mrs D's a ...' Eve started.

'A demon. Yes, honey. And a brilliant friend too. Not all demons are bad.' Monique stroked a hand down Eve's face.

'Come along. Let's go and sort these despicable people out,' Mrs D said in an acerbic voice as she hobbled off.

When we got to the doors of the Grand Ballroom, a staff member was checking tickets. Mrs D went up to him, murmured something in his ear, and he bowed his head.

'Welcome, madam.'

'How'd you do that?' Eve asked her.

'Mind manipulation, or compulsion, is my speciality. Like I said, you may be able to do it one day, dear.'

'Ooh, I hope so.' Eve grinned.

Grandma Monique giggled. 'This is so much fun.'

We walked around the ballroom, which was heaving with glamorous people, and I saw Earl's nephew standing next to his business partner among a small group of people. George was a lilliputian man with a thin, pointed face and a trimmed, goatee beard. He was dressed in an expensive-looking tuxedo and evidently thought he was extremely important. The woman was clearly older, but fighting it every step of the way. She had an ugly face, which the plastic surgery hadn't improved, with mean eyes and thin lips.

'Hello, George and Miranda,' Mrs D said as she breezed up to them. 'I think we need a chat about your Uncle Earl Montague's untimely demise.'

Both of them appeared to have stopped breathing, and I smelled fear on them—the demon within me absorbed the fear and became excited, and my blood heated up. I took a few deep breaths to cool the fire within me.

'Unless you'd like to discuss it here?' Mrs D growled.

People around them looked bewildered. 'Let's take this to my office.' George had a whiny, nasally voice, which suited him perfectly. 'We will be back in a moment,' he said to his guests.

'I wouldn't bet on it,' I heard Grandma Monique mutter.

We followed George and Miranda to the lush and spacious office. *All paid for with Earl Montague's money*, I thought resentfully.

'What do you people want?' Miranda asked.

'We know what you both did,' Eve started.

'Yeah, we know that you murdered your uncle and

his family to get your hands on Gracewood Hall,' I added.

I heard George whimper while Miranda glowered and stated boldly, 'You can't prove a thing, you little imbecile.'

'Oh, you're going to turn yourselves in, dear,' Mrs D said happily.

George snivelled and seemed about to faint, but it was evident Miranda was in charge.

'Don't be ridiculous—why would we turn ourselves in for a crime we didn't commit?'

Every word she said was loaded with contempt. She turned to leave, but Mrs D was like a ninja moving in front of her. My nanny demon grasped both their arms and they all disappeared ... literally in a ball of flames.

'Where's she gone?' Eve glanced around the room.

'I think I have a good idea. Probably the demon realm. And honestly, it's not a nice place,' I replied. Now, *that* was an understatement.

Grandma Monique rubbed her hands together, and her eyes shone with excitement. 'Well, that was unexpected.'

Within five minutes, they were back. George's and Miranda's faces were drained of blood, and they both had a look of wild terror in their eyes as Mrs D gave her parting instructions, 'Run along now. And remember, if you don't do as we ask, I shall leave you both there the next time I take you to the demon realm. Go on, go on —hurry up.'

George and Miranda disappeared without hesitation from the office.

'The demons were so excited when I brought George and Miranda to visit.' Mrs D smirked. 'I'm certain they'd both rather go to prison than visit that place again.'

'Oh, thank you, Lilith, honey ... That's the best fun I've had for years,' Grandma Monique said to Mrs D as they strode out of the office, chattering happily. Monique's infectious giggle made both Eve and me smile.

'Well, that was different,' Eve whispered to me.

'Yup. What can I say? We're officially genetic freaks. Welcome to the weirdest life in history.'

Eve burst out laughing, and we followed Monique and Mrs D from the office.

THE NEXT DAY AT BREAKFAST, the staff seemed happier and excitement buzzed in the air.

Eve and I sat with Mrs D and Grandma Monique, and they handed me a newspaper with the headline news blazoned across the front:

GEORGE MONTAGUE AND MIRANDA EVANS TURN THEMSELVES IN FOR THE MURDERS OF LORD EARL MONTAGUE AND HIS FAMILY, FINALLY

SOLVING THE TWENTY-FIVE-YEAR-OLD COLD CASE.

Eve and I turned to each other. 'Let's go see Earl,' she said, delight in her eyes.

We both rushed to the Grand Ballroom, where Earl Montague awaited us. 'How can I ever repay you both?' he asked.

'You don't need to,' Eve replied.

'What'll happen with Gracewood Hall now?' I asked.

Earl Montague beamed at me. 'George's sister, Zara, will inherit it now. And she is a good person, who will look after the business and staff well. Unlike George and Miranda.'

Just then, the ghosts of a lady and a boy of about ten years of age appeared next to Earl.

'Goodbye, Quinn and Eve, and thank you again. I can finally rest,' Earl Montague said in a relieved voice. The three of them waved as they faded away. Eve and I stood staring where Earl and his family had been.

'We don't see ghosts everywhere, like that kid in *The Sixth Sense* movie, do we? So, it looks like Mrs D's right—we *do* only see them when they need help. And George was our first. I guess you could say that we communicate with the unhappy dead?' I turned to Eve.

Eve laughed. 'Yep, and it was a good thing to do.'

That was a pretty successful ghostbusting, but I'd eventually find out that sometimes the ghostbusting business doesn't always go quite so smoothly.

CHAPTER 16

GREENVILLE SCHOOL

A few days after the wedding, Mum and Frank travelled with Monique to St Kitts. They were having a six-week honeymoon, travelling around the West Indies for a while, and then spending time with Grandma Monique. Mrs D was going to look after Eve, Millie, and me. Mum was also going to work part-time when they returned, so no more night shifts. Life would be much easier for her, which made me so happy.

Life returned to normal the week after the wedding, and even school was going well. Eve was helping keep me on track with schoolwork, which was even easier now that I was living with her because she made me do it even if I didn't want to. My attention-span problems made it hard, but I did my best. For me, one of the best things about school was still football. We had an vital cup match that Saturday, and everybody, including Mrs D, was coming to watch.

On the way to class with Harry, I bumped into Jack, the football team captain. Of course, he had Mia with him, plus Jessie and Chloe.

'Hey, Quinn.' Jessie touched my arm, and Jack rolled his eyes at me, biting back a smirk. 'Do you fancy going to the school dance with me?' she asked.

'Uh?'

'The school dance, silly. It's this weekend, after your football match. I thought it'd be fun to go together?'

Harry coughed in a pathetic attempt to cover up a snort.

'Erm, I'm not sure I'm going. Sorry.'

'Come,' Jack said. 'It'll be a laugh, and we can celebrate our win.'

'We haven't won yet, Jack. Somerton's a tough team.'

'I've got every confidence in us, mate. Especially you and Leo.'

Leo was on the team now too. He was almost as good as me, but not quite.

'Thanks, man.' Harry crossed his arms.

'All of you, Harry. We'll definitely win. We're unstoppable.' Jack slapped me on the back and walked off.

'Don't forget we're going together, Quinn,' Jessie called over her shoulder. 'I'll see you there.'

'I'm asking Leo,' I heard Chloe say. 'He's totes hot.'

I swallowed my grin, picturing Leo's reaction, while Jessie and Chloe walked off chattering.

'Damn. What was all that about?' I asked Harry.

'Looks like you've got a date, my man.' Harry was clearly amused.

'Have you got a date?'

'I'm asking Millie.' Harry sobered up. 'Damn, but she's fine.' A slow grin spread across his face. I just hoped Millie felt the same way about Harry.

I blew out a breath. I knew Eve and Millie hated Mia and her friends. I was going to be in so much trouble. Why hadn't I just declined Jessie's invitation? Then I thought about it, and I couldn't see the problem. It was *my* life, after all, wasn't it? *Eve doesn't see me as boyfriend material, so I can go with who the hell I want to, right? Even Jessie, who Eve and Millie hate.*

I swallowed the ball of dread in my throat and decided to try to break it gently to them both that night after school.

At lunchtime, we all met up as usual. Leo, Harry, Millie, Eve, and I had got into a routine of sitting together at the round table in the school cafeteria. Their company and the food made lunch break another favourite thing about school.

'Come to the dance on Saturday with me, Millie?' said Harry.

Millie, whose cheeks flushed, stuttered. 'U-um, I wasn't planning on going.'

'Come on, Millie.' Eve was trying to help Harry out, I think. 'Let's go; it'll be fun.'

'I've got nothing to wear.'

'But I have. We can sort an outfit out for you. I've got a fabulous dress that'll look lush on you. Don't worry—it's black.' Eve grinned.

'Quinn's got a date,' Harry announced through a mouth full of hotdog.

Eve peered at me with narrowed eyes. Leo saw the look on my face. 'Great, I'll be your date, Eve?' he helpfully added.

'Eh, have I?' I gave Harry a black look.

'Yeah, man—Jessie thinks you're going with her now, right?'

Sheez ... if looks could kill, I'd be six feet under. The looks Millie and Eve gave me were pretty evil. Eve got up from the table and walked out. Millie promptly followed her.

'Cheers, Harry. You know they hate Jessie.'

'Sorry, bro.' He looked mortified. I sighed and shook my head.

'Don't worry, bud. I'll look after Eve for you.' Leo laughed. 'How did you get yourself into this mess, anyway?'

'I have no idea.' I let out a slow breath.

I didn't see much of Eve, Millie, or Eloise that evening—they were upset with me. The only greeting I got was from Mrs D and Celeste.

‘Dinner is at six o’clock, dear,’ Mrs D shouted as I left the house.

I’d decided to go to Leo’s. I ran through the woods and along the back roads, and it took me less than five minutes to get to his house.

‘Hey,’ Leo said as he answered the door. ‘Come in. How’re things?’

‘I need a friendly face. Eve and Millie want to kill and chop me into little pieces.’

Leo laughed at me. ‘Girls. Boys are so much easier. Maybe they’ve both got their periods? I’ve heard it makes them a bit crabby.’

‘Hm, oh, yeah ... maybe?’ I hadn’t thought of that.

‘Women are strange and mysterious creatures, Quinn.’

‘You’re telling me,’ I sighed.

‘Why don’t you tell Eve how you feel?’

His question caught me off guard, and I just stared at him for a few seconds. ‘I can’t. She’s my best friend—she’d think I was a weirdo, wouldn’t she? We’ve known each other since we were kids. I don’t wanna talk about it.’

He exhaled heavily but didn’t push it. ‘Okay, if you’re sure? Let’s play pool, so I can whoop your ass again.’

‘Yeah, sure.’ I followed him, my stomach churning. I hated falling out with Eve.

‘Oh, Natasha’s in. She’s been asking about you.’ Leo reined in a grin.

'Damn. How come I'm so popular with the girls suddenly?'

'Have you not looked in the mirror, bud? You're gorgeous. I just wish you were into boys.'

'Erm, thanks. I think.'

Leo laughed at my discomfort. We played pool. Leo's games room is almost as large as Jack's. 'So, Natasha's a vampire,' I asked as we played.

'Yeah. Why? You interested?' Leo chuckled. 'Yes. Mom and Dad saved her from a slayer. She's been with them longer than me. She's harmless —to humans, at least. But I think she'd eat you for breakfast, if you know what I mean.'

'I sure would.' Natasha appeared out of nowhere and moved fluidly across the room. I went beetroot and scowled at Leo.

'Hey, Quinn,' she said in her sing-song voice as she ran a finger down my cheek. 'Leo's right—you are gorgeous. If you ever fancy a bit of vampire, you know where I am.' She smiled and walked out.

'She can be so bloody embarrassing.'

'It's okay. It's quite nice having female attention, actually. May as well make the most of it,' I joked. But the only female attention I really wanted was Eve's. *And that's never gonna happen—she's so not interested.*

I got home to find Mrs D in the kitchen.

'Dinner will be in five, Quinn.' She turned around to face me. 'I hear you have a date on Saturday?'

'Well, it was sort of an accident.'

I hadn't realised that Eve was standing behind me, and her voice made me jump.

'An accident?' she asked.

I turned around to look at her. 'Yeah, Jessie suggested it, and then she assumed I was going with her. She's really bossy. Sorry. You know I didn't actually *ask* her, don't you?'

'She's a pushy B-I-A-T-C-H.' Eve spelled out the word.

'Biatek?' I asked, confused. Yeah, spelling has never been one of my strong points.

She and Mrs D fell about laughing.

'I think we need to do more schoolwork tonight, Quinn; if you ever want to get any qualifications this year, you doofus,' Eve said. And she was okay again, thankfully.

Saturday came, and the biggest football game of the year was on. Eve, Millie, Eloise, and Mrs D watched from the side-lines.

'I must love you. Watching football, humph,' Mrs D had grumbled to me earlier.

It was a pleasant spring day, bright but dry, with a fresh wind. The ground was still wet from the rain the night before. We had our black-and-white strips on, and Somerton were in all-red. The friction in the air was intense.

The ref blew the whistle, and we were off. Somerton were tough competition, but our defence was robust. Harry was our strongest defender—a big lad and a brilliant tackler. Our goalie saved a howler in the first ten minutes.

'Keep going, lads,' Jack hollered.

Somerton pushed their players forward, leaving one defender. Leo looked up at me and we were on. The ball was kicked back, towards us. I ran with it, and Leo was on the other side of the pitch, running just ahead of me. I passed the ball to him. The defender charged at Leo, and he flicked the ball and ran. The goalie was ready for him, but Leo lobbed the ball over his head, and the ball rolled into the net.

The noise from the crowd was deafening; even Mrs D looked happy. Halftime came, and we walked back to our changing room, where a pep talk from Jack got us all amped. He was a great captain.

The school coach added to the energy and enthusiasm, 'We can do this, lads!'

During the second half, Leo and I had a few chances on goal We were both strong in the air, but their goalie was excellent.

Then things took a turn for the worst. Ethan, one of our centre midfielders, was running with the ball. Leo and I were nearest to him. One of Somerton's defenders tackled him; it was a blatant foul. I heard the crunch, and so did Leo. Ethan went down, howling in agony. The ref blew the whistle.

I could tell that the defender had meant to hurt Ethan. I'm not sure how, but I could feel the malice radiating off him ... or the demon inside of me could. I bolted towards him, my emotions surged, and I wanted to lash out. The defender gaped at me, bug-eyed. Leo stood in front of me and stopped me with a push to the chest.

'Quinn, your eyes. Calm down.'

I looked down at the floor and closed my eyes. I calmed my breathing, willing my red demon eyes to disappear. My temper was still trigger-happy and hard to control.

'Sorry.' I breathed in deeply and struggled to compose myself.

'His eyes—' I heard the defender say, 'they were freaking red!'

I glared at him and his teammates. 'Bite me, asshole,' I snapped. I scowled at him, and he kept his distance from me for the rest of the game.

Ethan was taken off, and a sub came on. The ref gave us a penalty. I sneered at the defender who'd hurt Ethan.

'I'm taking it,' I told Leo and Jack, and I took great pleasure in sending the goalie the wrong way. 2–0. The crowd were ecstatic, and the team ran and congratulated me. I did a backflip—showing off, but I didn't care.

At the final whistle, we'd won. The trophy was ours, and Greenville High was the school league champion.

Now all I had to do was get through the school dance.

'Yes, Mum, okay. I promise.' She'd called to nag me about studying for the dreaded exams at the end of the school year.

'Love you, Quinn. Don't forget to get lots of photos of tonight for me and send them on WhatsApp. Have a fun night, sweetheart.'

'Yeah, will do. Love you. Bye, Mum.'

I wore my chinos, a button-down shirt, and a leather jacket. My gut was in knots at the thought of meeting Jessie at the dance.

Mrs D was waiting for me when I got downstairs. 'I'll drive you there when the girls are ready. Just message me when you all want to come home, okay?'

I nodded, then turned to see Eve and Millie coming downstairs. Eloise was rabbiting on to them about the dance and how excited she was to come. Eve looked beautiful, and I desperately wished I was going with her. My mind then wandered to my date, Jessie, which made me feel incredibly guilty. Damn. As a big, bad demon, wasn't I supposed to revel in other people's miseries and use my charms to get what I wanted? The sensitive demon—honestly, you just couldn't write it.

Millie and Eloise walked off, leaving Eve with me. 'I wish I was going with you,' I said quietly.

'Well, you should have asked me, you idiot.'

'Really?'

This perked me right up. Maybe she'd actually realised, like I had, that I was the perfect man for her. She'd finally seen the light and succumbed to my incredible irresistibility.

But then she had to go and say, 'Quinn, even though you are, without doubt, a complete buffoon, you're my best friend, and I still love you.'

Yeah, best friend, I told myself as I swallowed my disappointment.

Leo arrived, looking as striking as ever. 'You look ravishing. I'm honoured to be your suitor tonight,' he said to Eve as he held out his hand and bowed.

'Geez, Leo, you *sound* like an eighty-year-old.' I glared at him.

Eve clicked her tongue at me and scowled. I frowned at Leo—he gave a wolfish grin while shrugging his shoulders.

'Put your fangs away,' I murmured, and he burst out laughing at my annoyance.

'Let's get some photos of you all for Frank and Helen.' Mrs D took Eve's phone and began clicking away.

I sat in moody silence in the car while the rest of

them chatted. When we arrived, there were loads of students making their way into school. We followed along and found Harry waiting for Millie. He handed her a red rose, which made her cheeks heat, and then Harry bowed.

'Harry Wood at your service, mademoiselle.'

Millie gave him a coy smile, then linked arms with Harry. When Leo made a gagging sound, Eve jabbed him in the ribs.

'Creep,' I mumbled to Harry, and the faintest glimmer of a smile crossed his lips.

The school hall looked pretty good, decorated, with a bar at one end serving soft drinks and fruit punch.

'Quinn,' I heard Jessie screech. I turned to see her rushing to me, her fellow pack and Jack following behind. She flung her arms around me.

'Oh, hi,' I said while admiring her appearance. She wore an off-the-shoulder red dress, which showed off her slim legs, and she looked stunning. I glanced over and saw Eve and Millie glaring at me, but I did my best to ignore them.

The loud music made my skin tingle; the bass thumped in time to my heartbeat.

'Let's get some fruit punch,' Jessie said as she dragged me to the bar.

Jack stood with me while we waited to be served. 'She's liked you for ages, you know.'

'Erm, who?'

'Jessie, Quinn. You're all she talks about.'

'Oh,' was all I could manage. I glanced around the room and saw Leo alone; well, he was standing with Eloise. Harry and Millie were dancing. Where was Eve? Then I saw her dancing with Seth, one of my teammates. Seth was a player—one of the jocks who loved themselves—and I wasn't too keen on him. Eve was laughing and seemed happy. I felt my body stiffen as I watched them and saw Leo approaching me.

'Keep it together, Quinn.'

I ground my teeth and sighed.

'Let's dance.' Jessie dragged me to the dance floor.

'Come on, Leo, you can dance with me,' Chloe said pulling him after us. The look of horror on his face was hilarious, and I smirked at him.

I'm not a very good dancer. Well, actually, I'm a terrible dancer, but I went with it, thinking I might as well enjoy myself. Thankfully, Jessie didn't seem much better—she was making bizarre and seemingly involuntary movements next to me.

'Are you okay, Jessie?' I asked.

'Yeah, why? I'm dancing.'

'Oh, sorry, I thought you were having a panic attack or something.'

'Quinn, you're hilarious.' She giggled. I frowned at her in confusion—I was totally being serious. Leo just snorted a laugh.

A slow dance came on, throughout which Jessie clung around my neck like a very tight scarf. Eve was slow dancing with Seth, so I wrapped my arms around

Jessie. The rest of the night went in a bit of a blur, and I quite enjoyed myself. Jessie was a great laugh, and Leo seemed to be having an okay time chatting with Chloe. Jack and Mia joined us at the bar.

Jessie took my hand and nuzzled her face into my neck. 'Mm ... you smell like cinnamon and woodsmoke. So manly.'

I just looked at her like she was batshit crazy, and Leo stifled a laugh. Chloe clearly liked Leo and flirted shamelessly, much to his discomfort.

'Look at us,' Mia said to Jessie and Chloe. 'We've got the three best-looking guys in school as our boyfriends.'

'Oh, totes,' Jessie said, snuggling into me. At that point, Leo nearly choked on his drink.

The lights came up, and the night was at an end. I strolled outside, holding Jessie's hand. I cringed when Chloe tried to kiss Leo, and he politely declined. Poor, gorgeous Leo, who just wanted a boyfriend, not a hot girlfriend. I looked down at Jessie and slowly lowered my mouth to hers. I smelled the sweet, zesty fragrance of the fruit punch on her breath and tasted her warm lips. I pulled her closer, deepened the kiss and slid my hands down her back. I got lost in the moment until I heard, 'Ahem'. I turned to see Chloe clinging to Leo's arm and Leo glowering at me.

'Sorry, Jessie. I've got to go.' I kissed her again and walked with Leo to the car.

'Where're Eve and Millie?' I asked Leo, who was looking a bit unwell.

'No idea.'

Just then, I turned to see Millie kissing Harry and Eve kissing Seth. 'Let's get in the car,' I muttered, clenching my jaw. I could feel my heartbeat booming in my ears. Geez ... I'd just been kissing a gorgeous girl; what was wrong with me? Jealousy bubbled in my chest and made my breath hitch when I thought about Eve kissing someone else. I was pitiful—pathetic.

Eloise was already in the car, waiting for us. 'You should tell her how you feel,' she said to me.

I just stared at her as if I didn't know what she was talking about. Of course, I knew she meant Eve. Eloise sighed, rolled her eyes at me, and faded away, muttering, 'Boys are total jerks.'

Leo creased up laughing, and Mrs D chuckled too.

Eve and Millie jumped in the car, nattering quietly to each other, and I zoned out of their conversation. The journey home was the same as the journey there. I was silent and brooding.

When I got home, I rushed to my room and flopped on the bed. *If Eve's going to see Seth, I'm going to see Jessie*, I decided. I needed to move on from Eve. Plus, there was the demon and angel thing, so it wasn't exactly a match made in heaven. There was also the issue of her complete disinterest in me as more than a friend. She was unattainable and would never be mine. I sighed. Anyway, Jessie was hot, witty, and popular. I'd had a great time with her. Maybe I could fall in love with

Jessie? Well, I was certainly going to try. The problem was Eve *really* hated her.

The following morning, I was still brooding and felt grumpy. Eve and Millie were sitting at the breakfast table chatting with Eloise.

'Morning, dear,' Mrs D said.

'Morning,' I grunted.

'Hey, Quinn,' Eve said happily, 'did you have a good time last night?'

I wasn't sure if this was a trick question. 'Um, yeah, it was all right,' I answered.

'Great. Millie, Harry, Seth, and I are going to the movies later if you fancy joining us?'

My heart sank to my stomach. 'Nah, it's okay. I'm going to Leo's. Natasha's there, and I think we'll hang out with her. She's pretty into me.' I've no idea why I said that. Jerk.

Millie scowled at me, and Eve looked confused and hurt. But I couldn't tell her why I was trying to make her jealous, could I? Eve stood up and went to help Mrs D. I just sat there; my jaw clenched.

'You need to tell her how you feel,' Millie said softly, and Eloise nodded in agreement.

I glared at them and frowned. 'Just leave it,' I snapped.

Millie let out an exasperated sigh and shook her head. Unrequited love in books is super-cute, but in real life—believe me—it totally sucks. Keeping my love for

Eve buried was a bit like suppressing pent-up anger. I needed to get over it, but I wasn't sure how.

I couldn't bear to be at home when Seth came to pick Eve up, so I headed to Leo's straight after breakfast. He and I just chilled out. I saw his parents briefly, but they were off hunting with Natasha. *Poor deer* I thought, again.

'Why aren't you going?' I asked Leo.

'I don't need to hunt as often as full vampires. Plus, I want to spend time with you. I've never had a real friend before, you know?'

'Ah, that sucks.'

'Yeah, well, most people would be a bit freaked out if they found out about dhampirs and vampires. But I'm on the Spook Crew now, so all's good.'

'Spook Crew?'

'Yeah—perfect name for our tribe, I reckon.'

I just laughed at him and shrugged. 'So, when did you realise you ... you know?'

'What, liked boys?' he answered. 'From a young age. It was more difficult when I was younger. Don't forget, I've been around for eighty years, and homophobia was rife when I was growing up; in fact, it was horrendous. It's much easier now, though, which is how it should be. We can't change who we are, can we? Plus, being a dhampir has its disadvantages as far as relationships go. I've flirted with plenty of guys, but I've never really met anybody I feel connected to. You know? And even so, I couldn't be honest about who I am. Not many guys would want to date a dhampir, would they?' He sighed and dropped his gaze.

'Nah, you're not that ugly.' I grinned, and he laughed and lightly punched me on the arm. 'The best part of last night was your face when Chloe tried to kiss you,' I said, swallowing my snigger.

'And you're supposed to be my friend.' He scowled at me, but then he laughed. 'I was helping you out, as a good friend does. But yeah, it *was* pretty gross. I politely declined and, in a very gentlemanly manner, told her I didn't return her interest. It confused the hell out of her.' He shrugged. 'I need to tell her I'm gay, in case she —you know?'

'Yep, that'll definitely do the trick.' I snorted a laugh.

Cordelia had left us loads of food, so after swimming and playing PlayStation, we stuffed our faces.

Natasha came back just as we were finishing. 'Let's go sit in the big room,' she said, grasping my hand. She was ice cold. 'Oh my, Quinn, you're red hot,' she purred, a small smile playing on her lips.

'Probably my demon blood. I dunno.'

Leo looked uncomfortable. 'Put him down, Natasha. He isn't interested. You're about two hundred years too old for him.' I gave Leo a side-glance and frowned, but Natasha ignored him.

'Come on, Quinn.' She laced her fingers through mine and pulled me closer.

We sat and chatted. I told Natasha all about myself, my dad, Mrs D, and my mum. It was nice, just talking. It took my mind off Eve, and I didn't mention her.

'You're all, you know, gorgeous,' I said as heat seared my cheeks. 'Is that normal for vampires?'

Natasha smiled, but it didn't reach her eyes. 'The vampires' physical lure is the snare for their prey, Quinn.'

I gulped. 'Erm, humans?' and she nodded.

'They are beguiled by us, and as apex predators ...' she looked away with a sad look in her eyes.

'So, how'd you end up ... you know?' I said, changing the subject.

'A vampire?' She smiled, but there was sadness in her eyes. 'It was a long, long time ago, Quinn. I lived in Seattle, America. A rogue vampire called Francoise Dubout decided that he would create a cult. He was a megalomaniac but a very charismatic leader. He turned many people and caused devastation in the city. When vampires are first born, they're like wild animals. The blood lust, the intense craving ... let's just say ... it's not good.'

She paused. 'The Lamia Ministerium intervened and killed most firstborns and Francoise, but I managed to escape. That's when Cordelia and Harrison found me and taught me a different way of living. The rest, you know.'

She closed her eyes. 'Now I'm as normal a person as I can be, thanks to them. My parents gave me the greatest gift anybody could give—they believed in me.'

'That's intense. What's the Lamia Ministerium?'

'It's the Ministry of Vampires. They reside near Venice, Italy. Every vampire is accountable to them. They have a stringent code of ethics and like us to behave. Mortals believe we are a myth, and the ministry wants to keep it that way. No vampire is allowed to turn a mortal, not without their consent. The one thing we mustn't do is piss them off like Francoise did. Otherwise, they're ruthless.'

'Wow. So, have any of you—you know—ever changed a human into a vampire?'

'I'd rather not talk about that chapter of my life,' Natasha said sombrely.

'Nah, not me, but it's harder for a dhampir than a vampire,' Leo added. 'Dad changed Cordelia, though.'

'Huh?'

'Yeah, she was dying of diphtheria—he was a doctor back then too. She was on death's door when he decided to do it. He had permission from the Ministry of Vampires, though. They fell in love while he was caring for her. It was well over a hundred years ago, but all's well that ends well.' Leo had a faraway look in his eyes.

'That's so sweet,' I murmured.

We chatted for a while longer, and then I checked the time. 'I'd best be getting back,' I said. 'They'll think I've left home. Not that I wanna go.' I still felt churned up about Eve seeing Seth.

As I was leaving, Leo grabbed my arm. 'Quinn, please make it up with Eve. I hate it when you fall out.'

I let out a breath. 'Looks like she's seeing Seth now, doesn't it?'

'Well, after last night's performance, it looks like you're seeing Jessie?'

'I guess so,' I sighed. 'I'll go and talk to Eve, promise.'

I left and ran home. I knocked on Eve's door, and she frowned when she saw me.

'I'm sorry, Eve. I hate it when we fall out. Will you forgive me for being grumpy?'

She smiled and threw herself into my arms.

I closed my eyes and enjoyed the feel of her. 'How'd it go with Seth?'

'Yeah, he's nice and all, but I'm not sure. I'll see how it goes,' she said with a wry half-smile.

I walked back to my room with a grin, hoping Seth turned out to be a complete jerk.

CHAPTER 17
MISS VULPES

The next school day was pretty average. That is, until lunchtime, when there was a buzz around the cafeteria. So I grabbed my lunch and went to sit down with the gang.

'What's going on?' I asked Leo.

'Mr Harvey, our biology teacher—he's been found dead.'

'Huh? What happened to him?'

'Rumours are his heart was ripped out of his chest. Dominic's dad works in the pathology department, and Dom overheard him talking to his mum.'

We exchanged glances, our brains whizzing.

'Do you think it might be something ... supernatural?' Leo whispered.

'Yeah, exactly what I was thinking.'

I heard Millie groan, and I looked up to see Jessie,

Chloe, and Mia enter the cafeteria. I saw the unimpressed look on Eve's face as Jessie and Chloe walked over to our table. They looked at Eve and Millie with daggers. 'Eve. Oh my, are you having a bad hair day?' Jessie crooned sweetly.

Eve just smirked at her. 'You know, Jessie, you should eat some of that makeup you plaster on your face; maybe then you'd be pretty on the inside too.' Millie nearly spat out her drink, and Leo and Harry were clearly trying not to choke on their food, but Jessie ignored Eve. I just blew out a big breath.

'Hey, Quinn.' Jessie ran the tip of her tongue across her top lip. I felt the blood rush to my extremities. Good job I was sitting down. 'I tried ringing you last night.'

'Oh, right. How'd you get my number?'

'From Jack, silly. Do you want to get together tonight after school?'

'Sorry, I'm busy. But soon, yeah?'

She fluttered her eyelashes at me and smiled. 'Yeah, let me know when. Soon, though—I'm missing your lips.'

Chloe bent down and whispered in Leo's ear, and Leo's pale face blanched.

'Chloe, thank you for your kind offer, but I'm gay,' he said.

Chloe looked horrified. 'What do you mean, you're gay?' she shrieked, and the cafeteria fell silent.

'I'm gay. I'm not into girls—I like boys.'

'Oh, no! You're too hot to be gay!' she complained. 'Damn.' She turned away and flounced back to Mia. Jessie stifled a laugh, bent down and kissed me on the lips, then went to join her friends.

Eve and Millie raised their eyebrows at us both.

'I'm seriously envisaging duct tape over Jessie's big, fat gob right now,' Eve said cattily as she glared at Jessie walking away.

Harry's cough sounded suspiciously like a laugh, so I eyeballed him. Leo said nothing, but he still looked a bit stunned.

'What did Chloe say to you?' I asked.

'You don't want to know,' was all he croaked. I swallowed a smile and turned to Harry.

'Harry, you're a computer whizz, right?' I asked, changing the subject.

'Yeah, bro. Ain't nobody better.'

'You any good at hacking?'

Eve almost choked on her drink. 'Quinn. That's illegal,' she said in a whispery growl.

'The best.' Harry ignored Eve.

'Fancy coming round ours tonight? We may need your help,' I asked quietly.

'Sure. I gotta go; see y'all later.' Harry kissed Millie on the cheek, then headed to his computer club.

'What's going on?' Millie eyed us suspiciously.

'I think we may have a case for the Keepers,' I said. Millie and Eve exchanged nervous glances.

'Mr Harvey?' Eve gave me a worried look.

'Yep.'

'Oh, great.' Millie sighed.

The next lesson for me and Leo was biology. 'I wonder who'll be teaching us now,' Leo muttered.

I shrugged my shoulders. 'Whoever it is, I hope they're not a pain in the butt.'

We walked into the classroom and sat down next to each other. Everybody there was subdued and chatting quietly, obviously talking about the untimely demise of Mr Harvey.

We were all surprised and quick to fall silent when a stunning, tall woman entered the room. Her magma-red hair tumbled over her shoulders. She had a large mouth, and an upturned nose; when she took off her sunglasses, her intense, amber-coloured eyes raked across her students. She broke into a smile, and her oyster-white teeth lit up the room. As her eyes met mine, I felt an electric current run through my body. Her aura was blood-red, and it unnerved me.

'Whoa,' I heard Jack murmur behind me. Even Leo looked impressed.

'Good afternoon, class. I'm Miss Vulpes. I'll be here for one term only. I'm covering for poor Mr Harvey.' She paused and examined us all, but her stare lingered on Leo and me for a split second longer than the others. I felt myself becoming hot and bothered.

'Right, let's get to know you all. One by one—stand and tell me your names.'

We all did as she asked, with Leo taking his turn first. 'Hi, I'm Leo.'

When it came to my turn, I stood on shaky legs. 'Um, Quinn Carter. Pleased to meet you.'

Jack was the last in the class to introduce himself. 'Hey, I'm Jack Taylor. And may I say, you're the best-looking teacher we've ever had.'

The rest of the class cheered. He was such an idiot sometimes.

Miss Vulpes just raised her eyebrows and smiled. 'Why, thank you, Jack.'

She had a tinge of an accent, but I wasn't sure where it was from. I just couldn't shake off my uneasy feeling about this new teacher, but the biology lesson was pretty good fun for once, so I didn't complain.

'I'm doing an after-school project, starting next week, for anybody that wants to be involved,' Miss Vulpes said at the end of class. 'I only need a handful of volunteers, so we'll whittle you down to the best students over the next two weeks.' She smiled smugly.

Almost every boy put his hand up, including Leo. I didn't—something about her was off. When she came too near to me, my demon within became agitated, and my gut tightened. Or was I being hypersensitive?

Miss Vulpes glanced at me, and then she smirked. 'Great—I'll see you all soon. I'll let you know about the project next class. You may go.'

'Aw, man. She's the most beautiful woman I've ever seen.' Leo inhaled deeply.

'But you're gay.'

'I know. It's crazy. She gives me this bizarre feeling.'

'Something about her isn't right, Leo. I felt the same about you when I first met you.'

'I knew something was definitely off with you, bud. I think you're overreacting, honestly. She's a normal, beautiful woman. You're not seriously saying Miss Vulpes's arrival might have something to do with Mr Harvey's death, are you? You're being ridiculous.'

'If I'm ridiculous, then you're dangerously unbalanced.'

Leo barked a laugh and walked off to his next lesson, leaving me stewing. I had a weird feeling that Miss Vulpes wasn't just an ordinary, beautiful woman but was perfectly capable of killing someone.

THAT EVENING, we waited for Harry to arrive as planned. Leo had stayed for dinner—even though he thought I was overreacting, he didn't want to miss out. I needed to speak to Mrs D about my misgivings about Miss Vulpes—I hoped she wouldn't think I was overdramatising things too. I shook off the shiver that snaked down my spine whenever I thought of the new teacher.

Harry arrived just as we were helping Mrs D clear

the dishes. 'Hey,' he said as he hugged Millie. Celeste was going wild, so he picked her up and laughed as she licked his face and whimpered.

'She's *mad* about you,' Millie giggled.

'She's got good taste.' Harry wiggled his eyebrows at Millie, and a blush seared through her cheeks.

Mrs D glanced at me and then at Harry. 'Hello, dear. I don't think I've had the pleasure?'

'Sorry, Mrs D. This is Harry. He's a good guy and a good *friend*.' I eyeballed her. I should have told her Harry wasn't supernatural before he arrived. Of course, she was oblivious to my attempted signal to be pleasant.

'Hey, Mrs D, nice to meet you at last.' Harry shook Mrs D's hand.

She narrowed her eyes at him. 'You're *mortal*?'

Oh. Dear. Lord. I nearly had a cardiac, but Harry laughed. Eloise groaned with embarrassment, faded away and vanished.

'I'll be in my granny annexe if you need me.' Mrs D turned and tottered out.

'She's a bit loopy sometimes,' I said to Harry. 'Sorry about that.'

'No stress, man, it's fine. My grandma comes out with hilarious stuff sometimes too.'

'Lord, she's so embarrassing sometimes,' Millie murmured to Eve, who laughed.

'Right, Harry,' I said, keen to change the subject and

get down to business. 'I've got my laptop. I need you to get into the coroner's database and find out exactly what happened to Mr Harvey.'

Harry stared at me with wide eyes. 'You what?'

'It's important. I can't explain why, but I need to know. Please?'

Nobody said anything, but I could tell that Millie wasn't happy about what I was asking Harry to do.

'Will they know it was us that hacked in?' Millie murmured.

'Hey, I'm the computer genius, babe. Don't worry,' Harry assured her. 'Let's do this.'

'Only if you're sure, though, Harry?' Millie gave me a hard stare, obviously angry at me.

'All we're doing is finding out what happened to Mr Harvey. We're not defrauding a bank,' I exclaimed.

Harry went to work—his fingers doing some quick rat-tat-tatting. It only took him about ten minutes to find what we were looking for. Then he turned away. 'Ugh—those photos are *gruesome*. Feel free,' Harry said as he stood up.

Millie smiled, her cheeks heating, and they went to the basement for some alone time. Meanwhile, the three of us looked over the report, and Eve turned a shade of green when she examined the photos. Harry was right; they were pretty grisly.

'It says here that his heart was taken out while alive. The marks made looked like huge claw marks,' Eve gasped. 'They can't explain it.'

'What's going on? This is not human, and it's not an animal either. What animal has clawed hands that can penetrate a chest and take a heart?' I asked.

'Aw, man,' Leo mumbled. 'It looks like you were right, Quinn. But I'm sure Miss Vulpes has nothing to do with this. Her nails were beautifully manicured.'

'Huh? You noticed her nails?'

Leo's pale face reddened, and Eve snickered. He just glared at me.

'Who's Miss Vulpes?' Eve asked.

'Our new biology teacher, but I'm not sure she's all she says she is,' I explained. Leo let out an exasperated sigh and shook his head.

Later that night, as Harry was leaving, he suggested that we all go to the visiting funfair the following evening. 'Oh, I adore funfairs.' Millie beamed.

'Me too,' Eve agreed.

'Cool. I'll meet y'all here at six o'clock,' said Harry, looking inquisitively at Leo and me.

'Excellent idea.' Leo seemed as excited as the girls.

I shrugged. 'Fine.'

After Leo had left for home and the girls had said goodnight, I went to talk to Mrs D. 'Come in,' she shouted before I even knocked.

'I need to talk to you, Mrs D.'

'What are you doing with a mortal? It's dangerous for you all, Quinn. Your exposure would be catastrophic.' I could tell she was furious with me, but I knew it was only because she was worried.

'I trust Harry. He's one of the nicest people we know. I think he would be great on the team.'

'Absolutely not.' Her eyes glowed red for a split second.

She must have seen the look of shock on my face because she sighed and calmed down. 'Let me speak to your father. Grandma Monique did mention a young man but said she couldn't fathom his abilities. I suppose, maybe, that's because he's mortal. Leave it with me. But do nothing until I say. Okay?'

'Harry might not have our abilities, but he's brilliant with computers and a total genius. Plus, he's loyal.' I paused. 'Anyway, I need to speak to you about the murder of our biology teacher.'

Mrs D's eyes lit up. 'Oh, tell me more.'

I explained what we'd found in the coroner's report, and Mrs D looked a bit troubled.

'What has a clawed hand that could rip a heart out?' I asked.

'A demon, dear.'

My heart sank. 'We have this new teacher. She's taken Mr Harvey's place this term. There's something off about her, Mrs D. I just know it.'

'Keep your distance, dear. If she is a demon, she'll sense your power, and then you will be a threat. I'll speak to your father.'

I went to bed feeling very churned up. I could feel something terrible coming and felt powerless. But right then, there was absolutely nothing I could do about it.

We didn't see Miss Vulpes the following day. Our next biology lesson was in a few days, and I'd decided that instead of going to the class, I'd visit the school nurse just before, pretending I was unwell. As a half-demon, my body temperature is pretty high anyway, typically 40–42, so it would be easy to get signed off.

That evening, the six of us walked the two miles to the funfair together. We could hear the music from a mile away, and our anticipation was building as we got closer to the noise. Laser lights lit up the evening sky like fireballs. Fragments of laughter, mingled with indistinct music, were carried on the gentle evening breeze.

We walked through the entrance to the aroma of hotdogs, burgers, and onions, mingled with the sweet smell of toffee apples, candyfloss, and popcorn. The jumble of sounds merged together too: laughter, chatter, screams, announcements over the loudspeakers, and booming music. The noise was deafening to my sensitive ears, and the sensory overload made me cringe. Leo looked at me with a grimace, but we eventually became accustomed to the aural attack. The atmosphere was electric—the fair was colossal. Adults and children milled about, chattering happily. Brightly lit, peaked tent tops hosted every game you could imagine, and there were different rides everywhere.

'Wow!' Eve screeched. 'Let's go on the Ferris wheel. It's the biggest one outside of London.'

Looking across the funfair from the top of the wheel was impressive. The people below us looked like ants milling about, and we had a bird's-eye view of the whole area. After the Ferris wheel, we wandered around, taking in the atmosphere of the fair and stuffing our faces with hotdogs, burgers, and doughnuts. We could hear long, loud screams high up in the sky as the twirling, looping rides span people faster and faster and higher and higher.

Next came the Waltzers. Huge. Mistake. The five of us got into the tub-shaped car mounted on an undulating platform. Eloise declined. It was dark inside, with neon strobe lights flashing on and off. Hardcore techno-type music blared from the speakers.

To begin with, we were spinning around gently and all laughing when a booming voice announced over the speakers, 'The louder you scream, the faster you go.'

A good-looking young guy appeared and started pushing our car around and around, faster and faster. The girls screamed their heads off, laughing hysterically. Harry, Leo, and I clung on for grim death; I'm pretty sure we all turned green.

'Jesus, that was horrendous. I'm gonna barf that burger back up,' groaned Harry as we all wobbled into the fresh air, feeling dizzy and sick.

'Never again,' moaned Leo.

'That was such fun,' Eve squealed.

'You're not right in the head,' I grumbled.

'Hello, Quinn, Leo, Harry.' I shook off a shiver and turned around to see Miss Vulpes right behind us.

I got goosebumps up my arms, but Leo grinned like an idiot and swooned. 'Hi, Miss Vulpes.'

'Hope you're having fun. I'll see you very soon, Leo,' she replied before disappearing into the crowd. She definitely gave me the freaks.

'I hope so,' Leo mumbled.

'Was that –' Eve whispered. I nodded. 'She's weird.'

'I know. But Leo thinks she's amazing,' I said, shaking my head. I couldn't understand how he was so blind to her creepiness.

We carried on walking, taking in the atmosphere. 'Let's do the bumper cars,' Millie said as she dashed off with Eve and Eloise. We followed them. The bumper cars were brilliant fun. We went on loads of rides and spent a large amount of dosh.

'Ghost train, Eloise?' I whispered to her so Harry wouldn't hear or see me. She just harrumphed and pushed me over. Of course, everybody fell over laughing, while Harry looked at me like I was a fruit loop—Eloise was invisible to him, so it must have looked really odd, me suddenly falling over for no reason.

'Tripped,' I said awkwardly to Harry as I struggled to ignore Eloise giggling while she pointed at me kneeling on the grass.

'He's so clumsy sometimes, aren't you, Quinn?'

I took the hand Eve held out to me and didn't let go as we started walking again. She didn't seem to mind, at least.

Suddenly, I heard someone screech 'Quinn!' and turned around to see Jessie, Mia, and Jack approaching.

'Why are you holding her hand?' Jessie growled, giving Eve a death stare. I dropped Eve's soft, warm hand, and she stepped away. I felt a tug in my heart as I let go. Jesus, I needed to sort my sorry ass out! My feelings for Eve were seriously driving me nuts.

The next minute, Seth and his mates turned up.

'Hey, gorgeous.' The creep gave Eve a kiss on the cheek.

I took in his perfectly styled hair and square jaw. Damn, but he loved himself. I mean, no disrespect or anything, but I need to mention—the guy has an IQ of a stuffed toy. Jealous? Me? Definitely. I resisted the urge to kick him.

'Quinn.' Seth nodded in my direction.

'Hey, Seth,' I said stiffly.

'Eve.' Jessie gave a forced smile. 'You're starting to look a bit chafed. What, are you skipping moisturising entirely now?'

I didn't know where to look, and everyone else tensed up too.

Eve raised her eyebrows, her eyes flashing with anger. 'You're really driving for that biatch-of-the-year award, aren't you, Jessie?'

Seth laughed and grabbed Eve's hand.

Jessie took mine as she glared at Eve. 'Come with us, Quinn. You'll have much better fun. Then you can walk me home. My parents are away for the night,' Jessie said, nuzzling my neck.

'All right, if you lot are okay with that?' I was addressing our group but looking directly at Eve. She shrugged and turned away with Seth.

'Laters, Quinn.' Harry saluted me as he and Leo followed the others.

I continued with Jessie and chatted with Jack. We had a pretty good time, but I still felt churned up about Eve. I just hoped Seth wouldn't try anything on with her. At about ten o'clock, we parted ways with Jack and Mia, and I walked Jessie back to her house.

'Come in,' she said, gazing up at me.

'Um ... I should be getting back.' I didn't want to lead Jessie on, but she was pretty intense and wouldn't take no for an answer. Reluctantly, I allowed her to drag me inside.

'Beer?' Jessie went to the fridge.

'Nah, don't drink alcohol. A Dr Pepper will be fine.'

Jessie at school—well, she isn't too pleasant sometimes, but talking to her alone, she is witty and good company. She was also about to show me that she was very into me. One minute we were chatting; the next, she was straddling my lap, with her arms around my neck and staring into my eyes.

'You need kissing so badly.'

'Erm, do I?' I felt the blood rush to my face and other places.

She pulled my T-shirt over my head and ran kisses up my chest, which made me shiver, and I tried to calm my racing heart. She unbuttoned her shirt, and I saw how her pale skin contrasted against her black lace bra. I pulled her closer and stared into her sultry, dark eyes, and then our mouths met. Things quickly became hungry and heated. I slid my fingers inside her open shirt; her skin was smooth and warm.

I hesitated. 'Um, are you sure, Jessie?'

She smiled seductively. 'Of course I am, Quinn. I've liked you for ages. *Wanted* you for ages.'

I gazed at her face. She was beautiful, and as she ran her tongue over her top lip, my blood surged like a volcano erupting.

'Um, I don't have protection.' I was really turned on, but there was no way I was taking any chances. I wanted us both to be safe.

'I do.' She giggled and kissed me again.

Jessie was leading the way, which made me less worried about whether I was moving too fast for her. She pulled me sideways onto the sofa, and a picture of Eve floated through my mind. How could I do this when, deep down, I knew I was in love with someone else? Well, the problem was, Eve didn't love me—not like that. I needed to move on, right? I decided that Jessie would be my priority. She made me happy, and that was what I needed. I pushed thoughts of Eve to the back of my mind. My hormones kicked in with the power of a lightning bolt to the brain, and I went with it; nothing in my head but Jessie.

As I walked into my house a little later, even though my life was in utter chaos, I couldn't help grinning.

'Where have you been?' Mrs D was standing in the kitchen and not looking too pleased. 'It's almost midnight, and you have school tomorrow.'

'I walked someone home. Sorry, I'm late.'

Mrs D harrumphed. 'I'm in charge while your mother's away. You're not just disappearing without letting me know where you are.'

'Jesus, Mrs D, I'm almost seventeen. Just leave it.' Being preached to irritated me. Then I felt incredibly guilty. 'Look, I'm sorry, okay? It won't happen again.' Her shoulders relaxed. 'Anyway, how come you're not asleep?' I asked.

'I'm a full demon, dear. I don't always need to sleep.'

'Oh, right. Of course,' I said, and she smiled affectionately.

'Goodnight, Quinn.'

My cue to beat it. I went to my room, took a shower and climbed into bed. As I lay there, thoughts about my time with Jessie spun through my mind, but they were utterly ruined when my mind switched to the potential demon threatening our town.

I tried to untangle my thoughts and sighed when

the heart-eating demon won out. This was potentially dangerous, but I knew the police didn't stand a chance if we *were* dealing with a demon. I knew as the Keepers, it was down to us to try and sort it.

My life was seriously plummeting into Sucksville.

CHAPTER 18
HARRY

The following morning, we were all having breakfast and chatting when Mrs D walked in with a newspaper. She placed it on the table. The headline read:

SECOND BODY FOUND WITH HEART MISSING—IS THERE A SERIAL KILLER IN OUR COUNTY?

The breath caught in my throat, and my belly churned. 'Serial killer ... or serial spook?' I studied the photo of the victim. 'Whoa—it's the young guy from the Waltzers last night.' I gasped.

'Geez, this is awful. Who the hell would do such a thing?' Eve said.

'A demon,' I replied.

Millie cussed under her breath, and I gave her a startled look. Millie never swore.

'Yes, it looks like we have a visiting demon, my dears. I think you need to do some research tonight,' Mrs D said solemnly.

'Harry's brilliant at computers and hacking,' I assured Mrs D.

'Very well, but you tell him nothing. Understand?' She glared at us all, and we nodded in agreement.

'Miss Vulpes was there last night,' I told Eve and Millie.

'Quinn so were half the town. That doesn't prove anything,' Eve reasoned.

I knew she was right, but I still had a feeling in my bones that Miss Vulpes was the demon we were looking for. And whoever it was, we had to stop this demon before anybody else got killed. But how would we do it?

School that day was a drag. I was agitated and wanted to get home to start researching what sort of demon we were dealing with. After sitting down to lunch, I broached the subject with Harry before the others arrived.

'Harry, you free tonight?'

'Yeah, course. I'll do anything to see Millie. She moved into your place, or what?'

'She's just about moved in. Her parents are busy people. They don't mind her staying with us.' I felt guilty lying, but it was up to Millie to tell him the truth.

'She goes back a couple times a week to see them.' Millie had told us that when she did return, her parents were never there anyway. But she was happy at our house, so I guess it was as cool as it could be. Millie and Eve joined us, chatting away with each other.

'Anyway, I need to do research, and I need your help. You can't tell anybody what it's about, though. It's top secret, okay?' I whispered to Harry.

'Intriguing. You can trust me, bro.'

I know I can, I said mentally before adding, 'Come round for dinner. Mrs D won't mind. Say, six o'clock?'

'Sounds good. Right, I'm off.' He gave Millie a kiss. 'See y'all later.'

Leo was late joining us. 'Where've you been?' I asked.

'Ah, I've been helping Miss Vulpes with an assignment.'

I felt like shaking some sense into him but refrained.

'I need you tonight.'

'Sorry, no can do. I'm going to the biology group. I'm definitely getting onto her exclusive project. Sorry, Quinn.' Millie and Eve watched our exchange.

I felt my temper rise, so I took some deep breaths. 'Leo, just watch your back. You're one of my best friends, and I love you, okay?'

Leo laughed. 'I'm a dhampir, Quinn. Superhuman strength, superhuman speed and agility, accelerated healing. Know what I'm saying? But cheers, bud, love you too.'

You may be a dhampir, but you're no match for some demons.

The next minute, Jessie walked over to me. 'Quinn, oh God, I've missed you.' She kissed my lips gently. 'You were a demon last night. I want to see you again tonight.'

I felt my face flush. *Wrong choice of word,* Jessie. 'I can't, Jessie; I'm sorry. But I promise we'll get together soon.'

She stuck her bottom lip out and frowned. 'Okay, but soon. Miss you already.' She kissed me again and flounced out of the cafeteria.

I looked up to find Leo, Eve, and Millie staring at me with their mouths open.

'What?' I asked indignantly.

'Did you have sex with her?' Eve looked incredulous.

'N-no. Of course not,' I growled through gritted teeth. 'And even if I had, it'd be none of your business.' I stood up and stormed out of the café just as Seth walked in.

'Hey, Quinn.'

'Sod off,' I snarled as I walked past him. I sat outside to calm down, then went to my next class. On the way, I bumped into her ... Miss Vulpes.

'Quinn, I'm so disappointed you're not trying for my

exclusive science project,' she crooned. She put a hand out to touch me, but I jumped backwards. She gave me a curious look.

'Sorry, just not my thing,' I mumbled as I rushed off. The last thing I wanted was contact with her. If she *was* the demon, the connection with me would cause her pain, and she would be on to me. I couldn't think straight. My brain was on overdrive, and I was so worried about Leo.

As soon as school was over, I made it home as fast as I dared without drawing attention to myself and rushed inside.

'Mrs D, we have a problem. Leo is going to the science project with Miss Vulpes tonight. He wouldn't listen to me. What if he's going to be her next victim?' I was breathless and panicked.

'Calm down, dear. I'll feel if Leo's in danger. And I promise you you'll have psychic visions, too, like you did with Eve. Your bond with your friends is strong. So come and have a cup of sweet tea.'

After a little while, I'd calmed down slightly; then I remembered about Harry. 'Oh, Harry's coming for dinner tonight. Hope that's okay?'

She scowled at me. 'I'm not happy about the mortal, but your father's told me to trust you.'

Cheers, Dad, I thought, and I swallowed my grin. Just then, Eve and Millie came home. Eve glanced at me but didn't say a word.

'I'm sorry I snapped at you today,' I said. I needed to

grovel. It was imperative we stuck together as a team. I'd do anything to accomplish that.

'Okay.' She gave me a black look. 'What's going on?'

I explained why I'd rushed back.

'Oh ...' Eve muttered, and tears glistened in her eyes.

'Ask Eloise to go and keep an eye on Leo. If anything happens, she can come straight back,' Millie suggested.

'Great idea. As long as we're not too late getting to him. I don't think your blood would heal him without his heart, Eve.'

We explained to Eloise what we wanted her to do, and she went off to spy on Leo.

'Just make sure he doesn't see you,' I warned her.

'Don't worry, I'll be very discreet.'

'So, what sort of demons eat hearts, Mrs D? You must know,' I asked.

'Well, most aren't bothered, really. They devour the whole of the contents in the human torso.' Eve turned green at the thought, and Millie gagged.

'You need to research, Quinn,' Mrs D continued. Clearly, that was the extent of her help.

Harry arrived, much to Millie's relief. 'Hey, what's up?' He laughed as he hugged Millie.

'Nothing, I'm just glad to see you.'

Harry grinned, and Mrs D tutted while she finished cooking dinner.

Over dinner, I broached the subject of our research.

'Demons?' Harry chuckled. 'They're mythical creatures.'

I heard Mrs D growl lightly, and then she coughed. 'Sorry, seem to have a frog in my throat.'

'Will you help us?' I looked at Harry whilst ignoring Mrs D.

'Sure. Anything for my babe.'

'Oh Lord, give me strength,' I heard Mrs D whisper. I bit back a smile.

'Come on ... let's do some searching for a demon that eats hearts.'

'O-okay.' Harry eyed me as if I was insane.

'Will you just humour us, please?' Millie said with a hint of desperation in her voice.

'Sure ...' Harry peered at her. I knew he maybe thought we'd all gone batshit crazy.

We worked solidly for a good hour. Harry was deep on the web and making notes. He had superlative research skills, which he *actually* loved using.

When Millie and I went to fetch drinks, I asked her, 'Can you use a spell or something? You know, to find out what's going on?'

Millie hesitated. 'I'm not sure, but I know who will know.' She smiled. 'My grandma. I'll ring her tonight and pop over to see her after school tomorrow. Okay?'

'It'll have to be, I guess.'

'Quinn, *did* you have sex with Jessie? From what Jessie said, it sure sounded like it. Are you sure Jessie's the right person for you?' Millie whispered.

I chanced a glance at Eve, who was busy on her

laptop. *No, Eve is the right one for me.* I felt like screaming. But instead, I let out a sigh.

'Why is everybody suddenly so interested in my sex life?'

Millie narrowed her eyes and crossed her arms over her chest. I wasn't sure how someone so timid and tiny could be *so* annoying.

'But no, I didn't,' I growled in a low tone. 'Not that it's anyone's business.' The guilt about lying caused a pain in my chest, so I softened my tone. 'Look, we have more important things to worry about.'

Seemingly placated, Millie returned to the others and began whispering with Eve. Harry was oblivious, but the girls put me on edge.

The next minute, Eloise appeared. 'Hi. I'm back! Leo is fine. He's at home.'

Harry jumped about five feet, shrieked ... and *splat*; his chair fell backwards with him still in it.

'You can see me, Harry?' Eloise squealed with happiness, and she danced around the room. Harry's wide eyes were fixed on her, and he opened and closed his mouth a few times, like he couldn't get any words out.

'Damn,' I muttered to Mrs D. 'He can see her?'

Mrs D did *not* look impressed.

'Means he's part of the supernatural team, Mrs D. Doesn't it? If he can see Eloise? You said that about Leo and Millie? But how come he can suddenly see her now? Not before? And he's mortal, not supernatural.'

Unusually for Mrs D, she appeared lost for words as

she studied Harry. She cleared her throat and turned to me.

'I'm not sure, dear. Maybe his link to Millie has strengthened. And his link to you too. I genuinely think, mortal or not, he loves you all very much. His loyalty must have been proven,' she said as she turned back to study Harry.

Millie rushed over to Harry and helped him up.

'It looks like you're part of our team now, Harry. I think we have some explaining to do,' I said as I gave Millie a slight nod to carry on.

'Now, don't freak out about what I'm going to tell you, okay?' she said to him.

Harry nodded, but his eyes were wild, like those of a cornered animal.

'Come on. Sit down in a comfy chair, and I'll try to explain the best I can.'

Millie recounted about Eve and me first. Harry stared at Eve and me with a confused expression and bug eyes. But when it came to poor Eloise, he looked at her as if she were a serial killer. The shimmering ghost seemed to rattle him more than me being a half-demon. Thankfully, Eloise didn't seem to mind—I think she was just buzzing that somebody else could see her. Millie explained about Mrs D too, and Harry let out a little whimper.

'Welcome to the team, Harry.' Mrs D went over to him.

It seemed she'd put her concerns about a mortal

joining the team to one side, and she patted him on the head. He closed his eyes and shrunk down a bit when she touched him.

'I'm not going to eat you, dear. I'm here to guide you all.' Mrs D tittered. 'Right, I'm off to my annexe. Night.' And she tottered out of the kitchen door.

Millie hadn't told Harry about her being a witch or Leo being a dhampir. I think she'd decided to break it to him slowly. Poor Harry. He sat on the chair and put his head in his hands.

Eloise cleared her throat. 'I know Leo's safe, but I agree with you, Quinn; I don't like that teacher; she's creepy.' Then Eloise grinned at Harry's bowed head.

'Which teacher?' Harry's head snapped up.

'Miss Vulpes. Quinn thinks she's the demon,' Eve said in a low voice.

'Really? I'm supposed to be joining her after-school science project.' Harry's voice sounded less tremulous.

'No, you're not,' Millie said bossily—then she hesitated. 'Sorry, it's just ... if she *is* the demon, you know?'

'If you don't want me to, it's not happening, babe,' Harry said without hesitation, and she threw her arms around him.

Eve gave me a look, gesturing with her eyes.

I got the message and grabbed Harry's arm, pulling him towards the kitchen. 'Let's get you another drink, Harry.'

'Millie,' Eve whispered, 'you really like Harry, and he

really likes you, but you need to tell him you're a witch. Harry knows about us now, and you've got to trust that he can handle it. Maybe just don't tell him about Leo yet. I'm not sure he can cope with vampires right now.'

I heard their conversation, thanks to my super-sensitive hearing, but Harry was oblivious.

'But what if he goes off me?' Millie whimpered.

'Woman up, Millie,' Eve growled quietly, and Eloise sniggered. Millie huffed a breath and walked into the kitchen.

'Harry, I'm a—erm—witch,' she tentatively declared.

Harry smiled. 'Millie, you're not. You're one of the kindest people I know.'

Eloise and I stifled a giggle, and Eve gave us a black look.

'No, Harry, I actually am a witch,' Millie continued. 'You know, magic and stuff? I'm a good witch, though, promise.' She chewed her bottom lip as she spoke.

Harry was silent for a few seconds, and his jaw dropped as he stared at her. Then he grinned. 'Whoa. I mean ... it's weird, and that, if you really are a witch. But if you are, I guess, like, it's pretty cool, and I'll get used to it eventually, won't I? Even though it's honestly a bit crazy. I didn't even know witches, demons, and ghosts were real! I thought it was all fantasy. This is totally mad ... So, you're a witch like the women in *Charmed*? But you're prettier than them. My little sister adores that programme. My girlfriend's a witch. Awesome!' Harry was rambling.

A slow smile spread across Millie's face. 'I thought you'd think I was insane. I've never told anybody before —well, apart from this lot. I'm so glad I've told you, Harry. Oh, and am I your girlfriend?'

Harry beamed and gave Millie a kiss. 'Will you be my girlfriend?'

Millie nodded and fell into his arms. I felt a small tug of jealousy in my belly. I was glad for Harry and Millie but I wished it was Eve and me. Then I felt guilty about Jessie. Seriously, my life was a sea of confusion.

'Harry, we think Leo's a target for the demon. So we need to find out as much as possible, as quickly as possible,' I said.

Harry cussed and wrinkled his brow. 'I've got a few potential big, bad demons. I could really do with checking the *Grimoire of Demons*, though. Bad news is, it's under lock and key in the collectables vault of the British Library. In bloody London.' Harry huffed out a breath.

'Not a problem—let's go.' Millie motioned.

'Huh?'

'Magic, Harry.'

Harry was bemused. 'Erm, oh yeah,' he said, narrowing his eyes. Listening to Millie's explanation about the teleportation gateway blew his mind.

'Nah, babe, that's just not possible ... is it?'

'You'll see, Harry.' I grinned and gave him a friendly punch on the arm.

Then Millie took her athame and murmured her spell, and the wall disappeared, giving way to the vault in London.

'Mad!' Harry gawped at the hole.

'Yep. Come on.' Millie walked into the vault, followed by the rest of us.

I looked around. The ceiling was twenty feet high, and we were surrounded by thousands of old books.

'How the hell do we find it?'

Millie chanted a few words while moving her athame around like a compass, and then, after a few seconds, a book floated from one of the highest shelves and straight into Harry's hands.

'Respect!' He laughed. He sat at the table and started making notes on his tablet and taking pictures with his phone.

After about ten minutes, I heard faint voices through the metal door.

'Quick!' I said. 'Someone's coming.'

'It's okay. Let's get out of here.' Harry jumped up, and we moved through the gateway back to Eve's house, leaving the grimoire on the table.

'That was unbelievable, Millie.' Harry looked in awe at the witch.

Millie's cheeks flushed, and she smiled. 'It's pretty incredible being a witch.'

'I'll make some drinks, and we can chat,' Eve suggested.

'I wish *I* could have hot chocolate,' Eloise whimpered as she faded away.

Harry eyed the spot where the ghost had been standing. 'Sick,' he whispered.

'Poor Eloise,' Eve said. 'She's really nice, Harry. Her spirit was cursed by a witch, and she can't pass over. She's been so lonely until now, but it must still be hard for her.'

We all agreed.

'Maybe Millie could break the curse one day? Being a brilliant witch, an' all,' Harry suggested.

'Maybe I could. But selfishly, I'd miss her ... really badly,' replied Millie.

'Me too,' Eve and I said in unison.

Eloise reappeared. 'You'd miss me?' She giggled and danced around the room.

'Please excuse the crazy ghost.'

I laughed at the look on Harry's face. He shook his head in disbelief.

Eve made drinks, and we sat together around the table. Harry had a gazillion questions for us. Once he got going, it was hard to shut him up. Eve pursed her lips and avoided my eyes.

'You're part of our team now, Harry. And sworn to secrecy,' I said as he was leaving.

'My lips are sealed, bro. And if I did tell anybody, they'd think I'd gone batshit crazy.'

'Good point.'

And so, Harry, the genius, became part of the tribe, even though he was a mere mortal.

THE NEXT DAY, school started out pretty quiet. I was still on edge, but at least Leo was around. I didn't mention Miss Vulpes; he wouldn't have a bad word said against her, so I didn't tell him about the research we were doing or the fact we were going to Millie's grandma's that night. I felt disloyal not telling him, but it was for the best. He wouldn't believe it anyway, not without proof.

The morning went quickly, luckily—I was counting the hours down until I could leave. This heart-eating demon was making me stir-crazy.

'Fancy coming round mine tonight?' Leo asked as we were walking to lunch.

'Sorry, bud, I can't tonight. Got stuff to do.'

Leo squinted at me. 'Stuff?'

'Yeah, Eve's promised to help me with my project for English. It's a ball-ache, and I'm struggling with it. Sorry, bud.'

'Ah, okay. Guess I'll be spending another night with my pain of a sister then. Cheers for that.'

We both laughed, but lying to him made me feel

incredibly guilty. We walked into the cafeteria and sat with the girls. Both of them looked sheet-white.

'What's up?' I started getting jitters in my belly.

'It's Jack. He's missing,' Eve whispered.

'Jack Taylor? My footie captain?' Sweet. Baby. Jesus.

Eve nodded. 'His parents are going frantic. He didn't come home from school, and the police have been looking for him all night. The search is ongoing. Nobody has seen or heard from him, and his phone's been disabled.'

'Who told you?'

'Someone who knows Mia. She's hysterical and has had to have the day off. His poor parents.'

'Where was he last seen?' I asked, looking at Leo.

He hesitated before saying, 'He was at the science project with Miss Vulpes last night.' He turned even paler than usual, but then he looked determined. 'It's not Miss Vulpes, though. I know it. She's the nicest person; she's not capable of it.' Leo stood up and walked out of the cafeteria.

'Damn, what has she done to Leo? Demons are bad news,' I said before adding, 'Present company excepted.'

'Bring something that belongs to Jack tonight. Maybe Granny can sense if he's still alive,' Millie whispered.

I felt my heart twist when I thought about Jack missing, and I couldn't stop thinking about where he was. Was he already dead? We picked at our food in silence.

After lunch, I went to the lockers and, when nobody was around, broke the lock on Jack's; my demon strength came in handy. There was a comb, hair gel, and other bits and pieces. I picked up the comb and slid it into my pocket.

I faked illness in the afternoon, texting Mrs D to come and collect me—otherwise, they wouldn't have let me leave. After taking my temperature, the school nurse was about to call an ambulance because it was so high. I couldn't tell her it was normal—being half-demon and all. Thankfully, Mrs D showed up before she could dial the number.

'Don't worry, dear. I'll take him to the hospital myself,' my demon nanny said as she guided me from the nurse's office. We drove home in silence. I was terrified for Leo but felt angry about Jack and could feel the rage building up inside of me. The demon in me was fighting to explode. I swallowed the fury, knowing it wouldn't help me to think straight, but it was like a fire in my throat. Once the car stopped, I rushed inside the house for a Dr Pepper, which put the flames out for a while.

'Spill the beans,' Mrs D said as she walked into the kitchen.

'One of my friends is missing. He was last seen at Miss Vulpes's science project class yesterday evening. Nobody knows where he is, and his phone is disabled. I'm worried he's already dead. But, I know it's her—Miss Vulpes. And Leo just *won't listen.*' I shouted the last bit, then sat down and put my head in my hands. 'Calm down. You're no good to anybody in this state, dear.'

I knew she was right, so I attempted to clear my head. 'One thing, Mrs D—I'm not sure if you know, but Leo is gay.'

'Oh yes, Quinn, I know.'

'So how has she entranced him? How? He doesn't even fancy girls. It just doesn't make sense.'

'Well, dear, some demons prey on males exclusively. They exude a certain pheromone; it makes the men bend to the demon's will. It makes no difference that Leo is gay. He's not in control, Quinn—she is. So don't be too hard on him.'

'But what about me? She hasn't affected me, has she? And Harry—he said he wouldn't go because Millie asked him not to, even though he still likes Miss Vulpes.'

'You are immune to her, Quinn, because of your father's blood. He is more powerful than any other demon.'

'What? Even the devil?'

Mrs D ignored my question. 'As for Harry, he is in love with Millie. The bond of love outplays even a demon's lure. The demon cannot break the bond, no matter how hard she tries. Millie will always win.'

At least that meant Jack wasn't in love with Mia, but even so, my head was spinning. But those words cut me to the core—was Dad the devil? The thought made me feel sick. As much as I wanted to know, I couldn't bring myself to ask. No, he couldn't be. He was an okay guy ... wasn't he?

I decided to do more research on demons that eat hearts I needed to take my mind off Jack, Leo... and now my dad. I developed a headache ... it was like a merciless heartbeat in my temples. This Keepers thing was maybe turning out to be seriously bad for the health.

God. *God,* everything sucked.

CHAPTER 19

KITSUNE

Later, Eve, Millie, and Harry came home from school with Eloise. We were all going to Millie's grandma's house after dinner, so we ate early.

I was stressed out because Leo had his biology project with Miss Vulpes that night, and I was worried he'd be the next Jack.

Eloise had agreed to help us to find out more about Miss Vulpes.

'Eloise, I need you to follow Miss Vulpes home tonight. We need to see where she lives. Okay?'

'Sure, Quinn. I'll go back now and keep an eye on her. Good luck at Millie's grandma's.' She faded away and went to spy on the new teacher.

'Still freaky.' Harry glanced at the space where Eloise had been and exhaled. 'How come she looks shimmery, but she's, like, physical like a person? I thought ghosts were supposed to be, you know ....'

'She's like that because of Quinn; we've no idea why. But she's still a ghost. People can't see her. Well, apart from us, I guess,' Eve answered.

'Come along, kids. Let's get to Cornwall,' Mrs D shouted from the kitchen before ushering us to the sitting room wall.

Millie took out her athame and held it to the wall, murmured the weird words, and it shimmered blue. Part of the wall disappeared, and a large hole led straight to Millie's grandma's house.

'Granny,' Millie shouted.

'Come in, darling. I won't be long,' we heard a voice shout.

Millie, Eve, and Harry walked through the wall. I was behind Mrs D, but as she attempted to walk through, she bounced back as if she'd hit an invisible force field. When I tried, the same thing happened.

Millie looked mortified. 'Oh, I'm so sorry. Granny, I need you quickly,' she hollered.

'Okay, okay, I'm here.' Millie's grandma stopped and looked at us. 'Demons?' she asked.

'Oh geez, y-yeah.' Millie was clearly embarrassed.

I bit my lip to stop myself from saying something I'd regret.

'They're my friends, Granny. They're both good and kind.'

Mrs D tutted and tapped her foot impatiently. Then Millie's grandma said a few words and waved her.

'Please, come in.' She smiled at us, but the smile

didn't reach her eyes. 'Sorry, there are magical wards around the house to repel demons. I'm not used to entertaining them.'

I raised my brows. 'Wards?'

'Yes. Spells, darling. Like a tapestry of magic protecting the house.'

Mrs D muttered, 'I'm the most well-behaved demon you'll ever meet, my dear.' Millie's grandma fought a smile.

'I'm only half-demon. And I'm not evil. It's very frustrating, you know?'

Eve took my hand. 'Quinn has the heart of a lion and the soul of an angel, I promise,' she said to Millie's grandma.

I think that was the sweetest thing anybody had ever said about me. I threw an arm around Eve's shoulder and whispered, 'Thanks.'

'So, you're only half-demon?' Millie's grandma asked.

'Yep.'

'Hmm.' She regarded me curiously. 'Please call me Annie. I'm very pleased to meet you all. Terribly sorry about the mix-up. Millie's not very good at communicating sometimes, are you, darling?'

Millie's face flushed again, but then she introduced us all. 'And this is Harry, my boyfriend, Granny.'

Harry beamed at Annie, who looked at him with interest. 'Another supernatural?'

'Nah, just an all-around mortal genius.' Harry grinned.

Annie laughed, and her face relaxed.

Annie appeared to be in her early sixties. She has blonde-grey hair and the most amazing steel-grey eyes. Tall, slender, and very alert, I can't imagine much would ever pass her by. I glanced around what I assumed was the sitting room, with its colourful walls, rustic furniture full of vibrant cushions, and photographs everywhere; mostly of Millie and some guy I thought was Millie's father, Annie's son. A black cat mewed and wove itself around Millie's legs.

'Hey, Notus,' Millie crooned as she picked up the cat. Eve stroked it under its chin. The cat gave me a death stare and narrowed its eyes. I decided not to try to touch it; I'm not sure it liked me much.

'So, let's go through to the kitchen. I'll make some tea, and I can get to know you all a little better. You can tell me all about your predicament too. Millie has been rather vague about the whole thing.' Annie turned around and walked off through the door.

Mrs D grumbled again. 'Witches,' she said in an exasperated voice.

Millie just giggled and raised an eyebrow at Mrs D.

'Present company excepted, Millie dear,' Mrs D added—and we all followed Annie into her kitchen.

'Right, fill me in,' Annie instructed as she filled the kettle.

I started, 'There have been two murders in our

town. Both people had their hearts removed by what looked like a clawed hand.'

'A demon,' Annie murmured.

'Yes, dear. Most definitely a visiting *rogue* demon,' Mrs D interjected.

'One of my friends is missing, and I'm seriously worried about my best friend, Leo. I think he might be next. Both go to an after-school science project class with a teacher called Miss Vulpes. I'm almost sure she's the demon. Jack never came home after her class. He disappeared ... how can he just vanish?'

'Aw, man, but she seems so nice,' Harry said.

'Yes, dear. She seems to be. But if she *is* the demon I suspect—going on what Quinn has told me—she will be able to control any man she wishes. It's probable she's also a shapeshifter, Annie,' Mrs D said, looking at Millie's grandma.

Harry filled us in on his research, adding, 'I've got a list of possible demons. There's a Wechuge and a Wendigo. Oh, and an Átahsaia. If it's a shapeshifter who likes hearts, I reckon if it *is* Miss Vulpes, then she's a kitsune.'

Both Mrs D and Annie were clearly impressed.

'Well done, Harry. A shapeshifting demon can take on the appearance of anybody, alive or dead, even down to replicating the DNA. A kitsune normally chooses a beautiful woman. So,' Annie mused, 'we have a shapeshifter demon who is a beautiful woman who eats hearts. The heart is the symbol of life force in a human.

It looks like you're correct, Harry. Would you agree with that, Mrs D?'

'Most definitely.'

'Has she got red hair?' Annie asked, and we nodded.

'Then you must be careful. This is a powerful demon. This demon can only shapeshift once it has absorbed enough life force and once it's reached five hundred years—'

'Five hundred?' Harry said. 'Insane—she only looks about thirty.'

'Hmm, a kitsune has the form of a fox. And fox in Latin is *vulpes*. Looks likely, Quinn,' Annie stated.

'I knew it,' I murmured.

'Have you got something of Jack's?' Annie asked.

I handed her his comb. Annie went to work mixing a potion of some sort while mumbling gibberish words. She placed the comb in the pot, and green smoke billowed out of it. She looked like she was reading the smoke. Millie shrugged her shoulders at me.

'He's not dead ... yet. But she is collecting young men. He is only the first. She needs three, but I'm not sure why. We must figure out what cosmic event is coming up and why she needs three young males, preferably virgins. She'll want a particular type of man. She wants a strong life force, as well as physical strength.'

'Whoa, Jack won't be too pleased about us knowing that,' I muttered. Eve gave me an incredulous look. 'What?' I grumbled.

'But what about the other guys she's killed?' Millie changed the subject.

'Oh, they were just snacks, dear,' Mrs D said. Millie pulled a face, and Harry went a bit green.

'Let me check the *Book of Shadows*.' Annie mumbled weird words, put her hand into the air, and took the book from its dimensional hollow. Still amazing to see.

'Whoa ...' Harry stood up with his mouth open. Millie patted his arm.

Annie leafed through the book. 'Hmm, we have mention of the kitsune—it has been vanquished before. But it eventually finds its way back to the mortal realm again. It's a wily demon. The Celestial Shadow Solstice may be the day she is aiming for. The cosmic energies are amplified on this potent day. I think she is gathering strength for something even bigger.'

'Makes sense,' Mrs D responded.

'When's the celestial thingy?' Eve asked.

'In two days.'

'Damn. We need to get to work. And quickly,' I muttered.

We said goodbye to Annie.

'Please come again. And Quinn,' Annie put her hand on my arm and flinched. 'You are powerful. Hard to believe you're only half-demon. She will sense your power; you will intrigue her. But, even though your power is immense, you must still be careful. Remember that a fox is a malicious and wily creature—expect blood and feathers if it gets into the hen house. Ergo, the kitsune is a formidable, clever and nasty demon.'

I gulped and tried to look okay, but inside I was a quivering mess. Eve squeezed my hand; she knew me too well.

Eloise was waiting for us when we got back. Celeste started barking and jumping around when she saw us.

'I followed her,' Eloise said. 'She lives at 28 Hollow Lane. But I couldn't get into the house to check.'

'That's because you're alone, dear. You could follow Quinn, Millie, Leo, or Eve, but as a tied spirit, you are limited. But well done,' said Mrs D.

'Right. Google Earth.' Harry brought the property up on his tablet and expanded the view. 'The house and garden back onto the woods, and the woods go on for miles.' He looked troubled.

'But if they're in the house?' Eve asked.

'Then we'll be okay. In theory,' I said as my stomach knotted.

'Another thing I learned is that kitsunes hate dogs,' Harry informed us.

I turned my gaze to Celeste. She was only small, but she was still a dog. 'I think we need to see if Miss Vulpes likes Celeste.' I smiled.

THE FOLLOWING MORNING, as I walked into school, I saw Leo waiting for me. My shoulders lifted with relief. 'Hey. How're things?' I said to him.

'Yeah, brilliant. Don't worry, bud—we can get back to normal once this science project's done. It's the last one tomorrow after school.'

Yeah, if Miss Vulpes doesn't manage to kill you before I get to you, I thought.

Inside school, there was a strange atmosphere. People were huddled in groups and whispering. Most of them looked worried.

'Hey, what's up?' I asked Ethan, my football mate.

'It's Jayden—he's missing now too. He's not been seen since last night.'

'Jayden Miller?'

'Yeah.' Ethan looked terrified.

'Is Jayden in your science group?' I asked Leo. He narrowed his eyes at me and tensed.

'Yeah, but so what? Just drop it, for God's sake.' Then he stormed off, leaving Ethan and me with our mouths open, watching him stomp down the corridor.

I sent Mrs D a text asking her to carry Celeste into biology and for her to pretend I needed to leave school later that afternoon. Eloise and I needed to check Miss Vulpes's house out while she was still in class.

School dragged. The only upside was seeing everyone at lunchtime, but Leo didn't show. I spoke to the others about Jayden; they already knew, and we were wired with pent-up energy.

'I've looked into it, and the peak time for the celestial shadow solstice is at nine o'clock tomorrow night,' Harry said.

'So, she needs one more victim before then. That gives us about thirty-two hours before she rips their hearts out. Assuming she manages to find a third victim,' I surmised.

'That about sums it up,' Millie grumbled.

'Where's Leo?' Eve glanced around the cafeteria.

'He's elusive. I have a horrible feeling he's next. I won't let anything happen to him. Everything will be okay. But I'm going to need your help.' I sighed. Of course, in truth, I had no idea if everything *would* be okay. I mean, far from it, as a matter of fact.

'Leo may not be her intended target? I hope,' Eve whispered.

'Whoever it is, we need to save them all. It's down to us. Otherwise, there'll be more deaths.' I stared at the three of them. They slumped their shoulders.

Mia and her friends strolled into the cafeteria like they were doing a TV appearance or something. Mia was back with a vengeance and loved the attention she was getting because of Jack. She was such an ass. Then, just as I was leaving lunch, Jessie walked up to me.

'Quinn, you've hardly answered my texts and barely made *any* effort to see me. What's going on?'

'I'm sorry, Jessie. It's not that I don't want to see you. It's just I've got so much on.'

Jessie folded her arms across her chest. 'I want you to stop seeing Eve.'

'What? I live with Eve, Jessie. That's highly improbable. Plus, she's my best friend.'

'She's a bad influence.'

I laughed. 'If I'd wanted controlling, I'd have come with a remote.'

Jessie huffed and walked away. 'Your loss, Quinn Carter.'

I shook my head and walked on to my next lesson.

I couldn't help feeling disappointed about being dumped, and I surprised myself when I realised my feelings for Jessie were growing—but maybe it was a blessing in disguise? I had so much going on it was hard to fit Jessie in, which was unfair to her.

Later that afternoon in biology, Miss Vulpes was as charming as ever. All the boys were swooning, including Leo. The way they drooled over her almost made me gag. It was sick, I tell you. Sick! There was a knock on the door, and Mrs D walked in, carrying Celeste.

'Sorry, dear. But I really need to take Quinn out of school. We have an emergency at home,' she said as she approached Miss Vulpes.

Miss Vulpes took one look at Celeste and stepped backwards. 'I'm allergic. Keep that thing away from me,' she demanded.

Celeste went crazy: whining, growling, and baring her teeth—then she started to tremble. The poor thing was obviously having some sort of doggie breakdown.

'Come along, Quinn,' Mrs D instructed. I got up and followed her out of the classroom, but when I glanced back, Miss Vulpes stared at me with open curiosity.

'Well, I think you were right, Quinn. Well done, dear,' Mrs D said softly.

Once we got home, Celeste settled down, and Eloise and I went to Miss Vulpes's house. I faded to spirit and walked through the locked door. The feeling of passing through the wooden door made my insides churn a bit. The sensation was like walking through a wall of warm gloop, but it was getting less freaky the more I did it. Eloise's link to me meant she could now follow me inside.

The house was empty. We searched carefully through every room, checking for any possible hiding place, but there was nothing.

'I'll see if there's a basement, Eloise.'

At the thought, I suddenly sank through the floor. 'Argh.' My stomach ended up in my mouth, and I swallowed the urge to puke. Eloise was in hysterics, laughing. 'Eloise, the basement's empty. How do I get back up?' I shouted.

'Concentrate. Imagine yourself floating back through the floor.'

I did as she instructed and eventually managed to do it. 'Whoa, that was different.' I felt light-headed. Floating up and down was nauseating and intense.

'We need to get back. This house is a front. She must

come in the front door and leave straight out the back door into the woods. I'll meet you back home.'

Eloise disappeared, and I stayed in spirit form and ran. I ran through houses, cars, and shops and arrived home in about three minutes. Mrs D seemed agitated. 'Quinn, Eloise told me about the house. We must find out where her den is before it's too late.'

'I know, but how? Maybe I could turn to spirit and follow her tonight?'

'She won't return to the den, not until she has her third victim. She won't want to take the chance, when she's so close to her objective.'

'You sure?'

'Absolutely.' Mrs D looked troubled.

'There's no science club tonight, so it looks like her last victim will be taken after school tomorrow, then?'

'Most likely,' Mrs D sighed and nodded. 'We'll have to wait until she takes the third boy—there's nothing else we can do—then you follow her from the house.'

I sighed. 'I'll go and wait at her house; see if she comes back and keep an eye on her.'

I changed into spirit and raced back, arriving just as Miss Vulpes was unlocking her door.

Now I've got you. I walked through the wall and saw her going upstairs, so I floated up through the ceiling. She stopped and sniffed the air—I had a feeling she could sense me. Even though I was a spirit, I held my breath and waited. She peered around the room, and my heart jackhammered, and my stomach convulsed as she narrowed her eyes in my direction. She frowned, looked away, started undressing, and went to run the shower. I let out a slow breath.

Damn. I floated back downstairs and waited by the back door. Ten minutes later, she appeared, dressed in pyjamas and a robe. I watched as she went to the fridge and took out a plate containing what looked like hearts. When she started eating one of them my stomach recoiled. She had blood dripping down her chin—*gross.* I was wasting my time; she was clearly going nowhere.

It was a relief to get out of there, and I ran back home to find everybody waiting for me. 'Well, she's definitely our kitsune,' I reported. 'I've left her eating what looked like a raw heart.' Everybody groaned with disgust. Eve wrinkled her nose, and I couldn't help noticing how cute it was when she did that.

'We need a plan of action. The kitsune will grab her third victim tomorrow. That's a certainty. Harry, you need to stay here with Millie,' I said.

'What, no!' both he and Millie complained.

'Look, it's going to be dangerous. Please—it's going to be bad enough worrying about Eve.'

Eve gave me a black look, but I ignored her.

'Eve may need to use her healing ability. Who knows what state Jack and Jayden are in. Eloise will be with us, so if we need you, Millie, Eloise will come back for you, and you can use a teleportation gateway.'

'But I'm the witch. I'm probably the only supernatural being that can vanquish her.'

'We can't vanquish her, Millie—you heard what your grandma said—she's a cunning fox demon. She'll find a way back, sooner or later. I need to absorb her.'

'W-what?' Harry stuttered.

'Yeah, it's pretty grim, Harry. But Dad promises that absorbing demons won't make me evil. It just makes me more powerful.'

'Whoa, that's disturbing and amazing at the same time,' Harry whispered.

I didn't sleep well that night. I'd tried to ring Leo, but he ignored my calls and texts. If anything happened to him, I'd be devastated. Of course, I dreamed of demons again.

I WAS BACK in the red-skied desert. The heat licked my face and coiled around me like a hot-blooded serpent. The screams, desperate and terrified, were horrendous. I felt the discomfort in my chest, and my fight-or-flight response was yelling at me to run. My pulse quickened, and my heart thudded. Gross demon guy saw me and backed away. Every other demon stopped what they were doing and knelt on the floor.

'What can we do for you, boss?'

'Boss?' I grunted.

'Oh, yes. We now know who you are. If you ever need us, you have a demon army at your disposal.' He grinned at me. His jagged teeth still glowed red with blood.

'Oh, so you can escape to the human world?' The whole place erupted into a cacophony of yelling and laughter. 'I don't think so,' I growled.

They actually looked dejected at my words, but demon guy smiled. 'Maybe one day you will need us, boss.'

I disappeared from the demon realm and back to my bed. I woke up with a banging headache and my gut in frigid knots.

CHAPTER 20

SAVING LEO

School was little more than background noise to my mounting anxiety the following day. My nerves were utterly frayed; it was excruciating. All I could think about was getting home, but there wasn't much I could do there either, apart from stew in my melancholy.

Leo was still avoiding me, which hurt me bad. I knew he was under the control of the kitsune, though, so I wouldn't bear any grudges. Still, I missed my dhampir best friend. It made me realise how strong my link to him had become.

At lunchtime—the only enjoyable bit of the day—Millie, Eve, and Harry seemed as depressed as me. 'Has anyone seen Leo today?' Eve asked. Harry and Millie shook their heads.

'I saw him in English, but he just ignored me. He's avoiding us—mainly me,' I said as I bit into my pizza.

'He hates me at the minute.' Saying that made my heart heavy, but then I knew he wasn't himself.

Eve grabbed my hand and squeezed it just as Jessie walked over.

'Hey, Quinn.' Jessie pouted and licked her lips, which heated my blood. 'Do you fancy coming to the cinema tonight? There's a great movie on.'

'I'm a bit tied up tonight'—understatement—'but soon, promise. Anyway, I thought you'd dumped me?'

Jessie gave a coy smile. 'No. Not yet. You're too hot to dump. I'll give you a second chance.'

'Erm, thanks, I think.' I grinned at her, feeling pretty relieved. I was actually getting somewhat attached to Jessie. Jessie gave Eve a withering look and walked back to her pack. Eve sighed heavily and narrowed her eyes at me.

'What?'

'Everyone's entitled to act stupid occasionally, but you really do abuse the privilege,' Eve sniped at me.

'Hey, drop it. I really like her. So, I'm seeing her whether you like it or not.' Eve shook her head and carried on eating her lunch. 'You're with the douche Seth, so butt out.'

Millie gave me a black look too. *Girls.* I decided to ignore the snarky Eve and changed the subject. 'We must return home as fast as possible once the school bell rings. We need to be ready.'

Everybody agreed. They all looked nervous and fidgety, but then we were about to take on a powerful demon. Plus, thinking about Leo being harmed—was horrendous.

That afternoon, I managed to make it through my last lesson without falling asleep from boredom. Then, when the bell rang, I legged it, bolting through the woods and getting home within two minutes.

'Mrs D, Eloise,' I shouted as I came into the house. Celeste ran to me, barking happily, so I picked her up.

'Eloise has gone off to find Eve,' Mrs D called out. 'I'm doing lasagne for dinner.'

I couldn't even imagine eating; the thought of it made me nauseated. 'Maybe later, after we've sorted the kitsune out, Mrs D. I'm not sure I can eat right now,' I called back.

'Okay, dear.'

At that moment, Eve, Millie, Eloise, and Harry arrived. I put my arm around Eve.

'I'm scared, Quinn.' She rested her head on my chest, so I rubbed her back.

'I know, Eve—we all are. We can do this, though. It'll be okay, I promise.' Another promise that I hoped I could keep.

'Do we need to go through the plan?' Eloise asked.

'Yeah, let's go and sit at the table. Millie, bring your iPad and crystal pendulum,' I said downheartedly. You're going to need them if Leo is taken. If it's not Leo she's after, I'm out of ideas. Unless we scout the woods? But that could take hours.'

I looked at the clock. It was 6.30 pm. 'We've got two and a half hours. Now, all we can do is wait.'

The house phone rang. *Probably Mum*, I thought.

'Hello,' Mrs D said as she answered the phone. 'Oh, no, he's not here. Yes, of course, we will. Don't worry, dear; I'm sure he'll be fine.'

'Leo?' I asked.

Mrs D nodded. 'His parents are worried. His phone looks like it's been disabled. They are going out to try to find him. His mother knows he can't have gone far. He was still at school at five-thirty because he was seen leaving with Miss Vulpes.'

Eve groaned, and painful tendrils of fear burrowed into my stomach. 'I'll go and—' I started talking when suddenly I had another vision—I was with Leo. He was in the house Eloise and I had visited ... with Miss Vulpes.

She turned to him. 'You don't know how grateful I am to you, Leo, for helping me finish this project. It is so important to me.'

'It's okay.' Leo's pale face coloured up.

'Right, let's get started,' she said.

Suddenly, she pulled out a taser and fired at him. He fell to his knees, looking disorientated, then bared his fangs and growled.

'Oh, a dhampir! I knew you weren't mortal—this is delightful! We may need a higher voltage,' Miss Vulpes said, a bit too happily for my liking. 'I can feel your beating heart. But a tiny stake through it won't hurt too much, will it?' She smirked.

Leo pounced, and she used the taser again. This time, he jerked around, and the look on his face was terrifying. He went down like a rag doll.

She picked him up. 'Oh, Leo. Your power will be mine.' She cackled and bolted from the house.

'Quinn, Quinn.' Eve was rubbing my shoulder.

'She's got him,' I croaked, bile rising in my throat and tears pricking at my eyes.

'You had a vision?' Harry looked astonished.

'Yeah, another of my super-freaky powers. I should have gone back to her house sooner, dammit.' I rubbed the heel of my hand over my brow. 'Millie, you need to scry for Leo. It won't take her long to get where she's going—she moved like a whirlwind,' I said once I'd calmed down. 'We've got two hours.'

'Here.' Harry found the area we needed on Google Earth and placed the iPad back on the table.

Millie was shaking. She started scrying for Leo, the pendulum over her iPad. She was concentrating intently. Her face was blank, but her eyes held a sparkle. She was linking to Leo, and the pendulum started doing its thing, but it was taking ages.

'Make it larger where the pendulum is pointing, Harry.'

Harry enlarged the view on the iPad.

'I'm nearly there,' Millie muttered. 'I've got him.' Millie took a pen and paper and wrote down the coordinates. 'I'll take you about a hundred feet from where she is. You can plan your attack from there. Okay?'

'Sure,' I said, wondering how sure I really sounded. Plan my attack? I had no idea what I was doing.

Millie took out her athame. 'Are you sure Harry and I can't come?'

I shook my head. 'No, please. If anything happened to either of you, I'd never forgive myself.'

Eve kissed them and Mrs D, and then we walked to the wall.

'Be careful, Quinn.' Mrs D touched my arm. 'Remember, she is a formidable entity. And also very wily.'

I sighed. Was I about to get pummelled by a kitsune? 'Eloise, come on,' I said to the ghost.

'I'm not sure I can watch you all get killed,' Eloise whined, paling visibly (well, for a girl who was already dead).

I laughed. 'Thanks for the vote of confidence, Miss Optimism.'

'Come on, we need you,' Eve murmured, placing a hand on Eloise's arm.

Millie placed the athame against the wall, mumbled the weird words, and as the wall shimmered blue, a large hole appeared, leading to the dark woods.

'Millie, I'll send Eloise back when I need you, okay? We'll need to use the magical wards your grandma uses on her house ... to trap the kitsune,' I said.

Millie gave a slight nod. The three of us walked through the hole and into the woods, and the hole closed behind us. It was eerie and silent. Except for a few shards of moonlight, the woods were as dark as a locked closet.

The moon was larger than normal, the colour of blood and fire—deep crimson and orange. Black trunks against a black backdrop didn't make for much to see. The darkness pressed in on me; it was almost claustrophobic. I wanted to run but knew I couldn't. With a few calming breaths, my night vision switched in, and I began to see everything clearly.

Eve was struggling.

'Hold my hand and watch where you walk.' I took her hand.

'I would if I could see anything,' she whispered sullenly.

'Okay, stay here, both of you. I'll go and scout around. Leo's here somewhere.'

I stopped ... another vision ... I was back with Leo. I was inside an old, dilapidated wooden cabin. Leo was waking up—he jumped up and threw himself at the kitsune. He grabbed her around the throat and squeezed. His eyes were wild, and his fangs were out. She merely snarled at him, pulled a wooden stake from her belt and thrust it into his heart. He collapsed, and she just left him on the floor. She walked to what looked like an altar. Candles and ancient-looking paraphernalia covered it. I couldn't see Jack and Jayden, but I knew they had to be there somewhere.

'Nearly time, my precious ones,' the kitsune crooned.

'Quinn,' Eve said, sounding alarmed.

I turned to look at her, and her face glowed red. I heard Eloise whimper.

'Your face.' Eve stared at me.

Reaching up, I could feel that my forehead was lumpy and gross. *What am I?* I knew I needed to calm down. I took some deep breaths and felt my heart rate drop. Then I felt my face again—it was back to normal. 'The kitsune has staked Leo through the heart. I hope he can survive another staking so soon.'

Chills radiated down my spine—I gulped down the ball of dread in my throat. 'Do whatever you need to do to save him. Even if ... you know ...' I didn't like it, I knew Eve's blood was likely the only thing to save our best friend. Eve squeezed my hand. She knew.

I heard Eloise snivel, and she wiped her eyes.

I blew out a big, slow breath.

'Quinn, you're worried about absorbing the kitsune and everything. But I also know that nothing will ever make you evil. I meant it when I said you have the soul of an angel. Your dad said that when you absorb demons, all it'll do is increase your powers, and I believe him,' Eve assured me as she took my hand.

'Me too,' Eloise said, touching my arm.

I decided not to think about it; it was time for the sensitive half-demon to grow some balls. 'Let's sort this kitsune out,' I growled. 'Right'—I took another deep breath—'there's a cabin very near here. That's where they are. Let me concentrate.'

I decided to try my heightened senses of smell and hearing. I tuned in, and the smell of earth and loam was overpowering. I heard the far-off hooting of an owl and the scampering of tiny animals through the undergrowth ... and then I heard Miss Vulpes's voice. She was humming at first, but then she started saying strange words in what sounded like Latin. It sounded as if she'd started her ceremony—her ceremony of murder. I looked at my watch. We had half an hour.

'This way.' I picked Eve up and ran. The cabin was straight in front of us. It looked long-abandoned: the wood was old and cracked with age; the roof was covered in a carpet of moss; and the cabin door was hanging off its hinges. I put a finger to my lips, but I could still hear the kitsune mumbling her strange words.

'Eloise, go back for Millie and Harry. Tell them to bring Leo's parents and that I'm going in,' I breathed, hardly daring to whisper.

Eloise nodded and disappeared.

Eve and I walked towards the cabin, where I put my hand up to halt her, gesturing for her to stay put. She seemed worried but agreed with the briefest movement of her head. Then I turned and ran before I changed my mind, the mossy earth cushioning my steps.

I silently ducked through the cabin door. The inside of the cabin was as dilapidated as the outside. It smelled of damp wood and musty earth. The kitsune had her back to me; she was engrossed in whatever she was doing. Leo was slumped on the floor, and Jack and Jayden lay unconscious in a cage.

I grabbed Leo and pulled him behind the open door. That's when the kitsune turned, hearing his clothes scratching along the wooden boards.

'Eve,' I yelled. Eve entered and gasped, then she backed away towards Leo.

'Ah, Quinn Carter. My favourite student. Immune to my charms. I so wanted you to be on my project. You're not quite what I wanted—but your power is almost tangible—I can practically *taste* it. Anyway, you're here now, so this has all turned out rather well.' She giggled and clapped her hands. 'Oh, and you've brought me a girl too. Not so keen on girls, but I'm sure her heart will taste just fine.'

I needed to keep her talking. I could sense Eve behind me, working on Leo, out of view of the kitsune.

'I don't think so, Miss Vulpes ... or, should I say, Madam Kitsune?'

Her face dropped, and she looked bemused.

'I'm here to stop you,' I declared.

She burst into a deranged laugh. 'Oh, Quinn. Nobody can stop me. I'm a powerful demon. There aren't many demons that could take me on, let alone a sixteen-year-old schoolboy. I'll finish my ceremony and be in this human form permanently. It's much easier to prey on young men looking like this.' Her lips curved into a hateful smirk.

She was supremely confident and yet, mad as a box

of frogs. 'But now, if you don't mind, I must continue with the ceremony.' She pulled out the taser and fired it at me.

It hurt—a lot—but the taser didn't have the usual effect on me. I was anticipating it, though, and I went down hard, making the floor tremble, as she expected. Then I closed my eyes, pretending to be unconscious.

She turned back around and concentrated on her ceremony again, obviously not worried in the slightest about Eve. When I turned back, I saw Leo drinking Eve's blood. Then he licked Eve's wrist to close the holes made by his fangs before turning to me with hurt in his eyes.

'I'm sorry,' he mouthed.

I shrugged my shoulders and pointed towards the kitsune. Leo launched at her and growled, taking her by surprise.

'How—' she started but didn't wait for a reply as she picked him up and threw him as if he weighed nothing. He crashed into the cage and lay stunned.

'I'm getting very annoyed with you, Leo. I don't need you now. I have Quinn, so decapitation it is,' she snarled as she went to pick up a huge knife.

That's when Eve launched at her, but the kitsune simply batted her away with a flick of her wrist. Eve crashed into the wall and groaned.

'I need to finish my ceremony!' Vulpes screamed.

In a blur, Leo's parents and sister stormed through the door, with Millie and Harry trailing behind.

Natasha, Harrison and Cordelia had their fangs bared. Harry looked petrified.

'Leo!' Harrison grabbed Leo within a split second.

I jumped up. 'Now, Millie!' I shouted.

'*Ex hac daemonium defendat. Magicis custodiis religato intra moenia,*' Millie chanted as she spread her hands wide in the direction of the kitsune.

'Nothing you can do will stop me! None of you is strong enough!' The kitsune laughed insanely. She ran at us but suddenly bounced backwards—she was stuck inside the magical ward, unable to get to us, thanks to Millie. 'What have you done?' she roared as talons appeared from the ends of her fingers like tiny daggers. She rushed over to the cage and broke the lock with one swipe.

'Jack, Jayden!' Harry screamed.

Millie dropped the shield. Then everything happened so quickly ... I jumped towards the kitsune, and she sliced into me with her talons. It hurt—really hurt—but only for a split second. When I looked down, there were no marks—nothing. Like the demon at Millie's house, she couldn't hurt me, and I could see a dawning fear in her eyes.

Leo, Harrison, Natasha, and Cordelia jumped her, grappling with her, just managing to pin her down for a second or two. She threw the four off like annoying insects, and they crashed into the walls. I seized her arms, and she yelped, but she hook-kicked me ten feet straight on top of Millie. A twelve-stone guy landing on you has got to hurt. I looked around. All of us were prone, and—I swore colourfully—we were so screwed. The smoky tendrils of dread wrapped themselves around me.

Crap. Crap. Crap.

Suddenly, the temperature dropped significantly, but I was so angry that my emotions clouded my brain. I glanced at Eloise, who had her jaw clenched and her hands fisted. The way she was looking at Miss Vulpes told me she was enraged. Like I said, never get a ghost angry.

Of course, the kitsune was utterly oblivious that she was about to get her skinny ass kicked by a ghost. A blast of high-velocity kinetic energy threw the kitsune against the wall and stunned her. I launched the ten feet to reach her and grabbed her arms—this time, I wasn't letting go. A shuddering power, like electricity, surged through me again. Every part of me tingled, even my ribs.

'No!' she screeched. 'What are you?'

She was scared ... scared of me. Her face contorted in agony and shook from side to side like it was on fast forward. I tried not to hurl at the sight of it. Her face changed several times between a fox and Miss Vulpes ... until she eventually stopped struggling.

I concentrated as hard as I could and felt myself absorb her essence. She released an agonising scream, and I felt her circulating throughout my bloodstream. She was still screaming inside me—I could hear her.

Then the screaming became quieter, like demonic whispers, and eventually stopped. Her physical form vanished, and that's when I blacked out again.

I WOKE up disorientated and groggy. Then I remembered absorbing the kitsune and gagged. Eve was sitting with me and stroking my brow. 'W-w-what?' I looked around. 'Why are we here?'

We were back at Miss Vulpes's house. Jack and Jayden's cage was in the middle of the floor, with the altar from the cabin now at one side of the room.

'Millie brought us here. Well, after I healed her. I think you broke a few ribs when you landed on her.' She tutted. 'Leo, Harrison, Natasha, and Cordelia carried the cage and altar in. It needs to look like Miss Vulpes kept them here. I think Jack and Jayden have been drugged all the time. This is the last place they'll remember. The police are on their way with an ambulance. There's evidence here of the human hearts she took too. We need to go,' she muttered.

'Are Jack and Jayden okay?' I murmured.

'I've healed them both. They were dehydrated, battered, and cut up, but they're fine now. Don't worry.' Eve smiled.

She was so pretty.

I heard Jack moaning; he was coming around.

'Come on, lazy bones, get your fat ass home,' Millie whispered loudly.

I stood up and wobbled towards the hole in the wall with Eve's help and walked back into our house.

Everybody was sitting around the kitchen table. Harry's typically dark skin had an ashen hue, and he seemed dazed. He looked like someone had whacked him on the head with a biff bat a couple of hundred times.

'You're *really* vampires?' I heard him ask Leo, Natasha, and their parents.

'Yes, we are, but Leo is a dhampir. A half-vampire. We don't prey on humans, Harry—only animals—so we are safe to be around.' Natasha bit back a smile when she saw Harry's face.

'I'm real glad I didn't join the science project,' Harry whispered.

'Well, hello, dear.' Mrs D came to hug me as I walked through the door. 'Well done.'

'Cheers. I think we need to thank Eloise, though. *She* saved us all,' I mumbled.

Eloise clapped her hands together and pranced around. 'That was so much fun.'

She's seriously not right in the head sometimes, but I guess being dead for so long can do that to a person.

'Quinn.' Leo grabbed me in a bear hug. 'Will you ever forgive me? I don't know what came over me. I actually thought I loved her. Totally gross.' He shuddered at the thought.

I laughed. 'You had no choice—she entranced you. It's not your fault, Leo. I'm just glad we managed to get there in time.'

'I love you, bud.'

'You too.'

'Now, who would like some lasagne?' Mrs D asked. Cordelia and Harrison grimaced, much to Mrs D's delight.

'I'm starving,' Leo said, and everybody else agreed. Unbelievable. He'd almost flatlined, and now all he could think of was filling his belly.

'See you in a while, Leo. Careful getting home,' Cordelia said as they were leaving.

'Thanks again, gorgeous.' Natasha walked up to me and threw her arms around me.

'Can't breathe,' I moaned. Natasha giggled and kissed my cheek. Eve narrowed her eyes at the vampire.

'Thanks again, Eve.' Natasha blew her a kiss, and Eve just smiled tightly.

'Don't worry, Cordelia—I'll send Leo home through a teleportation gateway,' Millie told them.

Harry still seemed traumatised and held Millie's hand tightly.

'And thank you, all, yet again,' Harrison drawled as he waved goodbye.

'I'm going for a bath and a lie-down. I think I've

fulfilled my gross-out quota for the decade.' Mrs D chuckled at my words.

'Aren't you hungry?' Eve asked worriedly.

I thought about absorbing the kitsune and only just managed to control my gag reflex. I shook my head and kept my mouth closed.

A little while later, Eve knocked on my door. I was lying on my bed, trying to read but actually staring blankly at the page.

'Hey,' she said as she walked in. 'I know this has affected you, Quinn, but nothing will ever turn you evil. I just know it, so can you try to stop worrying about it, please?' She sat on the bed with me.

'Will you stay with me for a while?' I murmured. Eve lay down and snuggled into me. I put my arm under her head.

'I think I'm gonna be in therapy till I'm thirty.' Eve giggled at me.

That sound was like music to my ears. *Damn, I'm so sad*, I said to myself. I felt like pulling her over me and devouring her mouth, but I refrained. Instead, I closed my eyes as she stroked my hair. Her presence was like a restorative to my badly jangled nerves.

Having Eve lying next to me was the best part of the day so far, and it was the last thing I remembered before I passed out.

CHAPTER 21

THE WITCHES

When I woke up, Eve was gone. I showered and went downstairs, thankful that it was Saturday. Millie and Eve chatted with Mrs D in the kitchen while they cooking breakfast. Eloise was playing with Celeste.

'Morning,' I grunted as I sat down at the table. 'I'll cook dinner for you all tonight.'

'Do you have to?' Eve laughed. I ignored her.

'How was Harry last night?' I asked Millie. 'He looked a bit confused with everything.'

'Ah, he's fine. He was a bit worried about the vampire thing at first, but he said he's never had so much excitement. He loves being part of the Spook Crew, as Leo calls us.'

I frowned at her, and she raised her hands and laughed. 'I know, I know. He's weird.'

There was a knock on the door, signalling Leo's and

Harry's arrival. 'Are we in time for breakfast?' Leo sat down.

'Yep,' Eve replied. 'Great timing, as usual.'

Mrs D threw a newspaper on the table while we ate scrambled eggs and sausages. The headline read:

POLICE IN MANHUNT FOR SCHOOL TEACHER WANTED FOR MURDER AND ABDUCTION.

There was a large photo of Miss Vulpes on the front page. I took one look at that photo, turned around, and threw up my scrambled eggs and sausages all over the kitchen floor, much to everybody's disgust. But give me a break; I'd managed to control my gag reflex so many times, but there comes a time when it becomes impossible. Just looking at her photo made me woozy.

Millie and Leo cleared my mess, and I collapsed onto the sofa, feeling rather peculiar.

'So, Leo, the kitsune staked you through the heart?' Harry enquired as Leo was mopping the floor. 'Doesn't that normally vaporise a vampire? And if you're a dhampir, haven't you got a beating heart? Sorry, I'm confused.'

Leo shrugged his shoulders. 'Yep, I've got a beating heart, being only half-vampire. But I've got vampiric strengths too. Sunlight and a stake through the heart are myths. For full vampires, bright sunlight is extremely uncomfortable, so they try to avoid it. A stake through the heart paralyses them, but you need to chop their heads off, or burn them, to kill them.'

Everybody groaned at the thought.

'I have accelerated healing, but Eve's blood saved me again.' He took Eve's hand and kissed it.

They carried on chatting, and I started to feel a little better. It was so nice to have everything back to normal ... for a while, at least.

'My grandma wants us to spend tomorrow with her,' Millie said. 'Is everybody up for it? You too, Mrs D.'

'Of course, dear. That will be lovely.'

'Sounds good,' Leo answered, and we all agreed.

'Let's go and walk Celeste in the woods, hey?' Eve suggested.

'Not until you've all tidied the kitchen.' Mrs D seemed in a strange mood. Something was up, but I didn't know what. I came back downstairs just as my phone rang.

'Hi, Mum.'

'Quinn, sweetheart. How are you? Tell me what you've been up to.'

'Not much—school and stuff.'

I felt bad about lying but couldn't exactly say my friends and I had been close to death while we battled a murderous kitsune.

'Everyone's round here. We're just going to go walk Celeste. Are you having a good time?'

'The best, sweetheart. It's been blissful so far. I'm so happy. Erm, Quinn'—Mum paused—'I just want you to know I miss you, sweetheart. I'm worried I've left you for too long?'

My heart twisted. I missed Mum badly, but I knew she was safe with Frank. 'Nah, don't worry, Mum—I'm fine, honest. Miss you loads, though.'

'Love you, Quinn. Don't forget to stay in touch, okay?'

'Love you, Mum.'

'Love you more, baby.' And the line went dead.

Mrs D walked up to me. 'Are you okay, dear?'

I sighed. 'I'm fine, Mrs D.' I'd never been apart from Mum for so long, but I was glad she was enjoying her time away.

Mrs D hugged me. 'I need to chat with you later.'

I wondered what she wanted to discuss, but then forgot about it once we left the house. We went to the woods behind Eve's house to walk Celeste.

'Race you,' Leo challenged me.

'Any mortals in the area?'

He sniffed the air. 'Nope—nearest one is at least two miles away. Well, apart from Harry,' he sniggered.

He ran, and I chased. As we disappeared, Harry whispered, 'Whoa ... that's just insane.'

The trees were a blur as we fell into a natural rhythm, with only instinct and reflexes guiding us. Leo was ahead, but I was gaining. Then he bounced off a colossal tree and changed direction, heading back towards Eve and everybody. I jumped into a tree and flung myself through the air, landing in front of him.

'Cheat!' he shouted.

I just managed to beat him back to our friends. Neither of us was sweating or breathless, despite the distance we'd covered.

'You two are complete show-offs.' Eve shook her head at us.

'I'm sorry I haven't got any superpowers.' I heard Harry whisper to Millie. 'Guess I'm boring compared to Quinn and Leo, huh?'

Millie grinned and threw herself into his arms. 'You're perfect just as you are, Harry. That's why I love you.'

I looked at Eve, and her cheeks coloured. I'd give anything for her to say that to me.

'So, our parents have got a few weeks left. You miss your dad?' I asked her.

'Yeah, I'm missing him, but I'm glad they're having such a good time. As long as I've got you and Mrs D, I'm okay, Quinn.'

My heart missed a beat, and Leo winked at me. 'Cool.' Yep—that's all I could think of to say ... seriously. Leo rolled his eyes and exhaled heavily.

'Do you fancy going to the cinema this evening, after dinner?' I said, looking at Eve.

'Oh, yes, that would be great,' Millie replied.

'Yeah, there's an awesome action movie on,' Harry enthused.

I sighed, but Eve smirked and threw her arms around me.

Later, after Leo and I returned from football training, Mrs D was waiting for me. 'It was your turn to cook tonight, but I've decided that if you go to the cinema, you may as well go out for a meal first. A treat, you know? You deserve it.'

'Yeah, nice thought, but I can't afford it, Mrs D. My allowance went on dates and new football boots this month.'

'Oh, it's fine, dear. Your father has given me money for you. He wants to treat you all.' She paused. 'He wants to be a part of your life, Quinn.'

I scrunched my face up and shook my head. 'What?'

'Think about it, dear. He wants you to visit him at his house and maybe stay over. Eve can go with you too. If you want her to?'

I went to say, 'No way', then I thought about it. Alone time with Eve *would* be good. And it would be nice to get to know Dad better. Could I forgive him for abandoning us, though? But he was my dad, wasn't he? The dad I'd always longed for.

'I'll think about it.'

We showered and changed. Leo was becoming a fixture in our house. He slept there, showered there, and nearly always ate with us, but I was totally fine about it. I was just glad to have my friend back. His parents were cool about it as long as he told them he was safe. After the kitsune and everything, we were all still a bit freaked out.

'Quinn!' Eve shouted. 'Hurry up. I've reserved a table

at the Italian restaurant near the cinema. We need to go.'

'Coming!'

Leo and I legged it downstairs, and then I stopped when I saw Eve. She wore jeans, a crop top and a suede jacket and looked radiant.

'You look nice,' I said. Eve blushed and murmured thanks.

Tonight would be extra special; I just wished we were alone. Then I felt guilty about Jessie—I should be taking her out. Damn, I was so confused.

Mrs D dropped us off, and we arranged for her to pick us up after the movie. Eloise was grumbling that she wanted to eat Italian with us. She'd never tried it before; I'm pretty sure it wasn't around in the sixteen hundreds.

'Hey, at least you get to see the movie for free.' Harry said.

Eloise harrumphed. 'I'll see you in the cinema,' she groused as she faded away with a scowl. Ghosts are seriously lacking in the sense of humour department sometimes.

The meal was scrumptious—pasta, pizzas, garlic bread. Dad had given me enough cash to treat everybody, and we all felt very full by the time we moved on to the cinema.

'Great movie choice, Harry,' I said sarcastically. The movie was full of supernatural things, like demons and vampires. 'This is so not like real life at all.'

'Shush—relax and enjoy yourself,' Eve whispered as she touched my leg.

My heart missed a beat, and I felt my face heat. I was glad it was dark in there. The downside was that the darkness and the inordinate amount of food I'd stuffed into myself didn't help with my fatigue—I think I fell asleep for most of the movie. I just hoped I hadn't dribbled. I woke up when Eve nudged me in the ribs.

'Huh?' I muttered. Eve shook her head at me and laughed.

After the movie, Eve popped to the bathroom with Eloise, and we waited for them in the spacious foyer. Most people had already left, so it was pretty empty.

'Quinn, Leo—quick!' Eloise suddenly appeared next to us. Ghosts don't have blood, right? But I swear, at that moment, all the colour had drained from her face.

'Stay here,' I ordered Harry and Millie, and both Leo and I chased after Eloise as she led us to Eve. She was in a hallway that was otherwise empty, apart from two guys who were harassing her. They were both older—big, muscly, and pretty sure of themselves.

As I approached, I realised that one of them was Noah King, our old school bully. I'd have recognised that aura anywhere; it was like a visual cacophony of swirling venti—the wind spirits, that is, not the coffee. He had severe personality problems.

'Come on, baby. I just want a little kiss.' I heard Noah jeer.

Leo put a hand on my arm. Rage burned through me, and he knew I was about to lose it.

'Hey, guys. Leave the little lady alone,' Leo said pleasantly in his American drawl.

'She's coming to a house party with us. Aren't you, Eve?' Noah answered.

Eve's eyes were wide with fear. I wasn't sure if she was scared of the guys or afraid of the demon in me, which hit me like a knife straight through my heart. But my trigger-happy temper had been activated. Fury enveloped me, and I snapped. I launched; the surge of anger was like a physical blow. I was strong and fast, with zero hesitation. I grabbed Noah around the neck with one hand and lifted him off the floor. His friend went for me, but Leo swatted him away like an annoying fly, and he went crashing into the wall.

'If I ever see you anywhere near her again—or harassing another woman—I'll find you and hurt you,' I growled.

His face glowed red and contorted in terror. Noah, to my great surprise, began screaming and waving his arms like a toddler having a temper tantrum, very close to my ear, nearly deafening me. I dropped him on the floor, and he scrambled to his feet. They both legged it. I closed my eyes and calmed my breathing.

'What a freaking douchebag,' Leo muttered.

Eve rushed over and hugged me. 'Thank you.'

'Let's go.' I pushed her away and walked back to the others, leaving a confused-looking Eve with Leo.

I admit the rage mechanism in my temper is sensitive, thanks to my demon within. But it doesn't help when people—just—keep—pissing—me—off. Although I knew Noah had it coming, I had a horrible feeling that sometimes the demon side of me was gaining control, and that thought hurt ... a lot.

Later, I still hadn't spoken to Eve about what happened with Noah, and when Leo had attempted to talk to me, I'd shut him down. He knew me too well to push me. 'Just know I'm here if you need to talk,' is all he said.

Grumpy? Me? Was I ever. This being half-demon, with incredible secret powers and a raging temper, is sometimes crappy—believe me.

Early the next morning, everybody was ready to visit Annie. Mrs D knew something was wrong, as did everybody else—I could tell they were a bit uncomfortable around me. I think I was broody and sullen, but I couldn't snap myself out of it. And I was bottling it up again. I wanted to be a typical teenager; I didn't want to be half-demon.

Millie chanted, the wall glowed blue, and this time we could see Annie's cottage garden. The cottage looked as if it was straight out of a fairy tale in a kids' picture book. Annie came out of the house and rushed over to hug Millie.

'Hello again, Mrs D.' Annie beamed at my surrogate grandma, who smiled back at the witch. 'Leo,' Annie said as she shook his hand. 'A dhampir. So pleased to meet you. You're the first I've ever met.'

'H-hey.' Leo's pale face coloured up.

'And Eloise. Delighted, darling.' Eloise did a twirl. Mrs D had told us that any supernatural with close links to any one of us could see Eloise. And sure enough, Millie's grandma, Annie, had no problem seeing the ghost.

'I thought we'd have a walk into town. After your ordeal I thought having a lovely, relaxing afternoon would be nice, so I'm making afternoon tea when we get back. I've invited some of my coven to come too—they're dying to meet you all.' Annie is an animated woman. She's full of energy and waves her hands around as she speaks. She and Mrs D walked off, chatting.

'Oh, great,' I mumbled.

'Quinn, you have your entire life to be an idiot. So why not take today off? Stop being so godsdamn selfish,' Eve said with venom.

I was taken aback and lost for words. She turned around and walked back to catch up with Annie and the rest of them.

'Come on, bud.' Leo took hold of my arm.

I sighed and followed along.

We walked into Boscastle. To be fair, it was pretty picturesque. The harbour was full of pleasure boats and fishing boats bobbing and creaking on the water. Gulls filled the air with their beating wings and screeching cries. The sun illuminated the water, and the white foam and turquoise of the ocean were beautiful. The smell of salt water was heavy in the air, and the sound of the waves and the sea air helped clear my mind and lift my mood, especially when we all got ice cream and sat on the harbour.

Everybody was chatting happily ... it was only me being quiet, although I was starting to feel loads better. Annie looked pointedly at Mrs D, and then Millie and Annie encouraged everybody to join her for a walk around the harbour.

As I went to get up, Mrs D gave me a sharp look, before saying, 'Sit.' I scrunched my eyebrows together and sat back down

'Talk,' she demanded. 'Everybody is worried about you.'

I sighed. 'I don't want to talk about it.'

'You don't get away with it that easily. Talking is the only way you'll cope, Quinn.'

I recounted again what was worrying me: losing it with Leo and the slayers; absorbing the demon in Millie's house; and then later absorbing the kitsune. Then I told her about losing control last night with the two jerks harassing Eve.

'I think I'm becoming more demon than human,

Mrs D. Absorbing demons is outright bloody freaky, and that makes me feel like a creep. Plus, sometimes I feel the demon side of me is taking control. I can keep a lid on my temper most of the time, but other times I just blow. And I'm scared.' I looked at my feet, feeling my eyes prick with tears.

Mrs D shuffled towards me and put her arm around my shoulder. 'Quinn, my lovely boy. I know a bad demon when I meet one, believe me. You are a good human being. Okay, your father is a demon, but honestly, you're handling it brilliantly. Absorbing demons won't harm you, dear. Please believe me. And as for your temper, you are almost seventeen—your hormones are everywhere, so sometimes control will be a struggle. It's *normal*, especially as a half-demon. The demon in you feeds off anger and fear.'

I gulped and squeezed my eyes shut.

Mrs D took my hand. 'But it will never control you, Quinn. You're a sensitive and caring soul, my dear—two qualities that will never be controlled by your demon within. Eve and the girls love you. So do Harry and Leo. The only things you must have are belief in yourself and acceptance of who you are. Nobody else can make you happy unless you're happy with yourself. You are a half-demon yet wholly human. I've never met such a kind, loyal, and strong young man.'

That's when I lost it ... I cried like a baby as Mrs D embraced me. Yep—boys cry too. It's a very healthy expression of feelings such as sadness, disappointment

... and finding out you're a *complete* super-freak. It's totally unhealthy to shut down your emotions, so I blubbed like my life depended on it. Old-school people may say, 'Man up,' but hey, I have a real sensitive side, which does *not* detract from my irresistible masculinity.

I managed to stop crying and scrubbed my hands over my face just before everybody returned.

'Right. Let's go and have afternoon tea with my coven,' Annie declared, and Mrs D stood up to join her. We followed Annie and Mrs D, but as I trudged along behind, Eve stopped and waited for me.

As I reached her, I tried to explain. 'I'm sorry I scared you again last night. And for being off with you. You didn't do anything wrong ... I sometimes worry I'm becoming a monster.'

'Why do you always make it about you?' she said through clenched teeth.

'Huh?'

I must have had a puzzled look on my face because she let out a big breath.

'Quinn, you're half-demon. Deal with it. I'm half-angel. Our relationship shouldn't work, but it does, even though you drive me crazy sometimes. I wasn't scared of you last night—I was scared of those two jerks. You and Leo rescued me again. You totally infuriate me sometimes.'

When I didn't reply, she gave an exasperated sigh and stomped off up the street.

Confused, my mind raced, and my chest tightened

as I watched her storm away. She saw me as her rescuer, and I hadn't scared her. My mood lifted as I took that in —I felt my tension drain away. I jogged up the street to join my tribe. Mrs D glanced at me and winked. Annie just smirked. Why do grandmas always know everything?

We walked into the house, and I joined the conversation. I sensed the others relaxing around me again, and I felt pretty guilty for behaving like such a jerk.

'Welcome back, bro,' Harry whispered to me.

Millie and Eloise grinned, and Leo hugged me. 'You seriously are a weirdo sometimes, Quinn Carter.' He chuckled.

'Nice. A guy with a pair of fangs, who survived a crossbow bolt through the heart, calls *me* weird.'

Everybody burst out laughing, and the sombre atmosphere lightened.

'I must be going, Annie. I wouldn't want to unnerve your coven. A full-blooded demon may put them off their afternoon tea.' Mrs D chuckled at her own humour.

Annie shook her head and smiled. 'I'm sure—' she started.

'No, no—it's fine, dear. I have much to do anyway,' Mrs D interrupted. I raised my eyebrows at Eve. She looked as bewildered as I felt. Mrs D said her goodbyes, and Millie created a teleportation gateway back to Eve's house.

Annie got busy putting afternoon tea out on the

kitchen table. She had fancy sandwich platters and cake stands. It looked lush.

Time to relax—no chance—that day just got better and better.

The doorbell rang. 'Go and let your aunties in, Millie,' called Annie.

That's when the other three witches arrived, and when they walked in, I almost spurted a laugh. If you've ever seen the film *Hocus Pocus*, you'll have their description: a redhead with funny teeth, a sizeable dark-haired lady, and a beautiful blonde. I was still desperately trying to rein in my laugh while Millie gave me a black look, but I could tell she was biting back a grin too. Leo turned around, his shoulders shaking with silent laughter, and Harry and Eve suddenly became very interested in helping Annie with the food. Only Eloise appeared bewildered, raising her hands in a *What?* gesture.

'Oh, I know what you're thinking, kids,' the redhead said. '*Hocus Pocus*?' And we all dissolved into hysterical laughter.

The three witches were fascinating. Esme was the redhead, Dora was the dark-haired witch, and Bella was the beautiful blonde. After we'd eaten, we sort of split between the sitting room and kitchen. I stayed in the kitchen, chatting with Bella and Leo.

'So, half-demon, hey? And a dhampir? How exciting,' Bella said. 'Annie says you're both good through and through. I must say, if I was ten years younger, you'd both be fighting me off.'

Leo's eyes widened at the thought, and I mumbled, 'Thanks ... I think,' which made her giggle. 'So,' I said to Bella, 'you lot aren't exactly what I imagined witches would be like.'

Bella smiled. 'Um, well, we are mortal, but we have magic—some simple magic, some complicated magic. We have wondrous recipes and cool little spells, and we are definitely a part of the supernatural world ... just like you two.'

'Come through here, everybody,' Annie interrupted, and we gravitated to the sitting room. 'Now, we must break into the Museum of Witchcraft and Magic here in Boscastle.'

'Huh?' murmured everybody, apart from Millie and the other witches.

Well, except Harry, who whispered, 'Awesome.'

'We only want to borrow a book for half an hour. It'll be fine,' Esme said. The other two witches giggled and looked at me with a smirk.

I pointed to myself. 'Me? Nuh-uh. I'm not getting arrested.'

I turned to Millie, and she mouthed, 'Sorry.' If I had known I was about to be asked to break and enter, I probably would have stayed home and finished my trig homework. Seriously. The Circle Theorem seemed like a walk in the park in comparison.

'Come on, Quinn. We are doing this for your tribe. We want to remake some of the magical talisman rings for you. It'll be worth it.' Annie looked like a sweet grandma, but she was turning out to be a bit of a nightmare. Eve shrugged at me, clearly trying hard not to smirk.

'You're the only one that can get in there ... with Eloise. In your spirit form, of course.' I could tell by her voice Annie was resisting the urge to laugh.

'How do you know about my spirit form?' I looked at Millie, and she gave me a worried glance.

'Me too?' Eloise said. 'Oh, how exciting.'

'Yeah, I'm blown away,' I grumbled.

'The alarms won't sense either of you. And the museum is closed now, so don't worry. I just hope the book isn't alarmed when you pick it up,' Annie added.

'And if it is?' I asked.

'Then we'll wing it.'

'Super.' I blew out a big breath.

'Right, you're looking for the *Black Pullet*, a grimoire from the seventeen hundreds. We will get you to the right floor, so don't worry,' Esme told me and Eloise. 'It's the only chance we'll get. The display ends soon.'

'What if I can't pick it up when I'm in spirit form?' I asked.

'I can.' Eloise twirled around.

'Well, you don't need me then?'

'*Please* come with me, Quinn.' Eloise gave me a pathetic look.

Damn.

Esme held her athame to the wall, and I concentrated. Within seconds, I felt myself shimmer, pulse, and disappear. I'd crossed into the veil.

'This is *weird*,' Harry laughed. 'Quinn, where've you gone?'

'I'm still here,' I said. But I knew Harry couldn't see or hear me.

'Where is he?' I heard Bella whisper.

'It's okay. He's still here.' I heard Eve say. Eloise and Eve were the only ones able to see me.

Once again, the hole appeared in the wall, leading into the dark museum. Eloise and I entered and saw the book in a glass case. It wasn't difficult to recognise the *Black Pullet*; it was an ancient-looking, hefty, black tome with strange writing and symbols on its leather-bound cover.

'Careful,' I said to Eloise. 'I'm not sure how to get the case open.'

'Give me a second.' Eloise focused on the case containing the *Black Pullet*, and it started vibrating, then popped open. Her kinetic psychic abilities were pretty stupendous.

'Respect, Eloise.' I high-fived her. Then I attempted to pick the book up, but my hand went straight through it.

Eloise grabbed it. 'This is so exciting, Quinn,' she giggled, but as soon as she picked the book up, the alarm sounded.

'Oh, great. Just great,' I griped. We legged it back through the hole, which Esme had kept open.

'What now?' I shouted as I returned to my physical form.

'Don't worry,' Esme said. 'Come on, girls. We need to stop security getting into the museum for half an hour.' At that, the three witches disappeared through another teleportation gateway.

'That was so cool, Quinn.' Harry gave me a wolfish grin.

'Yeah, cheers, bud.' I felt myself colour up.

Annie took the book and went to work while I paced around, worrying that we would all end up in prison. The wait was excruciating. I kept glancing at the clock —it felt like it was on go-slow. I was jittery and felt a sheen of sweat on my forehead.

Eve just put a hand on my arm. 'Big bad demon?'

'Whatever.'

'Okay, take it back,' Annie said as Millie opened up the wall.

Eloise and I returned to the museum, replaced the book, closed the glass case, and scarpered. Soon after, Esme, Dora, and Bella came back giggling.

'Took security a while to get in. They weirdly couldn't unlock the doors, thanks to our little spell,' Bella laughed.

'Then, once they got in, they couldn't unset the alarm. Thanks to magic, of course,' Dora sniggered.

'But it's all fine now, don't worry. It'll be a hoot when they replay the videos, see the book floating through the air and then back again.' Esme cackled like a bagpipe suffering from tonsillitis.

'What the hell will they make of the video?' I whispered to Annie.

'Quinn, people tend to rationalise what they can and forget what they can't. They'll think it's a spoof,' she replied.

I decided that witches were a law unto themselves. I can't tell you how glad I was to get home that evening—back to normality and, hopefully, no more demons or annoying witches for a while.

CHAPTER 22
EDWARD ATUA

The following weeks were boring, thank the gods—free from irritating witches. Well, except for Millie. No troublesome demons either, apart from Mrs D, of course. Quiet. Bliss. Everyday teenage life resumed. School was as dull as ever, although I learned quite a lot, so it wasn't such a waste of time. The most exciting thing at school that week, apart from lunch breaks, was when someone mixed the wrong ingredients in the science lab. It caused a school evacuation and lakes of toxic smog throughout the building. Cheers to that idiot.

I'd seen Jessie many times since the night I'd walked her home, but her insane jealousy about Eve soon became a problem. We'd had some good times together —she was witty and great company. I'd almost spent my whole month's allowance taking her on dates. Jessie had been warm for my form for so long, though, I reckon she would have happily settled for a Mackie Ds and a chocolate milkshake.

I liked Jessie and everything—like, really liked her—but the crunch came when she told me she thought she might love me. I couldn't say it back; I couldn't lie about something so important. It made me feel horrendous because I didn't want to hurt her.

The reality was the only girl I loved was Eve. I was doomed because I knew Eve would never love me as more than a best friend. I'd started becoming cool and distant with Jessie; it wasn't fair on her *and* made me feel incredibly guilty. Plus, things in my life could get complicated ... well, okay, my life was already one big complication, and it was one that Jessie couldn't be a part of.

Jessie became even more resentful of Eve, so when I refused to stop spending so much time with Eve ... Jessie dumped me, for real this time. But her parting words were, 'We are meant for each other, Quinn. One day you'll see that. I'll never give up on you—you'll come back to me, eventually.'

I didn't realise she'd already lined up a new boyfriend, though. Yep—Eve's guy, Seth. I was a bit relieved; it made me feel less guilty about loving Eve when I was with her. But I was also pretty jealous—not that I'd admit it. Luckily, I wasn't jealous enough to knock Seth out.

The good news was that Eve had dumped Seth's ass. She found out about him seeing Jessie and her, which made her hate Jessie even more. Eve's tirade to him on the phone made me so happy—she tore him to pieces. He turned out to be more of a jerk than I'd hoped.

'I'm sorry about Jessie,' Eve had said to me.

I just shrugged. 'I'll get over her. Don't worry.'

'She was lucky to have you.' She walked away, leaving me feeling baffled.

As the weekend of visiting my dad approached, Eve was really up for going, and she was getting increasingly excited about it while I became more and more nervous. Millie was happy to stay with Harry and Eloise while we were away—all of them were going to Leo's house again for the weekend. Harry was hyped about spending time with vampires.

We planned to go to Dad's on Friday after school and stay for two nights. I was filled with dread and apprehension. On the plus side, though, I was looking forward to it just being Eve and me. Maybe I could tell her how I felt? I sighed. Nope. She'd shatter my heart to pieces when she gave me the look ... you know ... the *I love you but as a best friend* look.

'But I need to tell Mum, don't I?' I'd asked Mrs D. 'I can't start seeing him without her knowing.' Mum and I had a close relationship, and hated not telling her.

'Wait until she returns, dear. We will sort it out then. Let her enjoy her honeymoon,' is all Mrs D said in return.

I felt guilty lying to Mum when I spoke to her about

the weekend's activities. But I trusted Mrs D was right, so I didn't say anything about where I was going.

Friday came, and Eve and I waited with our overnight bags. Dad had told Eve to bring her riding clothes because he had horses, so she was wired. The black limo turned up, and the ginormous chauffeur got out of the car—as always, wearing his wraparound sunglasses. He gave me a wide berth again as he opened the back door for us to climb in.

Eve and I chatted on the drive over. My stomach was in knots, but I didn't tell her how nervous I was. Gorgeous dense forest edged the roads for a lot of the journey, and when we slowed down, it seemed we were surrounded by forest as far as the eye could see. We passed two massive stone pillars, and a security guard in a hut opened the electric gates to allow us to drive in. It took, like, five minutes to get down the driveway—no joke.

As we drove, I did a double take—we were now on a sprawling country estate. Eventually, the house came into view. Well, when I say house, it was more like a colossal mansion, like something out of a period movie, where people all sit around getting served tea and sipping champagne. With turrets, gables, and beautiful high-arched windows—surrounded by formal lawns and gardens.

We jumped out of the car, and the chauffeur drove off. 'I guess we should go and knock?' I suggested.

Eve followed me up the wide stairs to the enormous

wooden doors, large enough to accommodate a family of elephants.

As I raised my hand to the knocker, the door swung open. A man, who looked like a butler, stood at the entrance.

'Master Quinn, Mistress Eve, please do come in,' he said in a very posh voice. He wore a black suit, a white shirt, and a grey tie. He had short blond hair, and his eyes crinkled when he smiled. 'Welcome to Myrtlewood Estate.'

We followed him in, and Eve whispered, 'This is sooooo posh,' in a not-so-whispery voice.

'Mr Atua is waiting for you both. Please, follow me to the snug.'

I glanced around the grand hallway, with its tall ceiling with mouldings around the edge and a table in the centre of two flights of spiralling staircases. Neutral tones, loads of paintings, and a polished, wooden floor complete the look. *Dad must be minted*, went through my head.

We walked down a wide corridor, and the butler opened a door, announcing, 'Mr Atua, your guests are here.'

Dad was standing beside a roaring open fire, immaculately dressed and still looking like a male model. It was hard to believe he was a demon. He was in a room I can only describe as refined. If this was the snug, I couldn't wait to see the rest of the house.

'Quinn.' His eyes lit up, and he came over and

hugged me. Awkward. Then he greeted Eve, kissing her hand. 'Please, sit down. Jarvis will bring us refreshments.'

We both sat on the plush sofa. *Where'd he get his money from?* I wondered.

'I'm a very successful businessman, Quinn.'

I gulped. Could he read my mind?

'I have companies all around the world. Don't worry. It's all legit.'

I grinned at Dad like an idiot, feeling embarrassed, before asking, 'So, how'd you meet Mum?' It just sort of fell out of my mouth before my brain engaged. Dad looked sad. I got a feeling that even thinking about her hurt his heart. If demons even had hearts?

Jarvis returned with a tray of mini hotdogs, burgers, and mini pizzas, and what looked like a jug of freshly squeezed lemonade. Of course, I was first to grab food after Dad told us to help ourselves. I inhaled a load of food, then downed a glass of lemonade. Eve was still politely nibbling on her first hotdog by the time I'd finished.

'Ah, a half-demons appetite.' Dad seemed pleased. Jarvis was still in the room but seemed unfazed. *I'm pretty sure Jarvis isn't a demon,* I thought to myself, although I could tell he definitely wasn't mortal.

'Will that be all, Mr A?' Jarvis asked in his highly polished accent.

'For now, Jarvis. Thanks.'

The butler bowed his head and left the room. Dad poured himself a glass of lemonade and sipped slowly.

'Your mum'—he paused—'is the most remarkable person I've ever encountered, Quinn. I think it was love at first sight. Well, love at first scolding,' he laughed. 'My associate—human, of course—was in her care. I came to see him at the hospital, but getting past your mother was a challenge. He was very sick, and I wasn't family. I remember the fire in her eyes and her tenacious spirit; she was bold and beautiful. I saw quite a lot of her over the following month and eventually plucked up the courage to ask her out. The rest is history.' He sighed.

'Plucked up the courage?' I asked. 'But you're a powerful demon.'

He smiled. 'Demons don't normally get attached, Quinn. I made a mistake asking her out.'

I must have looked horrified because he raised his hand to protest as he continued, 'But it's the one thing in my life I'll never regret. A few months of a normal life with Helen and then with you. I'll treasure both for eternity.'

I glanced at Eve, who seemed absorbed in his story. She scrunched her brows and mouthed, 'Bless.'

I felt a lump in my throat and needed to change the subject. 'So, this thing about being Keepers in the mortal world? Can't someone else do it?'

I needed to get this off my chest. I was finding it incredibly stressful. Being expected to rid the world of evil supernaturals is *less fun than* you think. Everyday teenage life was much easier.

'You are a chosen one, Quinn.'

'Erm, can't I be an overlooked one?' I heard Eve giggle, and Dad bit back a smile.

'I love your sense of humour.'

I totally wasn't joking ... anxiety balled in my throat. 'Yeah, I'm a regular barrel of laughs.'

'Meet Kismet.'

'Erm, who's Kismet?' I said, glancing around.

Eve snorted a laugh, and Dad smiled. 'Kismet is your destiny, son. You can't escape her. Quinn, you and your team are stronger than you realise. You are all brave, smart, and very loved. The job couldn't be in better hands.'

'Thank you,' Eve murmured. I glanced at her with a *What?* look. She narrowed her eyes at me.

'Come, Jarvis will show you to your rooms.' Dad stood up, and we followed him out of the snug to find the butler waiting for us.

'Go and explore if you'd like to,' Dad said, 'but don't go too far. Dinner will be served at half-past seven.'

'That gives us an hour to have a nosy around,' I suggested to Eve as we followed Jarvis up one of the spiralling staircases.

'Your rooms are next to one another. I'll collect you both here at twenty-five-past seven.' Jarvis smiled, bowed, and walked off to do whatever butlers do.

Eve went into her room, and I heard her squeal. I ran

in and found her face down and flopped on the bed. She lifted her head and grinned at me. 'This place is unbelievable.'

'Yeah, it's unreal.' I scanned the surroundings. The room was wood-panelled and painted in creams and whites. Her bed, a mix of greens and gold, and the curtains at the massive windows were the same. A chair, desk and a sofa sat by the open fireplace.

Leaving Eve, I went to investigate my room. Painted in colours that reminded me of a cloudy sky, the room had sea-blue and foamy white bedding. The furniture resembled Eve's, but broad French windows covered one wall, leading to a balcony with views of the gardens and beyond. Then I discovered an enormous marbled bathroom behind a closed door. I was impressed.

Eve popped her head around my bedroom door. 'Come on, Quinn. Let's go and explore.'

Jarvis appeared as we descended the stairs. 'If you go through the orangery,' he said, pointing to a door down a wide hallway, 'then you will get to the back gardens.'

We followed his directions and arrived in the most breathtaking room—all glass, plants, comfy chairs and sofas. Through the vast bi-fold doors, we found a colossal patio area, with tables and chairs and lots of potted flowering plants, then steps down into the gardens. In the distance, we could see pastures with horses grazing.

'This is intense.'

Eve nodded in agreement. We continued through the grounds for about ten minutes, enjoying the quiet and relaxing evening. It was a warm, spring day and the sweet smell of flowers and earth tingled my nostrils.

'He must have an army of gardeners,' Eve said, staring at the view.

The sun was setting, and the rich hues of red blending with oranges and crimsons set the clouds ablaze. It was incredible. I glanced at Eve and clenched my hands by my side. The overpowering craving to touch her never faded.

'We should get back. I want to freshen up and put a dress on,' she murmured, still gazing at the sunset. *Maybe coming here wasn't such a bad idea*, I thought.

We went to freshen up and change, and Jarvis was waiting when I opened my bedroom door.

'Your father thought an informal dinner would be in order this evening. You will be eating in the kitchen.'

I just shrugged and smiled. Eve strode from her room, looking stunning in a gold-coloured dress with her ink-black hair in a knot on top of her head.

We followed Jarvis downstairs and along another wide corridor.

'Wow,' I muttered as we walked into the kitchen—a sprawling open space with vaulted ceilings, making for a light room beautifully furnished with traditional cream units and an enormous island in the centre.

Dad sat at a huge wooden table by French doors overlooking yet another garden. A lady wearing an apron was standing next to the cooker. She turned around and beamed at us.

'Quinn, Eve, this is Mrs Potter. She runs the kitchen for me.'

'Hi,' Eve and I said in unison.

Dad invited us to sit down, so we joined him at the table. Mrs Potter dished the food, and Jarvis served us homemade steak pie, fluffy potatoes, and a kaleidoscope of buttered vegetables. It was divine.

'Thanks, Mrs Potter,' I said after I definitely couldn't fit any more in my belly. 'That was fantastic.' She smiled and patted my head.

'Let's return to the snug and chat,' Dad suggested. 'I've given most of the staff the weekend off. I thought it would be nice to have a quiet time with you both. I'm a bit tied up in the morning, but maybe we could go out on the lake in the afternoon?'

Eve and I nodded. 'We can go horse riding Sunday morning if you would like, Eve?'

'Sure. That would be amazing.'

We returned to the snug to relax while we tucked into the delicious cake Mrs Potter had baked—I was almost exploding by the time I'd eaten that. We chatted about all sorts: slayers, absorbing demons, and crazy witches, and I told Dad about battling the kitsune. I mentioned Eve's blood healing Leo as well as her healing ability.

'Nobody must know about that, Quinn,' he instructed firmly. 'If the wrong people discover the healing power of Eve's blood and her healing hands, it will put Eve in mortal danger.'

Eve looked at me in alarm.

Just then, there was a knock on the door, and the chauffeur poked his head around, *still* wearing his sunglasses. 'I'm finishing, Mr A. I'll see you tomorrow,' he said in his deep baritone voice.

Dad thanked him, waited for the door to close, and continued, 'It's best if nobody knows about Millie, Leo, or you. Okay?'

I gave Eve's hand a squeeze—then I changed the subject. 'So, how come there are so many supernatural beings in the world? Including demons?'

'The world is full of the supernatural. Humans believe we are myths, and most of us want to keep it that way. As for the demons—well, many hundreds of years ago, a cult of black magic practitioners opened a portal to the demon realm. I sorted the situation out, but many demons disappeared, and some not-so-pleasant ones escaped. Some are shapeshifters, like the kitsune, and they went on to cause numerous wars.' Dad paused.

'Unfortunately, humans still dabble with the dark arts even though opening gateways to the demon realm is hugely dangerous. Some humans will always be obsessed with releasing evil and hoping to profit from it.'

I gulped. 'Whoa. That's fierce.'

‘Hundreds of years ago?’ Eve piped up. ‘Exactly how old are you, Mr Atua?’

Dad tapped his nose, an enigmatic smile on his face.

After another half hour, we headed off to our rooms. I hugged Eve goodnight, then crawled into my sumptuous bed, where I passed out before my head hit the pillow.

I WOKE to birdsong and a haze of buttery sunlight flickering through my window. It took me a few minutes to remember where I was. Once I was fully awake, I jumped up, showered, dressed, then knocked on Eve’s door—no answer, so I hurried downstairs to find her helping Mrs Potter cook breakfast. Dad was sitting at the table with a coffee, reading a newspaper.

‘Mrs D reads that one,’ I commented as I grabbed a juice.

‘I should hope so. It’s my paper.’

‘What? You own it?’

‘Like I said, Quinn, I have many legitimate businesses.’

After a breakfast of champions—a full English—Eve and I decided to spend the morning exploring.

We seemed to walk for miles. My acute hearing

picked up the distant sound of water, maybe a river? The forest hummed with life.

Every now and then, the sun broke through the dense canopy and lit the dirt path we followed. I sniffed in the fragrance of minty grass and damp earth, happily absorbing the whole ambience of our surroundings.

As we slowly meandered through the forest, I suddenly heard a new noise—a soft rumbling, like a big dog growling.

I stopped and put a hand on Eve's arm. As I peered through the dense trees, my gut tightened. It was a fair way away, but my acute eyesight focused on a beast that was as black as coal, with shaggy fur and about as large as a pony. The problem was its glowing red eyes and razor-sharp teeth, which glistened as its panting tongue lolled from its mouth. It pricked up its ears as it looked at me and let out a bark that rattled my eardrums. Eve flinched at the noise.

'Jump on my back,' I murmured, worry tinging my voice.

Without hesitation, Eve did as I asked. Then I ran. The problem was—the beast was just as fast, if not faster, than me. I suddenly thought of how Celeste couldn't resist a game of fetch, so I found and threw a massive branch, wondering if this dog-like beast might fall for my trick. Sure enough, it watched the branch sail over its head and then turned to chase it. I started running again, feeling relieved, but it was only a matter of seconds before I could hear the beast beginning to gain on us again.

My heart was pounding, and I could feel Eve urging me on. We got to a ledge, and I saw below the source of the water sounds I'd heard earlier: a river. Unfortunately, it was about a fifty-foot drop to the riverbank.

The beast was gaining and looked terrifying. I was out of options, so yelled at Eve to hold tight, and jumped. We began to plummet when, suddenly, we weirdly started to slow down as if we'd slipped into slow motion. I couldn't understand what was happening.

'Huh?'

'Whoa,' Eve shrieked.

I turned mid-air to look around, and my heart skipped a beat ... Eve had wings.

'What's happening to me?' she cried.

Whatever *was* happening to her meant that we landed at the edge of the river—slightly wet but unharmed—and the beast seemed to have disappeared. I just stared at Eve, bug-eyed. Then I burst out laughing.

'It's not funny,' she growled and stamped her foot.

Once I'd calmed down, I cleared my throat. 'I think it's amazing you have wings.' But then I burst into a fit of giggles again.

'I'm stuck—I don't know how to get them back in. And where have they come from?'

Her wings took my breath away. A wonderful blend of creams and gold, speckled with white—radiant, like the colours of the warmest sunset. The smaller feathers blended intricately with larger ones as they rounded the delicate, narrowing curve toward the bottom tip. Sticking out about five feet on either side of Eve when fully extended.

'Come on. Let's go see Dad. If we can find the way back, that is. Unless you want to fly us? Try moving them.'

'I can't,' she complained.

'Eve, it's got to be like when I turn to spirit. You need to focus and concentrate. Try again.'

I stifled another laugh, and she glowered at me. Then she closed her eyes, her wings began to undulate ... and she took off. She screamed, and I clasped her foot and pulled her back towards me.

'Oh, I'm not sure about this,' she said as I placed her beside me.

Smack! Ouch. She'd socked me straight around the head with a wing.

'Careful with the wings, Eve,' I grumbled, which made her giggle.

'Erm, I think you'd better learn to fly quickly!' I said, pointing to the black shape I'd just noticed trotting toward us. The beast was back on our tail, although still fairly far away.

'Jump on my back and hold on. You can do this, Eve.'

She took one look at the approaching beast and didn't need telling twice. She jumped on my back, wrapped her long legs and arms around me, and gave it her all. Her wings slammed upward. When they came back down in a flash of gold and white, she was off the ground. It all happened so damn fast. The beast jumped in the air a split second later, only just missing us.

'Stop beating your wings and glide. I can see the house in that direction.' I pointed.

'Ohhhhh, I think I'm getting travel sick,' she groaned.

She pushed herself against the air currents, and we glided gently toward the house, passing over a prominent structure I guessed was a garage. The chauffeur was outside its doors, washing about six cars. As we sailed over him, Eve became more confident.

'Maybe being half-angel isn't so bad. Flying's pretty good fun!' she hollered as the wind whipped at our breaths.

The chauffeur looked up with his mouth wide open, and he watched us sail over him, about fifty feet in the air. This whole time, the black beast was following us.

I wasn't sure how we were going to land and not get eaten.

'Dad,' I yelled as the house got nearer. I saw him run outside, look up, and laugh. 'How do we land?' I shouted.

'Eve, concentrate. Imagine you're a bird; focus and descend. Feel the air currents under your wings,' he hollered.

We got lower and lower and eventually landed about fifty feet away from Dad. I ran as we landed to carry the momentum forward, and we finally came to a stop just as the black beast pounced. Eve jumped free, but it flattened me on my back. I closed my eyes and heard Eve scream. The next thing I knew, a rough tongue covered my face in thick saliva, which smelled like grandpa breath. I opened my eyes to see the devil dog ... drooling and panting ... and wagging its tail.

'Belua, heel!' Dad shouted as he tried not to laugh at me. The beast trotted to his side, and Dad patted its head.

'Belua?' I croaked as I stood up.

'Sorry about that, Quinn.' Dad coughed—I'm pretty sure he was covering a laugh. 'Belua is very affectionate. She obviously likes you. She is my hellhound; I call her Belle, though, because she's so pretty.'

I gave Dad a sideways glance. Pretty was *not* a word I'd use to describe the hellhound—she was more like a cross between a Shetland pony and a grizzly bear.

'She won't harm you, but she is very effective against poachers and trespassers—they never return after meeting her.' He smirked. 'She is also very protective of the people I care about.'

'She's a demonic pit bull,' I mumbled, at which point, Belle whined and rolled on her back, exposing her pink belly. I looked at Eve, and she grinned, then tickled Belle's tummy. Dad ducked when one of her wings almost thwacked him in the face.

'Well done, Eve,' Dad said as he patted Eve's shoulder. 'Your first landing!'

'Um, how do I get my wings back into wherever they came from?' Eve asked.

'Concentrate and focus, Eve. You'll get used to it.' Dad smiled at her.

Eve closed her eyes, and after just a few seconds, her wings vanished.

'Whoa.' I gazed at her. 'Eve, you're amazing.' She shrugged and turned beet-red.

Later that evening, Eve and I offered to cook dinner, so Dad gave Mrs Potter the night off. I was pretty handy in the kitchen, all thanks to Mrs D. We three had a great time chatting, laughing, and generally bonding. Dad was funny, charming, and intelligent; it was hard to believe he was a powerful demon. He seemed so ... *human*, you know?

When I'd wished Eve goodnight and went to my room, I felt glad that Mr Atua was my dad. Then I remembered Mum and that she didn't even know the man who'd abandoned us still existed. Plus, she was oblivious to the fact that I was half-demon. My belly somersaulted a bit with guilt and worry, but I knew Mrs D would eventually help me sort the situation out; well, hopefully.

Complicated? My life made *A Brief History of Time* look like My Little Pony. But what choice did I have if I wanted Dad in my life? None.

CHAPTER 23

HORSES AND HELLHOUNDS

The following morning, Eve was dressed for horse riding, and we found Dad waiting for us outside. We drove in a golf cart to the stables, with Belle loping by our side, woofing loudly and chasing her tail. She was adorable—well, for a hellhound.

When we arrived, a guy wearing jodhpurs and a big smile awaited us. 'Mr A'—he bowed his head— 'I've got the horses ready for you.'

'Come, Eve. Quinn, are you riding?'

'Nah. I'll run along beside you and play with Belle.' The hellhound woofed and stuck her rear end in the air, with her front legs flat on the ground, and she wiggled her ass. It was just like Celeste always did when she wanted to play, only much bigger and blacker ... and *much* hairier.

'Belle, you're so cute,' Eve said, kissing Belle on her nose.

'The horses, Eve,' Dad started. We admired two beautiful black horses with long manes standing in the yard. Then one of them turned its head to us and nickered. Flames shot from its nostrils, and its eyes glowed orange.

'Demon horses?' I croaked, and heard Eve say, 'Whoa ...' under her breath.

'Yes, but very well-behaved demon horses. Don't worry, Eve. They are much quicker than normal horses, so I hope you don't mind going fast? Just watch out for their nostrils.'

'Wow. This is so exciting,' Eve said, her eyes shining with delight.

'Eve, this is Fulgo. She is a beautiful mare, and she'll look after you.'

The horse nickered and bent down as it lowered a front leg like a bow. Eve giggled while avoiding the flames.

'My horse is Ignis. I've had him for many, many years. Let's go.'

They both mounted, and Dad's horse pawed the ground, seeming impatient to get going. Dad and Eve trotted off, and Belle and I followed. Once they reached the pastures, they started cantering, but Belle and I kept up easily. As we ran, I picked up branches for Belle and threw them a hundred feet. Each time, she'd race off, then return within a few seconds, crushing the sticks between her powerful jaws as if they were kindling.

'Once we reach the Gallops, they will go,' Dad shouted to Eve. 'Just relax and enjoy it.'

'Okay,' Eve yelled back.

A few seconds later, I gathered we'd reached the Gallops because the horses flew at around sixty miles an hour. Belle and I pulled alongside, enjoying the chase. Eve whooped—her eyes shone with delight. The look on her face was priceless.

'Come on, Belle, let's overtake,' I shouted. As we flew past the horses, they snorted fire from their nostrils, and upped their game. Still not fast enough, though.

'Quinn,' Dad hollered.

Suddenly, we were back at the river, with a twenty-foot gap between the riverbanks. I decided it was an easy leap, and my momentum drove me forward, so I leapt as, did Belle, and unfortunately, so did the horses. Just after landing on the other side of the fast-flowing river, I heard Eve shriek, and I slowed and stopped, realising how reckless I'd been.

Belle whimpered. Dad jumped down from his horse, his eyes glowing red, and I gulped. Boy, was I in trouble! I'm not normally reckless, honestly. Running supernaturally fast is just such good fun; I sometimes get carried away. Occasionally, I may take calculated risks, but to be fair, maths is *not* my strongest subject.

Luckily, Eve saved my ass yet again; she started laughing, then ran and jumped into Dad's arms.

'That was the best fun I've *ever* had.'

Dad looked a bit bemused, but then he broke into a wide grin. 'Let's get back. We will go over the bridge further down.' He still gave me a pointed look, though, and I just smiled pathetically while Belle nuzzled my hand. Then Dad shook his head and slapped me on the back.

'Come on,' Daid said as Eve and he mounted and trotted off. As she passed, Eve gave me a furtive smile and winked at me.

'We'll stay behind them this time, Belle,' I whispered, and the hellhound licked my hand in agreement.

When we got back to the stables, my phone rang. It was Mum.

'Hi, sweetheart. How are you?'

'Um, I'm good. Eve and I are at Leo's,' I said as I looked at Eve. Just then, her phone rang too.

'What have you been up to?' Mum asked.

'Ah, just chilling and hanging around, really. Walking Celeste and stuff.' I felt wrong about lying, but I couldn't exactly say I was at Dad's with a hellhound and demon horses, could I?

We chatted for a while, Mum filling me in on what they'd been doing and telling me we were all going to St Kitts next year to spend time with Monique.

'Wicked,' I replied.

Dad glanced at me and mouthed, 'Okay?' I nodded at him.

Eve walked over after we'd both finished our calls. 'I

feel guilty lying to Dad,' she said.

'I know. It sucks. But Mrs D will help us sort everything out when they return from their honeymoon. It'll be difficult, but I want Dad in my life.'

At this, Dad walked over and hugged me ... not so awkward that time.

'Why can I hug you? When I touch demons, I normally hurt them. Plus, I can't read your aura?'

'I'm all-powerful, son. Much like you. And as a consequence, your touch doesn't affect me, and my aura is invisible.'

Eve grinned and said, 'I want you in my life too, Mr Atua.'

Dad smiled and embraced her. My dad was a powerful demon, but I was pretty sure he wasn't the devil. At least, I hoped he wasn't ... but that was a conversation for another time. Right now, I just wanted to spend time with him and get to know him better.

It felt like no time before we had to leave Dad's place and head home. We enjoyed a light lunch together, and then Eve and I went to pack our bags. I felt sad about leaving. As we descended the staircase, we found Dad waiting in his grand hallway.

'Can I come, like, maybe once a month?' I asked.

'Obviously, it'll be harder during footie season—I'll only be able to stay one night. But maybe you could come and watch me play football?'

'I'd love that, son,' he said as he wrapped me in a bear hug.

'Can I bring the Spook Crew one time too? We could share rooms.'

'Spook Crew?' Dad laughed.

'Yeah—Leo's name for us.'

'Of course. Maybe next time? If they want to join you.'

'Cool.' I was amped.

Eve hugged Dad, and he walked with us to the limo. Suddenly, Belle came tearing across the garden and literally knocked me off my feet. She put her paws on my chest and slobbered all over my face with her rough tongue. Eve and Dad howled with laughter.

'She definitely likes you, Quinn.'

Eve kissed Belle's nose, and we reluctantly climbed into the limo. Dad, Jarvis, and Mrs Potter waved us off.

'Your dad's ace, Quinn. I really like him,' Eve said once we were on our way.

'Yeah, me too.' And saying that really surprised me. I'd honestly thought I'd totally dislike him after he abandoned Mum and me and all, but I just couldn't. He was a pretty special guy. And I honestly felt he loved me —like, *really* loved me.

We got home to find the house empty. Even Mrs D seemed to be out. 'Watch a movie?' Eve suggested.

'Sure.'

We unpacked our bags and went to the basement. 'My turn to pick. I choose *Twilight*.' Eve giggled, and I groaned.

'Not again.'

To be fair, though, it had been at least six months since she'd watched it. It was one of Leo's favourites too. He was crazy about Edward, while Eve was more into Jacob. *Ah well, I can have a snooze, I guess*, I thought, and I felt myself drifting off as the music started.

I woke up to a lot of shouting. 'Down here,' Eve hollered.

Millie, Leo, Harry, Eloise, and Celeste raced down the stairs. Celeste jumped around with happiness when she saw Eve.

'So, did you have a good time?' Leo asked.

'Yeah, amazing. My dad's pretty awesome. He's got a pet hellhound and demon horses.'

'Intense,' Harry said with an excited smile.

'Oh, and he's invited you all over next time we go.'

'Yay.' Eloise clapped her hands, and Harry and Leo looked pumped.

'But he's a powerful demon. Demons hate witches,' Millie muttered.

'Mrs D's a demon too, Millie. Dad's okay, honest. He'll love you.'

'I promise you'll love him too, Millie,' Eve told the witch.

Eve and I told them about the weekend, but she

missed out the flying part.

I frowned inquisitively. 'Nothing else, Eve?'

She sighed before reluctantly admitting, 'Oh yeah, I've got wings.'

'Huh?' everybody said in unison.

'This just keeps getting better and better,' Harry exclaimed.

'Yeah, I can fly, which is a bit unusual. I'm not very good at it yet and watch out if I'm landing. If you're in the way, I'll probably squish you,' she laughed.

'Wow ... that's so cool.' Leo's eyes widened.

'Why don't we go into the woods, and you can show us?' A wry grin tugged at Millie's lips.

Eve agreed, and we all rushed outside, Celeste in tow.

'Any mortals around?' I asked Leo—his sense of smell is much better than mine.

He sniffed the air. 'None within a couple of miles.'

When we'd reached a clearing amongst the trees, Eve closed her eyes. Her wings appeared, and everybody's mouths fell open. Her wings began to flutter, and she levitated about twenty feet. Then she flew around our heads, getting braver and braver. She swooped down, and Celeste went crazy with excitement.

'Whoa ...' Harry whispered, his eyes glued to Eve.

'Watch out,' she screamed as she came in for a crash landing. Leo caught her even after getting smacked in the face with a wing. 'I told you I'm not very good at landing yet,' Eve groaned, and we all cracked up.

Eve chatted with Millie and Eloise as we walked back to the house. She told them about Belle, the hell-hound, and her demon horse, Fulgo.

Millie just shook her head. 'Unbelievable.'

When we got home, Mrs D had appeared and was making dinner. 'I'm assuming you're all staying?' she asked, to which everybody shouted, 'Yes, please'.

As Eve disappeared upstairs with Eloise and Celeste, I motioned to Leo, Millie, and Harry to follow me into the kitchen. 'I'm worried. Dad said nobody must ever know about Eve's blood being a healing tincture for vampires. Or her healing abilities. Or that she's half-angel. He said it could put her in mortal danger.'

Millie wrinkled her brow. 'This is not good. Not good at all.'

'She needs protecting,' Mrs D said as she stirred the saucepan on the stove.

Leo looked worried, too, as did Harry.

'In fact, Dad said we should all keep a low profile. But, I'm mostly worried about Eve,' I added.

'Yeah, I agree with your dad,' Leo said, letting out a frustrated sigh. 'Eve's blood is different from any other. If her blood has the ability to heal me, immediately, it'll definitely be a healing tincture for vampires, no matter their injury or ailment. And that may be true for other supernatural beings too? Her smell would be a dead giveaway, especially if she got too close to a vampire. She smells of moonflowers ... mouth-watering.'

I growled a low, rumbling noise deep in my throat.

'I'm going to enchant some small crystals,' Millie interjected. 'One for each of us to carry. It'll work a bit like a GPS for me, and it'll be so much quicker for me to find people. We'll know where everybody is then, if we ever need to?'

'Great idea,' I said to Millie, and everyone mumbled in agreement.

'I'll get on it tonight after dinner. I'll pop to Granny's with Harry. She can help me.'

'Why don't we all go?' Leo suggested, and Millie shrugged and nodded.

'We'll tell Eve about the crystals over dinner,' he murmured, 'without freaking her out.'

While we were all eating, Leo started broaching the subject. 'Erm, Eve ... we've decided we're popping to Millie's granny's house after dinner. They're going to enchant some small crystals so we can all carry one. It'll be like a GPS signal in case we need it. You know what I mean? Then we'll be able to pinpoint where any of us are straightaway.'

'You mean me?' Eve looked worried. I heard Eloise give a nervous cough, and even Mrs D seemed unsettled.

'Not only you, Eve.' I paused. 'But after what Dad said about you and everything ... yeah, mainly you. We're all having one, though. It'll make life a bit easier, just in case, hey?'

Eve sighed. 'Okay. I guess it makes sense.'

'Come on, then. Let's go and see my crazy granny.' Millie stood.

'Have fun, but don't be too late back. It's your last week of school; then you have two weeks of doing nothing,' Mrs D said sternly. 'Well, unless we have any rogue demons or vampires to deal with.'

I tried not to dwell on that last thought, hoping the two weeks off would be quiet and fun, minus the drama of demons and such.

Millie used her athame and spell to summon a teleportation gateway; it was fascinating watching her work. 'Granny,' she shouted. 'Can we come in?'

'Yes, darling. Come on through,' Annie hollered.

As we entered Annie's sitting room, it was apparent Millie had told her about the intended visit because I walked straight through—no magical wards this time.

'Welcome,' Annie said to us all. 'Right, Millie, let's get started on these crystals.'

Annie held in her hand a selection of different-coloured, small stones. Witches are definitely a smart breed, I decided. There was evidently a lot more to magic than I'd ever realised.

'Let's pop into town?' I suggested.

'Not you, darling,' Annie said to Millie. 'This spell takes a little while to complete. We need to start it immediately.'

A little while later, we returned to Annie's house, where Millie worked over the stove, using the *Book of Shadows*. She was uttering strange words. A pot on the stovetop was bubbling, and blue clouds of smoke swirled above it.

Annie was watching her with a small smile on her face. Millie put her hand in the pot, and Eve gasped.

'Don't worry, darling,' Annie explained. 'Millie won't be burned. It's a magic potion, and she's a witch.'

'I think it's done, Granny.' Millie looked pleased with herself as she handed the crystals back to Annie.

'Right, Quinn—you go back to your house so we can test this out.' Annie handed me a small blue-coloured crystal, which I popped into my jeans pocket.

'Eve, darling. I'll give you the red jasper. It has protection qualities that I think you may need.' Eve's cheeks paled, but she took the crystal with a slight nod.

I returned via the teleportation gateway and waited for about ten minutes.

'Quinn, Quinn, Quinn,' I heard a voice shout somewhere in the distance.

'Uh?' I took the crystal from my pocket and heard the voice again. Millie's voice. *What the hell?*

'Talk into the crystal,' Millie's voice shouted.

I peered at the crystal in my hand. 'Um, hello?'

'It works,' Millie squealed triumphantly.

It felt bizarre, communicating through a crystal. The gateway opened up again, and I walked back through, shaking my head.

'The crystals will work as a GPS locator and a communication device,' Annie informed us.

'Does that mean we can hear each other talking all

the time?' Leo didn't look impressed.

'No, no, darling. It will only work when you want to talk to a certain person. It's magic, Leo—it won't eavesdrop on conversations, I promise. The crystal will know when you want to talk to the person.'

He looked at the jade-green crystal in his hand and grinned. 'These are pretty neat.'

Mum and Frank had just over a week left of their honeymoon, and although I couldn't wait to see Mum, I really wasn't looking forward to the conversation about Dad. I wasn't sure how Frank would feel about it all, either. Dad was handsome and mega-rich. But he abandoned Mum when I was a baby, and I wasn't sure she'd ever forgive him. I hoped she would eventually, though. Plus, Frank made Mum happy, and they were madly in love, so I guess Frank had the upper hand.

Jack and Jayden were still absent from school. They probably needed time to recover physically and mentally from the kitsune's attack. I'd texted Jack, and Leo and I planned to visit him that night, now he was feeling a bit better.

It was the last day of school—it had come around fast—so the atmosphere was buoyant. Even the food at lunchtime was pretty edible.

'Leo and I are going to see Jack tonight, so we'll be back a bit later. Can you tell Mrs D for me?' I asked Eve as we made our way to the final lesson.

Eve looked at me like she was annoyed but then did something that shocked me. She stroked my face, kissed me on the cheek, and walked away, leaving me feeling totally bewildered. I probably would have stood there all day if Leo hadn't tugged on my arm. He laughed at me and slapped me on the back.

'Come on, Carter, let's get this over with. Then we can relax for two weeks.'

'Yeah, hopefully,' I muttered.

As everybody swarmed out of school, Leo and I decided to walk to Jack's like ordinary people. It was a pleasant day, and life felt good.

When we arrived at Jack's house, his mum answered the door with a smile. 'Please come in. Jack's in the games room.'

Leo and I found Jack playing pool. 'Fancy a game?' he asked before hugging us. 'It's great to see you both.'

His mum brought drinks and nibbles, which the three of us devoured. We chatted while Leo and Jack played pool, and then I broached the subject of Miss Vulpes.

'Yeah, it's hard to believe she's a serial killer,' Jack said as his cheeks paled and his lips trembled slightly. 'She seemed so nice. But she was totally insane—kept muttering about staying in her human form and absorbing our life force.'

Leo and I made eye contact.

'She *was* insane, Jack,' Leo said.

Jack shuddered. 'I know, but I can't get it out of my head. She's still out there, somewhere, isn't she?'

'No,' I interrupted. Jack eyed me. 'Trust me, Jack, I can't explain, but you don't need to worry about her anymore. She'll not be back.'

'You can't *know* that?'

'I do know, Jack. Like I said, I can't explain, so don't ask me to, but you've got to believe me. You won't see her again.'

Jack gave me a quizzical look. 'You'll think I'm mad, but when I came around, I could have sworn I heard your voice, Quinn.'

Leo sneaked a worried glance at me, but I grinned at Jack. 'If I had been there, I'd have saved you and whooped her ass, Jack.'

Jack just narrowed his eyes at me, but then he smiled. 'Come on, let *me* whoop your ass at pool, Quinn.' Then he proceeded to do just that.

As we were leaving, Leo asked Jack about coming to football training the following Sunday.

'Actually, yeah, I think I will,' he answered. 'Thanks for coming round, guys; I feel tons better.'

I arrived home in time for dinner. Leo returned to his house to hunt with his family, while Millie had gone to Harry's house for the evening. The rest of us—Mrs D, Eve, Eloise, and I—enjoyed a quiet evening, eating and chatting.

'Let's watch *Harry Potter*,' Eve suggested.

Eloise jumped up and down and squealed with delight, 'I've been longing to watch this Harry Potter witch boy. He sounds wonderful.'

We all laughed at the crazy ghost.

'You fancy it, Mrs D?'

'Why not?' she smiled.

After the film had started, I think I only lasted about twenty minutes before I was snoring.

'Quinn!' Eve was jabbing me in the ribs.

'Huh?'

I woke up to see Eloise dancing around the sitting room chanting, 'Oh, I love Harry Potter witch boy.' Mrs D just chuckled at her.

Harry and Millie arrived back at ours, and while the girls jabbered like only they can, I chatted to Harry and Mrs D about Jack. Mrs D took a sharp intake of breath and seemed worried.

'Don't stress, Mrs D,' I said. 'It's fine. If I didn't tell him about Miss Vulpes, he'd be looking over his shoulder for the rest of his life. I'm not sure he believed me anyway, but I needed to try. He's in a terrible state.'

She just pursed her lips and nodded.

But on the plus side, the last week of school before our two-week school break had been quiet ... and for me, quiet was perfect. I should, of course, have taken this as a possible sign that all was not altogether right.

As the saying goes, the calm before the storm ...

CHAPTER 24

THE DAY FROM HELL

Of course, the demons were waiting for me in my dreams that night. No peace for the wicked, or so they say. I was back in the red desert. The hot, dry air burned my nasal passages, and salty sweat coated my lips. The difference was that this time it was silent. No torturous screams, no wailing; it was almost more unnerving than the other times.

The demons were staring at me. My stomach knotted up, and my heart jackhammered. Gross demon guy unfurled his bat wings and walked up to me. His dagger-like teeth were still covered with blood.

'Boss,' he said, bowing to me. The rest of the demons followed suit.

'I'm not your boss,' I growled.

'Oh, but you are. Whether you want to be or not is irrelevant. You are a higher demon, one who must be obeyed.'

'I'm not a demon,' I snarled.

Gross demon guy looked perplexed for a moment, but then he continued. 'Your army awaits, boss. A demon army is powerful—more powerful than any army.' He bowed.

I hesitated, 'If I ever needed you, would you follow my every command and return to the demon realm when I told you to?'

'We would have no choice. We must follow your commands.'

'And what if I said no killing of mortals?'

'We'd be disappointed, but if that was your wish, we could not disobey.'

'Mm ... maybe I'll use you one day, then. Only if I'm desperate, though.'

The whole place erupted into a racket of cheers and screeches, and gross demon guy stood and smiled.

When I woke up in my bed, I licked my lips and tasted the tang of salty sweat. Visiting the demon realm was honestly disturbing.

Leo turned up super-early; it was just as well Mrs D was up to let him in. He was in my bedroom and jumping on me at ridiculous o'clock.

'Leo,' I groaned, 'seriously—I'm going to stake you

through the heart in a minute.' Which caused him to jump on me even more.

'Come on, get up. Let's go for a run,' he said, much to my annoyance.

I didn't have much choice, really—I knew Leo too well—so I got up and put on a tee and joggers. Outside, the sky was grey, and the chilly breeze brought a mizzling rain.

When we arrived in the woods, Leo sniffed the air. 'No mortals anywhere near.' Then he sped off like a phantom wind, gaining a massive head start.

I thought about staying put, to annoy him; however, the adrenaline rush from running at supernatural speed was just too powerful, so I chased him like a tornado. Running that fast again felt liberating, and then I leapt from tree to tree and jumped on Leo as he sped past. We both tumbled and came to a stop.

'You're such a cheat,' he grumbled.

'Race you back?'

'Yeah, as long as you don't do your monkey impressions, swinging from branch to branch, you weirdo.'

'Like I said before ... weirdo? Fangs? Know what I'm saying?' I laughed as I took off with Leo just behind me.

'Breakfast better be good,' he grumbled after I'd beaten him again.

I swallowed my grin and threw an arm around his shoulders. 'Sore loser!'

We arrived back at the house to the smell of a cooked breakfast.

'Hey, do you fancy going to a live music club tonight?' Leo asked us once we'd eaten.

'We're sixteen, Leo,' Eve pointed out.

'I know, but it's a new club. You can get in from sixteen with an adult on a Saturday. They have a live band on. It'll be cool.'

'Alcohol?' Mrs D interrupted.

'Yes, but you need ID, Mrs D. And none of us are really into alcohol anyways.'

'Should be good,' I agreed, looking at Eve and Millie for their reactions.

'I'll talk to Harry, but yeah, sounds fun.'

'I hope you're not expecting me to take you all?' Mrs D grumbled.

'No, my parents said they'd take us. Nat's coming too.' Leo grinned at Mrs D.

'Then Harry will definitely be up for it—he loves your parents,' Millie said, 'and Nat.'

Then she frowned as she thought about it and pouted her lips. I went to laugh, but Eve slapped my leg under the table.

'Cool. Dad said they'd bring two cars. We'll pick you up at seven tonight.'

'It's a date.' Eve's grin kicked up a notch.

'Okay. As you're going with Leo's parents, you can stay out until half eleven at the very latest. No arguments,' Mrs D instructed, giving one of her no-nonsense looks.

The day blew by, and at seven o'clock, we all piled

into Harrison's and Cordelia's cars. We got there to find that the new club looked a bit like an old department store. A sign saying 'ECLIPSE' hung over the doors, with music-related graffiti-type murals around it. A big guy dressed in black stood at the entrance.

'Hi, Denzel.' Natasha gave him a mega-watt smile. 'I've brought my kid brother and his friends with me. They're all sixteen. Oh, and my parents are definitely over sixteen.' Denzel rolled his eyes at Natasha.

Inside the lobby, a young girl stamped our hands with green ink before informing us the live band started at eight-thirty.

'Cordelia and I will go get drinks.' Harrison headed to the bar.

I glanced around to take in my surroundings. The club was pretty dingy and had murals painted on every available surface. The air in there smelled of sweat, alcohol, and perfume. There were sofas, chairs, and tables scattered around, plus a dance floor, a stage, and a DJ playing popular music; I could feel the bass from the beats, vibrating from my feet up my back and into my chest. The loud music assaulted my heightened senses, but I gradually got used to it.

Harry and Millie went to dance.

'Come and dance, Quinn.' Natasha grabbed my hand and dragged me to the dance floor.

'I'm not very good,' I shouted.

She laughed, 'Shut up and dance.'

Natasha danced like no one was watching. She was

attractive and fun to be with, but when I looked up, I saw Eve staring at me with her arms folded over her chest. I smiled at her, but she glowered back.

I was just about to go to her to see what was wrong when Leo dragged her up to dance too. Eloise followed them and jumped up and down like a loon, squealing with delight ... it was just as well nobody could see her. Weirdly, even though Eloise appeared in physical form to us, well, apart from her spectral glow, mortals could still walk through her. This made her extremely grumpy, much to Leo's amusement. Music, friends, and good times ... coming here had been an excellent idea.

The music quieted when the band came on to sound-check, so we all went to join Harrison and Cordelia, who had found a table for all our drinks.

'The band's called Standby Therapy,' Nat said as she sipped water. 'They're supposed to be brilliant. They'll be on in ten minutes.'

As we chatted, Natasha squeezed herself next to me on the sofa, making me feel a bit hot and bothered. Every so often, her hand would touch my leg, and I became slightly flustered. Leo saw my face and motioned for me to come with him to the bar.

'Sorry about my sister,' Leo grumbled, 'she's definitely got a soft spot for you.'

I just laughed. 'It's okay. She scares me a bit, but I really like her. She's good fun.'

It wasn't long before the band started playing, and Nat was right—they were brilliant. We were standing by the dance floor when an attractive guy walked up to Eve.

'Would you like a dance, lovely lady?'

Oh, for the love of God. I felt like pounding his face in, but I reckoned Eve would probably be mad at me if I did. I couldn't stop the raging jealousy that fired through my body. My feelings for Eve were getting ridiculous. I needed to sort my life out. Eve glanced at me, but instead of hitting him, I clenched my jaw and diverted my eyes.

'Sure,' I heard her say before she walked off and danced with the sleazebag. My temper was trigger-happy, and I forcibly pushed my anger down and hid it back inside of me.

'Why don't you tell her how you feel?' Leo whispered in my ear. 'It's obvious you love her—like, really love her—bud.'

'What and get my heart shattered? She thinks of me as a best friend, not like that. Plus, our parents are married,' I snarled. 'For God's sake, I wish you'd all just drop it,' I snapped at him.

'You can't choose who you fall in love with. And yes, she's your friend, *not* your sister. But suit yourself. You're such a jackass sometimes, Quinn Carter.'

Everybody piled onto the dance floor, leaving me stewing in my misery. I stomped down the corridor to the toilets, thinking about Eve. I was pretty sure Eve loved me and everything, but only as a friend—not in the way I loved her. But to be fair, why would she? She was beautiful, intelligent, popular, and a freaking half-angel. What would she see in a bad-tempered, half-demon of average intelligence ... exactly.

I was so lost in my thoughts that I almost bumped into an extraordinary woman, stalking down the corridor like a panther. I did a double-take. She was stunning, with bright blonde hair piled on her head and blood-red lips—dressed in a figure-hugging, black leather dress. She narrowed her eyes at me and then walked into the ladies'.

I got goosebumps down my arms—something about her felt off—but I thought maybe I was imagining it. Plus, I was still raging, so I headed off back to the dance floor. Nat saw me and headed in my direction.

'Hey,' she said, grasping my hand. 'Come on, let's dance.' She put her arms around my neck and crooned, 'I like you, Quinn Carter.'

I was just glad it was dark in there because I felt my face burn with embarrassment. 'Don't forget what I said,' she all but purred, 'if you ever fancy a bit of vampire.'

I turned to Leo and Harry, who were wetting themselves. I scowled at them both. Then I looked at Eve, who seemed to be having fun with the sleazebag.

Natasha was great fun, and I started to relax as we fooled around together. That was until I saw Leo sniff the air. I frowned at Nat, who also looked worried. Harrison and Cordelia were motioning for them both to come over, and I followed Leo and Nat to the edge of the dance floor.

'There's a vampire in here,' Leo whispered.

'Apart from you lot?' My brows lowered in worry.

'Yep,' Nat said.

'I saw a drop-dead gorgeous woman some time ago, heading to the toilets. I thought there was something off about her.'

'You need to trust your instincts more, Quinn. Let's split up and find her,' Harrison instructed. 'We need to make sure it's not a rogue. Quinn, stay with Leo.'

We stayed put and waited. 'I'm not sure how to fight a vampire.' Unease balled in my stomach.

'You're definitely strong and fast enough. Just never let a vampire get their arms around you, or they'll try to crush you. You could disappear to spirit, I guess, but I think you need to learn to fight. A stake through the heart first'—he made a thrusting upward motion—'that'll paralyse them, then you need to decapitate them or burn the body.'

'Ugh, too much info, bud.' A shudder rolled through me.

'We only need to do that if it's a rogue, though. We'll do some sparring—I'll show you some moves.'

Before I could ask Leo more about rogue vampires, Nat came back looking a little dishevelled, with her parents behind her.

'She's gone,' Nat said. 'Escaped through a fire exit. I

found her feeding on a young guy. She went for me, but I kicked her ass.'

'Feeding?' I asked.

'Yeah, most vampires are controlled. They take just enough blood to survive. The human finds it pleasurable.'

'*Pleasurable?*'

'Yeah, I could show you if you want, Quinn.' She smiled seductively and licked her lips. Leo groaned with embarrassment, and Cordelia smiled and shook her head.

'Nah, thanks. I'm good,' I said, colouring up again. In my defence, it was a bit weird being sexually harassed by a vampire.

'As I was saying, most vampires only take a small amount of blood, which leaves the human a bit woozy but okay. However, a rogue vampire would kill.'

'We definitely don't want a rogue, then.'

'I don't think she was rogue'—Harrison breathed a sigh of relief at Nat's words—'but I don't think we'll see her around here again. Not after my booting of her bootie,' she laughed. 'Come on, let's dance.'

Nat grabbed Leo and me, and we danced for the next hour.

By the time I got into the car, I was shattered. I glanced out the car window to see Eve and the guy from earlier sucking each other's faces off. I felt fury kindling; my stomach twisted in knots. I took a breath to cool it and looked away.

'So, what's his name?' I heard Millie ask Eve once she'd joined us. 'He seems really nice.'

'Yeah, he is. He's called Josh. He's eighteen, and I've given him my number. He wants to take me to the cinema.'

The girls started giggling and whispering, but I didn't tune in to them. I couldn't bear to hear what Eve was saying. Instead, I sat in silence. Thinking about Eve with this Josh stirred up a dark feeling in my chest. What was wrong with me? I had a strange sensation in the pit of my stomach, and I felt like my heart was being constricted. I was pathetic—more than pathetic—and it wasn't good for me. I needed another girlfriend. I needed to stop loving Eve. I sighed and let out a jagged breath.

Leo just put an arm around my shoulder and squeezed. He knew me so well. 'Eyes,' he warned me under his breath. I closed my eyes and didn't open them again until we got home.

When we arrived, I hugged Cordelia, said goodnight to everyone, and went to my room. Leo followed me up.

'I need to be alone,' I grumbled. 'I'm going to lie down and listen to country music ... the music of pain.'

Leo cracked up laughing and pulled me off my bed, feet first. 'Come on, let's go and play PlayStation. It'll take your mind off things. Move it.'

I begrudgingly followed him to the basement, and we stayed up late playing a game that numbed my mind. But numb was good.

Leo and I went running early the next day, after which we practised sparring. Leo was strong, but I was his equal. He showed me loads of great moves. The previous night was buried deep within my mind—the exercise had worked wonders.

After showering, Leo and I decided to go out for breakfast, walking to a café in town for a change. As we were leaving the café, a car pulled up.

'Hey, boys,' came a voice as the window rolled down.

Leo groaned. 'Nat, what are you doing here?'

'I've taken the day off work, and now I'm giving you a lift. Get in.'

'So, what do you do, Nat? For a job, I mean,' I asked as we drove.

'I'm a florist, like Mom. We own the shop together. I mainly do the wedding business.' Her eyes clouded over, and she frowned.

I didn't say anything else because it was clear she was upset.

'See you at football training later, Leo,' I said as I slid out of the car.

I saw Eve standing by the front door, so I decided to try and make her jealous. Childish? Yep. I leaned into the car and gave Nat a slow kiss. When I turned around, Eve was gone.

'Mm, nice. Thanks, Quinn. But I know you're only trying to make Eve jealous.' Nat smiled sweetly.

I could almost hear Leo rolling his eyes. I shrugged and walked away.

In the house, Mrs D was waiting for me. 'You need to sort yourself out, young man,' she said and turned away.

'Yeah, whatever. Not me who's going on a date,' I grumbled under my breath. I hated being in a bad mood; jealousy sucked. But I couldn't help it—I guess it was my demon within. I needed some alone time, so I kept to myself until it was time to go for training.

Later that afternoon, Leo, Harry, and I met up at the training pitch, where I needed to exert some pent-up energy. Jack was there and looked loads better than the last time we'd seen him—he seemed back to his old self, thankfully.

Eve had gone to the stables, on the other side of town, where she exercised a couple of horses for people—according to Millie, anyway. I hadn't seen Eve since my pathetic attempt at making her jealous.

Leo, Harry, and I started circuit training with our football team. Then we played a friendly game of football, and everything was going great.

I'd almost forgotten about absorbing demons and all the other creepy stuff that had happened recently.

Even Eve was at the back of my mind, and my mood had lifted.

I was just about to lob the ball into the net when suddenly I wasn't there again. I was having another vision ... a vision that sent my stomach convulsing and turned the blood in my veins to ice ...

CHAPTER 25
THE COLLECTOR

'Quinn, Quinn!' Leo was holding my face. The floor felt like it had dropped out underneath me.

'Eve ... You and Harry get back to mine. Millie needs to find her.' I then bolted from the pitch, leaving my teammates looking bemused.

As soon as I got to the woods, I faded to spirit and flew as fast as I could towards the stables where Eve had been. When I got there, I searched everywhere. People were milling around, oblivious. I turned into my physical form before I ran into the yard. 'Excuse me,' I panted at an older lady standing nearby. 'Have you seen Eve?'

'Yes, love. She left about ten minutes ago. I saw her walking down the drive. I think she was heading back home.'

I ran as fast as I dared, without drawing attention to

myself, down the long drive to the main road. No sign of her.

Every fibre of my being yelled at me, *Eve's been taken*. Fear sank its vicious claws into my chest. By the time I got home, everybody was in a state of panic, which added to the overwhelming sense of desperation I was feeling.

'What happened?' Millie shrieked as soon as she saw me.

'Have you found her?' I asked, looking at her iPad and scrying crystal on the table.

She shook her head. 'I had her, but then the signal just disappeared. I'm will keep trying to connect with her, but it's going to take a while because I can't locate her crystal.' She started crying.

Guilt dug in like icy-tipped fingers. 'I didn't have my crystal with me.'

'Leo said you had a vision. Tell us about it, and quickly,' Mrs D said.

'Eve was walking, and a large, black car drew up. The door opened, and someone pulled her inside. I didn't see a face—I just heard her scream my name.' Looking at my friends' terrified faces, I broke down in tears.

Millie hugged me. 'We'll find her, Quinn, we will,' she said, attempting to reassure me.

'What if I never see her again? Thinking of that makes the air disappear ... I feel like I'm suffocating,' I choked on a broken sob.

'Come on, Quinn. We need you to be clear and focused; otherwise, we may never find her,' Leo told me as he held me. Eloise was sobbing, and Harry looked bereft.

'I'll keep trying.' Millie's voice cracked. 'Someone has crushed her crystal, I'm sure of it. Who would know about its powers, though?'

'Another witch,' Mrs D said. Millie stared at her with wide eyes and shuddered.

'I need to call Dad.' Mrs D nodded to me encouragingly. I shouted for him, and he appeared within a few seconds. I heard Harry gasp, and Millie took a step away.

'Quinn, what is it?'

'Eve's been taken,' I said in a shaky voice.

His eyes glowed red for a second—a muscle popping in his jaw. 'Then we need to locate her. You and Leo, come with me. Millie, you keep trying with the crystal.'

'I'm going to find her,' Eloise said in a tremulous voice as she faded away.

Dad took Leo and me by the hand and shadowed us to his house. It's a strange feeling, shadowing, like travelling through a cloying red mist thrumming with heat, power, and energy. We were surrounded by iridescent pulsating lights, like confetti and stardust.

We reappeared in the snug where Eve and I had been. Her absence hit me so hard I had to remember to breathe.

'Ugh, that was weird. I felt like I was being eviscerated.' Leo had turned a bit green.

'Huh? I felt fine?'

'Probably your demon blood, bud—won't affect you the same?'

'Maybe.'

'Sweet tea?' Jarvis interrupted.

'I can't—' I began, but Dad interrupted.

'Drink,' he instructed. He went to talk to Jarvis as Leo and I sipped the sweet tea.

'Now, who knows about Eve? Especially her blood?' Dad asked Leo and me.

'Just us lot and my family. But they're completely trustworthy,' Leo mumbled.

'Jarvis?' Dad turned to his butler.

'I think you may be right, sir,' Jarvis said with a frown.

'Bring him to me,' Dad ordered.

Five minutes later, Jarvis frogmarched Barney, the chauffeur, into the room. 'He tried to run, sir.'

'Now, Barney, start from the beginning, and tell me everything,' Dad said as his eyes glowed. I could feel his anger permeating the room; it hung around me like a thick mist. His face was a mask of livid rage.

Barney was humongous in every way, but he was trembling and definitely bricking it. 'He contacted me,' he mumbled. 'He's called the Collector. Told me to keep an eye out for any special collectables.'

'Collectables?' I growled.

'You put an ad in the paper, letting him know. He was going to pay me a hundred grand for the half-angel.'

'Does he know about her blood?' Dad asked.

Barney nodded. 'I overheard you talking to the half-angel when she was here. Then he upped the offer to a million.'

I gasped, and Leo went even paler than usual.

'I'm sorry, Mr A. I'll make it up to you.' Barney hung his head, ashamed by this betrayal, maybe.

I felt like stomping on his head but knew Dad would sort him out.

'You certainly will,' Dad snarled. 'Tell me everything.'

A LITTLE LATER, we shadowed home with Dad. Millie was still working on the iPad but leapt up as we appeared. 'I've found her,' she shouted. 'It looks like she's on a plane. She's over the sea.'

'She's heading in the direction of Italy, I think,' Harry said as he studied the map.

'Keep me informed, Quinn. I'll get Jarvis to send my yacht in that direction.' Dad examined the map. Then he vanished again.

'I think ...' I stopped. I had another vision. I saw Eve

again, and this time she was unconscious and handcuffed. Eloise sat beside her stroking her hair; obviously invisible to the others. There were three other people on the plane with them—two men and a woman. It looked like a private jet, all leather and luxury. The woman was attractive and seemed to be in charge. She had a glass of champagne and was talking on the phone.

'Yes, sir. She's perfect. You will love her. No—no one knows, believe me. She had an enchanted crystal,' she cackled. 'I sorted that out. They won't have a clue where she is. Yes, yes. The blood is like the golden egg. The Ministry of Vampires will pay handsomely for it. We can take a pint a week. She will cope with it, being half-angel. We'll make a fortune! As well as having her as a collectable, she'll make you money.'

The vision faded—anger swirled like a bitter acid in my blood. My muscles quivered, and my teeth were grinding; my demon within was struggling to be released and cause bedlam.

'Quinn.' Millie shook me.

I sat at the table, closed my eyes, and calmed my breathing. I tried to ignore the sudden trembling in the pit of my stomach as I struggled to keep my voice even.

'Eve's on a private jet. Like Barney said, they're "collecting" her and planning to sell her blood to the Ministry of Vampires.' I heard everybody gasp ... except Mrs D, who growled.

'Aw man, if the ministry finds out about her ...' Leo

put his head in his hands. 'I need to ring my parents,' he said as he rushed off.

'Dad!' I hollered. He was there within a minute. I told him about my vision, and he appeared agitated. 'We need a collectable. We need to put an ad in my paper.'

The next minute, Harrison and Cordelia rushed into the house. Dad shook his head. 'I think we all need to sit down and try to plan our course of action.'

'What about Mum and Frank ringing?' I asked before he started.

'Let me speak to Granny about that,' Millie said. 'I think she can charm them, for a few days so they think they've spoken to you both.'

'I think we *all* need to go and see Annie.' Dad turned to Millie. Her posture stiffened, and she hesitated as she peered up at him. I had a feeling she was worried about Dad meeting her granny.

'O-okay,' she stammered before speedily creating a teleportation gateway. Cordelia and Harrison looked on in awe.

'Granny!' Millie shouted.

'Come in, all of you. I've been expecting a visit.'

All of us walked through the gateway, including Dad and the vampires, to find Annie and some of her coven waiting, athames in hand. When they saw Dad, they all took a step back.

'Granny!' Millie scolded.

Dad laughed. 'Don't worry, Millie. Hello, Annie,' he said with surprising familiarity.

'Edward.' Annie glared at him. Millie scrunched her brows together.

'I think we need your help,' he said.

We all sat at Annie's kitchen table, but Esme, Dora, and Bella stood by the door. They were still eyeing Dad and the vampires, clearly on edge about their latest visitors.

'I've found out a bit about the Collector; he's a very secretive demon,' Dad said.

'Demon?' I whispered.

Dad nodded. 'He has a collection of supernatural beings and lives on an island, shrouded by magic, in the Mediterranean. An mighty witch works for him too. You may have heard of her, Annie—it's Morgana.'

The witches gawped. 'Surely not. She's a thousand years old?'

'Indeed. She sucks the life force out of girls to keep herself young. The demon collector provides her with as many as she needs in return for her services of black witchcraft. I need you and Millie to come with us. You must crack through the magical wards protecting island to get Eve out. And depending upon what happens, we may need you to fight ...' he said to Annie.

'No, Annie. It's too dangerous,' Esme pleaded.

'Granny?' Millie implored.

Annie sighed. 'Very well. Together, Millie and I stand a better chance. But we first need to enchant

Helen and Frank—we don't want them worrying. Girls—'

Millie handed Esme and Bella a comb of Frank's and a hairbrush that belonged to Mum. The two witches got to work over the stove.

'Your mother and Frank will believe they've spoken to you, but the enchantment will only last about two days,' Annie said.

Eloise appeared in a frantic state. Dora and Bella nearly had a coronary until Annie explained about the ghost and her link to us. If the situation hadn't been so dire, the looks on the witches' faces would have been highly amusing.

'I couldn't follow her. I couldn't follow her onto the island,' Eloise wailed. I frowned at Dad.

'From what I know of Morgana, she is very superstitious. She has, let us say, been haunted by many disgruntled spirits throughout the years. Badly haunted. I suspect she has protected the island against paranormal activity, which means you cannot to go with Quinn. I'm sorry, Eloise.'

'But, what about me? I'll need to get to Eve in spirit form?'

'You can cross the veil and walk in the realm of death. You are not a true spirit, merely a shadow. You will be fine, son.'

Next, Dad turned to Harrison and Cordelia. 'We need a hook. A hook of a collectable for our plan to work. I'm afraid it must be Leo.'

'No! Not going to happen ...' Cordelia started to say, but Harrison placed a hand on her arm. He seemed to radiate a calming influence in the room. She immediately relaxed.

'You're gifted with pathokinesis?' Dad looked at the vampire.

'Yes,' Harrison smiled. Looking at our faces, he explained, 'It's the ability to manipulate someone's emotions. It comes in handy as a doctor.'

'Whoa ...' I heard Bella whisper.

'Mom,' Leo said. He looked better but was still twitchy. He ran his hands through his hair, clasping the back of his neck. 'I have to do it to save Eve. She'd do the same for me. How many times have she and Quinn saved me?'

Harrison and Cordelia were even paler than usual.

'Yes, of course,' Cordelia agreed. 'Of course, you have to help. Is there anything we can do?'

Dad shook his head. 'Annie, I'll meet you at Quinn's house in an hour.'

Millie brought us back to our house, where Harry was still watching the airplane on the iPad. They watched it for about five minutes until, all of a sudden, it disappeared.

'It's shrouded by magical wards, but I have the coordinates of the last point,' Millie said.

'Harry—' Dad turned to my friend.

Harry gulped and whispered, 'Yes?'

'I need you to hack into my paper and put this ad in.

This needs to be an untraceable advert. Can you do that?'

Harry nodded.

'The phone call will be answered by Jarvis, my butler. Then we will be as prepared as we can be. I'll be back in one hour.' And he disappeared again.

We studied the ad Dad had given us:

COLLECTABLES FOR SALE
DHAMPIRS ARE A SPECIAL BREED
PLEASE CONTACT 08976 790542

Harry got to work, and the ad was placed within five minutes. Millie and I packed our bags, and Leo rushed home, promising to return within ten minutes.

I was pacing around and jittery. I couldn't get Eve out of my head. My heart burned just thinking about her.

'Sit down, Quinn. You're making me dizzy,' Mrs D complained.

Desolation hit me with crippling strength. 'I'm scared, Mrs D.'

She came over and hugged me. 'So am I, dear. But I know, you're going to be able to save Eve.'

I just hoped she was right ...

The kitchen wall shimmered, alerting us to Annie's arrival. She was carrying an overnight bag, and Dad appeared very soon after. Millie, Leo, and I were waiting for them both. Millie kissed Mrs D's cheek, then hung onto Harry for a while.

'Let's go. I'll come back for you both,' Dad said, looking at Leo and me. Then he took Millie's and Annie's hands, and I saw Annie flinch before they vanished. He was back seconds later.

'Good luck, bro,' Harry said sombrely as Dad took our hands. Eloise kissed Harry and faded away to join us. Mrs D wiped her eyes and held me for a second—then we shimmered and vanished, shadowing back into the red mist.

When I opened my eyes, Annie and Millie were waiting for us; we were all on board an enormous yacht. We were in a room with three large sofas and some coffee tables, with 180-degree windows looking out over the stunning blue sea. Under any other circumstances, it would have been a pleasure to be here.

'I will show you to your rooms.' Jarvis bowed his head and took the witches' bags.

We followed him to two huge bedrooms with en suites, where we dropped our bags.

I heard Annie harrumph. 'Demons,' she muttered as she walked from her room.

Jarvis bit back a smile as he said, 'Please follow me to Mr A's lounge. I shall bring you drinks and nibbles.'

We sat with Dad, and although I wasn't hungry, I knew I should eat. I think Leo felt the same. The tension was palpable; anxiety gripped us all.

'Be prepared,' Dad said to Annie. 'Morgana's magic is powerful.'

'Don't worry, Edward, we shall be,' Annie said with a stern look.

'Leo, as soon as we have contact, Jarvis will take you to the mainland. I'm afraid he's going to have to stake you.'

'No! He won't survive another staking so soon.'

My temper flared, and I nearly started shouting, but I calmed my breathing and got myself under control as quickly as possible.

'The Collector will want to test Eve's blood, Quinn. What better way? Jarvis will suggest as much.'

Leo took a deep breath. 'I'll do anything to save Eve. It's okay, Quinn.'

I let out an exasperated sigh and said nothing more. Annie held Millie, who was silently weeping.

'Dinner is at seven this evening; I suggest you all rest. Jarvis will collect you and bring you to my dining room. You must eat. We all need to maintain our strength,' Dad said before we all freshened up.

Eloise had taken a shine to Jarvis and spent most of her time with him. He seemed to be the only one of us that could calm down the hyperactive ghost.

I went for a stroll around the deck while Leo decided to chill in our room. We were both weary and over-wrought with emotion. I stood on the swim platform and gazed at the sea, wondering if Eve was okay.

As soon as I thought of her, the sea disappeared, and

a vision of Eve came into focus. A tall, fair-haired man stood in front of her. He was wearing what looked like a monocle, with weird-looking clothes, possibly something Sherlock Holmes might have worn—I kid you not.

'Eve, I'm delighted to have you here. You are the pièce de résistance of my collection.' He beamed at her and stroked her face; she flinched.

I was repulsed by the look on his face as he devoured Eve with his eyes. I wanted to wipe that smile off his face ... permanently.

'You are so beautiful, my little angel. Now that you have calmed down, we'll get on famously. You must not try to use compulsion on my staff. As you saw, the island is protected with magic. You cannot fly out of here, my angel. But it's exceptional that you have wings and may fly around the island daily. I shall watch you.' He gazed steadily at her. '*And* I don't like my angels using bad language, so behave.' His eyes flashed yellow for an instant.

'W-who are you?' Eve whimpered. 'Why have you kidnapped me?'

'Oh, Eve. You're half-angel. Your exquisite blood is a healing tincture for supernaturals. Especially vampires.'

The blood drained from Eve's face. 'H-how do you know?'

'Money talks, my little angel. I always get what I want. But worry not—you will live as my guest. I will lavish you with everything you need. You won't be in my exhibition rooms—you will live here with me.' He clapped his hands and giggled. 'Nothing but the best for my little angel.'

Morgana sauntered into the room, flicking her long, dark hair over her shoulder. 'Come, Eve. I will take you to your chambers.'

Eve stood on wobbly legs and followed the witch out of the door. Morgana put a hand on Eve, who flinched. 'Don't touch me, biatch.' Morgana's lips curved into a sneer, and Eve grasped her throat. She was choking—she couldn't breathe—and I was helpless—anxiety blossomed in my gut.

'Be careful with me, you stupid girl,' Morgana warned. 'I'm a powerful witch. No matter what the Collector thinks, I'm not fond of goody-goody angels. Your life force would feed me for a hundred years, so do as you're told.'

Eve was still gasping for breath and whimpering ... and I was back on the yacht, wanting to kill the Collector and Morgana with my bare hands. At least Eve had attempted to escape, unsuccessfully, but she was as determined as anyone I'd ever met, and I was so glad she hadn't lost her resilience ... yet.

I raced back to the room. I was acting all frantic and desperate. Of course, that's because I *was* frantic and desperate. I found Jarvis waiting for Leo, Annie, and Millie.

'I need to see Dad,' I panted at him, shouting for the others to hurry. My heart was racing so fast, I was certain I was going to have a cardiac. Everybody rushed from their rooms, and we followed Jarvis to Dad's dining room.

'I had another vision,' I said in a panicked voice.

'Quinn, you must stay calm. You will be no help to Eve otherwise. Use your head.' Dad was firm but kind.

I knew he was right—a calm Quinn was much more useful than a panic-stricken Quinn. I pressed the heels of my palms into my eyes and made an effort to calm myself. I told him about the Collector and Eve and about how evil Morgana clearly was. I also told him about Eve having used compulsion to try to escape.

Dad's lips twitched into a small smile. 'She's done well. Compulsion is a difficult skill to master.'

Annie growled, shaking with rage. 'It's about time someone put that bitch Morgana in her place.'

I breathed a quiet laugh while Millie hugged her granny. Good old Annie.

Just then, a host of waiters brought food to the table. Everybody ate, but slowly, like it was a chore.

Meanwhile, Dad explained, 'Quinn, as we discussed, you need to be with Leo, in spirit form, to get to Eve. As you enter the island, Annie and Millie will get a chance to connect to the island's protection and work on breaking down the magical wards.'

'But won't he see me in my spirit form? Especially if he's a demon?'

'Only the most powerful of demons can visit the spirit realm. Most demons must possess a spirit, which is why you get poltergeists. He is no exception. He doesn't have your power, Quinn.'

'Erm, you're not really the devil, are you? I honestly need to know,' I blurted out. I couldn't stop worrying about it. I saw Annie bite back a laugh.

'No, Quinn, I'm a very civilised, all-powerful demon and leader of the Ministry of Demons,' Dad said, sounding slightly offended.

'Really? Like a council? So why can't the ministry save Eve?' I asked.

'We intervene if the whole of humanity is at risk. But, unfortunately, this is no such situation, I'm afraid.'

'That's freaking rubbish,' I hollered as I banged the table, making Millie jump.

'So, what's the plan?' she asked, interrupting my outburst.

I controlled my annoyance. 'One option would be for you to just shadow us all out of there once I've located Eve and Leo?' I said, looking at Dad.

'Yes, that would be an option.' Dad squinted at me.

'Or we could try and take them down? Put an end to this once and for all,' Leo murmured, and Annie nodded in agreement.

'Quinn,' Dad said in a calm voice. 'Once you have decided, call me. When the wards around the island are down, I'll protect you with my life. That's all I can do.'

Annie narrowed her eyes at Dad, giving him a curious look. 'But will you get into trouble?' I asked.

'No, there will be no witnesses left if I get involved. Don't worry.'

I gulped.

'But can't Morgana—if she's so powerful and everything—vanquish you?' Millie looked at Dad.

'But she won't know he's a demon,' I added. Dad's face changed. 'Will she?' I asked worriedly.

'I met Morgana many hundreds of years ago. Yes, she knows me,' Dad said quietly.

'So, she could possibly kill you?' I almost squeaked. 'Annie?'

'Most vanquishing spells return the demon to the demon realm, where they become trapped until another portal is opened. But that type of spell would not affect your father as a demon king. So yes, Morgana would use a spell to vanquish Edward into oblivion,' Annie said with a slight tremor in her voice.

'No!' Millie, Leo, and I shouted simultaneously. Dad smiled.

'We can sort this out,' I started, and as Dad went to object, I carried on. 'But I promise, if we look like we're in trouble, I'll call you.'

Dad nodded, and the others tentatively agreed.

'If you need to come out of spirit form, though, be very careful, as Morgana will know then that you're there. Okay?' Dad added.

'Yeah. I'm ready.' I wasn't ready, not at all, but I'd die to save Eve.

I could tell how worried Leo was; he was paler than I'd ever seen him.

I just hoped the Collector would save Leo with Eve's blood; otherwise I wasn't sure I'd see my best friend again; and this made a whole other part of my heart twist painfully.

CHAPTER 26
BLACK WITCH

I didn't sleep well, and I'm pretty sure Leo didn't either. We all slowly made our way out for breakfast, and the room was so thick with tension that it was almost claustrophobic.

'Sir,' Jarvis said as he rushed in, 'we have contact.'

The rescue was on. And the day pretty much went downhill from there.

'We are to meet the courier at the old warehouse on Via Della Chiesa at eleven o'clock this morning.'

'Let's get moving,' Dad said. My belly did a topsy-turvy thing, and my pulse rate spiked. Leo seemed a bit wobbly when he stood up, so I put my arm around his waist.

'Come on, bud,' I whispered. 'Let's get Eve back.'

We both kissed Annie, Millie, and Eloise. 'Good luck,' they murmured. I wiped Millie's tears away with my thumb and kissed her cheek. She held my hand as I walked away, urging, 'Be careful. Please.'

I smiled to try and reassure her, then I followed Dad, Leo, and Jarvis.

Dad stood on the sun deck as he gave his parting instructions. 'Quinn, Leo—good luck, and please be careful. If you need me, just shout. I can join you as soon as Annie and Millie have removed the magical wards.'

'Okay, see you soon.' I sounded confident, but truthfully, inside I was a gibbering wreck.

We followed Jarvis down a ladder and into a speedboat. Leo had his hands clenched together and wouldn't make eye contact with me.

My stomach churned, and I felt light-headed and a bit dizzy. Going up against that kitsune had nothing on this. All I knew was that we needed to rescue Eve. I realised it didn't matter what she was—girlfriend or best friend—I needed her in my life, and I always would.

We arrived on the mainland, where another limo was waiting for us. As we drove, the town gave way to a barren road, and the old warehouse came into view. It had a curved roof, like an aircraft hangar, and walls of corrugated tin. The broken tarmac around it was empty, except for an old, rusting forklift covered in dirt. The limo dropped us outside the warehouse at nine-thirty ... we had an hour and a half to wait.

'How are you planning to ... you know?' Leo asked Jarvis in a quiet voice.

The butler placed a hand on Leo's arm. 'Don't worry, Master Leo, it will be fine, I promise.'

'You're a vampire ...' Leo said to Jarvis, who merely nodded. Leo then paced around the warehouse. Tension crackled in the air.

'A vampire working for Dad, who's a demon ... strange,' I murmured to myself.

I knew from chats with Mrs D that demons and vampires didn't usually mix. Then I thought about my link to Leo. Sometimes you bond with the most unlikely friends.

'We need to be ready at ten forty-five; they will be punctual,' Jarvis instructed.

I sat on a wooden box and tried to zone out. I closed my eyes and slowed my breathing. I was determined to master my anxiety, although I felt mentally exhausted. I'd almost gained control over my nerves when I heard a noise and opened my eyes. Jarvis had Leo around the throat and was strangling him. I watched in horror as my friend stopped struggling and dropped like a ragdoll.

'What the hell?!' I yelled as I ran to him.

'He won't feel the stake this way, Master Quinn. He is merely unconscious—don't worry.'

'Oh?'

'You need to get into spirit form now. I can smell them—they're coming.'

I concentrated and felt myself shimmer and pulse until I entered the spirit realm again. Luckily, as I did that, I missed Jarvis staking Leo through the heart. I couldn't even look at him, lying on his back with a stake through his heart ... again.

Just then, a large black saloon car pulled up. A massive guy with wraparound glasses got out and opened the door ... for the witch Morgana. 'Show me the dhampir,' she snapped at Jarvis, who proceeded to uncover Leo. He looked like Sleeping Beauty.

'Why is he staked?' Morgana roared.

'He's a feisty one, my lady. He would have caused you problems. He will recover, eventually, once the stake is removed. Quicker if you use him to test for the angel's blood?' Jarvis eyed Morgana with a slight smile on his lips.

'How do you know about the angel?' she snarled. Her eyes became swirling darkness, like storm clouds covering the sun.

Jarvis held his hands up, 'Don't fret. I know about her because I know Barney. He and I used to work together. Both of us are always looking for new collectables for you, ma'am. I helped Barney find out about the angel.' Jarvis tapped his nose.

Seemingly satisfied, Morgana moved closer to look carefully at Leo. Her eyes lit up.

'My, my, he's beautiful. The Collector will be pleased.' She licked her lips, which freaked me out a bit. 'Put him in the car ... gently,' she snapped at the chauffeur, 'and be careful not to knock the stake.' She turned to Jarvis, 'What's his name?'

'Leo, ma'am.'

I jumped in the car with Leo. My best friend was lying on the seat. He looked dead, and a physical pain stabbed at my chest. The chauffeur handed Jarvis a metal suitcase, which I assumed was the money, and Morgana climbed into the car with us. She hummed and stroked a finger up Leo's face.

'My, my—so young and so pretty.'

She smiled, sweet and cold, like a python before it eats you. Morgana made my skin crawl.

We arrived at the docks. I slipped through the car door and watched the chauffeur pick Leo up.

'Be careful with him,' Morgana growled.

People were milling around but didn't notice the huge man carrying an unconscious teenager. I guessed they were concealed by Morgana's magic. She would be hard for Annie and Millie to defeat, and thinking about it made my throat constrict. I was worried about everybody.

The chauffeur walked along the gangway onto a small yacht with Morgana following behind. 'Lay him on the bed, and be careful,' she said.

The boat started, and Morgana made a phone call. 'We have him,' she laughed. 'He's divine. So beautiful. An exquisite display for your collection, sir.' She licked her lips again. She was seriously giving me the freaks. 'Yes, yes, I'll see you in thirty minutes. I know, don't worry. Bye.'

She sat on the bed holding Leo's hand, her eyes fixed on him. I watched them both, not wanting to leave him alone with her. She just stared and stared, sitting still like a statue. She was stunningly beautiful, and I wondered how many young girls she'd killed to retain that beauty. Her dark-blue eyes appeared to be full of storm clouds.

When the chauffeur knocked on the door a while later, she jumped up.

'We are ready to enter the exclusion perimeter, madam.'

'I'll be there in a moment.'

The chauffeur closed the door, keen to keep his distance from the witch. Sensible guy.

Morgana caressed Leo's face. 'Don't worry, my love. We will be together soon.'

What the hell?

She strode from the room, leaving me with a heavy feeling in my stomach. What had I gotten Leo into? Oh, my sweet Lord. He was would be more than pissed with me if I didn't sort this out.

I passed through the door and watched Morgana raise her hands as she chanted. Then, when she was finished, she bellowed, 'You have two minutes to pass through. Hurry up!' The yacht lurched forwards, and I returned to Leo, desperately hoping that Annie and Millie could connect to the magical wards around the island.

Morgana didn't come back until the yacht had

stopped. She then appeared with the chauffeur, who went to grab Leo.

'Handle him gently,' she snapped at the big man. 'Harm one hair on his head, and I will vanquish you, demon.' She carefully wrapped Leo in the soft duvet.

The demon trembled and croaked, 'Yes, ma'am.'

I followed them off the boat and down the gangway. The island was idyllic—lush and green, with flowering bushes everywhere—but the birdsong and the calming sound of the lapping waves did nothing to ease my anxiety. I gazed up at the house set back from the beach on a small hill. It was enormous—the size of a warehouse—and I couldn't help noticing the abundance of security cameras everywhere. The house was almost all glass, the type you can see out of but not into.

People were rushing around, jumping to Morgana's orders. A couple of beach buggies waited for her, one of which had a trailer attached, laden with duvets and pillows. The chauffeur carried Leo and placed him in the trailer; I then jumped on to hitch a ride. My chest felt like it'd been hit with a defibrillator. Leo was so brave, but right now, he seemed so vulnerable.

We arrived at the house, and I followed them in. It was opulent, as expected, but felt clinical and cold. Everywhere was white. Well, except for the paintings, which looked original and expensive—clearly another thing the demon liked to collect.

'Bring the dhampir to the Collector's parlour,' Morgana snarled, then she walked off.

My senses were in overdrive, and I smelled Eve's intoxicating scent—moonflowers—which I now knew was the smell of her blood. I followed the chauffeur, who carefully carried Leo into a large room. There stood the man I'd seen in my vision. Sitting opposite him was Eve, who looked scared but was more beautiful than ever to me. I felt like a fist had seized my heart. She noticed me and gasped; I put a finger to my lips.

'What is it, Eve, my angel?' the demon asked.

'I-I'm feeling slightly woozy. May I be excused? Just for a minute, please?'

'Of course. Philippe, accompany Eve to the powder room.'

Eve walked past the demon and locked the door behind her. I walked through the wall. Eve tried to hug me but passed straight through me—I didn't dare change out of spirit form in case Morgana sensed me.

'Shh,' I whispered. 'Just listen. Leo is the dhampir they've been discussing, and he has a stake through his heart.'

Eve's eyes widened, and she dragged in a ragged breath.

'You need to heal him. We are going to get you out of here, Eve. Both of you.'

A tear trickled down Eve's face.

'Has he hurt you?' I growled.

She shook her head. 'Not yet, but I'm scared, Quinn.'

A knock on the door interrupted us. Eve flushed the toilet and walked back to the Collector's parlour, where she found the demon and witch towering over Leo, who was still out for the count. I heard her stifle a sob.

'There, there, my angel. Do you want to see the dhampir?' the demon asked Eve before turning back to Morgana. 'He's perfect.' The lust and greed in his eyes made my inner demon snarl.

Morgana nodded at the Collector's words and looked longingly at Leo. I didn't like how she seemed to undress him with her eyes.

'Oh my, yes, what a beautiful collectable,' the demon chuckled, clapping his hands together. 'Another exquisite item for my exhibition. Well done, Morgana.'

'I think we should test the angel's blood on the dhampir,' Morgana suggested as she placed cuffs on Leo's wrists and feet. 'He was staked because, apparently, he's a feisty one.' She then began to mumble strange words before she smirked. 'He won't be going anywhere.'

'Eve, my angel, remove the stake and let him feed. Not too much, though.' The demon caressed Eve's face.

Oh, how I wished I could zap him into next week.

Eve walked to Leo and sat beside him. She winced as she pulled out the stake, and Leo slowly opened his eyes.

'A small amount of blood, dhampir,' the demon said, 'or you will be roasted before you've even had time to finish.'

Leo grabbed Eve's wrist and drank for five seconds. Then he licked her wrist to close the holes. Eve stroked

Leo's face, but he growled deep in his throat. She jumped away, pretending to be scared of him.

'Oh look—my lovely angel even cares about a dhampir,' the demon giggled like a schmuck, and Morgana sneered. Leo stood up and bared his fangs, snarling like a cornered animal.

'Well, the blood certainly works.' The demon smiled and rubbed his hands together. 'The Ministry of Vampires will pay handsomely. This day just keeps getting better and better.'

Just wait, I thought.

'Come along, Leo.' Morgana took hold of the chain between his handcuffs, and Leo hobbled after her. His face was drawn, and his shoulders were slumped.

'Go and get ready for dinner, Eve.' The demon gazed affectionately at her. 'Wear a blue dress; there's a good little angel. Morgana, you will accompany us too,' he called as the witch reached the door.

Morgana scowled. 'Very well, but I'll get the dhampir settled in first.' Leo's eyes widened, and I saw him gulp.

Eve walked from the room, accompanied by Philippe. They walked up a spiral staircase towards a large door at the top, and Eve hurried through it alone and closed it. I noticed Phillipe had avoided Eve's eyes, which made me wonder if he had been the one she had used compulsion on when she'd attempted to escape. I passed through the wall, and Eve motioned to the bathroom.

'This is the only room without cameras. Or I hope it is,' Eve sighed. 'I've missed you, Quinn.'

'Not as much as I've missed you. I'm sorry I was such an ass. Please forgive me?' She gave me a weird look. 'I wish I could hug you ... but I daren't come out of spirit—Morgana will know I'm here,' I said. Eve ran her hand through her hair. She was trembling. My fingers ached to touch her; I got a fluttering in the base of my belly. Hellfire, I loved her so much.

'What's the plan?' she asked, chewing her lower lip.

I told her about locating and freeing Leo, then how, as long as the magical wards were broken down, I'd get Dad to shadow us out of there.

Eve shook her head. 'We can't leave everybody,' she said in a cracked voice.

'Who?' But before Eve could answer, I heard a knocking on her bedroom door. 'I need to go and check Leo's not been savaged by Morgana anyway,' I muttered.

'Huh?' Eve sucked in a breath.

'Long story.' Her face was etched on my memory. I closed my eyes momentarily until the knot of raw, messy emotions climbed back down my throat. Then I dropped back through the floors just as Morgana led Leo to an elevator. I watched which level the elevator stopped at and fell through the two storeys to join them. We seemed to be underground, and what I saw there blew my mind. There were huge windows—at least twenty—and behind each was a different supernatural creature. Each exhibit housed a vast area; for example, some had trees and flowing water, others were surrounded by rocks and dirt, and some had a holding tank, like you might find at an aquarium.

I peered through one window and saw several small creatures, a bit like gnomes but made of half-flesh, half-wood. Another area was set up like a woodland, with fairies flitting about or sitting on tree branches. A beautiful dryad stepped out of a tree trunk; she had a gaunt appearance. She sat down on the forest floor, her mouth downturned and her eyes fixed on the fallen leaves. A faun—half-man, half-goat—lay on the ground, looking sad and dejected. Then I came to a holding tank, within which was the most exquisite mermaid, she had long hair covering her torso. Again, she simply sat on the bottom of the tank; her tail scales had no lustre to them. I could feel my temper rising.

Now I'd seen these captives, I understood what Eve had meant. The Collector needed to be stopped, and the Keepers were going to be the ones to do that. But we had one slight problem: Morgana. Thinking about the witch made me wonder how Annie and Millie were getting on with breaking through the magical wards.

I walked by the next area, where an enormous brown wolf lay. His eyes were closed; I could tell he'd given up by the diluted colours in his aura.

Then the elevator opened, and Morgana and Leo came walking towards me. As they passed the wolf, it jumped up, baring its teeth, and bounced off the glass in desperate fury. Morgana simply laughed at its distress. This was so unbelievably cruel and hard.

'He doesn't much care for me, as you can see.' Morgana smirked. 'And he can tell you're half-vampire, Leo—you are his mortal enemy.'

Leo stopped and stared into the wolf's eyes. It bared its teeth again before closing its mouth and lying down with its back to the glass. Then it whimpered—a sad, meek cry that any abused dog would make. That sound cracked my heart, and I saw tears prick Leo's eyes.

'Come along, let's get rid of your shackles,' snapped Morgana. 'Don't try anything silly ... I'm a powerful witch. I can do serious damage. Take off your shirt.'

Leo hesitated, but then he did as she asked.

'Mm, you are divine, Leo.' She ran a finger up his bare chest. His face was a mask, but I knew he must be bricking himself.

'You can behave yourself, or I can get the guards to stake and burn you. It's up to you. What do you say, pretty boy? Shall we have some fun?'

Oh. Dear. Lord. I almost vomited in my mouth. I knew I had to act fast to save him—Leo would need therapy for the next fifty years if I didn't. Before I could change my mind, I quickly walked back through the wall and switched to my physical form. The wolf jumped up and glared at me, so I put a finger to my lips. 'We'll get you out of here, buddy,' I whispered.

I glanced around to see other creatures gaping at me through their glass cages, and I turned back to spirit form just as sirens started to blare. I heard Morgana growl with frustration and storm out of Leo's room. That's when all hell broke loose, with guards running and searching everywhere.

'Find the intruder!' Morgana roared as she stomped towards the elevator.

The guards checked every inch of the exhibition area, then returned upstairs, leaving one guard by the elevator. The element of surprise had gone—once I'd materialised, of course—so it was improvisation time. All I knew was that I couldn't risk Dad being obliterated by Morgana, so I'd only call him as a last resort.

It's now or never, I decided. I stood behind the guard and turned back to my physical form. As I grabbed him around the throat, I knew he was a mortal, not a demon —I could smell his fear and hear his heart pounding. *Damn.* I squeezed, and he struggled before he went down. I hoped I hadn't killed him. I rushed to Leo's cage and broke the door open.

'Quinn, thank God!' he panted.

'We need to get out of here and find Eve.' I just wished I had a solid plan; I was pretty much winging it. We could all be killed, but I shelved that thought.

'Let the wolf out,' croaked Leo.

'But you heard what Morgana said—it's your mortal enemy,' I argued.

'I'd rather be killed by the wolf than ravaged by her.'

The wolf tipped its head to the side, almost as if it understood us.

‘Nice wolf, we are the good guys,’ I said. ‘We won’t hurt you.’ I raised my hands to the animal as a peace gesture but noticed them trembling. I broke open the door and stepped backwards.

The wolf snarled and leapt through the door, heading straight towards Leo.

CHAPTER 27
CRAZY WITCH

I knocked Leo out of the way just in time. The wolf flattened me, but I held the snarling beast around the neck.

'Listen to me. I know you understand. I'm half-demon.'

It snarled as it struggled.

'Leo is half-vampire, but we are NOT killers. Do you want to get out of here or not?' The wolf stopped fighting me for a second. 'If you do, we need to work together. Starting now. I'm going to let you go ... it's your choice: try to kill us both or help us to free everybody.'

I slowly released the wolf, and it stood panting and glaring suspiciously at Leo and me. Then, it sat down and lowered its head, letting out the quietest of whines.

'I need to go and check on Eve,' I said quietly. I had no choice but to trust the wolf even though it was ginormous, with teeth like daggers. It could crush a man with one swipe of its giant paw. I knew Leo could hold his own ... but this beast was something else.

'You two, be careful. Use the elevator, press stop halfway up, and wait. Don't come out of it until I tell you to,' I said as I glared at the wolf, and its amber eyes met mine.

'Great. I'm sharing an elevator with a wolf that wants to kill vampires,' Leo mumbled. The wolf just growled, making a low rumbling noise in its throat.

'Behave.' I pointed at the beast. 'You kill one of my best friends, and Morgana will be the least of your problems.' I think my eyes must have glowed red because the wolf whimpered.

I turned into spirit and floated through rooms, desperately looking for Eve. The whole place was bedlam as guards searched everywhere for the intruder. Then I heard Morgana's voice issuing fierce instructions. She was with a burly guy who looked like the head of security.

'The exhibition rooms are clear, ma'am. The intruder isn't down there.'

'The Collector is in the panic room. We need to turn this place upside down. My magic is never wrong. Find whoever it is and kill them,' she screamed at the big guy.

'Yes, ma'am.' He ran off, shouting directions to the rest of the men and women.

I passed through the wall and into Eve's rooms.

They were empty. Dread and apprehension gripped my throat, making it hard to breathe. Where was she?

The panic room—I needed to find it. I ran everywhere, poking my head through walls and doors. I had a tight, nebulous feeling in my chest, like you get when your body floods with too much adrenaline. After about five minutes of frantic searching, I eventually found the panic room. There, drinking a glass of amber liquid, the Collector sat on a comfy chair, watching the pandemonium on a host of monitors. Eve was sitting opposite him, with her back to me.

'Don't worry, my angel. Morgana will sort things out, and we will eat dinner in no time. I have a special evening planned for you.' The way he looked at her made my anger surge. I moved closer. Eve had her eyes closed, and her arms were wrapped protectively around her body.

I went up to the demon and appeared in front of him. He shrieked, and Eve screamed.

'I think your meal's off,' I growled, punching the Collector. His nose crunched, he howled, and I vanished again. His lips and chin trembled as blood gushed down his face. He looked frantically around the room for me, his eyes wide open and his nostrils flared. It seemed he was trying to process the power I must have.

'Where are you? Who are you?' he screeched and stood up. 'I can make you rich. Rich beyond your wildest dreams.'

I appeared in front of him again. 'Call off your

guards. Control Morgana if you know what's good for you.' I touched his shoulder, and he screamed and backed away.

'What are you?'

'I'm your worst nightmare, and don't even think about shadowing out of here.' I warned him.

A flicker of fear clouded his eyes, but then he smiled with an edge of sinister. 'Don't worry; I'm not giving up my kingdom that easily, young man. You have to face Morgana yet,' he chuckled without humour. 'The most powerful witch ever to grace the Earth, you know.'

I could feel a ball of dread in my chest when I thought about the witch. It made it hard to breathe, but I ensured my face held no sign of my worry. I narrowed my eyes at him and snarled, 'We will see about that. Tell everybody to leave the island, apart from Morgana. Do it. *Now*!' I honestly should have had an Oscar for that performance—my pulse was actually pounding in my ears, and my heart was doing jumping jacks.

The Collector picked up a two-way radio. 'As you wish.' He smirked. 'Morgana. Call off the guards.'

'We have a problem?' I heard Morgana answer.

'Yes, yes. A small problem. Tell everybody to man the boats and leave. But you must stay. Do it now.'

We watched the monitors and saw the guards piling into speedboats as they left. The house appeared to be empty, but I was going to check.

'Stay here,' I ordered the Collector. 'You won't see me, but I'll be watching you. Make one move, and it'll be your last.' I took his radio and crushed it beneath my foot.

I disappeared and raced to find Morgana. She was outside, watching the army of security people leave the island.

'Make sure you're ready to return as soon as I sort this situation out,' she said, speaking into a portable two-way radio.

Next, I ran back into the house, to Leo, seriously hoping the wolf hadn't attempted to rip his throat out. I appeared in the elevator, where I'd told them to wait, only to find Leo sitting with the wolf's head on his lap. He was stroking the beast's muzzle and singing to it. 'Whoa ... Quinn,' he said, jumping when I appeared. The wolf growled.

'Come on,' I panted as I pressed the button, and we opened the doors into an empty hallway.

'Where is everybody?' asked Leo.

'I'll explain later. But, first, you need to take Eve to Dad's yacht.'

'I'm not leaving you.'

'Just do it. Please. Wait here, and I'll get her.'

I appeared before the Collector, and he gave me a sardonic smile.

'Oh, you *are* still alive,' he said, with an evil glint in his eye. He was so sure of Morgana.

I ignored his attempt to unnerve me, but the trigger to my rage mechanism was activated, and I lost my shit.

I grabbed him by the scruff of his neck, and he yelped.

'I've got a few things to say to you,' I growled. 'Number one, you're a freaking psycho. Number two, you look like a bad extra from a Sherlock Holmes movie. And number three, you've really, *really* ... pissed ... me ... off.' To emphasise the last three words, I banged his head on the desk. When I dragged him up, he was bleeding more heavily from his nose and mouth.

'Open the door ... *now,*' I snarled in his face.

He did as I asked. I checked the monitors and took Eve's arm with one hand, still holding the Collector by the scruff of the neck with the other. We walked to Leo and the wolf. The wolf let out a low rumble when it saw the Collector.

'Not yet,' I said as I gazed into its amber eyes.

'I'm not leaving you, Quinn.' Eve had a defiant look in her eyes.

'Me neither,' Leo grunted.

The wolf howled—maybe it was wolf speak for, *I'm staying too.* Who knows?

Now it was time to play my ace, my big bad demon —I just hoped Millie and Annie had broken through the magical wards around the island.

'Dad,' I yelled, and he appeared instantaneously. The Collector recoiled as if he'd been smacked in the belly and started to shadow. Dad was as quick as a mongoose—I've never actually seen one in action, but

I've heard they're pretty fast—he grabbed the Collector around the neck and growled in his face.

'M-Mr Atua,' the demon whimpered.

'Hello, Mortimer,' Dad said in a dangerously even voice. 'I wondered where you'd disappeared to. You've done very well for yourself, considering you're a lower demon.' Dad stared daggers at Mortimer. 'But, oh dear, you have caused us a lot of upset.' Anger radiated off him in an almost palpable wave.

'I-I'll make it up to you,' the Collector squeaked.

'You certainly will.' Dad gave a cool smile, which didn't reach his eyes.

'Give me a second,' he said to Leo, Eve, and me. He took hold of the Collector with both hands, vanished, and returned to us within a few minutes.

'Demon realm?' I asked.

'Yep. I've stripped him of his demonic powers.'

'You can do that?'

Dad smiled coldly. 'I'm a demon king, son. He is trapped there in his human form and will be making it up to me for a very long time.'

I almost pitied the Collector ... but couldn't quite manage it.

'I need Millie and Annie,' I said. 'Are they prepared?'

'Give me a moment.' Dad reappeared a few seconds later with the two witches and Eloise. Eve gasped and hugged Millie and Eloise.

Annie looked grim but determined. 'Let's do this,' she said in a low voice.

'Dad, go back, and take Eve with you.'

'No.' Eve glared at me, and I huffed a sigh.

'I'll go now, but call again if you need me.' Dad vanished.

The rest of us walked outside to find Morgana. Her eyes lit up when she saw us, as she purred, 'I've been expecting you.'

'Don't forget, Millie: keep hold of my hand, no matter what happens. Just don't let go. We are stronger together,' Annie said, looking lovingly at her granddaughter.

Millie nodded, but she was pale, and her lips had a slight tremble. Her anxiety was unmistakable.

Suddenly, the wolf snarled and sprang towards Morgana. But she barely flinched. She lifted her hand as the storm clouds swirled in her eyes, making them darken, and the wolf stopped, contorted in agony. Its whines and screams were horrendous. The air got stuck in my lungs.

'Stop!' Leo roared. The poor wolf lay on the ground; I wasn't sure if it was still breathing. Leo went to run to it, but I grabbed his arm.

'Leo, you are not leaving me. I'll kill each one of your friends. I'll let you watch,' crooned Morgana in a mocking, melodramatic voice. A smile twisted on her lips as she glared at him.

Leo bared his fangs and growled.

'You're a freaking lunatic,' I snarled at her. She cast me a distasteful sneer as her gaze roved over me.

'And you're a pestiferous creature.'

I was flattered; I'd never been called pestiferous before. I had no idea what it meant, but I was pretty sure it wasn't a pleasantry.

As she switched her attention to Leo, I vanished into my spirit form and darted to Morgana. I quickly changed to my physical self and gripped her around the neck, squeezing as hard as possible. I sensed a brief flicker of fear, but then she snarled and glared deep into my eyes.

I was instantly paralysed—it felt like I had a noose around my neck. I couldn't breathe, change back to spirit, or do anything ... she was strangling me with magic. Eve and Leo ran to her, but she threw them away with a flick of her wrist, like an invisible gust of wind. Both went flailing through the air and landed with a sickening thud, but the short break in eye contact had at least given me a chance to breathe.

I gasped, bent over, trying to reinflate my lungs, when Morgana smiled maliciously. Lifting her hands, she created a raging fire, which instantly engulfed me. Luckily, though, as I had experienced before, the fire only served to invigorate me. The flames licked my skin; I absorbed the power. Then, I vanished again, leaving Morgana looking around in surprise—her frown was epic. But believe me, my demon within could feel her simmering rage, and boy, was she mad.

My gaze fell on Eve, Leo, and the wolf, lying motionless on the ground. Nausea swirled, unrestrained, in my empty stomach. I knew I was no equal to such a powerful witch, and a feeling of dread crept up from the pit of my gut. Annie and Millie started chanting, and Morgana watched them with morbid curiosity.

'Witches?' She laughed humourlessly. 'You are no match for me.' She motioned her hands at them, but they'd protected themselves. 'Well done,' she said as she smirked. 'Good, but not good enough.'

The grey in Morgana's eyes swirled and darkened, and she pointed at Annie. Millie's granny clutched her chest, her face contorted, and she fell to her knees before collapsing.

That's when the temperature began to plummet.

I looked at Eloise, who was as still as a statue, tears streaming down her face. The ghost's eyes were riveted on Morgana. At that moment, the wind began to pick up, sending clouds of sand swirling around us. Dark clouds raced across a clear blue sky, rain pelted down, and thunder ominously rumbled. Eloise was so angry she'd whipped up a supercell thunderstorm. She was like a paranormal goddess of vengeance.

Morgana looked questioningly in our direction and then raised her hand, mumbling under her breath. Suddenly, Eloise began to swirl like a fine sea mist, and she was gone in a whirl of tears, sand, and raindrops. The storm suddenly vanished, and I felt like a crippling hole had been punched through my chest.

Morgana laughed. 'A spectre? Oh, I'm offended. One

more for my box of souls. I have quite the collection,' she said as she smiled coldly.

And we were utterly screwed. The sense of impending doom was overwhelming—that is—until Millie turned into a psychotic, demonic witch from hell, which scared the living crap out of me. She screamed—an inhuman noise that almost burst my eardrums—then bared her teeth. She looked demented.

Millie raised her arms out by her side. The wind whipped up, and she started to lift into the air, about twenty feet—she just dangled there. Her eyes became pools of solid jet black, like liquid pools of darkness. It was almost like she'd conjured her rage into raw energy. Lightning and static crackled and sizzled around her tiny body—and my heart stuttered a beat.

Morgana's mouth fell open as she watched Millie in amazement. Then, as Morgana lifted her hand and chanted under her breath, Millie turned her face to Morgana, the petite witch's now black eyes drilled into the evil supernatural. Millie raised a hand and pointed it at Morgana. A streak of lightning crackled wildly from her palm, vaporising the wicked witch where she stood.

Millie was still elevated, the wind whipping her blonde hair around her face. Her eyes remained black, like bottomless pits to the bowels of hell, and her face was contorted in a mask of pure evil. At this point, my heart almost stopped—this version of Millie made Roald Dahl's psychopathic and monstrous Grand High Witch look like a cute granny.

'Millie!' I screamed. At my call, the energy seemed to leave Millie's body. She went limp and started to fall. I ran to catch her and laid her gently on the ground. Then I turned around to see Eve and Leo staring with their mouths open.

'Eve, quickly!' I called.

Eve rushed over to Annie, and as soon as Eve touched her, a golden light shimmered around the older witch, who moaned and sat up.

'Millie!' Annie cried. But Eve had already started doing the same to Millie, who now groaned and opened her eyes.

'Where's Eloise?' Eve asked with desperation. I explained what had happened, and Annie ran into the house with Millie following.

Leo was crying and holding the wolf's head in his arms. Eve ran over and tried her best to heal the poor beast. It was beginning to look hopeless when, at last, the wolf whimpered ... and changed into a young man. A very naked young man.

I averted my eyes and yelled one more time, 'Dad!'

CHAPTER 28
MIGUEL

On the boat, Annie carried a wooden casket that was not much bigger than a jewellery box. 'Eve—this is the box of souls. They have been trapped by Morgana for centuries. It's time to let them rest.' Annie placed the box on a table.

Eve gently opened the lid, and everybody watched in awe. Then, one by one, balls of celestial light floated straight through the ceiling and disappeared into the afterlife. Well, not all of them went upwards; some went downwards, but I guessed they'd deserved to go that way. Then one remaining celestial ball of light bounced off the ceiling, landing with a thud on the floor, and Eloise appeared to us again.

Eve and Millie rushed to help her up and tried to hug the life out of her—well, if she hadn't already been dead.

Jarvis approached Dad. 'Most of the mercenaries are human. I've dealt with the demons, sir.'

Dad walked out to the assembled captives, motioning for Annie to follow him. I, of course, went with them. I could see the others watching through the windows.

'We need to erase their memories,' Dad murmured to Annie.

Annie started chanting when one of the guys suddenly pulled a gun and fired it straight at Dad.

The bullet bounced off him, and Dad looked very put out as he glanced down at the hole in his shirt. 'That was a costly silk shirt,' he growled as his red eyes drilled into those of the man responsible. The mercenary passed out.

Annie carried on waving her hands until the mercenaries glanced at each other, grimacing and frowning. 'Where are we?' I heard one of them ask.

We chatted with wolf man. Or attempted to, that is —he sat in silence and wouldn't make eye contact with us. At least he was now dressed in a pair of joggers and a T-shirt. He seemed a bit older than us, had pale-brown skin, and his dark hair fell past his shoulders. Above his high cheekbones, his beautiful eyes were the colour of ochre, with hues of caramel syrup and flickering golden tones. He was attractive in a dark and brooding kind of way. He bit his lip as he stared at the floor, and seemed lonely and scared. Eve sat with him and held his hand. I tried not to be jealous, but it was hard.

'We are your friends. Please trust us. What's your name?' Eve smiled kindly.

'Miguel.' His voice was a smooth baritone, clear and calm.

'What happened to you?'

He sighed as he looked at Eve. Tears fell down his face as he spoke. 'I am a Ticuna Indian from the oldest tribe in Peru. Our village was decimated ... by vampires.' His eyes narrowed. 'I escaped, along with some others, only to be hunted by the Collector.'

Aw man, poor Miguel. Eve hugged him while I asked, 'So, are you, like, a werewolf?'

Miguel's head snapped up, and he scowled at me. 'No, I am not a werewolf. I am a Lupus sapien. There is a big difference. I can change into my wolf form at will, unlike a werewolf. Do not insult me.'

'Erm, sorry,' I said as Eve tried to swallow her laugh.

'Miguel,' Leo thankfully interrupted, albeit a little edgily, 'my family are vampires ... but good vampires. They don't kill humans. We are not all the same.' But Miguel wouldn't make eye contact with us; he just stared back at the floor.

'Dinner is served,' Jarvis announced, which brightened the mood in the room.

We went to eat, and there were so many questions I needed to ask. Over dinner, I questioned Dad about the Collector's captives.

'Don't worry, Quinn,' he replied. 'All of them are being returned to where they belong. It's being done as we speak. You all did well.' Dad looked around the table. 'You rescued over fifty innocent, supernatural creatures. The rogue vampire, however, will need to go to the Lamia Ministerium. They will decide on its fate.'

'I didn't see the vampire, thankfully,' I said.

'Annie and I have decided to keep the island shrouded in magic after what has happened there. We will get an agreement from the Supernatural Council, of course.' Annie nodded in agreement as Dad spoke. I was just about to ask about the Supernatural Council when I noticed that Miguel seemed uncomfortable and had started fidgeting.

'You, Miguel,' Dad addressed him directly. Miguel looked ready to turn wolf and leg it, but Dad continued. 'You can decide your own destiny.'

'Come and live with us,' Leo implored.

'Vampires and wolves do not mix,' Miguel murmured.

Leo gently took his hand. Miguel flinched but didn't pull away.

'Maybe vampires and wolves *can* mix?' Leo whispered. 'Maybe anything is possible when we are on the same side?'

As Leo spoke, Miguel finally made eye contact with him, and the tension seemed to leave his body. Yep, I could feel their attraction from across the table.

'Millie,' I said, looking at the witch. 'You seriously weirded me out back there. But, man, that was some seriously badass magic.'

Millie blushed and smiled. 'I have no idea what happened, Quinn.'

Annie clutched Millie's hand. I'd told Annie about Millie becoming the super-scary, powerful witch earlier. 'Millie needs to be in control of her powers. Lack of control could potentially be catastrophic. But I'm so proud of her.' Annie gazed lovingly at her granddaughter. 'Without you, darling, things could have ended so differently. You saved us all.'

Millie looked embarrassed. 'Yeah, like I said, I don't know what happened. I remember being overtaken with such undiluted fury at Morgana because of you ... then Eloise ... then it's blank. Don't worry, though,' she said as she looked around at us all, 'I'm going to work on the control thing with Granny.'

'You were right, Edward.' Annie looked at Dad. 'She is destined to be the most powerful witch to walk the Earth.'

'A full-blooded witch,' Dad said, 'the most powerful supernatural being alive ... well, once she masters her powers, anyway'—he paused—'or some may say the most dangerous.' Dad's eyes drilled into Millie's.

She peered at him with big eyes and blushed furiously.

Annie flashed Dad an angry look, and he raised his hands, smiling kindly. 'Just saying. If she wasn't my son's ally, I'd be worried.'

'A full-blooded witch?' Leo asked.

'Yes, both her parents were witches. Millie, you are destined for great things,' Dad answered.

'My dad too?' Millie asked. Annie nodded her head at the petite witch.

Eve laughed. 'My very own best friend and super witch,' she said as she hugged Millie.

I was desperate to take Eve into my arms, but I sighed and chatted with Dad. At least Eve was safe and back with me.

Once we were home, we filled Mrs D and Harry in on everything that had happened; life got back to normal pretty quickly—as if it had all been a bad dream. Mum and Frank were due home within a couple of days. I was so excited about seeing Mum, but I was more worried about the 'Dad conversation'. I knew I couldn't tell Mum about being half-demon—not yet, if ever. But I desperately needed to talk to her about Dad.

Really late on the first night we were home, I found Eve in the kitchen. Somehow, after our ordeal, I had a tangible emotional connection to her, and I knew she'd been struggling with night terrors since her abduction. I also knew—don't ask me how—that she loved someone. She was experiencing a deep, unconditional, and passionate love—it radiated from her, and I could see it in her aura. I had no idea who the lucky guy was, and at that point, I didn't want to know. I knew in my heart that she didn't feel like that about me, so I decided to just bury how I felt and move on. She loved me, and that was enough.

'Hey, want some hot chocolate?' I asked her. 'It might help you sleep?'

Eve was sitting at the kitchen table, staring blankly out the window. We sat and talked, and then I plucked up the courage to grab her hand. We stayed there for quite a while.

'Stay with me tonight, Quinn?' she asked.

'O-okay,' I croaked.

Once upstairs, I tucked Eve to bed and lay on the covers. I held her in my arms until she went to sleep, wishing I could crawl under the duvet and kiss her. I wanted to wrap her in my arms and never let go. Sadly, I knew I was only her friend, so that had to be enough. I never wanted to lose her again. I stayed with her all night and watched her sleep for a long time until I passed out from exhaustion.

CHAPTER 29

EVE

I managed to get Mrs D alone, the following morning. 'Maybe I should just get it over with and tell Mum about being half-demon?'

Mrs D seemed horrified. 'Oh, dear. I need to speak to your father.' Then she vanished.

I gave up waiting for Mrs D to return, and we all went to Leo's to hang out with him and his family. Miguel had gone to live there but had ended up spending most of his time in the forest as a wolf. Harrison, Cordelia, and Nat had spent some time with him, but it took Miguel a while to adjust.

'He's cute enough,' Natasha had said when Miguel wasn't there, 'but, my God, he stinks of dog.'

Leo smacked her around the head. 'Well, I like him.'

'Oh, I *know* you do.' Natasha's lilting voice made Leo colour up.

'I don't know. It's weird how I feel about him. I

know I shouldn't—he's my mortal enemy—but I have this connection to him. I think I'm in love for the first time in my life. I can't explain it, but I feel like we belong together.' Leo looked down at the floor and sighed.

'Ah, baby bro.' Natasha enveloped him in her arms.

'How does *he* feel about it?' Eve asked kindly.

'I've told him how I feel. But I don't know. When we are alone, he's more relaxed. Yet, I'm not sure he feels the same way I do.' Leo's eyes filled with tears, and Natasha and Millie enveloped him in their arms.

'Come on,' Eve whispered to me. 'Let's go and find Miguel.'

'We'll be back in a bit,' I called to them all.

Eve and I walked into the forest to find the wolf boy. It was a cloudless day; rays of mellow sunlight filtered through the verdurous canopy, casting a green-glow luminescence across the pathway. Twigs crunched underneath our feet as we walked further into the forest.

'Miguel,' Eve shouted. Miguel appeared in wolf form, and I looked into his amber eyes. He gently head-butted Eve and me, then he made a rumbling sound in his throat, like a lion purring.

'I've brought you some clothes. I wondered if you'd like to come and meet our tribe.'

He tilted his head to the side, and then with zero warning, he changed into his human self. 'Whoa ... put some pants on, bud,' I yelled.

Eve covered her eyes before she and Miguel fell

about laughing.

Harry and Eloise loved Miguel, and we all knew immediately he was one of us as soon as he bowed and kissed Eloise's hand. The ghost was ecstatic, and right then, Miguel became part of our team.

'Looks like you've got a new pack now,' Leo said. Miguel smiled shyly in response.

'I'm happy,' he replied. But then, he glanced nervously around at us and took a deep breath. 'I know these people are your family, Leo. So, I need to tell you something, and I feel like I can be honest in front of your friends.'

Leo stiffened, and his eyes widened. His brows knit together as he frowned.

'I've thought about what you have said to me, about how you feel. I have tried to fight it. Believe me, I have tried. But I can't. I feel the same. I want to be with you too. This connection is unexplainable, but maybe there is a reason behind it.'

Leo's shoulders relaxed, and he walked over and took Miguel's hands in his. Miguel put his arms around Leo, kissed him on his lips, and rested his head on Leo's shoulder. While Miguel embraced him, Leo turned his gaze to the rest of us—he looked the happiest I'd ever seen him. Eloise stood with her mouth gaping open.

Eve put a finger to her lips and whispered, 'I'll explain when we get home.'

So, it seemed Leo had found a boyfriend at last.

'See you both later,' Eve shouted to Leo and Miguel as we returned to our house. Leo and Miguel just grunted and stared contentedly into each other's eyes.

'What do you mean, he's gay? I thought that meant being happy?' I heard Eloise ask Millie and Eve as they all walked upstairs to Eve's bedroom. Harry and I burst out laughing.

'They make a cute couple, huh?' Harry said.

'Yeah.' I smiled and was delighted for Leo and everything, but selfishly, I was worried that Leo wouldn't want to spend as much time with me if he had a boyfriend. Then I shook my head. *Stop being a selfish jerk.* I mentally slapped myself.

Later on, Mrs D arrived back home with Dad in tow.

'We need to plan for your parents coming home,' Dad said to Eve and me. 'I'm not sure telling Helen you are half-demon is a brilliant idea, Quinn. Not yet.'

'Okay.' It seemed I'd have to keep my secret for a while longer. Would I ever be able to tell her? I'd always been close to Mum, and I felt like there would be a hole in my world without her support. And let me tell you, I needed her support.

We chatted for quite a while and devised a plan to introduce Dad back into our lives. I just hoped Mum and Frank would go along with it.

Millie, Harry, and Eloise then took Celeste to Leo's, leaving Eve and me to meet Mum and Frank.

As Millie was leaving, I heard her say to Eve, 'Give Josh a ring. He's rung you, like, a hundred times.'

'Yeah, maybe I will.'

I went upstairs to my room—I couldn't bear to be around if Eve decided to ring Josh, so I lay on my bed and brooded.

'QUINN! THEY'RE HERE,' Eve hollered up the stairs. I raced down just as Mum and Frank walked in. Mum rushed to hug me, and Frank hurried over to embrace Eve. Mum soon rattled on about their honeymoon and how amazing it had been. After about half an hour of catching up, Eve tensed up and gave me a look to say, *Get on with it.*

'Erm, Mum ...' She narrowed her eyes at me, obviously having detected the nerves I was feeling.

'Dad's back.'

'What?' She touched her face, and the blood drained from her cheeks. Frank shifted and looked agitated as he took Mum's hand.

'It's complicated, but he wants to meet with us all. He wants us to go for dinner tomorrow. I think it's a good idea, Mum. I want to start seeing him.'

Mum sat in silence for a few minutes with a faraway

look in her eyes. 'W-when did he return? Where has he been? Why did he desert us?' She started crying, and Frank gave me a stern look. He drew Mum towards him and held her.

Not going too well, I gulped. *Damn.*

'Helen,' Mrs D said. 'I think you should give him a chance to explain, dear. He wants to be part of Quinn's life.'

'A bit late for that,' Frank growled.

'No, it's not,' I said, raising my voice. I felt my temper sizzle. Eve placed a hand on my arm, dousing the flames. 'Sorry, Mum, I really want you both to come for dinner. With Eve and me. Please?'

'It's up to you, Helen,' Frank murmured. 'I'll support you whatever you decide.'

'Okay. We'll come with you,' Mum said softly. 'But it's going to be hard.'

DAD'S LIMO TURNED UP. Mum was trembling, but Frank had her back. We walked out to find a female driver waiting for us. Presumably, Barney had been banished to the demon realm by Dad.

As we approached Myrtlewood Estate, I heard Mum gasp while Frank just looked glum. Jarvis was waiting for us. 'Welcome,' he said as he bowed his head. We followed Jarvis to the kitchen. Dad stood by the picture window, but turned around and smiled at us as we entered the room.

'Edward.' Mum stared at Dad, and the blood disappeared from her face.

Dad shook Frank's hand and kissed Mum on the cheek. 'I think I have much explaining to do,' Dad said. He seemed genuinely worried.

Over dinner, Mum and Frank seemed to relax. My belly was still cramped with nerves, but Eve was chilled, as always. Dad explained that he'd been working for the ministry—not a lie; and that he'd had to leave, or he would have put Mum and me in danger—also not a lie. Mum and Frank assumed Dad was like James Bond—a 007 spy or something. They then discussed life in general, their honeymoon, Frank's work, and, of course, me. I just sat in silence. Eve found my hand under the table and gave it a squeeze.

'Would you be okay if I started seeing Quinn again?' Dad asked nervously.

'If Quinn wants to see you, that's fine,' replied Mum.

'Can I come with Quinn too, Dad?' Eve asked Frank.

'Of course, my angel,' he replied, taking her hand. Her lips quirked into a smile.

Dad was clearly relieved. 'Thank you, both.' He paused before adding, 'I have a yacht.'

'You would,' Frank mumbled.

Dad wiped his mouth with his napkin to cover a

smile. 'I would like you to use it. Anytime. It's fully staffed ...just let me know when and where, and I'll get it ready for you wherever you need it.'

'That's very kind,' Mum said. 'Maybe next year when we all go to St Kitts? We could sail around the islands?'

'Sure.' Frank kissed Mum's cheek.

As we walked to the door, Dad's voice reverberated in my mind, *Quinn.*

My head snapped to look at him, but his voice sounded in my head again, *Don't say anything. Come back to talk to me when they are in the limo.*

I answered, *Okay,* without uttering a word, and a flicker of a smile crossed his lips.

'Erm, won't be a minute,' I said as I ran back to Dad while Eve, Mum, and Frank waited for me in the car.

'Telepathy?' I frowned at him.

'Another demonic power that will come in handy,' he said as his lips quirked into a smile.

'Cool.'

Dad's face became serious. 'Jarvis has informed me that the Ministry of Vampires knows about the half-angel.'

A nugget of unease sprouted in my gut.

'But they don't know her identity, so don't worry ... for now.'

I sighed. 'She needs to know eventually, but I won't say anything. I don't want to worry her—not yet, at least—she's been through enough. Oh, and by the way, how *do* you know Annie?'

'As I said, I'm the leader of the Ministry of Demons. She is the leader of the Ministry of Witches.'

'Oh.' I was left speechless as I gazed into his dark eyes. There was so much more I needed to find out about our supernatural world.

'And I may not be around as much as I'd like, for a month or so anyway. The Fallen Angel is taking a vacation, and I must oversee things in the Dark Kingdom.'

'Huh?' I eyed him with scrunched brows. 'Lucifer goes on holiday?' I said incredulously. I had visions of the devil sipping a cocktail, relaxing on a sun lounger, and wearing a pair of speedos. That image made me feel a bit queasy, to be honest.

Dad laughed at my expression. 'Yes, son. He likes to holiday in the mortal realm quite frequently.'

'That's just plain weird.'

Dad chuckled again. 'I'll see you soon, son.' Then he hugged me.

I started walking away, but Dad stopped me. 'Quinn, please tell Eve how you feel, son. Life's too short, believe me.'

'Huh?'

He just gave me a look—you know ... the same look Mrs D sometimes gives me. I gave him a sheepish smile and walked back to the limo.

On the way home, I heard Frank whisper, 'Edward's very handsome.'

Mum laughed. 'He's not a patch on you, Mr Williams.' Then she kissed him. Like a proper snog. *Ugh.*

Eve and I chatted as we walked into the house. 'My list of freaking crazy is full,' I joked. 'I hope we have a month or so of normal life to concentrate on exams.'

Eve laughed. 'Yeah, me too. The last six months *have* been a bit traumatic.'

I hesitated. 'The prom, Eve. If I've not got a date, shall we go together?'

Eve snapped her head around and narrowed her eyes. 'Sure, I'll be your backup date, Quinn.' Then she stomped off upstairs.

Could I have been any lamer? I mean, seriously? Why didn't I just ask her?

I said goodnight to Mum and Frank, who were deep in conversation. Upstairs, I stopped outside my room. Should I brave up and tell Eve how I felt? Nah—it'd rip my heart out when she gave me the 'It's me, not you' line. I couldn't handle the rejection.

I lay on my bed and stared at the ceiling. Then there was a knock, and I was surprised to find Eve at my door.

'Quinn,' she said in a shaky voice. I just gawked at her like a complete tool. I wanted to grab her but clenched my fists and controlled myself.

'Can I come in?'

'Um, yeah. Of course.' I stood aside and closed the door after she had walked inside.

Eve was trembling. She was edgy and fidgety. 'Do you think I'm pretty?'

I just stared at her, temporarily deprived of the power of speech.

'Do you find me attractive, Quinn?'

I tilted my head and frowned, trying to unravel my thoughts. What was she going on about? Thinking back, Eloise was right—boys *are* total jerks, sometimes.

'Quinn!'

I think my brain must have short-circuited because my mind was totally blank. She sighed and went to walk out of the door.

'Eve, I love you.'

There—I'd said it. I held my breath. I could feel my heart jackhammering at my ribs.

She spun around. 'What do you mean?'

'I love you. Erm ... I've loved you for ages. Like, more than a best friend ... you know? I want to be with you, Eve. But I understand if you don't feel the same.' I rubbed my sweaty palms on my jeans.

Eve threw herself into my arms. She gently kissed my lips. We pulled apart and took shaky, shallow breaths.

'What about Josh, though?'

'Josh, who?' she whispered.

'I adore you, Eve.' I smiled and looked deep into her intoxicating eyes. I held her face in my hands, and then I pulled her into a deep and passionate kiss ... her lips were soft and luscious. I buried my fingers in her hair and felt her shiver against me.

My brain ignited, and warmth spread throughout

my entire body. Eve was in my arms and kissing me—at last. Everything was perfect. I felt her beating heart against my chest, and as I held her, the whole world fell away. No demons, no Vampire Ministry, no monsters of any kind ... just my angelic Eve.

EPILOGUE

The Lamia Ministerium, near Venice, Italy. A day after the battle with Morgana ...

The castle's entrance was so enormous that it engulfed everybody who entered; the windows were like the eyes of the devil. If this fort could talk, the misery it betrayed would have you begging for deafness. The smell was of lavender and roses, though, thanks to the ornate gardens. The castle was surrounded by high walls and miles of dense forest. This citadel was the headquarters of the Vampire Ministry, located near Venice, Italy. However, because it was shrouded in magic wards, humans were blissfully unaware of its existence.

Rhys walked into the meeting chambers and bowed. The grand master vampire, Arynth, was waiting for him, and her eyes were shining red—probably because she'd just feasted on an unsuspecting kidnapped victim. The victims were plucked from around the world by her exquisite PA, and lover, Dimitri. Dimitri, as a vampire, had an appeal that mortals found irresistible. Of course, these mortals were never to be seen again. Like so many other humans, they simply disappeared off the face of the earth.

Most vampires had human feeders. The feeders were well taken care of and kept on the property purely to feed the residing vampires. The feeders were like drug addicts, addicted to the euphoria created by the vampire's bite. However, human feeders were not suitable for Arynth—she and the other elders were old-school in their ways. The blood tasted fresher when it was instilled with fear.

Arynth's hair was as black as coal, despite her many centuries on Earth—although how many centuries that was, nobody knew. Rhys nervously eyed the bodyguards standing around Arynth—hulking vampiric brutes. As always, the other two elders, Alaric and Lazarus, were with Arynth. Neither was as old as Arynth, but they were both as superior.

Lazarus had the ability to constrict the circulation of blood in a vampire's veins, causing paralysis and immense pain. Rhys was, therefore, careful not to get on the wrong side of him. Alaric had been a mage before becoming a vampire, and Rhys had witnessed the creepy vampire ripping the heart out of a rogue vampire with a wave of his hand. All in all, the three elders were extremely dangerous.

'Our deal with the Collector has failed, I hear?'

'Yes, Ma'am. Morgana and the Collector have disappeared. The half-angel too.' Rhys gritted his teeth, ready for Arynth to release her fury.

Arynth sat drumming her fingers on the arm of her ornate wooden chair. 'We need to find her. Our civilisation depends on strong leadership. Without her blood, I feel my seat is in jeopardy.'

Arynth gave Rhys a look that made him tremble and lower his head. Arynth had the ability to listen to anyone's mind, and Rhys now felt the vampire probing his brain. Rhys, however, could empty his head of all but the most relevant information, leaving only scraps for Arynth to devour.

'There is talk of a disease. A disease rampaging through South America. Fatal for vampires.'

Rhys's head snapped up. This was the first he'd heard of the threat.

'Yes, it has decimated many so far,' continued Arynth, narrowing her eyes. 'The half-angel's blood is of immense value to us as a race. This disease, which attacks our kind, could end us. You must find her. You are the best tracker we have ever known. Find out where she is, and then we will decide how to proceed.'

'Of course, Ma'am.' Rhys bowed and left the meeting chambers. He walked outside. God, how he hated the weather here. The sun was streaming through the clouds, irritating his uncovered flesh. Rhys pulled on his hat and sunglasses. His linen suit, thankfully, protected most of his skin.

He climbed into his car and smiled with anticipation.

Let the hunt begin.

ACKNOWLEDGMENTS

Firstly, a huge thank-you to my family and friends for believing in me. The pep talks and wine-drinking sessions definitely helped me overcome my self-doubt. A massive thank-you too, to fellow authors Charlotte Taylor (*Broken Twigs*) and Eva Alton (*Vampires of Emberbury*). Both your kindness and patience are so appreciated. Without you, I would never have found the courage to bare my soul to the world and publish my book. You are stars in the night sky, and I love you both dearly.

Other wonderful authors who have supported and helped me are Hayley, Ila, Lynne, Kelly, Wendy, Tess, Victoria, Rachel, and Rebecca. Thank you all so much.

And of course, if you are reading this, then thank you too.

Love and kisses to you all,

Helena

ABOUT THE AUTHOR

HELENA M CRAGGS writes Young Adult urban/paranormal fantasy.

THE YOUNGLINGS series is an action-packed, gripping, full-length coming-of-age YA paranormal fantasy. It will transport urban fantasy fans to a fascinating supernatural world within our own, filled with magic, suspense, danger, sizzling adventure, a large dose of humour, and slow-burn paranormal romance.

Helena lives with her husband, three cats, chickens, and two dogs in the beautiful hills of Yorkshire, England. She loves everything magic and is addicted to fantasy.

Also by Helena McCraggs

The Younglings Series

The Younglings: Shadows & Magic

Released September 2021

The Younglings: Fire & Magic

Released June 2022

The Younglings: Mayhem & Magic

Released May 2023

Also by Helena M Craggs

The Younglings: **Storms, Starlight & Magic**

Coming Soon

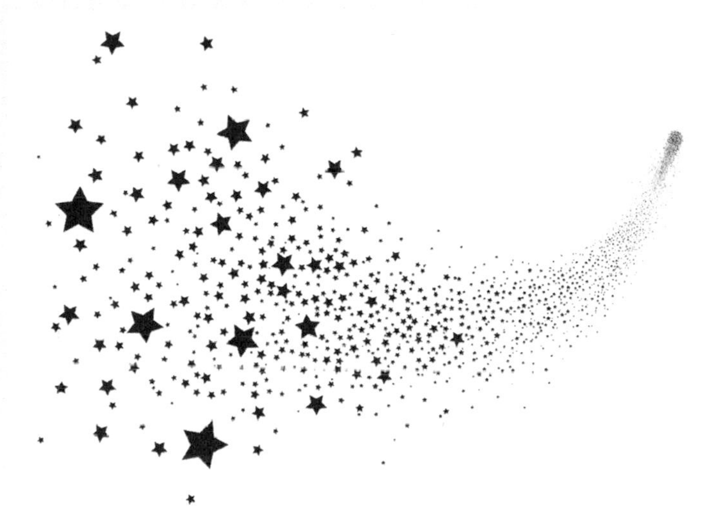

Printed in Great Britain
by Amazon

21536921R00236